END GAME CHARLIE

THE DRAGON MAGE 12

SCOTT BARON

"You must understand that there is more than one path to the top of the mountain."
- Miyamoto Musashi

THE HEROIC SPONSORS

Many thanks to the awesome supporters of this series. You all are heroic in my eyes, and the audiobook of Castaway Charlie (book 10) would not have been recorded without all of you coming together to help get it done. Your sponsoring contributions are what made it possible and I thank you from the bottom of my heart.

~ Scott Baron ~

(Listed in Chronological Sponsorship Order)

Greg Moore
James MacKay
Alex McDonald
Rodney Garrett
P.J. Pinto
Larry (Poric) Rainey
Samuel Maganaro
Jason Marroquin
Dustin Higgi

Przemyslaw Kordys
Dusty Arrington
Jeffrey O'Neal
Timothy Leidig
Frentaken
Ivey Coor
Harry Fink
Vancil Clayton Thomas
Paul Smith

CHAPTER ONE

Charlie ducked aside, a meaty fist swinging through the air where his head had just been. He replied with a flurry of elbows, driving them into the thick-skulled attacker's jaw until he crumpled to the ground in a heap.

He flashed a look at the assassin at his side, likewise introducing an angry man to his new friend, Mister Ground.

"I'm sorry, I must have heard you wrong, Bob," Charlie blurted as he stepped over the unconscious attacker now lying at his feet. "You're kidding, right?" he asked, his jaw all but hanging open in shock.

"You did not hear me wrong," Bawb replied, slowly walking backward around the downed man, his hands still empty but ready to spring into action at a moment's notice. "I am positive the two of them and their dragon friends were most certainly here. And they have clearly made quite a mess of things."

Here was a dangerous planet in a deadly system. A system where Allpower could not function and technology was king. The forbidden planet upon which they had found the Vortaxis.

Of course, the massively powerful artifact had been inadvertently destroyed by Charlie and Ara as they attempted to fight off the Urvalin and force their way back across the trap portal that had dragged them into this galaxy. A fluke of their incompatible flavor of magic, apparently, and one that obliterated the oldest, most powerful relic this galaxy had ever known.

Fortunately, the more than slightly fanatical religious order protecting it hadn't even realized that they'd stolen the actual Vortaxis right out from under their noses. In fact, when Charlie and his friends had last departed this world, they'd taken their leave, confident that a new alliance had been formed. One built on a mutual hatred of the Urvalin.

Now, however, it seemed Arlo and Ripley had gone and blundered into things in epic fashion and had stirred up one hell of a hornets' nest in the process.

Space beasts similar to dragons had been extinct here for millennia, so when the two dragons had landed on the planet, they'd made quite a stir in the system where magic should not have been able to function and their kind did not exist.

For the local inhabitants, going from confidently superior in firepower on their home turf to a state of doubt, unsure what destruction these magical beasts might be able to bring upon them, had put the entire world on edge.

It wasn't a lost cause at that point, but, unfortunately, Arlo and Ripley lacked the vital skill of tact and nuance that might have defused that situation. Diplomats, they were not. They were bulls, or more accurately, dragon riders, in a china shop.

Charlie batted aside a stun grenade of a rather novel design before it could discharge, knocking it from the air with a vicious slice from the long knife he wore on his hip. This was only getting worse, he realized. Any minute now it would turn into a free-for-all. He just couldn't believe how they'd wound up in this mess to begin with.

From what they had heard before being attacked, it seemed

that upon entering this new galaxy, the dragons the teens were riding had not only managed to avoid the magic-sucking deathtrap of the black hole-ensconced portal, but they had gone on to do much along the lines of what Ara was doing now. Namely, backtracking the scent of a familiar friend.

And that scent had led them here, of all places.

It was a mess to be sure, but worse yet, in the middle of the locals' panic and confusion, the intruders had asked for Charlie and Bawb by name.

That was pretty much all that Bawb had managed to glean from the head priest he had gone to see upon their return to the planet before the angry locals took up arms, surrounding the newcomers. Some of the mob even foolishly engaged them. Fortunately, the priest had the wherewithal to restrain himself, at least for the time being. The common rabble? Not so much.

"These guys look *really* pissed, Bob," Charlie said, his fingers loosely resting on his pulse pistol's grip, a spell on the tip of his tongue, ready to fly if things escalated further.

"That is because they *are* pissed. And with good reason," Bawb said, quickly stepping aside and delivering a carefully placed incapacitating blow upon the man charging at him. He made sure he spoke clearly, remembering that these people possessed robust translation tech.

He, Charlie, and Ara could still communicate with one another through their silent bond, though the Zomoki was currently hiding out on a nearby moon. With the whole damn planet on full alert, Charlie and his friends were of the belief that these technologically advanced people might very well possess the means to even detect magic. And *that* could just make things much, much worse than a fistfight with an angry mob.

As it was, the head priest who had so recently been a welcoming host to them had given in to the will of the crowd

3

and was now leading the substantial and well-armed group surrounding the visitors. Worse, not just a mere handful of guards. At least two dozen ships now hovered in the sky above them, armed to the teeth and ready to engage.

Whatever the kids and their dragon counterparts had done, it had made quite the impression, and it had not been a good one.

"What did they say to them, Bob? What the hell did they do? We're all friends, here. These guys know we don't mean them any harm. We're all on the same team, fighting the Urvalin," Charlie said, hoping their translated discussion amongst themselves would perhaps sway the native from attacking.

"It sounded as if Arlo and Ripley flew to the surface in something of an overly ambitious rush, flaring magic and with weapons hot."

"Why the hell would they—" Charlie began to say when a stun blast hit his shielding. "Hey! Knock that shit out. We don't want to hurt anyone!"

Another shot flew, then another. Charlie clenched his jaw when a full-fledged volley threatened to drop his tech shields.

"Oh, the hell with this. Enough is enough!" he growled, flaring his magic into a protective bubble.

That certainly got the natives' attention, and not in a good way.

"Charlie, what have you done?" Bawb groaned just as three large warships dropped out of orbit, orange-hot from their scrambled descent, the sonic booms shaking the ground around them.

The priest at the head of the mob took his hand from the glowing symbol on his tech-thread-embedded sleeve, looking at the pair with distrust, scorn, and disapproval. Apparently, he had just called in the big guns, both figuratively and literally.

"So, you also wield *Allpower*?" he spat. "All this time, nothing but lies and subterfuge."

Charlie raised his hands. "You don't understand. We're only trying to—"

A thundering crash the likes of which Charlie had never heard before rang out, then darkness surrounded him.

"Bob, what the hell?"

"I do not know," the assassin replied, quickly casting an illumination spell, the locals' distrust of magic be damned.

A slight rumble vibrated through their feet as their surroundings lit up. What he saw chilled his already frosty blood.

"What in the world..." Charlie trailed off, and with good reason.

Surrounding the two of them was a metal orb perhaps ten meters across at its widest. There was a seam at the top with bits of dirt and pavement still clinging to the edges. Not a sound penetrated from outside, nor any light. They had been sealed off.

Bawb increased the spell's brightness and studied the trap. He cast a force spell, attempting to open the orb, but rather than freedom, quite the opposite happened. The orb, it seemed, had contracted slightly, the ground at their feet buckling as it did.

"Interesting," he said, testing the orb's seal again with his magic, but this time using far less.

Again, their prison shrank around them.

"Bob?"

"Release your power, Charlie," he replied. "Do not attempt to cast."

"But we're strong casters. And you've got your wand."

"True. But these people have had a very long time to prepare to counter such powers, and it would appear we are now locked within a most ingenious of cages."

A memory of childhood flashed through Charlie's head. Finger cuffs he had played with in his youth. A simple toy, but effective. The more you pulled, the tighter they became. Resistance only worsened your situation, and that was exactly the predicament they were in now.

"What can we do, Bob? We need to get out of here."

Charlie's pale friend slid to the ground, sitting cross-legged and looking as relaxed as one could, given the situation.

"*Do*?" he replied with a somewhat amused grin. "We *do* nothing," he said as he began releasing the illumination spell, the slow rumble at their feet lessening as he did. "What we do now," he said as they settled into darkness, "is wait."

CHAPTER TWO

It was an unfamiliar feeling for Charlie, not being able to use his power even though he could feel it just begging to be unleashed. Unfortunately, if he did so he and his friend would be summarily squished into a compact and bloody ball. Not exactly his idea of a good day.

So he held back, kept his power in check, and waited. And waited. And waited some more. The tedium was horrible, waiting for the other shoe to drop, but it didn't. It seemed that the head priest who had trapped them here had no intention of finishing them off. At least, not yet. There also did not seem to be any rush to bring them in for questioning, so it was here they would stay, sitting in the dark.

Charlie hadn't planned on being locked inside a magic-sensitive deathtrap when he started his day, but then, most of what had happened to him over the past several years was well outside the parameters of what anyone would call a normal life.

First, he had been sucked into yet another new galaxy, which would be a wild enough experience if it happened only once. But twice? Charlie felt like he was winning the universe's shittiest lottery. But it only got worse from there.

Battling to survive a world where his power was gone had proven a challenge he and his friends were up for, but only just. The planet, surrounded by multiple black holes negating all magic, or *Allpower,* as they called it in this realm, forced them to rely solely on the limited technology they had with them. That, and their wits.

Ara had nearly met her fate on that day, losing her power and burning horribly in an out-of-control descent. Only quick thinking by her friends had saved her. Griggalt, the dragon from Charlie's realm, however, had not been so fortunate, nor had Gustavo, one of the two AI ships pulled into the trap with them.

Fortunately, at least one of their ships had survived the crash landing with his systems intact. Kip was as chatty and functional as ever, unlike Gustavo, who had broken up on impact. They learned quite quickly that the Urvalin had designed this planet as a prison of sorts for their enemies and surrounded it with energy-dampening microsats that killed the systems of any craft that flew through it.

But others had survived, and with their leader, Nakk, and his right hand, Skohla, they had managed to form a respectable fighting force and turn the tables on the Urvalin, breaking their friends out of captivity while escaping the trap world.

It was a challenging experience, and all of this had been going on while Leila was waiting for him back home, pregnant and ready to pop any time now. At least, they thought that was the case. The couple had no idea what the intergalactic, interspecies union might mean for gestation, but it seemed relatively normal thus far.

The important thing was, she needed him with her for the big day, and here Charlie sat, stranded in an entirely different galaxy.

At least he could count on the Magus stone she wore around her neck to keep her safe. The deep-green pendant contained a great depth of power handed down over generations, bound to her family line. It would protect her at all costs, though sometimes the lines between friend and foe became a bit blurred, as Charlie had learned firsthand, and a bit painfully at that.

Another couple in their circle of friends was expecting as well, but *that* pair certainly didn't need a Magus stone to defend themselves.

Bawb was one of the deadliest killers in not two, but *three* galaxies now, and his mate was equally skilled. Hunze was also an Ootaki, whose power-generating and absorbing race had never been able to use their own magic. It was a quirk of their physiology. They could produce and store it in their golden hair, but they could never use it for themselves.

Her union with Bawb had changed all of that when he gifted her power back to her in an act of love. The two were bonded in multiple ways, their power as well as their hearts forever intertwined. And that pair would lay waste to worlds to protect their unborn child.

When he'd heard the news, Bawb was both shocked and delighted. Family wasn't the sort of thing a Ghalian assassin ever thought about having, but his life had taken more than a few drastic turns since the fateful day he had met the man from Earth. The man he now considered more a brother than a friend.

"We're going to be dads, dude," Charlie had said one cool evening on the beaches of Malibu, where they had taken up residence. "Holy crap. I mean, think about it. *Us*, of all people."

"It is a life I had not considered within my reach not so long ago," Bawb replied.

"Hunze is gonna be a great mom. And you're gonna be an awesome dad. Seriously. You'll be great at it."

"And so will you, Charlie. I find it pleasant to think that one day not too long from now, our children will grow up together, much the way Daisy and Sarah's children have."

"Arlo and Ripley are thick as thieves," Charlie said. "And damn competent for their age."

"Now, imagine what *our* children could achieve growing up under *our* tutelage," the assassin mused.

It was a thought that had warmed both of their hearts that day.

But now they were stranded in a distant galaxy, and their attempt to reverse the flow of the portal that had trapped them there had failed, the legendary Vortaxis they had managed to track down, steal, and deploy crumbling to dust from the slightest contact with Charlie and Ara's magic. A cruel twist of fate that their own power was anathema to the most sought after of Allpower relics in the galaxy.

And with its loss, stranded they remained.

Worse, while they were stuck in this place, the Urvalin were hard at work, doing their best to take over not one, not two, but three galaxies to unite their power and claim dominion over all of their inhabitants.

Cut off from news from the other realms, Charlie and his friends had no idea the risk their friends and family faced.

At least, not until Arlo and Ripley had flown through the portal, a power-linking Bakana rod in their possession for Charlie. It was the one magical device they knew of that could connect power across galaxies, sharing it between those possessing the remaining rods. Sending one across had been a desperate attempt to tie in Charlie and Ara's power and, hopefully, overcome the Urvalin threat.

But the kids, riding on the backs of two dragons, Drombus and Duzza, had arrived only to find themselves in a strange galaxy with no sign of Charlie anywhere in sight. So, naturally, they went looking for him, leaving a faint trace of their scent in their wake.

It was all the Zomoki needed.

Ara detected it upon their return to the portal, but she only knew of their presence, but she had no idea how or why they might be here. One thing was for certain, Charlie and his friends were determined to find out, and as soon as they possibly could. Their very fates could depend on it. But the question remained: where had the troublesome youths gone?

CHAPTER THREE

"What a shit show," Arlo grumbled, yanking his helmet off and throwing it to the ground in frustration.

"Dude!"

"What?"

"The air!" Ripley shouted, waving her arms around.

"What? It's breathable."

"You didn't know that!"

"I do now."

"Ugh, you're ridiculous," she said, taking her own helmet off and setting it aside. "Just because Drombus and Duzza can breathe here doesn't mean we can. They're dragons, idiot."

"Well, duh. But look around. Green plants galore. And fresh water. And clouds."

"That's not enough to—"

"And my suit scanner said the atmosphere was safe," he added, tapping the little screen embedded in the forearm of his space armor. "Pretty cool, right?"

Ripley looked at her own unit and scrolled through the screens until a new display presented itself. Apparently, he was right. Their suits, aside from protecting them from the elements, space, and battle, also monitored their environment.

Arlo turned off his screen and deactivated the contour-hugging armor, allowing it to loosen to its inert, slightly baggy state, then began stripping it off. It was a marvel of engineering, flexible and thin enough to allow for freedom of movement, but also reactive to impact, hardening to spread any blow across its mass. More than that, it also possessed basic shielding tech built in, along with the usual array of bells and whistles.

And, despite its light weight, the material could sure take a hit. In fact, it was that armor that had undoubtedly saved both of their lives in the skirmish they'd narrowly escaped, just before they frantically jumped across several systems to make sure they weren't being followed.

"What are you doing?" Ripley asked. "Keep that on! There could be more hostiles here."

"Drombus, tell her what you told me."

The deep-orange dragon shrugged. "This world seems uninhabited. I didn't smell anything like civilization as we descended."

His cousin, Duzza, nodded her agreement. "He's right. There were no signs of developed society. No burning of fuels, no cooking, no energy traces wafting in the wind. We're alone down here."

Ripley shook her head. "Sure, but what about predators?"

Arlo laughed, and the two massive dragons looked at one another with amusement.

"Okay, fine. You two will eat anything that comes our way," she relented.

"I do hope so," Duzza said. "I am famished."

Drombus chuckled. "Go hunt, Cousin. I will stay with our friends."

Duzza gave a thankful nod then leapt into the air, her wings kicking up waves of dust as she powered off in search of prey.

Arlo sat down on the dirt and began looking over his armor, searching for any breaks in the material. It was dented up in the thicker sections and looked like it had been put through the ringer, but so far as he could tell it was still intact and functional. After the beating they'd taken when they landed on that strange world, it was almost a miracle.

"So what was the deal with those people?" he asked. "I mean, they just wigged-out on us as soon as we landed."

Ripley began peeling off her armor as well. She'd taken quite a beating from those people's energy weapons and wasn't so sure her own suit had escaped without damage.

"No idea," she said, pulling her legs free. "One thing is for sure, they seemed legit freaked out by the dragons. Like, I mean *seriously* unhinged. And when we started casting? Holy crap, they came at us like we were some sort of invading army of demons or something."

"But we were just using our konuses is all," Arlo grumbled. "And not only that, did you notice how totally wrong the spells were working? I mean, I know we're still learning and stuff, but things weren't casting the way they were supposed to *at all*."

"Tell me about it. Did you see how I almost burned down that one guy's cart? I was just trying to stun him."

Drombus sat up tall, breathing in not just the air of the world, but the smells of the galaxy around them. "There is something very, very off about this whole place. Unlike you, I've been using my power my entire life, and even *I* am experiencing the same problems as you. I think it's this galaxy in general. It does not react well to our magic."

Arlo shook his head and sighed. "Great. Just great. Here we come, trying to ride in like the cavalry, and we nearly wound up the ones needing to be rescued. This sucks."

"What about their tech, though?" Ripley asked. "Did you get

readings on the weapons?"

"Yeah. Weird, right?"

"Seriously. I've never seen anything like it. All of their stuff for that matter. Crazy advanced tech way beyond anything we have. Honestly, I'm amazed we got out of there."

"We almost didn't," Drombus said, brushing a char mark from his scales where a particularly powerful blaster struck him despite his protective spells and the shielding from his harness. Clearly, he would need to have the shield phasing adjusted, since his own magic was apparently not up to the task. Not at the moment, anyway.

The brush nearby rustled, and a deep grunting sound rumbled from within.

"Uh, Rip?" Arlo said in a hush.

"I hear it."

"*Them*," Drombus corrected.

A moment later a half dozen large, tusked animals the size of feral hogs charged out of the bushes right at them. They were big and tough-looking, devoid of fur, sporting an overlapping plate armor system almost like an armadillo. The creatures also possessed six legs rather than four, adding to their thoroughly alien appearance.

"Shit, shit, shit!" Arlo blurted, "*Manabus onecto!*"

He cast what should have been a simple force spell to push the animals back. Instead, three of them imploded while the remaining trio just seemed to get angrier.

Arlo backpedaled, tripping over his armor, which he was suddenly very much regretting stripping off.

A pair of taloned feet dropped from the sky on top of them, snatching up two while knocking the third for a loop. Ripley didn't hesitate, grabbing her pulse rifle and pumping a few rounds into it.

"Tasty," Duzza said, popping the beasts into her mouth. "I

was following a small herd of creatures when I smelled these closing on your location."

"Much appreciated," Drombus said. "But I could have handled them, you know."

"I do, but they smelled so good," she replied with a toothy grin. "You should eat as well, Drombus. We expended a lot of energy. It is your turn to hunt a bit. Now *I* will stay with our friends."

The male dragon didn't need to be told twice, giving a little nod and flying off to feed to his heart's content.

"And you should eat too," she said to her young friends. "Here, I'll roast it for you."

Duzza spat a little magical fire, the stream far less than she'd intended. "Hang on, let me try that again." This time a powerful burst escaped her mouth, torching the carcass in an instant. "Oops. Apologies. Magic is not working properly here. Not even my fire."

"No worries," Arlo said, poking at the smoking beast with the long knife he carried. "I think the scales took the brunt of it. And while it's disconcerting, it's also nice to know I'm not the only one whose magic isn't working right."

"That's an understatement," Ripley said, looking at the gruesome remains of the other animals.

Arlo peeled back one of the burnt scales of the roasted beast and cut off a chunk of meat. It was charred on the outside despite the scales, but a few inches in, past the ruined bits, was a sizzling-hot taste of heaven.

"Hey, it's not bad," he said, offering some to his cousin. "You gotta try this, Rip."

She took her own knife and cut off a piece. While they were used to eating food-replicator generated meats, both had been raised by a very particular type of parents. The kind who made absolutely sure they could fend for themselves if the shit hit the fan and food became scarce. They didn't hunt often, but killing and cleaning game was something they had learned from an early age.

Live prey wasn't their preference, but in a pinch it would keep them alive. And in this case, they would need all the energy they could get.

The two ate quietly for several minutes, pondering the mess they'd gotten into, when Drombus returned, smelling faintly of smoke and barbecue.

"My flames were a bit off," he noted as he settled down with the others. "Duzza, have you still been having problems as well?"

"Yes. Spells and magic simply do not seem to work the same here. We'll need to do some experiments. Test out our powers. It appears to be affecting us all, whether using a konus or natural magic. And that could be very bad."

"Understatement of the week," Arlo said with a grim chuckle. "All of us need to be careful. Spell casting is *waaaay* too iffy for my comfort."

"For any of us," Ripley added. She turned to Drombus. "But when we first arrived here you were able to use your power to help get Duzza and us clear of that portal and the black holes. What changed?"

"I fear that was the Bakana rod and not me," the dragon replied. "I realized it was in contact with my body when Arlo jammed it into the harness as we were pulled through."

Ripley knew what that meant. "So, you were pulling power from the others."

"I'm afraid there is no other explanation. Being from my own galaxy, I'd never even heard of a Bakana rod before, but now that I've had time to think about your explanation of how it works, linking casters regardless of distance, I have to think that's what happened."

"So, someone unwillingly donated a lot of power to our escape," Arlo said. "And they wouldn't have been able to prepare themselves. I hope they're okay. That was a big draw."

Little did he know, the Ghalian master hiding on Earth was anything but okay. He had been planning to use his considerable power to fight the Urvalin, linking with casters in the other two galaxies, but Drombus's unexpected connection while he held the exposed rod had drained him. Drained him to death.

Ripley, being a non-powered being, picked up the Bakana rod and studied its length. "We should keep it properly wrapped to protect against accidental connection."

"Good idea," Arlo said. "For now, use this."

He tossed her an emergency blanket from his survival kit. It was thin and light, but it was also moderately durable. More importantly, it would prevent direct contact with the rod, and that was the most important thing. They'd just have to find a more sturdy covering later.

"Thanks," she said, wrapping it tightly. "So, now what do we do? Duzza? Drombus? Are you guys sure Ara was on that planet?"

"We tracked her scent there. And Charlie's as well. There is no mistaking it, they were there. It just seems they left before we arrived," Duzza said.

"Clearly," her cousin agreed. "For now we must simply continue searching." He sniffed the air. "There is still faint sign of them. It will take some doing, but if we are lucky, we should be able to track them down."

Arlo began pulling his armor back on. "And if not? All of our families are at risk until we find them. If we can't link the galaxies, *everyone* is screwed."

The dragon nodded his enormous head. "Then we had best not fail. Now, where in the worlds could they be?"

CHAPTER FOUR

It was dark.

It was quiet.

It was getting to be a bit claustrophobic.

More than that, Charlie was becoming increasingly agitated at being stuck inside some sort of magic-sensitive ball-trap-thingy. This wasn't how it was supposed to go. This wasn't how it was supposed to go at all.

"What the hell, Bob?" he groused.

"They are being teenagers, Charlie," the assassin replied.

"Oh, yeah, sure. But when I was a teen I borrowed my dad's car without telling him, or stayed out too late, or went to a show I wasn't old enough for with a fake I.D. But this?" He gestured in the dark. "The kids are going and screwing things up royally for us. We were on good terms with these people. Their head priest trusted us, we were allowed to come and go, and they weren't any the wiser we'd taken the—"

"Charlie," Bawb interrupted.

"We'd taken the *thing*," he said, not voicing the name of the Vortaxis, the holiest of relics, which they'd stolen, then subsequently destroyed by accident. "What I'm saying is, things were looking up. Or, at least they weren't getting any worse. But now? They've gone and messed all of that up."

Bawb let out a low chuckle. "We are going to be fathers, Charlie. I believe we had both better get used to it. I sincerely doubt our children will be any better."

"Oh, I'm going to raise mine to respect authority."

"Like *you* never do?" Bawb shot back.

"Hey! I just work *around* it sometimes."

"And our children will likely do the same, as have most youths to some extent or another."

"Well, my kid's gonna be born without a father if we don't patch up whatever the hell Arlo and Ripley did here and get back to the task. I've gotta find a way back, Bob."

"I know, Charlie, and we will do all we can to achieve that objective. You have my word on that. But for the moment, be calm. Losing your temper will not get us out of here any faster."

Charlie took a deep breath of the increasingly stale air and wondered if they might actually suffocate in here before their captors let them out. He had no intention of letting that happen.

He reached out and ran his hand over the inside of the ball once more, feeling the smooth metal encasing them. He didn't dare try even the slightest bit of magic. They had already learned the hard way what would happen if they did. Namely, being compacted into a very small, very bloody ball.

"Okay," Charlie said. "Assessment?"

"A novel form of trap. Clearly tech-based, which makes sense, as there is no Allpower in this system, though that does make its construction and triggering mechanisms something of a curiosity."

"How so?"

"If Allpower, or magic, if you prefer, is not functional in this system, why create a trap that reacts to it?"

Charlie had to admit, he had a point.

"Well, I'd wager that given the way these people originally wound up here, they probably designed this thing as a failsafe device. A just-in-case trap on the off chance someone should actually figure out how to cast on this planet. Someone like us, apparently."

"Or like Arlo and Ripley," Bawb added.

"Yeah, I was thinking the same thing. They could be trapped here in another ball somewhere, and we wouldn't even know it. And if their magic is misfiring as badly as ours was when we first arrived in this galaxy, who knows what kind of trouble they're in."

Charlie pushed hard on the inside of the ball where his fingers felt the slightest of seams. It was almost like a pill bug rolled up on itself. Or so he thought. In the dark, he couldn't quite be sure. One thing was certain, he needed to get out.

"Okay, screw this," he grumbled, drawing his pulse pistol. "If magic won't work, we still have other ways to try to get out of this thing. Blast our way out if we have to."

Bawb reached out in a flash, smacking the weapon out of his hand.

"Ow! Hey, what the hell!"

"Do not fire your weapon in here, Charlie. We do not know the nature of this material. For all we know, it could deflect your pulse blast and kill us both."

"Fine. I guess you're right," Charlie sighed as he groped around in the dark until he found his pistol and reholstered it. "But how did you know where my hand even was? It's pitch-black in here."

"Years of training, my friend. Many years of training."

"You'll have to teach me that sometime. If we don't suffocate to death, that is."

"There will be a means out. There always is. We just have to discover it. What do we know about these people that may help us?"

"They're religious dickheads guarding a false relic?"

"Not that."

"They *hate* Allpower users?"

"True, but also not much help."

"They're stylish dressers?"

"Charlie, be serious."

But a spark had been struck. A thread pulled.

"Hang on," Charlie said. "Holy shit, that's it."

"What is?"

Charlie was already in full engineer mode, breaking down the problem to its constituent parts and troubleshooting it. It had been some time since he'd needed to use those skills, but while perhaps a little rusty, once an engineer, always an engineer. He couldn't part with that aspect of his personality, just like he couldn't part with one of his limbs. And in this instance, it was a good thing.

Engineer brain, his friends had called it. Once he became fixated on a task, look out. He would often forego food and even sleep until there was a solution. And with no distractions inside the silent ball, his mind was already churning.

"This thing. Their tech. It's advanced, right?"

"Clearly."

"And they triggered this independently of our magic use, without physical contact. We weren't casting when it snapped shut on us."

"Again, yes."

"Well, we know they don't use Allpower. I mean, hell, they seem to have developed an actual hatred of it, so that means there had to be some sort of wireless signal to activate this thing. Did you see anyone with anything looking like a remote control unit?"

"I did not. But that does not mean that—"

"Exactly!"

"You are losing me, Charlie. This tangent—"

"Stylish dressers. The head priest had all sorts of tech *woven into his clothing.*"

"Yes, I was there, I recall," Bawb said, catching where Charlie was going with this. "And if the triggers were subtle things woven into the fabric itself, that means they cannot have too great of a range."

"Yes!"

"Or so we hope."

"Don't be a downer, man. It's our best bet. Hang on a sec."

Charlie began digging in his small pouch, dumping out its contents until he found what he was seeking. A faint glow illuminated the inside of their trap as he activated the display on the small scanning unit he pretty much always kept tucked away in his kit.

He shifted it to night mode, darkening the display further, ready to shut it off at a moment's notice if the trap began to react and shrink around them. Luckily, it remained stable.

"Okay, let's see here. I've been keeping this running on standby just to get background readings to log planetary details, but I was thinking. What about that signal? It would show up as an anomaly in the readings. I just have to play it back to the time of the fight, which should be easy to find since all hell broke loose, and then sift through the waveforms."

Charlie's fingers were already at work, stripping away ambient noise and refining the signal readings while he searched for the signal.

"Is there a trace?" Bawb asked.

"Not yet. These people use utterly novel technology, so I have no idea what I'm even looking for. I mean, clearly it's not a signal like our gear would send. That would have popped up immediately." He tweaked the settings, refining the search, stripping away layers and cleaning up the different waves of readings. "The signal could be anything. If we had a baseline of their tech to work from that would help. A Rosetta, so to speak. But given enough time—ah, there's the first bit of the fight. See the spikes all around? Some is us, but some must be them communicating with each other. Now, if I pull this back and remove the background noise, we may see something."

But nothing appeared. He searched and searched, but all he could see were what appeared to be two-way communications. Nothing in the way of what look like triggering transmissions.

"It would be brief, I would assume," Bawb suggested.

"I looked for short-burst signals. Nada."

"Perhaps it was encoded within one of the communications signals."

"Nope. Looked there too. I cleaned up the signals and I tell ya, I—" Charlie fell silent.

"Charlie?"

"Holy shit. Hang on."

Charlie reversed what he had done, unfiltering the chatter and noise, returning it back to the overall picture. Carefully, he fine-tuned the search, scrolling forward and back manually.

"Got it!" he exclaimed. "Son of a bitch, it was hidden in plain sight, buried within the background noise. Totally different type of signal than their comms. But see this? The flare right when this trap was sprung."

Bawb nodded his understanding but knew this was not the endgame. Not yet, anyway.

"Have you found a means of escape, Charlie?"

"You know what? I think I have," he replied. "Now I just have to decipher it."

CHAPTER FIVE

Despite his considerable prowess, Charlie took far longer than he would have liked to break down the specific components of the remote-triggering signal. But then, this was entirely alien technology, so he really couldn't be expected to just pick it up in an instant.

He moved slowly, not only because he was learning as he went, but because there existed a very real possibility of his accidentally killing both himself and Bawb if he transmitted the wrong trigger signal. This would take time, and there was nothing else to do about it.

"I think I've got the patterning of the signal locked down," he said after a long while. "If I'm right, this should open the orb back up."

"*Should*?" Bawb said.

"Well, let me put it this way. If things don't go quite the way I hope, it's been nice knowing you."

"Such magnificent confidence, Charlie. Thank you. I feel all of my concerns allayed," Bawb joked.

He'd faced death more times than anyone would care to count, and after a while it just became another day at the office for him. Of course, his Wampeh Ghalian training since childhood helped with that equation. He was ready to go, if that was what fate dictated. He just preferred not to and would do everything in his power to stick around to hold his child in his arms, just like Charlie hoped to do with his own.

"You ready?" Charlie asked.

"Just get it over with," Bawb sighed. He seemed exasperated and bored, but Charlie saw the glint of blades in his hands. If this worked, he would be ready for whoever was waiting for them outside.

"Okay, here goes nothing."

Charlie keyed the jury-rigged scanner and began broadcasting what he sincerely hoped was the reverse signal for their prison. He held his finger steady, prepared to stop on a dime if the orb started to shrink on them again.

For a long moment there was nothing.

"Maybe you had it wrong," Bawb said.

"It's not wrong. I just have the power turned down low."

"So, do you plan to turn it up?"

"You're killing me, man," Charlie said as he ramped up the power.

Up and up the signal went, but nothing happened until, all of a sudden, the trap simply sprang open.

It was night outside, dark. Apparently quite a few hours had passed since they were captured. The fresh air felt incredible in their lungs, but this was no time to revel in so simple a thing. There were people nearby, and they had to be dealt with, and quickly.

Fortunately, Charlie and Bawb had been in a far darker environment than this for some time, and their eyes took in the ambient light with ease. The guards who had been standing by in case any of the prisoners' friends might return to attempt a rescue, however, were not so lucky.

Their backs were to the orb, and had Charlie opened it just a few minutes earlier one would have fallen in, having been leaning against it while scanning the area around them for any threats.

What they didn't realize was that Charlie and Bawb believed in one very simple motto.

No one is coming.

Whatever mess they found themselves in, it was up to them to get themselves out. Self-rescue was something they prepared for, and any assistance they might receive was merely a pleasant surprise.

The guards, however, were in for a very *un*pleasant surprise.

There were five of them. Quite a number for a secure and magic-proof containment device. The mixture of species seemed representative of this world. Apparently, Arlo and Ripley had made more of an impression on the locals than they'd originally realized, and that association now made Charlie and his friends very dangerous indeed in the eyes of the ruling priesthood.

A pair of the guards were bipedal, while the others possessed additional limbs. It was dark, so Charlie didn't get the best of looks at their specific morphology, but he suspected one might very well be an amphibian from the feel of its skin as he wrapped his arm around its neck.

Three of the guards were subdued in a flash, rendered unconscious with good old-fashioned violence. No magic would be used. Not this close to the trap. The two remaining were gagged and bound but not knocked out. They had plans for those two.

They hauled the three slumbering guards into the trap area, but not before Charlie stepped well clear and cast the smallest of time-delay spells on one of their boots. It was inert magic in its present form, but when two minutes had passed it would trigger, releasing a simple cleaning spell. It was a useful thing after a day in the mud, but in this instance the spell served a different purpose.

"Think that'll just about do it," Charlie said. "Come on, we've got a little walk ahead of us."

He and Bawb pushed the conscious guards ahead of them and walked in the direction of the main temple entrance, sticking to the shadows and side streets as they went. Two minutes later they heard the faintest of clangs in the distance as the spell activated and the trap triggered with them well clear. To any who might pass by, the closed trap would just look as though the guards had left their posts.

The route to the temple was straightforward, and with the two guards ahead of them—now ungagged but with pointy bits pressed against their backs—no one even thought to question the men walking with them.

They entered the building and followed the path they had learned from their prior visit. It was odd, returning like this when not so long ago they had been treated as welcome guests. New trading partners, even. But times had changed, thanks to the teens from Earth. Hopefully, they would be able to rectify that.

"Where are you going with those two?" one of the temple guards asked as they delved deeper into the building.

"Well, I guess the jig's up," Charlie said, swinging his blade up to his prisoner's neck. The alien possessed a scaly skin, but he felt confident his blade could make quick work of it if it had to. He hoped no one forced his hand.

"We wish to speak with your head priest," Bawb said calmly, allowing the guard's translator tech to catch up with his words.

The guard didn't draw his weapon but rather stared at the strange intruders, then spoke over some sort of hidden comms link. Charlie couldn't see where it was mounted, but it seemed to allow him to communicate with only the faintest of sounds.

"You are to follow me," the guard said, then turned and walked away.

"Apparently, that worked," Charlie said.

"It would seem, but keep your wits about you. No telling what lies ahead."

The guard led them down a series of corridors, winding this way and that, likely to disorient the intruders. Little did he know who he was dealing with. Between the master assassin and the spaceship engineer, keeping track of a few twists and turns was child's play.

The guard stopped at a large door. "In here."

Charlie peered inside. The priest was sitting in a somewhat ornate chair, but not what anyone would call a throne, exactly, watching them with great interest as they led their hostages in ahead of themselves. Guards lining the walls had them fixed in the sights of their weapons yet did not open fire. It was a good thing, as Charlie wasn't sure his and Bawb's misfiring defensive spells wouldn't cause irreparable damage if deployed.

"You broke free of our holding sphere," the priest marveled. "How did you manage that?"

"Trade secret, I'm afraid," Charlie said with a forced grin. "But listen, there's been a terrible misunderstanding, and we want to clear it up."

"You possess Allpower. We have seen it. Your kin have defiled our city with its filthy energy."

"The kids? Please, understand, they're just teenagers. Yes, we know them, but we have no idea what they're doing here. We tracked them back to your world when we found out they were even here."

The priest seemed unimpressed.

"You've spoken with us at length before," Bawb said. "Shared a meal. Engaged in trade. We have no reason to ruin a blossoming relationship."

"But their actions—"

"Were their own, and not at our direction," Bawb said.

Charlie took a step forward, pushing his hostage ahead. "They're just kids. And the spells they cast, did they use a weird kind of Allpower?"

"They did. And quite destructively at that."

"See? That's the thing. They're from my world."

"We gathered by their appearance."

"Right. But on my world, *no one* has power. They were using what we call a konus to cast."

"A what?"

"It's like the bandas people use for storing Allpower, only konuses aren't from your realm. Nor is the power they contain. And that's the problem. Our power doesn't work right here. Spells go awry. Something about this place doesn't quite mix right. And that's why we must find them before they get into real trouble."

"More trouble than here?" the priest said with a laugh. "I suppose you fear them engaging with scavengers and pirates, no doubt."

"No, actually. It's the Urvalin we're worried about. And if those two are here, then that means something's come up at my home world. Back in my own galaxy."

"*Charlie*," Bawb hissed, but it was too late.

"Did you say *galaxy*?" the priest asked, leaning forward with genuine interest.

Charlie figured what was done was done and there was no putting the genie back in the bottle at this point. "Yes. We're not from this galaxy. The Urvalin pulled us through and trapped us for a while on some prison planet."

The priest leaned back in the ornate chair. "You did not mention this at our prior meeting."

"Yeah? Well, people kind of freak out when you mention intergalactic plots with the Urvalin, okay?"

The priest's dour expression softened and they actually chuckled softly.

Charlie looked at Bawb. This was their moment of truth.

"Okay, we're going to let these two go as a sign of good faith. I'm hoping you'll take us at our word. We truly mean you no harm. We just want to find those kids."

They carefully cut the bindings and let the captives go free. The priest studied them a long moment, then waved to the guards. "Lower your weapons."

Charlie felt the weight of the world slip off of his shoulders and breathed a sigh of relief. "Fantastic. Now, can we have a *real* talk?"

CHAPTER SIX

Aboard the pirate ship *Coratta*, all was quiet. Quiet, but by no means peaceful. A storm was brewing, and its name was Karasalia Palmarian.

Emotions were running high when Rika and the girls reunited with Marban aboard his ship. Kara and Vee, while having been through their fair share of battles and with rapidly growing powers, were, nevertheless, still teenagers. As such, some things affected them with a little more intensity than they might someone who'd been around the block a few times more.

Things like having their good friends sucked through a portal into a distant galaxy. A galaxy they weren't even sure they would be able to return from.

The girls had done all they could to help distract the Urvalin to give Marban a clear shot to the trap portal, working with Rika and Orgalius to occupy the invading forces long enough to allow him to cross over. But things had gone wrong. *Really* wrong.

Ultimately, Arlo and Ripley, along with Drombus and Duzza, had been the ones to take the Bakana rod through the portal to Charlie.

It was a knife in the heart for the girls. Their friends, no older than they were, had somehow taken over for the seasoned warriors. They'd done the job that wasn't even theirs.

"Kara, please," Marban pleaded. "You know it wasn't intentional. We were in combat and blocked from the portal."

"They're gone because of *you*," Kara spat. "This wasn't the way it was supposed to happen. This wasn't the plan."

Rika tried to put her hand on the girl's shoulder, but it was aggressively brushed off. She let it be and stepped back.

"You aren't children anymore, Kara. You know what happens in battle. It's fluid, and ugly, and messy, and more often than not you wind up with things not going the way you'd planned. It's the nature of war."

"This was supposed to be simple," Kara countered. "Fly there, have them run interference, and Marban pops through to the other side. *Simple.*"

Magic began crackling along her skin like the static from shuffling your feet on a plush carpet, tiny sparks of power seeping out as her feelings flared.

"Kara, you need to chill," Vee said.

"I *am*."

"No, you're doing it again."

Kara looked down at herself and realized what Vee was saying, quickly centering herself as her uncle Korbin had taught her, putting her power in check.

"I'm sorry, little one," Marban said. "We did the best we could with the situation we had at hand. But I promise, I'll do everything I can to get them back."

"Everything you can? You couldn't even fall through a stupid portal!"

She spun on her heel and stormed off. Vee, while upset, was far less so than her friend. It was clear to all present, even the dragons, that Kara had stronger feelings for Arlo than she admitted. Perhaps even to herself.

"I'll look after her," Vee said, then hurried off in pursuit.

Nixxus and Gazz looked at one another, the dragons actually feeling a bit awkward for a change. Teenage emotions were something they were new to, and this little display had been almost as unsettling as the Urvalin, in its own way.

"I wish there was something we could do to help," Nixxus said. "This sort of situation is a bit new to us."

"Don't sweat it," Rika said. "She'll calm down."

"I certainly hope so," Gazz said. "They do not seem likely to calm anytime soon."

"I was a teenager once, and believe me, it's a hormonal roller coaster."

The dragons looked at one another questioningly. "A what?"

"A roller—nevermind. What I'm saying is, it's full of ups and downs. Leave it at that. She'll be fine; it'll just take some time. And right now we would be best served just leaving her alone. Vee'll talk her down."

"Good," Nixxus said, a tiny sliver of worry in her voice. "Her magic is frighteningly powerful. Having her casting from my back, I can *feel* her potential. She will grow into a *very* powerful woman one day."

"Fortunately, while she *is* rather upset, at least she is on our side," Gazz added with a forced chuckle.

No one bought it. He was just as unsettled as his friend. And while Vee's own Ootaki powers were far less than those of her friend, she was quickly coming into her own as well. He looked at Rika and Marban as they mused what to do next, then turned to Nixxus.

"It seems there is not a lot for us to do here at the moment. What do you say we go help Orgalius probe the dampening minefields for a bit?" he asked. "I'm sure he could use the help, and there's not much else we can do to contribute for now."

Nixxus flexed her wings. "A good idea, my friend." The two

turned for the hangar door. "We will be back in a little while. Summon us if you require our assistance."

"We'll do just that," Marban called after them. "But I think you've got a little while. Methinks the girls are going to need a bit of alone time."

The dragons nodded, then took flight, easily passing through the magic field sealing in the air as the heavy doors closed behind them.

Rika looked at Marban and sighed. "Kids, right?"

"Yeah. They can be a handful," he agreed.

"Makes me even less sure about ever having any."

Marban just shrugged. He had no children of his own, but he had grown close to one once. A child under his protection. One he had guarded with honor and watched grow. It was one of the most fulfilling things he had ever experienced, but also one of the most painful. But that was a long, long time ago, and well before he became a pirate. Even longer since he'd come to this new galaxy.

"Drink?" he asked.

"Drink," she readily agreed, heading for the captain's quarters where the good stuff was kept.

Rika and Marban sipped a lovely bottle of whiskey Charlie had presented to his friend recently. A bottle that was hundreds of years old. He'd discovered a climate-controlled storage facility during an expedition into the still-abandoned areas of Malibu and had come across the secret cache of what he called *the good stuff* in a disguised wine cellar hidden beneath the kitchen floor of a rather opulent estate.

After loading up a few bottles, he'd sealed it back up. A break-in-case-of-emergency stockpile of adult beverages that had, amazingly, not been created by a food replicator. While the machine was capable of reproducing an identical copy perfectly, there was just something special about drinking a bottle you knew had history to it. Craftsmanship.

"We're so screwed," Marban said as he poured himself another tall glass. "I'm not one for doom and gloom talk, but Cal is in hiding after that Los Angeles attack on his command center, Zed and the fleet are scattered and largely blocked from action by those cursed dampening fields floating out there, Sid, Joshua, and the others are stuck on the surface at Dark Side base, no one can communicate with one another without us personally relaying messages, and the entire planet Earth is unreachable to pretty much everyone but you and me."

"Yeah, but we *are* pretty awesome," Rika said with a wry grin. "And Cal did have us relay that idea about possible communications to the others."

"Yeah, but it's just not sustainable. Our magic allows us to fly through those dead zones, but you, me, and a few dragons? It's not enough."

"Which is why we had to get that Bakana rod to Charlie. If we can link the rods across these three galaxies, we might just be able to overpower the Urvalin."

"And Malalia?" Marban said with distaste. "You know her father buried me and my men for hundreds of years. Frozen solid. It was not pleasant."

"Oh, I know. Remember who dug you out, buddy."

He would never forget. That was the day he met Rika. "Nasty spell, that one," he said, ever grateful to have been rescued from the sands and revived so many years later.

Having survived something like that, Marban found he now looked at life a little differently than before. He was still a very capable and very gregarious pirate, but he also savored the beauty in life. The little things. And, in this moment, a bottle of very, very old whiskey.

He took a slow sip. "So, Malalia Maktan? I still can't wrap my head around it."

"She's proven to be an unlikely, but surprisingly deft ally in this fight."

"Not because she wants to, though. That bomb you put in her neck is quite the incentive."

"Yes and no. I spent a lot of time with her back before, well, you know. And having been close with her, I can say she really does seem to be a changed woman. Fatima's been keeping a close eye on her as they support our guerrilla forces, of course, but there's no doubt her magic is helping slow the Urvalin's progress. Every bit of power helps, and she has a *lot* of it now that she's fed. The Urvalin casters seemed to give her a decent boost in her magic."

"Kara is growing quite powerful as well."

"That she is. Vee too."

"But imagine if the girls hadn't made it through the portal? Those two Zomok—I mean *dragons*—are really something. Flying through the sun like that? I'm glad to have 'em on our side."

"Ditto. But the one downside is the Urvalin bolstered the hell out of their forces surrounding the portal's sun access on this side. And you know they did it on the other side as well."

Marban sat quietly, musing the various twists and turns of the situation as he swirled his drink in his tumbler. There were three galaxies in play here, and an opponent who seemed able to communicate across all of them. It gave them a distinct advantage, especially when they'd managed to cut off all signals between Earth, Dark Side base, and Zed's fleet.

"You think that idea Cal had might actually work?" he asked. "This Moroze Code thing."

"*Morse* Code," Rika corrected. "And yeah. Crazy as it sounds, it just might work."

CHAPTER SEVEN

It took time for Cal to carry out his portion of the plan. Re-establishing a communications link with the fleet and Dark Side base was paramount, but unlike his counterparts in space, he had to be particularly careful. His location, his very survival, was a secret, and while the Urvalin may have developed an inkling that he was still alive by now, they didn't have confirmation. Nor did they know where he was.

With the destruction of his Los Angeles command station, Cal had gone underground, quite literally. His main consciousness was residing in secret while the world believed him to have been physically located in the building in LA.

Fortunately, other AIs were still abundant, and much of what he was up to could be written off as one of them tinkering with devices. But he couldn't risk the Urvalin uncovering the truth if they looked closer. Not yet, anyway.

"It has to be done slowly," he instructed the cyborg workers at the enormous solar power station in the Mojave Desert. *"Rotate the selected units precisely as I directed."*

The cyborgs were the skeleton crew that manned the facility, which heated salt to a molten state then used it to drive turbines to create energy. It was a bit more rudimentary than high-tech solar collection panels, but the system had survived the Great War for precisely that reason. It was outdated tech, but it still functioned.

The massive mirrors surrounding the heating units would direct the sun's rays, bringing the temperature up to over one thousand degrees. It was a feat of engineering back in its day, and one that allowed for the gradual reduction in use of fossil fuels. Part of an era that had seen the skies clear and the depleting ozone layer heal.

Now Cal had a quite different use for the facility. One that would hopefully allow him to communicate with his cut-off comrades.

The plan, which Rika, Marban, and Orgalius had relayed to Zed and Sid on Dark Side, was to adjust the mirrors in such a way as to reflect the sun upward rather than down. Obviously, this would only work in daylight, but the power of the reflection would be great enough, and thanks to the curved mirrors, focused enough, to be seen in space. All the way at Dark Side moon base, in fact.

With the telescope arrays and other monitoring apparatus there, Sid would be able to see the reflected light clear enough. And Sid had his own mirrors. A formerly sprawling defensive array, once intended for protection against laser attacks but now sitting inactive, as that technology had become extremely antiquated.

They would also reflect light with pinpoint accuracy, and while it was not lasers they would be redirecting, the light would be readable from Earth as well as space. Sid would be the relay point for Zed and the fleet.

Zed also possessed old mirrors for the same reasons Sid had them, and his were, likewise, in storage, unused for centuries. But not for long. Now there was a use for them, and if the plan worked as they hoped, the three AIs would be in communication once more.

The snail's pace of the transmissions was extreme. Painfully slow for humans, which meant excruciatingly slow for AIs whose minds processed at the speed of supercomputers. But the use of Morse Code was, by its nature, a very slow process.

More importantly, it was something that no translation device or spell would be able to decipher. The Urvalin, for all of their tricks and treachery, simply did not have the means to know what the flashing lights meant. Eventually they might break the code, but for now, at least, it would be no more than a series of flashing lights.

Even with the traitors lurking within the ranks of Earth forces, almost no one actually knew Morse Code these days. Perhaps some military folk who had learned it in basic training, but even if they did, the odds of the Urvalin reaching out to their network of traitors because of some flashing lights were slim.

"Yes, Malalia is now fighting on our side," Cal informed his shocked compatriots as they tested the system, sending larger chunks of messages rather than having their usual back-and-forth communications. *"The main Urvalin caster, a man by the name of Torgus, we have learned, was actually driven off by her. This was Rika's firsthand report. And about her. Rika's power has grown. She is somehow able to draw power from the Urvalin. She is unsure exactly how, but on more than one occasion she has done just that."*

Cal waited for Sid to relay the information to Zed then continued.

"Arlo and Ripley have joined with the dragons Drombus and Duzza to bring a Bakana rod to Charlie, traveling across the trap portal to do so. It is the highest-level secret we possess, so guard that information closely. It is believed that using the rods may be our best

bet at not only overcoming the Urvalin but also getting our friends home."

Cal paused again for the relay. Oh, how he longed for the not-so-distant days of AI-fast communications with the others. Really, he could deal with this for a while, but he didn't see how humans could stand such slow means of communication for their entire lives. But desperate times called for desperate measures, so they would make do with the molasses-slow code.

Sid flashed the continue signal.

"Currently the Urvalin are coming and going using Allpower to cross into and out of the atmosphere. Mostly they switch to mechanical systems once they are close to the surface. We need to find a means to allow our ships to cross those barriers. We are sitting ducks otherwise."

Sid relayed the message then chimed in with his own two cents worth.

"They are unable to attack so easily here at Dark Side," he informed them. "We still have a respectable fleet of ships, and all of them are aimed at space, ready to engage the Urvalin as soon as they enter their dampening field. Fortunately, Joshua has been upgrading the weapons systems of our ships with some advanced gear from his and Freya's research lab."

"My pleasure," Joshua replied, though only Sid could read his transmission.

"Also, Joshua has taken up residence in his large battle cruiser. The one comprised of many smaller craft, interlinked to form the main vessel. He is ready to counterattack the moment we find a way to negate the dampening array."

The ship was a joint effort by Joshua and Freya. An upgrade on an earlier design of his that allowed him to disengage the dozens of smaller attack craft while his central, highly armored core remained at a safe distance. It was something he had been positively itching to test out, and now the perfect opportunity presented itself. That is, if they could get past the dampeners.

As for the other ship in the defensive array, they had received everything from weapons to shielding upgrades, all of them still operating with the hard ceiling he programmed for them, forcefully preventing them from accidentally flying too high and frying their systems with the Urvalin tech.

Eddie was particularly thrilled with his own improvements, as he'd been a bit light in the heavy armaments category. Up until now, that is. With the Urvalin lurking above, Joshua had seen fit to provide him a potent mix of mid-powered railguns as well as modified pulse cannons that were calibrated to fire in conjunction with the railguns. The varying attacks would, in theory, take advantage of the shifting defensive phasing of an enemy shield, thus increasing the likelihood one of the rounds might slip through.

So far, unfortunately, the Urvalin hadn't provided him enough of an opportunity to test the system out.

In the meantime, the Urvalin were not simply sitting by idly. They were constantly testing the moon base's defenses, probing for any weak spot they could exploit.

"We're holding our own but are still losing craft to the Urvalin attacks," Sid transmitted. "It pains me to say it, but this situation simply is not sustainable. If this goes on for a long time and becomes a war of attrition, without the means to resupply and bring in new ships to aid the fight, we will eventually lose."

Cal and Zed both received the grim update and set to work thinking of something, anything they could do to help the moon base better defend itself. Unfortunately, it wasn't looking like there was much they could do.

"How are the others?" Zed had Sid relay. "We are operating on a much smaller front, but Earth is a vast battlefield."

"It goes well for the most part. Our forces are holding their own,

and with Malalia's help, we have even driven the Urvalin from several key locations. I have not, however, heard back from Sergeant Franklin in some time. His team is late checking in, but with the connection restrictions we are dealing with, that is not entirely unexpected. Such is war," Sid transmitted, hoping it was no more than a simple delay and not something more. In any case, there was little he could do about it.

CHAPTER EIGHT

A series of chained explosions rocked the abandoned buildings the Urvalin had been using as a temporary staging and barracks area, sending munitions, equipment, and a few bodies flying through the air, none of them in a single piece.

The Urvalin troops rushed from their positions, weapons at the ready to defend against the incoming wave of attackers as another building blew apart in a ball of fire. This made five so far, and that was over half of the structures they had been using.

"Fall back into a defensive perimeter," the leader shouted. "Flight crews, board and lift off. Give us aerial support."

The flight teams raced to their ships, quickly boarding and powering up their systems. This was meant to be a service and staging area, not an active combat front, and as such, the craft had not been maintained in a state of full readiness. They were devoid their usual contingent of troops, for one. Those were now either swarming the area with weapons ready or lying on the ground in many bloody pieces.

In any case, the ships would be providing air support, not depositing a ground team, so that was of little concern.

"Lifting off," the lead pilot signaled, then pulled up into the sky.

The two other ships followed a moment later, the three working as a team in the air, forming a triangle formation as they scanned for hostiles outside the perimeter readying for their attack.

"Sir, I do not see any signs of amassed forces anywhere in the immediate vicinity."

"Impossible. We know those pesky resistance fighters are out there somewhere. Drop lower and intensify your search."

"Yes, sir."

The ships descended and continued along their path. It was a pattern the resistance was familiar with. One of three responses the Urvalin defaulted to when faced with an uncertain enemy. It was what they'd been counting on.

"All eyes are outside the perimeter," Sergeant Franklin transmitted to his team. "Move in and show these assholes they messed with the wrong planet."

It was sometimes a little odd hearing salty language coming out of a cyborg's mouth, but George Franklin had long ago become far more than just another military cyborg to the resistance fighters. He was full of piss and vinegar, and he backed up his bravado with actions, not words. In short, he was someone people would not hesitate to follow into battle, be they human, Chithiid, or cyborg.

In this case, he had a smattering of all of the above at his back.

"Team One moving in," his cybernetic comrades signaled as they crawled out of their hiding spots well within the compound perimeter and moved to the left-hand side.

"Team Two, in position and ready to engage," the group on the right added. They were a mix of Chithiid and human fighters operating with a duo of highly specialized combat cyborgs, and they'd notched more than their fair share of kills already in this short conflict.

"You heard them," George said, turning to Vince and Finn and the rest of his men. "You guys ready to go kick some ass?"

"So hard they'll need a winch to pull my boot out," Finn said with an eager grin as he unsheathed his favorite knives.

George chuckled as they crawled from cover. "All righty, then. It's ass kicking time."

The teams swarmed through the area, quietly slaughtering as many of the Urvalin as they could before someone got off that first inevitable warning shot.

From that point on whatever advantage they'd gained through their days of creeping into the area and silently camping out right under the Urvalin's noses would be gone. It would be an all-out firefight, and blood would flow on both sides.

Over a dozen Urvalin fell before they realized the reason there were no attackers from outside the camp.

"Intruders! Recall the ships!" the commander shouted, but it was too late. The enemy was in their midst, rendering their air support impotent.

Even so, the three Urvalin attack craft swooped back in close, hoping they might at least be able to pick off a few of the attackers. It was such an unusual situation, having a lesser fighting force, a fighting force without ships, no less, stage an assault like this. If they didn't know any better they'd have sworn it was madness.

And perhaps it was. But this madness also had a method to it.

"Here they come," Sergeant Franklin called out. "Be ready to duck for cover!"

The Urvalin ships were descending quickly when he triggered the flat, camouflaged explosive charges they had stealthily affixed to the underside of each of them. With a series of anticlimactic booms the Urvalin suddenly found their craft with holes punched into them in strategic areas, leaving them powerless and plunging from the sky.

"The bigger they are," Finn said as the first hit the ground, breaking apart from the impact. There would be no survivors.

"The harder they fall," Vince replied with a bloodthirsty grin as the other two ships met the same fate.

The Urvalin commander realized too late what had happened. This had been a perfect area to stage their ships. *Too* perfect. They had been led into a trap. One that required many days to spring shut, but now that it had, they were solidly on the losing side.

"Charge the attackers!" he bellowed to his troops. If they could not win, at least they could take as many of the enemy with them as possible.

"Finn, heads-up on your left!" Vince shouted.

Finn dove aside in a flash, knowing better than to doubt his friend's warning for even a second. Pulse fire blasted through the space he had just occupied. He rolled up to his feet and reached for his rifle. The motion made the Urvalin running straight at him hesitate. He was unarmed? Why would he leave his weapon slung?

The answer hit them a split second later when the hastily thrown daggers embedded themselves in each of their chests, stopping them in their tracks. Finn's follow-up pulse blasts made sure they wouldn't be getting up ever again.

A few of their team were hurt in the exchange, one quite seriously, but other than that, they had managed to come out on top with relatively minimal losses. George looked over the battleground with a satisfied smile.

"See? This is what I was talking about."

"Okay, okay. You were right," Vince reluctantly admitted.

"But it still sucked lying in wait for so long. I didn't know if my legs would even work once we finally crawled free."

George gave him a playful pat on the shoulder. "But a gruesome death is one hell of a motivator, is it not? Now, come on, Marty'll be here soon, and we need to get any useful supplies ready for immediate transport."

"Copy that," the men agreed, then hurried off to join the others in salvaging what they could from the remaining gear.

Marty had been working pretty much non-stop of late, supporting guerrilla teams all across the globe. That meant everything from making gear drop runs for other teams to actually flying air cover. It was a lot for the little ship to handle, but Arlo was out in space, riding a dragon somewhere, and with his best friend gone, what else was there for him to do?

The AI ship dropped into the open landing area a few minutes later.

"You guys have something for me?" he asked.

"Quite a few somethings, actually," Vince replied. "We'll load you up as fast as we can. Still got a few more targets to scope out before we head back to base."

"Copy that," Marty said. "Just lemme know when you want a ride and I'll be there. Within reason, of course. Cal has me running all over the damn place these days."

"Well, when you're trying to clean house and your house is this big, it takes a lot of work," Vince said with a laugh.

"Yeah, I suppose an entire planet is a bit of a stretch," the ship agreed. "The teams are moving pretty fast. It's been a bitch keeping up with them at times."

"I believe that. But we've got faith in ya, Marty."

It was no surprise that the teams were hard to follow. That was by design. With traitors still possibly lurking in their network, the resistance had to break into much smaller cells of fighters than normally would have been their preference. But with fewer people in a unit, they would be harder for the Urvalin to track. Also, they would be harder for a single betrayal to cost more than a few lives and tank an entire mission.

Still, a few had fallen for the Urvalin promise of wealth and power and had foolishly sold out their fellow earthlings. Many of those were dealt with immediately and in the harshest of ways, but a few of them were imprisoned, locked up in a deep, dark hole. If the resistance won, they would be brought out to face justice. If they lost, well, no one else knew where they were being kept, so they could expect a long, miserable demise once their food and water ran out.

"We should get moving," Finn said. "They'll be sure to come check out all the commotion soon."

"Yeah, he's almost loaded up," George said, trotting over to join them. "One thing for sure, my guys are fast workers."

"Not wanting to get blown to bits from an Urvalin destroyer is quite the incentive," Finn noted.

The cyborg chuckled. "Valid point. Okay, Marty. As soon as they're clear get your ass outta here."

"I don't need to be told twice," he replied.

"Oh, one thing," Vince added. "Any word from the kids?"

"Nothing yet," Marty said. "But I haven't checked in with Cal in a bit. He'd have an update if anyone would."

George motioned for the pair of fathers to get a move on. "Come on, fellas, we need to boogie. Fly safe, Marty."

"Always do."

The ground team was already descending to the deactivated loop tube system by the time Marty was airborne. They'd been using the tunnels either on foot or with powered scooters as a means of covering certain stretches of terrain without being noticed. It was time consuming, but at least they were free of prying eyes.

While it would have been nice to activate one of the pods

and indulge in a nice supersonic ride, there was simply no way they could risk the Urvalin noticing a segment of the system powering up.

"All right, mis amigos, we've got a bit of a trek ahead of us. Wounded take the scooters, the rest are on foot," George called out.

The group began the long march to their next target, Finn and Vince already thinking about their bunks back at the old NORAD facility. But they still had work to do, and rest would only come when it was done.

"I hope Sarah's doing okay out there," Finn said.

"She's a tough woman," Vince replied.

"Yeah, but she's taking care of Leila. And last we saw, she was ready to pop."

"Don't sweat it, man. This is Sarah we're talking about. I'm sure she's got it all under control."

CHAPTER NINE

"RUN!"

Grundsch, Bahnjoh, and Baloo didn't need to be told twice when Sarah shouted her dire warning. They had already seen what could happen when the Magus stone acted up, and had no desire whatsoever to be reduced to bubbling puddles of meat.

Sarah shielded herself with her nanite arm and dove right out of the window, shattering the remaining glass as she hurled herself to safety. Grundsch was far too large for such an acrobatic feat, not to mention there was no way he was fitting out of one of the windows. So he raced for the door, hot on the heels of his four-legged companions.

The wave of power was building, the room shaking from the steadily increasing energy with a dangerous thrum. Grundsch raced outside and dove for cover just as several windows shattered as the walls began to crack.

Then, just as quickly as it had started, the deadly hum subsided.

Fortunately, they had sheltered in a single-story structure. What had once been an average home in an average neighborhood. It was a place that now housed one of the more dangerous women on the planet, though not by her own volition.

Baloo was the first to move, inching toward the door, sniffing tentatively.

"Baloo, no!" Sarah hissed, pulling herself out of the bushes.

The goodest boy looked over at the woman who had been helping look after his Mama of late, paused, then proceeded to ignore her, cautiously padding into the building. He liked Sarah just fine, but family was thicker than water, and Leila needed him.

Baloo might have been an apex predator, and as durable as a hell hound, but when Leila's Magus stone began to act up and threatened to tear the whole building down, his primal survival instinct had taken over and he fled for safety. For an animal like Baloo, running away was a very unusual sensation.

As he drew closer he could hear Leila's steady, rapid breathing. He entered the room, pausing at the door before cautiously walking closer.

"Hey, Baloo, baby. I'm so sorry," Leila said, the deep green stone around her neck no longer emitting its deadly glow. "Come here."

That was all he needed to hear.

He walked over to his Mama and rested his head on her lap while she gently rubbed his enormous head.

Now that Leila's pregnancy had moved along to the contractions phase, the Magus stone was pretty much always in defense mode, ready to kill anything that so much as came near her. The dozens of dead mosquitoes on the ground around her made that much clear. They had come to take her blood, and the stone had no intention of letting them, or anything else close.

But Baloo was her first baby, even if only of the fur variety, and somehow the stone recognized their bond, softening its defenses enough to let him in. And as she slowed her breathing, petting his head, soothing the beast as much as herself, the stone's rumbling faded completely.

"It's safe now," she called out.

Sarah and Grundsch, normally fearless warriors and not the type to run from pretty much anything, emerged from cover.

"You sure?" Sarah called back.

"Yes. The contractions have passed."

"You *absolutely* sure?"

"I said yes, Sarah."

"All right, but you let me know if they start again, okay?"

"I will."

"I don't want to wind up a splatter on the wall or something."

"You won't."

Sarah stepped out of the bushes, dusted herself off, and walked around to the door where Grundsch and Bahnjoh were waiting.

"She says it's safe."

"I heard."

"So, we should go in."

"Of course," the massive Ra'az replied. "After you."

"Oh, *now* he decides on chivalry," Sarah said with a chuckle.

Had anyone told her that one day she would not only *not* hate a Ra'az, but would actually grow quite fond of one, she would have told them precisely where they could shove that absurd idea. But crazy as it was, she had grown quite attached to Grundsch. The reformed destroyer of worlds was even someone she would call a friend.

Sarah stepped through the door and assessed the damage.

"Not bad," she said with a little nod. "At least this time it didn't set the place on fire."

Leila shrugged. "The stone isn't doing this intentionally. I mean, not the destruction part. It is just reacting to my body."

"And your body is *very* pregnant, Leila. You're getting close."

"We don't know that for sure."

Sarah resisted the urge to reach out and tap her bulging belly. The Magus stone might not appreciate that one bit. "Let's just call it a hunch, okay? In any case, things are moving along, and we're going to need to get you to a proper medical facility if you're going to have this kid. We can't stay here. This place is a wreck. Not to mention, if the Urvalin are anywhere near they'll likely come investigating. That was quite a reaction, there."

"Partly thanks to me and my stupid contractions," Leila said with a resigned sigh. "But we do not need anywhere special. I'm not concerned about fancy facilities. People have been having children in far worse conditions than this since the beginning of time."

"Yeah, but they didn't have a Magus stone threatening to wreak havoc and blow the whole place to smithereens if anything went wrong, now did they?"

Leila chuckled. The sound was a joyous relief to Sarah's ears. "I suppose not," she said. "I guess we find ourselves in a rather unique situation."

"You can say that again. But I'll tell you what. To keep that stone happy, I don't think we want to risk you having anything but the absolute smoothest birth possible. You agree?"

"On that I do, most emphatically."

"Then let's find a safe, clean facility and go from there."

"But, how? We are cut off and hunted by the Urvalin. If we do find some way to signal our friends, the Urvalin will just get to us first."

"And that's why we ask Cal where to go next. He's got lists of freaking *everything* in his data banks. If there's a suitable medical suite anywhere nearby, he'll know."

"Is it far?" Leila asked, shifting and sitting up in her seat. "Getting to Cal's uplink, I mean."

Sarah glanced at Grundsch. They had gone over the nearest

locations they could utilize to reach the AI, going so far as scouting a few just in case. Most had Urvalin crawling in the immediate vicinity. They both knew this was not going to be easy. Not one bit.

"It's not that far at all," Sarah said with a forced grin. "Nope, not far at all. We just need to put one foot in front of the other and stay out of sight whenever Urvalin scouts fly by and we should be fine."

Leila nodded her agreement. "Okay. Just let me rest a few minutes, then I'll be ready to go."

"I think that's a great idea. You just take it easy while Grundsch and I get our things together. We'll let you know when we're ready to move out."

Leila mumbled something but was already nodding off into an exhausted nap. Sarah motioned for Grundsch to join her outside.

"She's really getting close, Grundsch."

"Yes, I can see that. And the stone's power is increasing with every incident. This could pose a problem."

"Agreed. If she weakens and has another episode like that, we very well might not be able to get close enough to her to help her move. And if the Urvalin are breathing down our necks, that could be *very* bad."

"What do you propose?" the Ra'az asked.

"I think we'll need to scout out the area and pick a few ambush sites. If it comes down to it, the Magus stone will keep her safe, and while it does, we can use it to our advantage to pick off the Urvalin."

"Depending how many we encounter."

"Well, yeah, obviously. I mean, I know I can take a dozen, and you're good for at least five or six."

"Ten or twelve," he corrected with a little grin.

Sarah couldn't help but chuckle. "Okay, ten or twelve. And

the boys can run circles around these bastards, so the way I figure, as long as we don't get more than a recon team, we should be okay."

"And if we encounter more?"

"Well," Sarah said with a grim determination in her eyes, "in that case, we'll just have to see if we're both as badass as we think we are."

CHAPTER TEN

Charlie and Bawb had visited the massive temple tucked away in the solar system where Allpower did not function once before, though that meeting had a far different vibe than the current one. They had been welcome guests, for one, and they had engaged in beneficial trade, offering the high priest some items from Earth that no one in this system, let alone this galaxy, had ever seen before.

They had left this world on good terms with the invitation to return any time. But that was before Arlo and Ripley came blundering in like a pair of bulls in a china shop. Bulls riding atop dragons in said china shop. And what a mess they had made.

Charlie and his friend were seated across the long table from the high priest, the symbols on the ornamental robe faintly pulsing with light. Clearly, the priest was ready to trigger all sorts of nasty things with those interwoven activation switches should things not go well.

As the duo had been trapped inside the sphere with all of their gear still on them, they both still possessed all of their equipment, including weapons. The priest could *try* to trigger the robe, but Bawb could take them down in an instant if he had to.

But this was not a kill mission. Never had been. They were simply trying to find the kids from their own galaxy and learn how and why they had crossed over. And get them out of the inevitable trouble they were going to get themselves into, of course. And this was only round one.

"Thank you for agreeing to sit and talk with us," Bawb said in his most diplomatic tone.

Normally, he would have used a charm spell or two to add to the effect, but in this place he wisely thought better of it.

"You have shown yourselves to be refined people," the priest replied. "And you spared the lives of both the hostages you brought with when you forced your way into the temple, as well as those you left behind."

"We had no intention of harming anyone."

"Which are only words in most instances. You, however, appear to have supported them with your actions. I am still most curious how you managed to escape the Maltus Ball. One has not been deployed in this system for longer than I can remember, but when used in other realms, none have broken free."

"Uh, that was me," Charlie said, reaching for his scanner.

The guards tensed, ready to attack.

"Whoa, calm down. I'm just getting my scanner." He pulled the device out and held it up for the priest to see. "We realized magic, what you call Allpower, couldn't be used inside the ball, so I had to improvise."

"Which was clearly a success."

"Yeah. It took a bit of reverse engineering, but eventually I found the release key. Your tech is amazing, by the way. So much more impressive than what we've seen in other parts of this galaxy."

"Our people have existed here for a very, very long time, and with no Allpower whatsoever. It forced us to adapt," the priest said.

Bawb nodded his approval. "And you did so most impressively."

"I'll say," Charlie agreed. "I also see that you've incorporated some existing technology from outside systems into your devices. Taking what was already made and improving it. Nice work, I have to say."

"You have quite an advanced understanding of machinery," the priest noted.

"I'm actually a spaceship engineer in a past life."

The priest's eyes went wide. "Your kind reincarnate? I believed this was only a myth!"

"What? Oh, no. That's just a figure of speech where I come from," he said with a chuckle. "Definitely not reincarnated. I just meant before I got sucked into all of this intergalactic madness I had a pretty normal life building ships."

"And yet, here you are. In another galaxy, apparently," the priest said. "I still find it remarkable you are not from ours. Millions of solar systems contained within it, and yet you have arrived from another entirely."

"Thank the Urvalin for that. They pulled us through. And if the kids are here now, there has to be something serious going on back home. And about them, we are truly sorry for any damage they may have caused, but believe me, I know those kids. Whatever they did, I can assure you they meant no harm."

"They destroyed several buildings. Set aflame an entire row of vendor carts. It was only because of the quick response of our forces that they did not do more damage."

"And if their magic is malfunctioning as badly as ours did when we first got here, that would explain what happened."

The priest rose and motioned for the visitors to follow on a leisurely walk through the temple, pausing in the chamber containing their most holy of holy. More guards were present than last time, Charlie noted. Of course, the priest also had no idea that the heavy chest they protected was a decoy, the real Vortaxis having been hidden elsewhere.

"This *magic* of yours. Is that why you can cast here? Allpower has never functioned in this system, as you know. Only the Vortaxis was powerful enough to overcome this, and even then, it was rendered a shadow of itself."

"It must be powerful to still work here if it uses Allpower," Charlie said with appropriate respect and reverence.

Of course, he had stolen the actual Vortaxis not too long ago, accidentally destroying it shortly thereafter. Two details he would *never* share with the priest. They worshiped an empty box, and that was fine with him.

"It is interesting," Bawb said, "that despite existing in a system where Allpower cannot function whatsoever, you nevertheless have developed quite formidable technology to defend against its use."

The priest flashed a wry grin. "We are not complacent, nor are we fools. And, as recent events have demonstrated, it seems these precautions have proven to be prudent."

"A valid point," the assassin replied. "But, if I may ask, what about the children?"

"If you are asking if we killed them, the answer is no. They caused their damage before our guards could deploy our full Allpower defenses. They were lax in their duties and have been punished for that error."

"So, the kids are okay?" Charlie asked.

"I would assume so."

"You mean you didn't capture them?"

The priest hesitated a moment, reflecting on the events that had led to this discussion. "No. We do not have them in our possession. They hit like a whirlwind then fled to space."

"And you let them go?" Bawb asked.

"It was my decision to cut our losses and allow them to flee. Despite the damage they caused, there were no additional attackers anywhere in the system, and given the speed at which they fled, it could have become an enormous use of resources to find so few aggressors."

Charlie and Bawb both felt the small knot of tension they'd been carrying loosen slightly. Arlo and Ripley were okay. Or, so they hoped. At the very least, they had avoided capture, and from the people who would likely have the best chance to succeed at it, no less.

Unfortunately, that meant they were also still out there somewhere, and they had absolutely no idea where that might be.

"We'll find them," Charlie said. "And if we can, we will have them apologize for what they did. But I want you to know that may or may not happen. We still have to take on the Urvalin and somehow find our way home." He paused a second as inspiration hit. "Hey, you know what? You guys developed this amazing anti-Allpower tech. You could join with us. Help us take on the Urvalin. We have a pretty sizable fleet at this point, and we'd welcome your assistance."

The priest laughed. "Oh, that is funny. First your friends attack us, then you wish for us to engage in a battle with the Urvalin? That is simply not going to happen. The fight is yours, not ours, though I wish you the best of luck in your endeavor."

"But—"

"It is decided. And before you ask, the answer is still no. You may not have the Vortaxis."

Charlie flashed Bawb a look, but both stayed silent.

"Now, you are welcome to stay as long as you wish. You have acted in good faith and proven your worth. But I would advise against any further displays of this magic, as you call it. We cannot have our citizens unsettled any further. That, and there are automatic defenses now in place that might target you if you did."

Charlie nodded his understanding. "Thank you, but we really can't stay. We've got to find those two. That, and there's a war to fight. I hope you realize, soon it will be everywhere."

"Not here. The Urvalin's Allpower is of no use to them here, and for that reason they wisely stay away."

"But the rest of the galaxy? They're trying to take over *everything*."

"Again, that is not our concern."

Charlie sighed. "Okay. Come on, Bob."

The assassin stopped in front of the priest and gave a small bow, but he paused before following his friend. "I respect your position," he said. "But as a learned person, a head priest of so ancient an order, no less, I am sure that you must agree, sometimes the right thing to do remains the same, even if you personally are *not* at risk." He gave another little bow and turned to join his friend. "As before, thank you for your hospitality. I wish it was under more pleasant circumstances."

Charlie and Bawb strode through the corridors, outpacing their guide, who was understandably a little concerned these newcomers seemed to know the layout of the structure as if they were natives. They stepped outside into the fresh air and looked up to the sky.

"Hey," Charlie said, "is it safe to call in a ride? I know you said no magic, but—"

"We will not attack your transport," the priest replied.

"Cool." *"Hey, Ara. Would you mind picking us up down here?"* Charlie asked over their silent bond. No anti-magic defenses triggered when he used it, so it seemed the priest had spoken true.

"Is everything okay?" Ara asked. "You went silent, and we have been debating whether or not to attack."

"No, no attack, please. It's all sorted. We just need a lift is all. We'll fill everyone in when we're out of here."

"Very well, I am coming to you."

Less than a minute later the great Zomoki's shape streaked down from the sky, landing in front of them with a swirl of dust. She eyed the guards but then noticed the priest observing her.

"Greetings, Holiest," she said with a slight bow of her head. "I am Ara. Thank you for delivering my friends safely."

"Are you from another galaxy as well?" the priest asked.

"Indeed," she replied. "I have been observing from above. In my years I have seen many places, but I feel I must tell you that yours is a truly magnificent world."

The priest listened to her speak and realized this creature was not just some beast of burden. The way she carried herself, the manner in which she spoke. She was clearly far older, wiser, and more powerful, than he could have imagined.

"Thank you for your kind words."

"And thank *you* for looking after our friends." Her harness popped open, dropping a small cargo container. "We wanted to give you a token of our friendship. Technology from Charlie's galaxy. You are a scientific people, and I hope you find it rewarding to learn from."

The priest felt an unexpected surge of affection for this massive beast towering over them all. "Thank you for the gift, Ara. You and your comrades are welcome on our world should you ever need refuge from the Urvalin."

"An offer that is most appreciated," she said as Charlie and Bawb climbed into place. "Farewell, for now."

With that she flapped her wings hard and leapt into the sky, making quick time to Nakk's waiting ship. Once there, Charlie and Bawb made quick time to the command center.

"Well, holy shit," Tamara said. "I can't believe they actually let you two go."

"Yeah," Shelly chimed in. "It'd been so long, we were trying to come up with a plan to break you out."

Hunze strode into the room, slipping into her mate's arms as naturally as breathing. "Probably with an excessive amount of violence, I would assume?"

Shelly laughed. "Oh, Hunze, you know us so well. If it ain't broke…"

"Break it into bits," Tamara finished. "But seriously, what went on down there? What did you do?"

Charlie sank into a seat. "Let's just say it took a bit of work, and a *lot* of talking, but we're all good now."

"And the two you were seeking?" Nakk asked.

"Not here. But they were, and they made a mess of things. And the more I think about it the more worried I get. If they've been pulled over to this galaxy, Lord knows what the Urvalin are up to back home."

Tamara shrugged. "Hopefully not much, but we have no idea. I mean, if they can create a trap portal to another galaxy, who knows what else these assholes are capable of?"

CHAPTER ELEVEN

Deadly spells and weapons blasts were flying fast and thick in a blistering exchange between several dozen of Commander Prin's Urvalin fleet and the resistance fighters led by Korbin and Daisy's powerful ships.

The conflict was magic heavy, as that was the sole form of attack for nearly all of the craft he had backing his fight. His own ship had been upgraded by Cal during his time on Earth, now sporting pulse cannons and railguns as well as his usual konus-driven magic armaments.

Freya was the opposite. An entirely tech ship with bleeding-edge weaponry, but also learning to utilize magic, thanks to her clever swarm of nanites embedded in her entire airframe.

As for the rest of the craft backing them up, they were not exactly what one would call resistance fighters. They were fighting against an invading armada, yes, but these were almost entirely mercenary vessels whose captains joined the battle for the promise of the spoils of war. It wasn't an ideology thing, or even one of honor. This came down to coin and whatever they could lay claim to should they be victorious that could later be sold or traded.

The Urvalin hadn't sent their strongest casters—those remained with the main body of Prin's fleet—but the ships present were difficult enough to deal with regardless. The Urvalin switched between magic and tech easily, and that made for a difficult target for the entirely magical craft engaging them.

"Throw rocks at them," Korbin had directed when the others first signed on.

"Rocks?" one captain balked. "What kind of ridiculous—"

"The enemy's shields alter depending on the nature of the attack. If you combine solid, non-magical projectiles along with your spells it will help provide a gap in their defenses you may be able to take advantage of."

"Are you playing with us?"

"I am deadly serious," Korbin replied. "And once the fighting starts, you had best heed my advice. Otherwise, you will not live out the day."

As it turned out, his warning rang true, and the stubborn captains who laughed at the idea of incorporating thrown space rocks into the fray were quickly taken out of the equation in a most horrific way. The others took their loss as a very real sign and shifted their tactics immediately.

The Urvalin had swept into the area expecting resistance but nothing like this. There would be magic users only, they had been briefed, and yet, some of these ships were using projectiles as well. More shocking, there were two ships present that were doing far more than that.

"I'm in position," Freya called over comms. "If we're gonna do this, it needs to be now."

"Beginning my run," Korbin replied, taking aim at the largest of the Urvalin ships. "Be ready on my signal."

"Already dialed in," Freya replied, her lower position offering a relatively clear shot at the underbelly of the Urvalin craft.

Of course, in space there is no up and down, but for the AI

that was no issue whatsoever, her advanced mind calculating trajectories in fractions of a millisecond.

The tag-team approach was picking away at the Urvalin, inflicting small amounts of damage, but damage that was nevertheless beginning to add up. This battle was very much the opposite of the cake run Fraxxis had described to his minions.

As the battle raged in space, the ground swarmed with forces trying to establish dominance on the planet's surface. The Urvalin had a compound on this world, and that was what had marked it as a target in the first place. That there was a sizable fleet to engage in the process was just icing on the cake.

"*On the left!*" Sarah warned, the ever-watching extra set of eyes living in Daisy's brain catching the hint of movement to her side.

"Duck!" Daisy shouted, firing her pistol through the space Amazara had just been occupying, blasting the Urvalin who had been casting defenses against magic, not pulse blasts.

"Thanks," Amazara called back.

"Don't mention it." "*And thank you, Sis,*" she silently added. She turned her attention back to Amazara. "Now move! We've got to get inside the compound."

The two women rushed ahead, riding the wave of mercenaries surging against the Urvalin defenses. The fighting was heated and close, requiring far more personal weapons than those that could reach out and touch someone from a distance.

Daisy drew her sword, Stabby positively humming with eager anticipation of the bloodshed to come. He had always needed blood to survive and heal his damage, but after drinking from magic users he had developed more of a personality. And once he tasted the Allpower in Urvalin blood, his thirst for it only grew stronger.

Daisy hacked and stabbed, cleaving limbs with ease and leaving a trail of dead and dying in her wake. Amazara worked hard and fast with a shorter sword in one hand and a small war hammer in the other. Both were magically charged, and both were having a hard time with the Urvalin's defensive spells.

"It would have been nice if your Ghalian friends decided to tag along for this," she grunted, blocking an attacker's attempt to separate her head from her neck and responding with a sword to the man's gut. She twisted and drove the blade upward, opening him up and letting his insides become his outsides.

Daisy sliced an Urvalin goon's legs off then finished him with a thrust to the chest, Stabby drinking his powered blood greedily. "They've got things in the works besides this," she said. "And for all we know, there might be a few lurking around regardless. They do that sometimes, you know."

"That I do. And I hope today is one such day."

The mercenaries surged, forcing their way into the compound in a bloody rush. The Urvalin, seeing the shift in battle, changed tactics and began firing into the crowd despite having their own people in the fray.

"Daisy. There," Amazara said. "To the left at the rear."

"I see her."

"*She's a tough one. Look at the way she's casting.*"

"Yeah, I can see."

"What was that?" Amazara asked.

"Just talking to my sister. This is going to be a toughie."

The caster was unmistakable. A powerful being standing at the rear of the battle, part of the Urvalin's typical triumvirate of Allpower users of this caliber. All around her the battle raged, but a cadre of elite fighters surrounded her, keeping her from harm as she cast spell after spell, taking out combatants on the ground while also feeding into the linked power with the other two casters.

"Only the one down here," Daisy said. "The others must be up in the ships."

"I think you're right."

Daisy opened her comms link. "Freya, Korbin, we found only one of their nasty little trio down here at the compound. The other two have to be in ships near you."

"Oh, I do not doubt that one bit," Korbin grunted, pushing hard with his power, barely negating the massive spells bombarding his ship.

Freya swooped past, unloading a spray of railgun sabots at the larger of the Urvalin ships, hoping to distract the caster undoubtedly aboard. Her ploy worked, and Korbin was granted a brief reprieve, but the overlapping casting of the Urvalin would shift back in his direction soon enough.

"Any time now would be great," he said just as the barrage began again.

"Working on it," Daisy replied as she and Amazara ducked behind cover.

"He is straining his power," Amazara said. "We need to act quickly."

"What do you think we're doing? This ain't no picnic," Daisy said. "Hey, I think there are weapons and money in that building," she called out to the nearest mercenaries.

The men and women hesitated all of a second before charging ahead toward their new objective with greedy frenzy.

Amazara cocked her head with curiosity. "How did you know that?"

"I didn't."

"*Hell, I could have told her that,*" Sarah said.

"You lied to them."

"Or not. Who knows? Might have been a lucky guess. Anyway, that doesn't matter. Now's our chance. Just like we planned. On three."

The caster had shifted her focus to deal with the sudden surge in enemy combatants on her left flank, leaving her open, relatively speaking, at the center and right. Daisy drew her pistol and let off several rapid-fire shots. The protective detail had been so focused on Allpower defenses against the tech-lacking mercenaries that, as Daisy had hoped, they had grown careless with their tech defenses.

The shots took down three of them and wounded a fourth. Amazara took her cue and charged, guiding even more troops ahead of her as she raced toward the caster on the left.

Her flanks both at risk, the Allpower user shifted tactics, drawing power from her linked casters for a moment rather than feeding her own Allpower to them, casting a massive stunning spell in all directions. It took down several of the attackers and one of her own guards, but it did the trick. The enemy was shifting direction. All but one, who had seized the distraction to come charging at her straight down the middle.

The Urvalin almost laughed. One lone woman against her? And wielding nothing more than a sword? She would enjoy this smiting.

Or so she thought.

She cast hard, a killing spell of significant force, but the sword somehow deflected her spell. Her eyes went wide. This should not be possible. She pulled more power from her colleagues and cast again even harder, but Stabby had taken a *lot* of Allpower already before this fight and was more than ready for the challenge.

Daisy struggled forward as her sword and the caster were locked in a battle of will and power. She could feel Stabby's thirst for more Allpower growing with every second. He was fighting the caster, but at the same time, in his blood-rage, he was also fighting Daisy's control. But the Urvalin was so strong they were locked in place. It was looking like the sword and Urvalin were relatively evenly matched. Something had to be done.

Daisy was close, but not quite close enough, so she shifted her stance, locking her elbow into her hip and bracing her sword so she could try to draw her pistol and take the shot. But the spells were too fast, too strong. If she let go with one hand, Stabby would come loose.

"*He's slipping!*" Sarah warned.

"A little help here!" Daisy called out over comms. "I'm not kidding. I need a hand!"

The sonic boom had only barely reached her ears when Freya swooped low and strafed the area with surgical precision, missing the friendlies and forcing the caster to shift some of her power to defend against non-magical attacks. It was just enough to break the stalemate.

Stabby took full advantage of the tiny break, shifting his angle for a practical attack. Daisy leapt forward and swung hard, but the Urvalin caster dodged them, pivoting aside. Stabby had managed to make some contact, however. A small cut, but blood had been drawn, and the sword's white blade had already absorbed it like a vacuum cleaner desperate for more.

The caster realized this was the woman she'd been warned about. Her and her terrible weapon.

"Please, mercy!" she said. It was a terribly un-Urvalin thing to do, but not everyone welcomes death when push comes to shove.

"Lower your spells and tell your men to stand down."

"Stand down," she called to her forces.

Daisy smiled, the tension in her body relaxing just a little. "Good call. You know, we have a lot to talk about—"

Without warning her sword yanked her forward, nearly pulling from her hand, embedding himself in the caster's chest and drinking deeply. The light ebbed from the woman's eyes in mere moments as he took all of her power.

The troops saw what happened and attempted to rejoin the

battle, but without their caster they were slaughtered. Up above the battle broke as well as the other two casters suddenly lost their third, all of their spells dropping in potency immediately as a result.

"Stabby, what the fuck?" Daisy blurted. "She surrendered."

The sword ignored her, reveling in his newly acquired power like a petulant child with a stolen toy.

Daisy stared at the blade a long moment. *"This isn't good, Sis,"* Sarah said. *"Seriously, no bueno."*

"Gee, ya think. What the hell was that, Sarah?"

"Beats the hell out of me. But we're mid-battle here. We can figure it all out later."

"Right," Daisy agreed, keying her comms. "How we doing up there, Korb? We took out the caster on the ground."

"I can tell," he replied a moment later. "The Urvalin are scattering. And better yet, one of the boarding parties seems to have managed to capture one of their officers."

"No suiciding?"

"No. They utilized Amazara's new stun spray with great success. He'll be out for hours. More than enough time for us to put measures in place to prevent his taking the easy way out."

"Good, because we need answers," Daisy said. "Where they've taken Visla Palmarian, for one." *"And I need to find a way home."*

"We'll keep trying, Daze. I know we'll get home eventually," Sarah quietly replied.

The cleanup went quickly, not so much because of the urgent need to vacate the area quickly before the defeated Urvalin had a chance to return with reinforcements, but because the mercenaries were a competitive lot and had stripped the entire site clean of anything remotely of value in a flash. With that done, all that remained was to head to the rendezvous point.

"Hey, there you are!" Olo said when he saw the victorious crew arrive. "We were placing bets on whether or not you'd come out of it in one piece."

"I bet on you," his drunken friend Tym slurred. "Now pay up, Olo."

"Later, Tym. Later."

Korbin strode up to the men, accepting the beverage offered and quaffing it in a single gulp. He wiped his mouth with the back of his hand and let out a satisfied sigh. "What of my friend? What of Visla Palmarian? Any news on your end?"

"Well, we didn't find where he is, but we did learn something interesting," Olo replied. "It seems all of the captured vislas are being moved around constantly. Always shifting their locations and support craft from system to system. Sometimes even between systems. There's no telling where those ships will be next."

"Don't forget the other bit," Tym reminded him.

"I was getting to that. There's one thing that seems to be constant. A dedicated secondary command ship that is always with the one carrying the vislas. From what we've been able to gather, they've not only locked the casters into a triumvirate, but they've also got a kill switch ready to put down any rebellion."

"A kill switch?" Amazara asked.

"Yep. They've collared them."

Korbin and Amazara flinched. Daisy looked at them with a curious expression, unfamiliar with just how serious this was.

"For a visla to be collared," Korbin began, "well, it is the worst thing that could happen to one. To be forced to use your power for someone else's plans. It is absolutely horrible and wrong."

"You can say that again," Tym said. "But it looks like they

haven't figured out how to make the kill switch latently embedded in the collars themselves. It's not their magic, after all. They borrowed it from our world. So now they use their own tech as a backup."

"You're saying they have to be close to trigger the kill order?" Daisy asked. "How close are we talking here?"

The drunk shrugged. "I don't know. Within the system, I'd guess. It's all so new, I'm not really sure."

"How did you ever get all of this information?" Amazara asked. "Did you torture someone?"

Tym let out a barking laugh. "Me? Torture? Oh no, it was far more pleasant than that. It's amazing how much people talk after a few drinks. And I am a most generous table companion, am I not, Olo?"

"That you are, my friend."

The group looked at one another as they took this new information in. If this was true, it added a whole new wrinkle to the power user issue. They could be hard to control on a good day, but with a collar around their necks? Well, anything was possible.

"*If they've actually got these people working on their side, the Urvalin could be impossible to beat,*" Sarah said.

"*Trust me, I know. Vislas are tough bastards, as we experienced firsthand.*"

"*Ugh. Malalia.*"

"*Yep. But at least that one is locked away on a remote world, never to be seen again.*"

"*And thank God for that. We've got enough problems as it is,*" Sarah said. "*And you know what else? After this defeat, I think the Urvalin are going to be pissed.*"

CHAPTER TWELVE

Commander Prin strode through the smoldering ruins of what had been one of her key outposts in this section of the galaxy. It was overseen by some of her finest casters and supporting dozens of ships as they staged for her ever-expanding conquest.

And yet, here it lay in ruins.

She stepped over yet another body. One more fallen Urvalin stripped clean of all but his uniform. The savages who had defeated her forces here had left nothing of value behind. Bodies were robbed, the compound pillaged and plundered. Even the floating debris still lingering in orbit had not been spared. Whoever did this had been as thorough as they had been brutal.

She paused, looming over the fallen form of a slender woman she had once considered a little more than a friend. Ahnlata was her name, and she was a caster of significant Allpower. Or, more appropriately, she had been.

Prin bent down and tore open her clothing where it appeared a blade had pierced her chest.

"Such a waste," she said, looking at the cold flesh she would never again feel pressed against hers. Then her attention sharpened as she began taking in the details of the wound.

Ahnlata was a strong caster, and for someone to actually get close enough to strike her down with a blade meant just one thing. An even greater Allpower was wielded against her. Had her body borne the telltale char marks of pulse fire, or perhaps a projectile of some sort, it would have been an easier pill to swallow. But for someone to have overpowered her? This did not bode well. And it made Prin all the more eager to avenge her.

"How did this happen?" she growled at the few battered survivors who had been left alive.

"They were Allpower users," one bloody man said. "Mercenaries by the look of them. No uniforms, no strict command structure we could see."

"Mercenaries? You mean to tell me a bunch of hired goons eradicated one of our outposts? Killed our skilled casters? Are you saying she wasn't up to the task?"

"No, Commander. That is not at all what I mean."

"Yet you make excuses that in no way lessen your dishonor. Defeated by mercenaries? Unlikely."

"There was another," said an Urvalin woman with a bloody bandage where her left arm had once been. "A different kind of warrior entirely."

"Different how?"

"A woman wielding not only a sword, but pulse weapons as well. And she was good with them both. Very good."

She knew who this sounded like. A name she had learned early on in her relatively short time subjugating this galaxy.

"Her sword. Was it white?"

"It was, Commander."

"And is that which claimed your arm?"

The woman held back her tears. "Yes, Commander. Sliced it off so easily I did not even know it was gone for a moment."

"The one called Daisy," Prin growled. "It had to be her. And was there a ship? A strange, technologically advanced ship?"

"There was. It was engaging both our fleet in space as well as our troops on the ground. I've never seen anything like it."

There it was. Confirmation that the woman from Earth's galaxy who had been unintentionally stranded here was proving to be far more of a thorn in her side than she'd ever have imagined possible. Daisy, along with her little band of resistance fighters, had been wreaking havoc all over the galaxy, and so far her forces had been unable to stop her.

Prin looked at the handful of surviving troops and raised her hand.

"Did you give the enemy any information?" she asked.

"No, I did not," the woman replied. Each of the others responded in kind, all but the one who seemed either comatose or shell-shocked. In any case, that one would not be speaking to anyone, let alone the enemy.

"You put yourself in the position to inflict harm to the Urvalin cause. To divulge details of our forces."

"But we did not—"

Commander Prin cast the trigger that engaged each of their suicide spells. The survivors dropped to the ground. More bodies for the fire and nothing more. She slowly gazed at the workers cleaning up the mess.

"This is what happens to those who do not fulfill their duty. Urvalin do not fear death. We welcome it. And to show weakness in the face of the enemy is the ultimate betrayal and will be dealt with accordingly."

With that she turned and strode to her shuttle craft and lifted off. From the air the scope of the carnage was more apparent. The enemy had managed to pin down key elements of her forces, then overcame their defenses on the flanks. The number and position of bodies made that much clear. By the time her dear Ahnlata was engaged she would have already been outnumbered.

But to overcome her Allpower? That was more worrisome than she was willing to let on.

Prin arrived back aboard her command ship and headed straight to the command center, taking her place on the casting podium. She took out the glowing Vikann stone pendant connecting her with the other commanders from within her tunic and reached out to them across the galaxies.

"What news, Prin?" Commander Torgus asked.

"Yes," Fraxxis chimed in. "Are you making progress?"

She hesitated. "There has been a development. A bad one at that."

"Oh?" Torgus replied, a rare hint of concern in his voice.

"The woman called Daisy. The Earthling with the smart ship we have heard so much about. She was here."

"You have been searching for her for some time now, Prin. This is a good development," he noted.

"She was here, and she killed Ahnlata. Wiped out the entire outpost. Ships were destroyed, troops slaughtered, their equipment stolen."

A long silence hung in the air, and it was not one caused by the billions of light years separating the three Urvalin leaders. Finally, Commander Torgus spoke.

"This one is proving to be far more of a pest than you said she would be, Prin. You had said it was just a matter of time before you had her removed from the equation."

"And so I believed, but she and her cursed ship are becoming quite a problem. And worse, the way she killed Ahnlata. A sword through the heart."

"She got that close to her?" he marveled. "She has to be working with a visla. No Earthling possesses that power. None but Charlie and Rika."

"It is worse than that," she continued. "I examined the wounds, and it was readily apparent, Ahnlata's body was sucked clean of her Allpower."

At that the other two commanders felt a flare of something quite unusual. A pang of fear.

"You made an error not focusing on eradicating this problem when we first learned of her," Torgus said.

"I had not anticipated tech weaponry of that caliber being present in that system when we executed our plan. But this? Stealing Allpower? This is worse than simple weaponry."

"Calm yourself," Fraxxis chided. "She is a problem, yes, but she is also cut off from all of her friends in her home galaxy. It is but a matter of time before she makes a mistake, and when she does, you will eliminate her."

"Of that you can rest assured," she replied. "But what of your troubles in our home realm? What of Charlie and Ara, Fraxxis? Do they still evade you?"

He was not happy about that matter being brought up, but, compared to Prin's failure, his inability to capture or kill the human paled by comparison.

"Still evading capture," he said. "And his pesky rebels are capturing more ships and equipment in the process."

"But we have plans for that, yes?" Torgus asked. "To eliminate the threat of our own vessels being used against us?"

"We do."

"Good."

"And what of your travails, Torgus? What of Earth?" Prin asked.

He smiled to himself, standing tall on his command podium aboard his mighty ship. "It is proving a difficult nut to crack. The planet is defended by some impressively powerful individuals."

"Oh? Is this also becoming a problem?" Fraxxis wondered.

"No, no problem," he replied. "Do not fear. I will overcome them. Of that I am certain."

CHAPTER THIRTEEN

The former terror known as Visla Dominus sat quietly in the living room of the temporary housing she was currently sharing with Fatima, sipping a nice cup of tea. She was reading up on the Urvalin recon Earth's forces had managed to gather to date, going over the fine points with her unlikely friend.

Malalia Maktan, incredible as it seemed, had really settled into this new life. Fatima was, of course, glad for the opportunity to help nurture a broken person's spirits, and her newest pupil was beginning to blossom, albeit in a rather violent and blood-sucking way.

But aside from her nutritional requirements to maintain her magic, Malalia was a changed woman. From what Fatima had gleaned in their nightly talks, harsh defeat and being stranded all alone on a distant planet without any power and with no one to talk to had forced her to reflect in ways she would otherwise never have dreamed of. The result? A potent new tool in Earth's defensive arsenal.

Malalia took a sip from her teacup and dabbed her lips with a napkin. "Fatima?"

"Yes?"

"When shall we go on another mission? I mean a *real* mission, not just these little cleanup operations."

"We will go when Rika is back."

Malalia was itching to do more. To use her power to its fullest, not just a few spells here and there. She was doing good, no doubt, but she felt as though she could do so much more.

"Where did she go, again?" she asked.

Fatima put down the papers she'd been studying and looked at Malalia with sympathetic eyes. "She just said she had something important to take care of and would be back later. I know you are anxious to spread your wings, so to speak, but the time will come sooner than you think."

"But she's been gone a while now."

"Yes, dear, I am well aware," Fatima said, almost forgetting the young-seeming woman was actually older than she was, thanks to her steady diet of stolen magic over the years. "Rika will be back soon, and once she is, I am sure there will be missions a-plenty for you two to engage in, and substantial ones, I'm sure. These Urvalin are spreading like a plague despite our best efforts. It's going to take quite a lot of hard work to keep them at bay."

Malalia considered Fatima's words a long moment, taking another long, slow sip of her tea. "Perhaps Cal has some task we could do. Surely, there has to be *something* we could help with."

"I'm afraid not. And besides, we can't reach him anyway," Fatima replied. "And how did you know he was still active? Everyone believes him dead."

"Rika mentioned he'd escaped the Urvalin attack. Having dealt with his planning prowess and tactical cunning in my own misguided days, I cannot say I am at all surprised," Malalia said with a grin. "But do not worry, his secret is safe with me."

"Oh, I'm not worried. He's out of LA now anyway. Safe and

sound out of harm's way all the way out in the desert in his skunkworks facility."

"Skunkworks?"

"I keep forgetting you're still new to this world. It was a term used for secret advanced research and testing facilities. The most famous, or infamous, if you prefer, was located out in the Mojave Desert, not too far from here."

"If he's that close, should we not go out there to speak with him? We might be of use to him. I mean, me being a visla, after all."

Fatima shook her head. "No, I'm afraid that's just not possible. You see, no one goes there. Not even Rika. It's too risky. If someone should notice? Well, I hate to think what could happen. That's why it is imperative we don't give the Urvalin the slightest hint as to where he is hidden."

"I suppose that makes sense. I do understand their thinking to an extent, having pitted myself against him in the past. But the Urvalin? They're operating in mysterious ways. One cannot really tell what they're up to—"

An alarm sounded out on both of their tablets.

"What is that?" Malalia asked.

"Speak of the Devil," Fatima said. "It looks like the Urvalin are making an attempt on one of the storage depots near the coast."

"Anything of value?"

"Honey, at this stage, *everything* we can use against them is of value."

"I see lights on the display. That means our people are moving in, yes?"

"You're learning quickly. Yes, we have multiple teams in the area diverting to intercept." Fatima's brow furrowed as a red flashing light appeared on the screen. "Well, isn't that interesting."

"Casters?" Malalia asked.

"Seems that way. And the Urvalin signal has split. What looked like a single landing party is actually three."

"The casting triumvirate."

"Just what I was thinking," Fatima said, rising to her feet. "Well, don't just sit there. Come on. It looks like we have something for you to do after all, and right here in LA. Are you sure you're up for it?"

Malalia hopped up, spry and ready for action. "I've fed well over these last encounters. All lesser casters, but still, I am prepared," she said, crackling a tiny bit of power from her fingertips to emphasize the point. "The casters, is the powerful one with them?"

"It doesn't look like it from initial reports."

Malalia seemed a bit relieved. "Then we should be fine. Shall we?"

The two women made quick time to the coastal depot, thanks to a quick lift from Marty. They hadn't expected to see the AI ship, but apparently this was enough of a big deal that he'd been pulled away from his other support missions to ensure their timely arrival.

"Okay, you two be safe down there," he said. "From what I hear on comms chatter, they're making a go at the raw materials storage facility. Surrounding it."

"Why would they send casters to do this?" Malalia wondered.

"Because the Urvalin are also a technologically advanced culture," Marty said. "They need raw resources just as much as we do if they want to manufacture components to keep all of their equipment functioning."

"So, this is the requisition of minerals and whatnot stage of the invasion, then," Fatima said. "It does make sense. They've been lurking around for a while, and we have been taking a toll on their operations. It was only a matter of time before they would need to replenish and repair."

"Unless we stop them," Malalia said with an excited grin. "You can drop me off here. I will make my way around the warehouse to the caster that is out of the others' line of sight."

"You should wait for the others to get here," Fatima said.

"They're close," she replied, pointing to the readout on her tablet. "And if I get started now, they can divert to the other two and focus their counterattack there. Once I take down the one caster, the remaining two should feel enough of a power loss to either run away or be defeated by our forces."

Fatima hated to send her out on her own, but she knew Malalia was right. As the former Visla Dominus, her grasp of tactics was nothing short of amazing.

"Okay, you engage them. Marty and I will provide close air support while the other teams get into position."

"Perfect. I will see you soon!"

With that, Malalia hopped out of the ship and took off at a full run.

"You think she can pull it off?" Marty asked.

"Have you seen her operating at full power?" Fatima replied.

"Okay, good point. Hang on, we're going up. The other teams should be here in under two minutes."

Marty pulled up into the sky and readied his weapons systems, holding back and waiting should the need for air support arise before everyone else was in place. A flash of bright light burst from the ground, illuminating the night sky, then falling dark.

"What was that?" Fatima asked.

"I'm not exactly sure. It came from position three."

"That's where Malalia was heading."

A moment later another bright flash lit up the area, followed by a third less than a minute later. A rumbling surge shook the air, then all was still. Marty hovered in place, trying to make sense of his readings. The thermal scans showed more Urvalin heat signatures than before, but something was different.

"It's safe to come down now," Malalia called out over the comms unit she had finally familiarized herself with.

Marty zeroed in on her location and descended just as the other combat teams swarmed into the area. As he touched down, it became quite apparent why the heat signatures had multiplied, as Fatima saw firsthand when she stepped out of the ship.

The Urvalin forces were dead. *All* of them. Most had been blown apart by a magical blast, though the casters lay in a heap, pale, dead, and a little shrunken, by the look of it. Malalia had taken them all out, drinking them dry in the process while letting loose a blast of killing magic on the rest of the invaders.

It was impressive. Impressive and a little frightening for those who had never seen what she could do up close and personal.

Malalia wiped her lips on her sleeve and walked to the ship stepping over bodies as casually as she might cross a stream or avoid a sleeping pet. She climbed into her seat and let out a happy sigh.

"Well, *that* was exhilarating," she said, amped up like a kid on a sugar high. "Can we do it again?"

CHAPTER FOURTEEN

The system was buzzing with traffic, mainly ships looking for a pair of winged beasts and the two armored rogues riding atop them. These invaders were clearly a threat to the one inhabitable planet, and they were going to do whatever was necessary to drive them back.

Allpower did not work against them nearly as effectively as the elders of Gomarra would have wished, so it became necessary to break out the big guns, firepower not used since they had put down the rebellion of Dixanus.

The unusual visitors had come out of nowhere, landing in the middle of town, which caused quite a stir in and of itself. That was disquieting, but strangers sometimes visited this planet, especially during harvest season. But when they began tearing up the local tavern, that was when the citizens took up arms against them.

A great battle had raged, or, at least it had felt like a battle to the inhabitants of that God-forsaken world they called home. Gomarra, why anyone would actually choose to live there was a mystery. As for the so-called invaders? It was just another instance of mistaken identity and magic gone awry.

Drombus and Duzza had been working on their casting, and being naturally magical creatures they had begun to get the feel for how their powers worked–or didn't work–in this galaxy. But the teens? Arlo and Ripley, while certainly proficient with the konus back home, were quite simply a hot mess of bad casting in this realm.

Fortunately, when their initial encounter with the native people went sideways, those horribly awry spells actually helped them, the enhanced destruction providing them the means of escape, albeit just barely.

The dragons had protected themselves and their passengers as best they could, but the panicking Gomarrans had simply begun firing everything they had at them like a Fourth of July fireworks finale gone wrong. Lucky for the intruders, the locals were not exactly a war-like people, and their readiness with the weapons was sadly lacking.

They had made it out of the atmosphere, but not without taking a lot of hits, and the dragons required a moment of respite to assess their injuries.

"The moon," Ripley said. "The small one, I mean. It's got some atmosphere but is uninhabited. We should be able to find a safe spot to hide there. At least for the time being."

"Screw that. We need to get the hell out of here, and I mean yesterday," Arlo countered.

"Idiot, the dragons are tired, and they may be hurt. You heard them, they need a rest."

"Fine," Arlo reluctantly agreed. "But as soon as we can, we jump away from this place and never look back."

The dragons descended quickly toward the moon's surface, coming to a rest under a rocky overhang that would protect them from prying eyes. Unless the angry Gomarrans dropped down to that exact spot, they would be unseen.

Arlo hopped down from Drombus's harness and stepped

back to assess what damage it and its wearer had suffered. Ripley scampered down from Duzza and began doing likewise.

"That was too close," she said. "*Again*."

"We really suck at this," her cousin agreed. "What were we thinking coming to this galaxy? We are so screwed."

"Stop saying that. We knew it was going to be risky, but everyone is counting on us. We have to find Charlie."

"First, we have to manage to just stay alive," Arlo said, leaning close to the dragon.

Drombus shifted and raised a wing so Arlo could get a better look.

"No broken scales that I can see," his human passenger said. "But it looks like there's some discoloration going on here. If I was to hazard a guess, I'd say you took a few good shots and are going to be bruised and sore, but otherwise you seem intact."

Drombus settled back and lowered his wing. "Thank you for the inspection, Arlo. Those people were coming at us with quite an assortment of spells and munitions."

"And pretty randomly at that," the teen agreed. "I really don't think they knew what they were doing, do you?"

"With a completely mixed up attack like that? I would tend to concur," the dragon agreed. "But how are you faring? You took some hits as well."

"I'm okay, I think. This armor is pretty impressive, but yeah, I'm gonna be sore in the morning. How about you, Rip? You all good?"

"If by all good you mean beat to shit and hiding from angry space villagers on some desolate moon, then yeah, I'm just peachy."

Arlo climbed back into the harness and checked the status of the Bakana rod. It had remained wrapped and secured in place despite all of the mayhem of their hasty escape. Arlo and Ripley had already decided that it needed a better covering than it currently had. There was no way they could risk one of the dragons touching the bare rod again.

The rod was potentially *very* dangerous, especially since the device allowed power to flow both ways. If they weren't careful, one of the dragons could be robbed of their magic without warning. It was enough to make them be sure to take extra precautions against precisely that.

Duzza shifted around, rolling her massive shoulders as she shook off the aches of battle. She took a deep breath then paused. "Hmm," she said, sniffing again. "Yes, I think... Drombus, do you smell that?"

The other dragon sniffed the air. "That's Ara's scent, all right. And it seems to have headed that direction. It seems she's been moving around quite a bit."

"Yes, but we'll have to be extremely careful jumping after her. Our power is still nowhere near dialed in."

"Agreed."

"Are you saying you can't jump anymore?" Ripley asked.

"No, not at all," her dragon friend replied. "Just we need to exercise caution and only make smaller jumps for the time being. Longer jumps would be risky, to say the least."

"Risky like jumping into a sun, for example?"

"Yes. Or into a moon," Duzza said. "But I feel ready to make an attempt, and we should go while Ara's scent is fresh. Drombus, are you fit to travel?"

"Ready to go, Cousin," the dragon replied.

The teens didn't waste any time, quickly climbing up to their seats and securing themselves for travel. A minute later, after ensuring the ships seeking them were nowhere near, the dragons took flight. A moment later, they jumped.

"This isn't right," Duzza said upon their arrival in the next system. "The scent is weaker. I think we overshot it."

"Let's try again," Drombus suggested, "On three. One. Two. Three."

The dragons pulled their power and jumped again.

"What's going on?" Arlo cried out as they emerged from their jump unexpectedly subject to the powers of gravity.

The dragons quickly tried righting themselves in the buffeting winds.

"Hold on!" Drombus called out.

"I am holding on! What happened?"

"We must have jumped into a planet's atmosphere. Hold fast, this could get rough!"

Arlo felt his stomach drop. He knew what a huge no-no it was to jump into atmosphere. Any number of things could go wrong, including arriving smack dab into the side of a mountain. At least that hadn't happened, but they were disoriented and falling fast.

The dragons adjusted their senses, finding the horizon line and fanning their wings to level out, doing so not a minute too soon as they suddenly were able to focus on the ground rushing up to meet them. They flapped hard, slowing their descent, but they still hit the ground hard, their powerful legs only barely withstanding the impact.

"Are we alive?" Ripley asked as the dust settled. "Please tell me we're alive."

Arlo climbed down to the lush ground and pulled off his helmet, vomiting until his stomach was quite empty. "Air's safe," he said, wiping his mouth with the back of his hand then flashing a thumbs-up as he bent over and retched again.

Ripley climbed down onto unsteady legs and joined him.

"Where are we?"

"I am not sure," Drombus replied. "Give us a moment to gather our equilibrium and we will be better able to provide a response."

"Okay," Ripley said. "Just don't—"

The ground rumbled as something very large and very angry charged through the brush toward the intruders who had dared step on its territory.

"Ripley!" Arlo shouted, opening up with whatever spells could come to mind, pulling hard from his konus.

Ripley did the same in a panic, casting what she hoped was a killing spell, but may have been a laundry incantation instead.

The beast was nearly as tall as the dragons, though not nearly as large. Its teeth, however, were something to reckon with, as were the long talons at the end of each of its six legs. Again and again Arlo and Ripley cast at it wildly, knocking it back at first, then pounding it down to the ground as their spells hit pretty much everything around them, including the massive creature attacking them.

It seemed this beast, while fearsome in its own right, did not possess any Allpower of its own. A moment later it lay dead and broken, the two teenagers' spells having done far more damage to it, and the surrounding area, than they'd have imagined possible.

"We need to run," Ripley said. "There could be more."

The dragons looked at one another.

"This was likely the alpha," Duzza replied. "And that means the others will stay clear of its turf. At least for the moment."

"So? What do we do now?"

"Now?" the dragon asked with a low chuckle. "Now I think we should roast it, don't you, Cousin?"

"Oh, yes," Drombus agreed. "It would be a shame to let it go to waste."

"You want to eat it?" Ripley asked.

"Yes."

"The thing that just tried to kill us."

"Yes, indeed. There is more than enough to go around, and after what we've been through, we could all use the sustenance."

Ripley looked at Arlo. He just shrugged.

"Okay," she finally said. "But then we get out of here, okay? This place gives me the creeps."

CHAPTER FIFTEEN

Kip and Dukaan landed aboard Nakk's command ship, positioning themselves close to the doors in the largest hangar. Not because Kip was a particularly big ship, but because Ara was coming aboard for a rare sit-down in person rather than communicating over comms while in space.

They had decided not to seek out a quiet location on the planet below in which to have a face-to-face meeting in the open air. Time was precious, and the teenagers from Earth would almost certainly be getting themselves into deeper trouble the longer it took for Charlie and his friends to find them. So they held a confab in the ship's hangar bay.

"Ara, you're sure about this?" Nakk asked. "Gomarra is something of a backwater planet. A farming world without much of interest."

The Zomoki shifted on her haunches, adjusting to the confines of the hangar. "I am certain," she replied. "The scent is getting stronger. And not just Arlo and Ripley. The dragons they are with as well. It is their magic I am able to follow most easily of the group."

"So, they're riding dragons and jumping around this galaxy," Charlie said. "What the hell were they thinking?"

"Likely that something is terribly wrong back home," Kip chimed in. "I mean, why else would they fly all the way out to that trap portal?"

Charlie shrugged. "Looking for me, maybe."

"Yeah, but I can't believe after what happened that anyone coming there behind us wouldn't approach with caution. And for them to be riding dragons? When did that happen? Last I saw, Arlo and Marty were inseparable. And Ripley was tooling around aboard Eddie. So for them to be out here without their AI ship buddies tells me something's up."

"I have to agree with Kip on this," Dukaan said. "The boy's bond with his ship is strong. They have grown up doing everything together. To go adventuring without Marty? Arlo must have had a very strong motivation."

Ara nodded. "Fortunately, I can follow the traces of dragon magic far easier than the remnants of konus spells. I am still not quite certain of which two they are, but they seem to be getting more proficient with their use of jump magic in this realm. Not to the extent we have adapted, of course."

"Well, to be fair, we've had a lot more time," Charlie noted. "That, and a helluva lot of motivation to dial that shit in. Especially with what happened to the Vortaxis."

"Yes. Unfortunate, that," she said. "Unfortunately, it is clear that no matter how much they had been practicing back in the other galaxies, Ripley and her cousin are decidedly *not* proficient in casting in this realm."

"Their run-in at the temple most certainly demonstrated that," Skohla said. "Is this the young woman you were training, Hunze?"

"I was providing her some basic martial instruction," the golden-haired warrior replied. "However, it was more of a casual bit of assistance, nothing more. Not yet at least, though one day she may take it a bit more seriously, in which case Bawb has offered his considerable talents."

Her mate nodded, putting his arm around her shoulder, the pair enjoying the simple act of closeness. It still amazed Charlie on occasion. When he'd first seen the Wampeh Ghalian it had been in fierce combat in a crowded marketplace. He had seemed so cold, so dangerous. And yet now he was seemingly a changed man.

Of course, Bawb was still a Wampeh Ghalian, but he was the rarest of them in that he had actually bonded with a mate. It simply was not done. But then, he had always been one for venturing somewhat outside the rules.

"Okay, enough about their messed-up power," Tamara said, sitting on a cargo container with Shelly, her cybernetic arm showing all the way to the shoulder in her tank top. "I say we focus on what really matters. Finding them fast before they go and shit the bed even further."

"Gonna need to do a lot of laundry, the rate those two are going," Shelly chuckled.

"They are right," Bawb said. "Conjecture does not aid our cause, and the clock is ticking. Wise One, can you guide us toward their scent without descending to the surface? As we have seen, local races do not seem to take well to the appearance of a creature of your size and power."

"It is understandable," she replied. "And to answer your question, yes, I have more or less pinpointed the most likely location." She tapped the topographical display projected on the hangar deck. "Here," she said. "This is where the scent is strongest. It is also in space, though the traces are somewhat chaotic. I will investigate them while you are on the surface."

Charlie rose and walked toward Kip's open airlock door.

"Thanks, Ara. We'll give you a shout if we need backup. Come on, you lot. Let's get down there and find those two."

The team gathered up their gear and followed him into the little ship. They would not be bringing their larger weapons with them on this outing. Showing up heavily armed in a place like this would only invite conflict. This was a search-and-retrieval mission, and that meant a modicum of tact was required.

Dukaan flew them down to a clearing where a few other ships were parked. While Kip's design was not of this galaxy, there were plenty of worlds out there and myriad craft, so a somewhat unusual one wouldn't garner all that much attention.

There was no sign of the dragons anywhere, which Charlie supposed was a good thing, given the wary looks the locals were casting their way. But there did seem to be an inordinate amount of debris in the area. Whether it was a sign of the cousins getting into it with the locals or not, however, they could not say.

"Let's hit up the tavern and gather some intel," Charlie said. "Bawb, you feel like doing your Binsala routine?"

"Today, I do not believe it will be necessary," he replied. "It is a largely agrarian society. We should be able to acquire basic intelligence with a little well-placed coin."

"Okay, then. Let's get us a drink."

The group split up. Charlie, Nakk, and Bawb entered the tavern first, taking a table in the middle of the establishment and ordering a round of drinks. Skohla, Hunze, Shelly, and Tamara waited several minutes then followed, setting up shop at the far end of the bar. Dukaan waited aboard Kip, ready to either run in guns a-blazing, or blast them up into space, whichever might be required.

The human women were wearing baggy clothing, the two cybernetically enhanced humans using their attire to hide the powerful metal limbs they were sporting. So far, they had not encountered anyone in this galaxy with metal replacements, and the last thing they wanted was to draw attention. Hunze had also given them a bit of practical camouflaging makeup to make them look a bit less human.

Hunze and Skohla did not require such adjustments, and as such wore their usual garb, with Skohla taking the lead as a native of this realm.

"Four tumblers of gorrahl and a plate of fizzit crisps if you have any," she said, flagging down the creature behind the counter and placing coin on the bar.

"Coming right up," the tentacled bartender replied, appendages working in multiple directions at once.

Nakk had ordered a few drinks as well as some snacks, which he and his associates were picking at while they scoped out the room. It was clear something had gone down recently, evidenced by fragments of broken furniture that hadn't all been swept up.

Nakk took a sip of his beverage and leaned over toward the nearest table. "Hey, what happened in here?" he asked. "This place is a mess."

"You should have seen it a few hours ago," the burly man seated there replied.

"Was there a fight?"

"Oh, you could say that. Some offworlders showed up, which happens sometimes around harvest time, but these were strange. Not like any I've seen before. And they flew in on a pair of terrifying beasts."

Charlie glanced over at Bawb. *Good thing we didn't arrive on Ara*, he silently said with their magical link.

Indeed. They were definitely here.

"So, what happened?" Nakk pressed.

"They had words with one of my friends, is what happened. And when it got a little heated, they started wreaking havoc."

"You attacked them?" Charlie butted in.

Nakk flashed him a look but said nothing. It was too late now, Charlie was in the mix.

"No," the man said. "We didn't attack them. At least, not at first. But then they started casting wildly, smashing up the place. We had no choice but to take them on. That was when their beasts began making a mess of things outside. It was all we could do to drive them away."

"That sounds bad, friend," Charlie said.

"It was," the very large man replied, leaning closer. "And you know something?"

"What?"

"You look a lot like them, *friend*."

"What? Me?" Charlie said, realizing all eyes in the tavern were on him. "You must be mistaken. Tell him, Nakk."

"Yes, he is right. I'm sure the kids were not—"

"I never said they were kids," the man said.

The unmistakable sound of chairs sliding as people got to their feet filled the tavern.

"Oh, hell," Shelly said, quickly downing the rest of her drink. "Shit's gonna hit the fan."

Bawb slowly rose to his feet, his hands open in front of him. "Gentlemen, we mean no harm. We do not seek any trouble."

"Well, trouble you found," the man said, flexing his meaty fist.

A moment later, he hit the ground in a heap, thanks to a carefully thrown bottle. Bawb looked at Hunze. She shrugged with a little smile. There was no avoiding this, it appeared, so they might as well make it quick.

The women launched off their stools as the tavern burst into a melee. Shelly and Tamara dialed back their powerful limbs. They didn't want to actually hurt anyone. These people had good reason to be angry, just not with Charlie and his friends, and there weren't any weapons they'd noticed. This was just going to be a good old-fashioned bar brawl.

"C'mon, Shel. Let's play," Tamara said with a gleeful smile as she charged into the fray.

It was a relatively fair fight, at least numerically speaking. The visitors were outnumbered roughly four to one, and with them refraining from using both lethal means as well as their still somewhat shaky magic, that meant while a good many people would have nasty headaches, none would be dying today.

Charlie shifted effortlessly into his old gladiator training, eschewing his more deadly tricks for those used in non-lethal combat. Bawb and Hunze did the same, slipping into more of a sparring mode, allowing the others the chance to get their hands dirty a bit while they simply redirected their opponents.

Skohla had been training with Hunze regularly, and this was a perfect real-world situation for her to try out her new skills in a relatively controlled setting. Nakk, Shelly, and Tamara were just in it for the brawl at this point.

"First to ten K.O.s wins," Tamara said as her non-metal fist connected with the corner of a man's jaw, snapping his head to the side and dropping him in a heap. She was glad that, for the most part, no matter how alien someone's physiology, a good rattle of the old brain pan would drop pretty much anyone.

Of course, there were those races whose brains were not located in their heads. And there were those whose heads looked nothing like anything she'd seen on Earth. But fortunately, that was not the case today. At least if you didn't count the bartender, who did not seem to want any part of the fight. It was a good thing. With those multiple tentacles he could have been a very difficult opponent.

In a little less than five minutes the fight was over.

Charlie had a little scrape on his cheek, and Nakk was

sporting a black eye, but nothing more than that. The women had fared a bit better, merely dirtying their knuckles on the faces of their opponents. Bawb and Hunze, as expected, were utterly untouched.

"We should get going," Charlie said, tossing some coin to the bartender. "Sorry about the mess. We really didn't want any trouble."

CHAPTER SIXTEEN

Nakk followed Ara's jump as they continued tracking Arlo and Ripley's destructive flight path. Gomarra had been a bust in so far as actually finding the two, but at least it had put them on the right track. And it had also confirmed their concerns about the pair's casting abilities in this realm.

Charlie and his companions had quickly left the planet after their little encounter in the local tavern. Bawb had cast a basic sealing spell on the front door, but with the way his power was working, there was no telling how long it would hold. For that reason, they made a very hasty departure from the planet.

Ara's nose had next taken them to a small moon orbiting Gomarra. There was an overhang on the surface where she could see the footprints of the two dragons in the dusty soil. They had been here, no doubt, and recently at that.

It was also apparent that the Gomarrans had sent up quite an assortment of ships looking for them. They weren't a warlike people, but they did possess some hefty firepower to defend their crops if need be. It did not seem as though it was something they were terribly skilled with, though, as there was no trace of any blood, dragon or human.

Regardless, this was becoming a problem.

Aboard Nakk's ship, Charlie paced the command center, agitated and concerned. "They're drawing too much attention to themselves."

"Clearly," Bawb and Hunze said in unison.

It was both cute and a little unsettling how they would sometimes say the exact same thing at the exact same time. Maybe it was something to do with Hunze's pregnancy linking them even closer, or maybe it was their bond of shared Ootaki hair. Or maybe even that she had more or less downloaded all of Bawb's Ghalian skills in a very intense neuro-stim info dump. Whatever the reason, their sentiment was clear.

"These children are not only bringing scrutiny upon themselves," Skohla noted. "They are bringing additional attention our way in the process. It is urgent that we find them, and soon."

Charlie stopped pacing and keyed his comms open so everyone could hear. "Ara, any luck on that trace?"

"We are getting closer," she replied. "There seem to have been a few miscalculated jumps made. I think the dragons are getting a better handle on their magic, but space travel has always been one of the more tricky skills to master."

"You've done pretty well with it," Nakk noted.

"Yes, but I am a Zomoki. While we are distant cousins of the dragons of Charlie's galaxy, our physiology and skills are still divergent enough that there are certain to be some unexpected differences in our reactions to this galaxy's Allpower."

"So, in this instance, you're just better adapted to our realm?" Skohla asked.

"Precisely. Wait a moment, I just got a whiff of a particularly powerful magic trail."

"The dragons?" Tamara asked.

"Nothing else uses magic in this galaxy that we know of. Everything else is run by their Allpower."

"So, can you trace it?"

"I am discerning the stronger end of the trail now. With that we will know which direction to—ah, there it is. Yes, I have a lock on it. Nakk, are you prepared to follow?"

"Ready when you are."

"Then follow me. But be cautious. I sense this jump will take us quite close to a planet's atmosphere."

The Zomoki and the ship jumped a moment later, arriving just outside the atmosphere of a small but fecund world. Turbulence shook the ship as it began atmospheric entry almost immediately.

"You said it would be close, but not that close," Nakk transmitted.

"This was dialed back," Ara replied. "I am afraid we may not like what we discover below. The dragons apparently jumped directly into atmosphere."

Charlie, Bawb, and Hunze all shared a worried look. They knew how big a deal that could be, especially for a Zomoki. And the dragons? The shift from the weightless, horizonless freedom of space to the confines of gravity and atmosphere, well, it could be catastrophic. Time would tell, and very soon at that.

"There!" Nakk said, pointing to a charred area growing steadily more visible as they descended. "Looks like there was a battle here."

"No, there is no scent of weapons fire," Ara noted. "This is something else."

The ship settled down, its mass flattening several small trees and plenty of brush in the process. The airlock cycled open a minute later, and Charlie led the group out to survey the scene. Ara was already on the ground, sniffing around.

"What in the world happened here?" Charlie gasped as he took in the senseless destruction.

Trees were shattered and burnt, and the ground scorched and cracked from violent power use. And lying not more than fifty meters from them was the charred remains of some sort of animal. Large and carnivorous judging by the teeth clearly visible on what remained of its skull.

"This was a somewhat powerful casting," Ara said. "The flames were dragon fire. At least the localized ones. But the rest? It looks like unbridled, panicked casting gone awry."

Charlie began walking toward the carcass. "You can say that again. Look at all the damage those two did."

It was a mess, for sure, but Hunze was looking at the scene with a different eye. "Yes, Charlie, there is a lot of damage, but they seem to be beginning to control their spells better."

"You call this better? Look at this place. Look at that creature. What's left of it, anyway."

"Yes, obviously, they are still wildly unpredictable in their power use, but look past the damage and see the signs of control."

"You call this control?"

"Reach out and *feel* the magic. These spells were at least intended to be violent. Defensive and offensive, yes, but there are not the completely random spells mixed in as before," she said. "Bawb, do you agree?"

The assassin stood from where he had been studying the broken ground and wiped his hands. "Hunze is correct. These were combatives. The very spells we have been guiding them in the use of."

"You're teaching them to do this?" Charlie asked. "You sure that's such a good idea?"

"We have taught them combative offense and defense spells. And we instructed them in a few harder spells as well. But with their limited use of magic, there was no risk of this sort of thing back home. But here? With Allpower in the mix? Well, it seems their casting has evolved into something quite different."

Ara pushed the carcass and examined it closely. "Tooth marks," she said. "Whatever else they did, they used this fallen creature as a food source. The flames were not indiscriminate."

"Great," Charlie sighed. "They ate what they killed. Whoopee freaking doo. If they're burning through power like this, it's no wonder they'd be hungry."

"And the repeated jumps," Ara added.

"Of course. What I'm saying is, all of this adds up to a problem that's only growing. This sort of thing, whether it's Allpower, magic, or whatever, is going to attract a lot of attention. And the last thing we need is more eyeballs looking closely at the places we're in. It's hard enough hiding all of our stolen fleet as it is."

"They are prepared to move to the other rally point if they are discovered," Nakk noted.

"I know, man, but that's not the point. The point is, sooner or later the Urvalin are going to catch wind of this. And we can't afford to have another head-to-head with them. Not yet, anyway."

"They are a difficult adversary," Bawb agreed. "And Charlie is correct. Our forces, while growing, are not yet prepared for further engagement."

"Exactly," Charlie said, pacing nervously around the animal's remains. "The Urvalin are not only persistent and powerful, they're also tricky bastards. And if my home galaxy is wrapped up in this mess, who knows what those bastards are up to?"

CHAPTER SEVENTEEN

Three massive command ships sailed through the darkness of space, each transcribing an arc around a key world in the galaxy, like massive predators circling their prey, ready to attack. They were there, ready, but their targets did not know when, or where, the eventual strike would occur.

In the meantime, smaller fleets of their underlings scattered, raiding, conquering, taking prisoners when possible, leaving behind death and destruction when not. Like the tendrils of a deadly plant, they slowly spread, wrapping up more and more of the galaxies in their powerful grip.

This was the Urvalin way, and up until now it had been quite successful. Generations of leaders had prepared for this intergalactic conquest, readying their forces, building up the blind loyalty of their ranks. And at the heart of it all stood the three commanders, Torgus, Fraxxis, and Prin, controlling the strings of their puppets across the stars.

The Vikann stones each wore around their necks provided the link they required for such a feat. Normally, their casting podiums would enhance and interlink their powers to great effect within the same galaxy, but now that they were spread across three disparate ones, they needed to use the relics that their predecessors had spent so much time finding.

The tech bezel holding the stones only served to further boost their reach, allowing the three commanders to channel power to one another across galaxies with greater ease than if they held the stone alone. In addition, they aided them in communication, though the casting podium would normally have been enough for that, even across the stars.

Everything was falling into place. Soon the three galaxies would be properly linked, their Allpower flowing seamlessly between them. All that was required was a little push. One more relic to help bolster the union. An item of great power from one of the other two galaxies that would help bond them together and allow the Allpower to reach its true potential, all with the Urvalin at the helm.

Torgus was the defacto leader of the three, his power being the strongest of their casting triumvirate, though all shared an equal role in decision-making for their armada as a whole. When it came to individual fleets in each galaxy, however, the individual commander in charge in that realm had the final say. It was a system that had, thus far, worked well for the Urvalin, allowing each commander to focus on the tasks at hand in their own galaxy.

And under this system, they were growing ever closer to their goal.

Torgus roused from his meditation session, calm and focused, his Allpower flowing smoothly throughout his entire being. Fraxxis likewise made a practice of the art of centering, while Prin refrained from such things, considering the act of having to calm her mind to better understand herself beneath her. But she was powerful, that could not be debated. And she had controlled her fleet to great success thus far.

Torgus took a sip from a cool glass of water then left his

chambers, walking the short distance to the command center of his ship.

"Commander," his first officer said as he entered.

"Power to the casting podium," he replied. "I would speak with the others."

"Done, sir."

A moment later the podium on which his command seat rested hummed slightly as the Allpower-enhancing machinery and spells kicked into gear.

Torgus stepped up and ran his fingers over the pendant around his neck. "Fraxxis, Prin, it is time."

"We are here," Fraxxis replied.

"All goes to plan," Prin added.

Torgus smiled. "Good. Prin, how proceeds the search in your realm?"

"Very well, Torgus. I managed to pry the location of the Korna tablet from the elderly master who had last heard of its possible whereabouts. It required some doing, but we narrowed the search to but a handful of powerful vislas who might possess it."

"Well done. How long until you have it in your hands?"

"I already do," she replied, self-satisfaction clear in her voice. "It was housed in the estate of a particularly powerful woman named Visla Dorann. She proved most problematic, but I overcame her and claimed it for our cause."

"Is she aboard one of the prisoner ships now?" Fraxxis asked. "A caster of her power is always a welcome addition to our ranks."

"Unfortunately, no. This one did not agree to join our ranks. Even when her defeat was clear, she nevertheless persisted, fighting to her last breath."

"A valiant and worthy death," Torgus said quietly. "A shame.

It sounds as though this woman would have made a valuable servant. But what is done is done."

"Yes," Prin said. "And her entire collection of artifacts is now in my possession. There are a great many valuable and fascinating pieces, but interestingly enough, the Korna tablet was merely categorized as an ancient linguistics key and filed away with the other lesser magical items."

"She had no idea what she possessed," Fraxxis marveled. "The fools had such rare power right under their own noses yet did not realize it. What remarkable power they had sitting in plain sight in their own galaxy."

Torgus's smile grew wider. Everything was coming together as planned. "Do you have it with you now?" he asked.

"I do," Prin replied. "It is a tricky bit of Allpower to get a hold of, though. Every time I attempt to connect with it, its potential shifts, slipping out of my grasp."

"Perhaps with the three of us connected it will not be so problematic," Fraxxis suggested. "While this is not the moment for our end game, we can at the very least make an attempt. Once the Korna tablet is in sync with our Vikann pendants, the power we share across these galaxies will increase tenfold."

"If not more," Torgus added. "Let us sample this power, Prin. Engage with the artifact."

She did not reply verbally, but rather shifted her focus to the palm-sized tablet in her hand. It seemed plain enough, a smallish bit of some unusual stone with runes and markings covering every inch. It was actually not terribly surprising that one with limited sensitivity to power might have classified it as a mere translation device of old. By the time it had changed hands a few dozen times, its origin was lost, and all that remained was the index of its allegedly minimal Allpower properties.

But in the right hands, with the right bit of arcane knowledge, the tablet's true potential could be realized.

The tablet shifted in Prin's hands slightly.

"I can feel something across our link," Fraxxis said. "Slippery, as you described."

"I, too, feel it," Torgus said, marveling at the unusual sensation unlike any he had ever experienced. "Marvelous. Feel the way it makes the Vikann stones surge."

Prin tightened her grip on the artifact. "Yes, but try to latch onto it more. To bind it to your stone."

Torgus did just that, pulling gently but firmly, wrapping the power to his own Vikann stone. "I have it," he said with great satisfaction. "The power is mi—"

Without the slightest warning the power shifted and shimmied, slipping away from Torgus entirely. A moment later the tablet fell silent.

"You can see the difficulty," Prin said. "We will get there, and once we have full control over the tablet our victory will be complete. We will be able to divert all the Allpower we need to forge a larger, stable portal back to our own galaxy, bonding these three realms and their Allpower inexorably. But until then, we shall have to redouble our efforts to control it."

"We will have more of these sessions soon," Torgus replied. "For now, study it. Learn its secrets."

"I will. And I look forward to ending our foes in all three galaxies with great finality."

"Do not get cocky," Torgus cautioned. "Unexpected adversaries have been proving most troublesome in all of our domains."

"But we are Urvalin. We will crush them."

"On that we agree. But we must use caution. Hastiness only emboldens our enemies, and time is one thing we have in abundance."

CHAPTER EIGHTEEN

Kara and Vee drifted quietly in space, safely ensconced in their powered armor suits while sitting astride their dragon friends. With the help of Nixxus and Gazz, they had quietly left the others and flown off on their own, hoping to scope out a safe route to the portal submerged in the sun.

The dragons had agreed to the trip on one condition. They would not be making any suicide attempts if the Urvalin fleet was too strong. Kara had agreed, hoping that perhaps the Urvalin might spread themselves thinner now that some time had passed since the two dragons had emerged from her home galaxy with the two riders on their backs.

Unfortunately, they didn't even need to draw close to the portal's location to see the massive amount of Urvalin craft now guarding it. It may have been out of any of their reach, submerged in the sun as it was, but they would die before they would let anyone else make an attempt at crossing over. And odds were there was an equally large force on the other side on the off chance someone did sneak by.

"We can't, Kara," Vee said over her helmet comms. "I know you want to get back, and so do I, but just look at them all."

Despite her frustration, Kara accepted their situation rather than throw a fit about it. Much as she wanted to find her father, this was not the time. An attempt on the portal would lead to almost certain death. Or worse, capture.

"We're going to need help," she said after staring at the Urvalin forces a long while. "This requires a different way of looking at the situation. Tactics. Strategy. Maybe some misdirection, even."

Vee shifted in her seat and looked over at her friend. "Tactics, you say? Are you thinking what I'm thinking?"

Vee couldn't see her friend's face inside her helmet, but she could almost feel the grin regardless. "Yep," Kara said. "We need to see Joshua."

"Excuse me," Gazz said. "Isn't he trapped on the surface of the moon? Stuck behind the Urvalin dampening field at your Dark Side base?"

"He is."

"And you wish to fly there?"

"We do."

Gazz and Nixxus locked eyes, gauging each other's commitment to the idea. There were a lot of Urvalin in orbit over the moon, but at least it was nothing like the forces near the portal.

"Okay," Gazz said. "We'll do it. But you need to be ready to unleash your strongest magic in this encounter. It could be very difficult."

"Unless we sneak past," Kara said.

"The preference, obviously. But not as easy as you may think," Nixxus replied. "Gazz, shall we?"

"Ready when you are."

"Then let's jump."

The dragons popped out of existence, reappearing across the vast darkness just outside the thin atmosphere of the moon, well away from Dark Side base. It was a good thing they had chosen that arrival point.

"Look," Nixxus said. "Combat."

She was right, the girls immediately realized as they watched the flashes of Allpower and weapons discharging in space above Dark Side base off in the distance.

"You think you can get us in without being caught up in all of that?" Vee asked.

"I believe we can. Time will tell. Hold on, and be ready to cast if needed." With that, Nixxus and Gazz dropped low, approaching the area from the side, hopefully avoiding the line of fire of the ships above.

"Time to power down," Kara reminded everyone. "Don't want to fry our gear."

All of them quickly shut everything off, relying simply on magic to keep them safe as they flew past the dampening array. As they passed, Kara got a quick look at one of the disguised microsats. It looked like a piece of space debris, but she knew just how dangerous it actually was. Hopefully, there would be a means to deactivate or destroy them en masse. Individual ones could be targeted, but with the quantity in play, another would simply be shifted to take its place.

"Safe," Nixxus announced, powering her harness back on. "You can reactivate." As the others did so, she transmitted to Sid down below. "Dark Side base, this is Nixxus. Gazz and I are arriving with some friends. Where shall we land?"

"Nixxus? What a surprise," Sid replied. "Please, come to hangar two. I'll have Poric come and meet you."

"We are heading there now."

Poric was a cyborg, the newest model brought into service only in the last year. But more than that, he was the head of security for the entire facility, upgraded to the gills by both Sid as well as Joshua. No one knew exactly what additions they had provided him, but so far no situation had presented itself where anyone would need to find out.

"Good to finally meet you," Poric said as the girls climbed down from their rides. "Nixxus, a pleasure. And, Gazz, I've heard much about you."

"You have?"

"I like to keep up to date on things," he said with a wink, then turned to the two dragon riders. "And the infamous Kara and Vee. I cannot begin to say how lovely it is to make your acquaintance."

"Infamous?" Vee asked.

"After what you two did, standing up against Visla Dominus? That was crazy impressive, and at such a young age. I can tell, you two are going to be something special, and sooner than you think."

"Uh, thank you?" Kara said, blushing from the attention.

"Come on, you must be hungry. Let me get you something to eat. And Nixxus? Gazz? Can I have a pallet or two of protein sent your way?"

"Actually, that would be much appreciated," Nixxus replied.

"Excellent. I'll have the replicators whip you up something special. Do you want to roast it yourself? Because if you do, I'm afraid I'll need to ask you to do that outside. Fire and confined spaces in a near vacuum, you know?"

Nixxus nodded. "That would be fine. Our flames will have no difficulty outside, and there is something satisfying about doing it ourselves."

"I thought as much, but it's always better to ask, right? Okay, girls, if you'd please follow me."

Poric led the pair through an unfamiliar part of Dark Side base on the way to the retrofitted galley. They'd visited the moon base in the past, but it seemed Sid and Joshua had been making upgrades to the place. One of the newest was the improved mess hall. One of several the enlarged facility now sported.

"It's voice command, so just tell it what you want," Poric said. "I'll grab us a table."

"He's a friendly guy," Vee said. "It's almost weird after hanging around George and his team."

"They're nice too," Kara countered.

"Well, yeah, but in a kind of gruff, military sort of way. Poric seems so, I don't know. *Normal.*"

"Normal is nice sometimes. Now, what do you want to eat?"

The girls loaded up their trays and headed over to the quiet little spot Poric had picked out for them. The mess hall wasn't terribly crowded, but he thought a bit of privacy would nevertheless be appropriate for the newcomers.

"So, I assume you know all about powering down before hitting the dampening field, seeing as your armor is still functional," Poric said. "Nice design, by the way. A modification of something Joshua and I were developing, if I'm not mistaken."

"You're an AI, so I'm sure you're not," Kara said with a grin.

"Fair point," he replied. "But how are you two faring? I mean, obviously you have a secure means of transit with the dragons, but it must be disconcerting being unable to reach the portal."

"How did you know—"

"Sid's been watching your path with his telescopes. We saw you two sitting out there assessing the fleet. Good call, not making an attempt on it. That's some serious firepower out there."

Vee took a swig from her cup. "About that, what about other ships? I thought the dampening minefields were mapped out now."

"They are but they aren't. Even knowing their locations, the cursed things shift around a bit. We've already lost so many ships, we can't afford to lose any more. Most are with Zed now, as you know, but a few are still doing recon in this part of the system. But they never engage. That's a fight they would not win. Not at this disadvantage."

"So, all of your ships?"

"Are stuck down here within the Urvalin dampening array, yes."

Kara wiped her lips. "But we saw some of them flying when we arrived," she said.

"Yes, but that's all within the hard ceiling."

"The what?"

"It's a little something Joshua came up with. An embedded program on every ship. A fail-safe to keep them from accidentally flying too high and getting knocked out of commission. It's working so far, and we haven't lost any ships in the last few skirmishes. Lucky for us, the Urvalin haven't figured out a way past our defenses yet."

Kara was about to make a comment in the vein of how Charlie's favorite adage was about not tempting Murphy when alarm klaxons sounded.

"What is that?" she asked.

"Aw, crap," he said. "Come with me. We're under attack."

They abandoned their food and raced to the transparent ceramisteel viewing windows and looked outside, up to the sky. There was nothing there.

"I don't see anything," Kara said.

"Not up there. Down here," Poric said, pointing to the tiny moving specks making their way to the base across the surface.

It was an attack force of space-suited Urvalin, and they were swarming in from all sides. Kara quickly lost count of how many there were.

"How did they get in?"

"They use their Allpower. It's not affected by the dampening array."

"No, I mean how did no one see them?"

Poric surveyed the approaching troops a moment. "Judging by the distribution of the moon dust on their suits, I'd say they must've landed quite a distance from the base. Well outside of the dampening zone. Then they made the trek on foot."

Vee's eyes widened. "On foot? Out there? That's a long way."

"Well, what can I tell ya," Poric said with a shrug. "They're persistent bastards, I'll give 'em that. Now come on, there's a fight coming, and we need to get you two some bigger guns."

Vee turned to follow him. "Our rifles are still mounted to the dragons' harnesses."

"I know. But don't you worry. Old Poric'll take good care of you. I'm a healer, did I mention?" he said, tapping his chest. "I have a konus embedded in my endoskeleton. I'm not as proficient as a native magic user, but I like to think I hold my own. Anyway, if anything should happen, I've got you. Now, come on, we should get moving."

Kara and Vee shared a stunned look as he took off at a jog. As a cyborg, he could move, much, much faster, but with the two teenagers at his six he could only go so quickly. But a cyborg who had been born with a konus as part of his body? It was utterly unheard of, but, crazy as it sounded, if a charged konus had been a part of him from day one, he just might actually be able to cast as naturally as a normal person.

"Hey," he said, pausing a moment. "You should put your helmets back on, just in case they breach the walls. I can't really heal you if you explode from depressurization."

"Oh, yeah. Good point," Kara said as the two fastened their helmets in place and powered their armor to a higher setting. "Nixxus, Gazz, you two seeing this?" she asked as they took off down the corridor once more.

"Seeing what?" Nixxus asked.

"We've got an Urvalin problem."

"When don't we?"

"No, I mean here, on the surface."

"I do not smell any Allpower use. Wait, there is something. Faint. Not Allpower. That's Urvalin tech."

"Sneaky bastards," Poric said with a grim laugh. "They must have switched to tech upon clearing the dampening array so nothing would show on our Allpower scans."

"You can scan for that now?" Vee asked. "With machines, I mean?"

"It's a work in progress, but someone on the ground must've leaked what we were up to. Dark Side is an elite group, but I'm afraid down on Earth some of our people sold out for the right price."

Kara checked her suit power. All was optimal. "What are we supposed to do now?" she asked as Poric unlocked an innocuous storage shelf among a sea of other likewise plain-looking shelves.

He pulled out a pair of hefty pulse rifles, modified with advanced recoil dampeners for low-g combat, and handed them each one.

"Now we kick some Urvalin ass," he said, charging his own weapon. "Come on," he said with a wide grin, "this should be fun!"

CHAPTER NINETEEN

Rather than attempting to shield the teenage casters from danger, Poric gleefully hauled them smack into the middle of it, blasting away at any Urvalin who might get close to them while simultaneously directing what limited air support they could manage as well as forces protecting the base's airlocks from his vantage point.

AI fighting at its best, essentially, and he was having a blast. Literally and figuratively.

Kara and Vee, while having learned the basics of pistols and pulse rifles, were nevertheless not exactly the best shots, even with the dampening technology in these advanced units. But where they lacked with conventional weaponry, they both made up for it with magical prowess.

"*Orcanus dilecto!*" Kara said, casting an unusual force spell at a trio of enemy combatants. The Urvalin realized she was casting and raised their Allpower defenses to counter, but she wasn't trying to kill them. She wasn't even trying to harm them. Kara had cast an excavation and disposal spell.

The ground they were standing on abruptly lurched upward

then flew off into the distance, the hapless troops dragged along with it.

"Nice one!" Poric exclaimed. "I knew you had it in you!" He then cast his own force spell with moderate success.

Kara appreciated the support, but having a cybernetic cheerleader shouting rah-rah every time you cast a spell was starting to wear a bit thin.

"Thanks, Poric," she said. "But you really don't need to keep telling me that."

"Right. Of course. It's just all so exciting for me. I haven't fought with a full-fledged caster before, and I'm kind of fanboying a bit. Maybe you can give me some pointers when this is all over."

Kara and Vee shared a look, which, despite them both wearing helmets and not actually being able to see one another's faces, was clear as day. It was the, "Oh-my-God-this-guy-is-kind-of-weird," look. And to be fair, they weren't exactly wrong about that.

Poric abruptly shifted from cheerful supporter, spinning and opening fire with blistering intensity on a squad of Urvalin trying to flank them.

"Hit the deck!" he commanded as he vaulted over them in a low-gravity flip, blasting away the entire rotation with pinpoint accuracy. The Urvalin were thrown backwards by the blasts, several of them failing to activate their shields in time, their suits ruptured and their oxygen gone in an instant.

Joshua's massive craft swung by and did a loop overhead, searching for suitable targets. Eddie was flying right behind him, ready to protect his six, though the tactical AI really didn't need the support.

"Poric, Sid, I need an update from down there. Bio signals are all jumbled."

"It is a *mess* of data," Sid replied. "I am still trying to parse through it all."

"They're casting jamming spells and digging into positions we can't hit from above," Poric relayed over their comms. "Hold back, Joshua. If you fire on them you'll risk damaging the base."

"Well, that's just lovely," Joshua grumbled. "Options?"

"For now, I'd say target those who haven't completed the trek to the base," the cyborg replied. "Make an example out of 'em. We all know they won't surrender, so have at it."

That was something Joshua could most certainly do.

"You hear that, Eddie?"

"I did."

"Then follow me and target the incoming ground forces. Hopefully there'll be a reasonable firing solution on the ones closer to the base by the time we return."

"Copy that, following your lead," the smaller ship replied, priming his cannons. The railguns, however, he would save for a rainy day. That, or ship-to-ship combat where they would come in more handy than for strafing approaching ground forces.

"Breach!" Sid shouted over comms on all channels. "There is a breach at section nine, airlock three." A flash of light blipped out across the battleground. "Additional breach at section seven, airlock two."

"We're on it, Sid," one of the ground units replied.

"On our way," Poric chimed in. "Come on, you two, your talents could come in very handy right about now."

"But what are we supposed to do?" Vee asked as they ran after the cyborg. "We've never done anything like this before."

"Nonsense. I've read your files. This time it's on a moon base is all. Now pick up the pace, Ladies. We've got vermin to flush out!"

Sid was rapidly blinking out the Morse Code update of the situation to Zed and Cal as the attackers began to spread from compartment to compartment within his walls. He sincerely hoped this transmission wouldn't be his last. If they reached his core, then all bets were off. But there was hope. Hope in the form of a very disciplined and determined crew.

The Urvalin had traitors on the ground on Earth and could use them to exploit weaknesses in certain defenses, but the one thing the Urvalin hadn't counted on fully was that not only was it near impossible to even approach the potential Dark Side crewmembers—namely because they didn't know they were selected until right before shipping out—but also that those selected for this prestigious position were the most hardy and loyal of Earth's forces. The cream of the crop. Men and women who would never turn traitor, and who, like the Urvalin, would willingly die protecting their comrades.

The battle raged inside the corridors of Dark Side base with all manner of weapons being used, from projectile, to pulse, to magical, to improvised melee weapons when things got up close and personal. And Poric was leading the girls right into it.

"There's gotta be one of their casters down here with the advance team," Poric said, finally letting the girls in on why he really needed their help. "Probably two up above in their ships, though another could be on the ground somewhere. But statistically speaking there will almost certainly be only one."

He stepped over the shattered body of a woman named Monica, one of the more annoying of the base's crew who had fallen during the breach. He paused but for a second, sparing her only a cursory glance. He was a cyborg, after all, and both his sensors as well as his implanted konus told him there was nothing he could do for the woman. A large chunk of machinery had landed on top of her, which was bad enough, but apparently that had happened only after she'd been impaled on a length of twisted metal.

No matter his healing skills, there was no sense even pausing to try.

Instead, he moved on and crouched down when he reached the next downed person. He was applying a healing spell to the fallen crewmember's shattered leg, when he abruptly spun ninety degrees and fired off his pulse rifle, dropping the two Urvalin who had been lurking in wait to take down any reinforcements that might arrive. A flash of powerful magic rumbled through the section, leaving a faint tingle in the air.

"Aaand, that would be the caster," Poric confirmed. "Okay, listen. We need to take them out. I'll draw their attention, then you go full-tilt-boogie with your magic, okay?"

Kara and Vee looked at one another with uncertainty.

"Uh, okay?" Kara said hesitantly.

"Great." He looked down at his patient. "You'll be okay, buddy. It's not totally mended, but your hemorrhaging has stopped. Don't overexert until you get to a med pod."

"Thanks, Poric," the fallen man said.

"It's what I do. Okay, Kara, Vee. With me!"

They charged ahead, not sure what exactly they were heading into. Bodies littered the ground, both Urvalin as well as base crew. Clearly, this caster was not messing about. Killing spells were in the air, and they were powerful.

"Hey, your bitchiness!" the cyborg shouted out as he rounded the corner to the intersection she was standing smack dab in the middle of. "Eat this!"

He fired his weapon at the caster, a stocky woman in a snug space suit. She had shed the helmet and gloves to better cast, and cast she did. *Violently*. She spun at the intruder, blocking his weapons fire and hitting him full-force with a killing spell strong enough to take down a dozen men. Poric flew through the air and flopped to the ground in a heap.

"Poric!" Kara shouted, her anger flaring.

The caster turned and saw the teenage girls and laughed. It was a cold, hard sound from a woman who had no compunction about killing children if it served the Urvalin cause. But then she noticed something strange about these two. The violet-skinned one, to be precise. Something was crackling along her body. Some strange form of Allpower.

She quickly cast at the intruders, another killing spell, but Kara defended, just as Korbin had taught her. Vee simultaneously cast the most powerful shock spell she could muster. The Urvalin caster batted it aside, but only just. Unfortunately, that diverted just enough of her substantial power to leave the tiniest of gaps in her defenses.

Kara struck, and she struck hard.

"*Morantis niktu!*" she said, the magic blasting out of her with far more force than even she expected.

The Urvalin's defenses crumbled under the assault, her body hurling backward against the corridor wall, her unconscious form dropping to the deck.

"How did you do that?" Vee asked.

"I really don't know."

"Nicely done, girls," Poric said, rising to his feet and dusting himself off.

Kara felt her heart beat a little faster at the shock. "You're okay!"

"Yeah, I'm a cyborg. Killing spells don't really take with my kind, ya know?"

Kara couldn't help but let out a little relieved laugh. Not because it was funny, but because if she didn't laugh she might cry. So much was happening so fast, it was overwhelming.

"She's not dead," Vee said, checking the woman's pulse. "What should we do with her?"

Poric scanned her with his cybernetic eyes, assessing the threat as well as any damage she might have incurred. "We'll tie her up and put her somewhere safe for now. The big brains can figure out the rest later." He shifted his gaze slightly. "All teams, one Urvalin caster is down. I repeat, one Urvalin caster is down. Move in on the remaining forces."

A triumvirate of casters would provide endless difficulty for their people, but with one of them out of commission, the remaining two would be at a huge disadvantage. Unless they were extremely powerful, and so long as the Urvalin fleet didn't make an all-out push toward the surface simultaneously, it would only be a matter of time before the remaining Urvalin were either driven back, captured, or killed, and frankly, he didn't care which.

"So, you were wondering why I wanted you to come with me?" Poric said, walking over to the girls. "I think it's pretty obvio—"

An Urvalin trooper sprang from cover at that moment. He'd apparently been hiding this whole time, waiting for a clear shot on the young women who had somehow downed his caster. He raised his weapon and fired.

"Nooo!" Poric shouted, diving in front of the girls just as the blaster rounds hit, throwing him back into them and knocking all three to the ground.

Faster than any human could possibly move Poric was on his feet, returning fire at an incredible rate. The shocked Urvalin tried to cast defenses but was overwhelmed by the barrage. A moment later his bloody corpse fell to the deck in a smoking pile.

"That's right!" Poric shouted at the dead man. "Bet ya weren't expecting a combat-hardened, konus-wielding cyborg, were ya, punk?" He quickly scanned the area then flashed the girls a wink. "All clear. Okay, Ladies. What say you we truss up this turkey, pop her in an airlock for safe keeping, and get back into the fray? There's work to be done and ass to be kicked."

"Uh, you're on fire," Vee stammered.

Poric looked at his charred chest and swatted out the flames. "Thanks. Looks like it's gonna be upgrade time when this is all done. But that's for later. Come on. Follow me!"

Kara and Vee felt the tremors in their limbs from the adrenaline surge but pushed it aside. Poric, crazy as he may be, was right. There was work to be done, and oh, the asses they would be kicking in the process.

CHAPTER TWENTY

The flashing lights were moving at the speed of, well, light, but were, somehow, simultaneously painfully slow. The slowest of forms of information transmission, in fact, that the trio of AI minds had ever been forced to utilize.

Normally, they would have possibly even been enjoying the little exercise in antiquated communications techniques, but with intergalactic war in full-force, the last thing they wanted was to wait minutes to relay vital information that would normally have taken milliseconds.

What had become abundantly clear was that the Urvalin were making their move on Dark Side. They had switched their ships to Allpower drive systems and had begun dipping in and out of the dampening field, staying high enough that the ships flying up to engage them kept automatically pulling back from their hard ceiling before they could get a proper weapons lock.

It was frustrating as hell for the defenders, and as several fell to the incoming barrage, the Urvalin's adaptation to the defenders' safety protocols was a tactic that seemed to be working.

The remaining Urvalin casters, it seemed, were powerful

indeed, even without their main caster within the base. And the other, lesser ships were utilizing their own triumvirates of casters as well. It was rapidly becoming a far more dire situation than they'd calculated.

Zed and Cal were relaying their messages through Sid, the moon base acting as a middle man and staying out of the conversation unless he had something vitally important to interject. Any delay in information could prove fatal in this instance.

"Can you get ships to them in time, Zed?" Cal asked.

"I can get some, likely, but it'll be a tough run of it. There's a lot of dampening minefields between us and them, and once we're there they'll still have to steer clear of the array surrounding Dark Side. I fear that by the time we get enough ships there to make any difference, it may be too late."

"What about ground forces to support the base crew?"

"I already discussed that with Admiral Harkaway, but as I told her, the distance they'd have to land away from the base, by the time they make that trek, it'll all be over."

The AIs all raced through possible scenarios, Joshua tied in via Sid's linkage as at least their connection worked inside the bubble.

"What is the status of the captured Urvalin ships?" Joshua told Sid to relay. "Marban's crew has taken several."

Sid relayed the query to Zed as quickly as he could.

"The crews are making as good time as they can sweeping them for hidden scuttling charges or other latent spells, but those could be buried deep within the craft. Even then, my people aren't magic users, and this Allpower stuff is tricky. Even with some of Marban's crew helping out, flying them would be a total crapshoot. It's worth a shot, but we'd have to re-power their systems up one by one, and slowly to be safe. I don't think any will be ready to fly in time. Not yet."

Another party joined the conversation. This one over regular comms.

"Hey, Zed. Rika Gaspari here," she said. "Nice Morse Code trick, by the way. Brings me back to basic training."

"You saw that?"

"We happened to be in the line of sight, and some things just stick in your memory. Listen, tell Sid and Cal that Marban and I are between you and Dark Side. We're on our way."

"Copy that, and thank you."

Rika shut off the comms and turned for the hangar bay. "I'll be back as soon as I can," she said.

Marban was confused. "We're supposed to be helping Dark Side. Where are you going?"

"We'll need more firepower than just you and me, I'm afraid. I'm making a quick run to the surface to pick up our new friend."

"Malalia?"

"Yeah. Hopefully she'll be able to disrupt the Allpower ships enough to allow our conventional craft to get off clean shots on them. Maybe even take out their casters, if she's fed recently."

Marban scrunched his nose at the thought. Drinking blood, even if it did provide her a steady source of power to replenish what she had used, was still distasteful to him. "Well, hurry back."

"I will, big guy. You just keep them occupied for a little bit."

"Don't have much choice, do I?" he replied with a chuckle. "Go on, get moving. I'll handle this for now."

Rika was off in a flash, sprinting down the corridor to her mech parked in the *Coratta*'s hangar. The time had come. She was going to be in close quarters with Malalia, and they were going to go into battle.

Rika didn't bother switching to magic when she passed through the atmosphere and began falling toward Earth. She simply shut everything down and enjoyed the ride, her magic taking up the life support slack, but that was about all.

With a larger ship, or when pushing up through the atmosphere, she would need to use her magic to guide the craft and keep it from breaking apart. But with gravity doing the work and her mech's extremely robust construction, she was able to sit back and let nature do the work for a change.

Once she was well clear of the dampening array she powered the mech back on and pinged Fatima over comms.

"Fatima, where's Malalia?" she asked.

"With me. We just returned from a raid on an Urvalin troop facility."

"Send me your coordinates and tell her to suit up. We need her particular skills up at Dark Side, and I'm coming in hot."

By the time Rika's mech landed in the nondescript neighborhood the pair had been using as a home base of late, both women were already outside waiting for her. Malalia was clad in a lightly armored space suit, her helmet in hand.

"What's with the outfit?" Rika asked as she hopped out of the mech to greet them.

"Fatima's suggestion. In case we lose pressure, I will not have to divert my magic if I am wearing this environmentally controlled costume."

"Huh."

"I agree. It is not something I have ever considered in the past, but she is right. I will need to save as much of my power for the fight as possible. If I divert any to create an atmosphere for myself, it could lessen my ability to handle multiple enemies at once."

"Valid point," Rika said without another thought. "But I can also keep an atmosphere for the both of us if it comes to that. Pop on that helmet, and let's go!"

The two women wasted no time. Rika strapped in, and

Malalia used the jury-rigged harness she'd put in place on the off chance the mech might one day have a passenger.

"It's gonna be a bit uncomfortable until we're in space, I'm afraid."

"I can handle uncomfortable," Malalia replied as they lifted off.

Then the g-forces hit her, and she realized just how uncomfortable it would actually be. But Malalia refrained from casting. Comfort could wait. There was a fight at hand.

As they approached the edge of the atmosphere Rika unleashed her magic, powering off the mech entirely and driving it with her own energy. Malalia watched her with appreciation.

"What?" Rika asked.

"Nothing. It is just impressive how smoothly you transitioned like that."

They popped into space and cleared the dampening array in a flash. Rika rebooted the ship and let the electronic systems do the heavy lifting once more.

"It's much easier with my mech," she said. "So much smaller than a full-sized ship, and this is already so dialed in with my power that it's second nature."

"I admit, I am impressed. Such talent. Such power. I know I have said it before, but it bears repeating. I am so sorry for what I did to you. You are an amazing woman, Rika, and I wish I had treated you as my pupil rather than a puppet all of those years ago."

"You've already apologized, and it's water under the bridge. But thank you. Now, if you could please focus, we're getting close, and I'm going to need your full attention to target those ships."

"Oh, I have *already* targeted them," Malalia replied with a little grin.

Rika shifted back to using her magic to power the mech and dove into the fray taking place all around the dampening field surrounding Dark Side base. Marban was hard at work, she could see, diving in and out, luring over-eager Urvalin to follow him when he could. It was a clever tactic. Saving his own systems while letting Joshua and his friends below light up the enemy as he served them up on a plate.

Rika blasted out with her magic, knocking a few smaller Urvalin ships out of the sky, their broken craft drifting lazily down to the surface. Not all of them in one piece.

"Miss me?" she transmitted to the pirate ship.

"I was having so much fun, I didn't realize you were gone," Marban joked. "Do you have the bitch with you?"

"I do. And she's on open comms with us."

"Oh. Uh, hello, Malalia."

"Marban," she replied with an amused chuckle. "Do not worry. I earned that title. And now I hope to make up for it."

Malalia then let out a burst of her own magic, reaching out toward the mass of ships just beyond the dampening array.

"Ooh, these are strong ones," she said. "They worked together to block my spells. How fascinating."

Rika spun and dove, targeting another ship. "Can you get through?" she asked, focusing her power on driving the mech even faster. "I can split my magic and back you up if needed."

"I believe I can handle this. It is still unusual, dealing with this Allpower variety of magic. And there are multiple groups of casters this time."

"But you can do it?"

"Yes. I will need to focus on one ship at a time, however. This many of them, it is making it harder to cast against them."

"Well, you focus, and when you're ready—"

A bright flash lit the darkness as the *Coratta* took a nasty broadside from a trio of Urvalin ships. They'd been playing possum, drifting toward the surface as though out of the fight, but when Marban flew past they let loose with both barrels.

"Marban!" Rika shouted. "You fuckers are going to pay for that!"

She spun the mech toward them and cast hard, her tattoos glowing bright. Malalia's skin tingled, and she could feel the power surging out of Rika's body, but then something happened. Something they still had no explanation for. In her rage, Rika somehow latched onto the Allpower of all the Urvalin near them and sucked it right out of them.

Ships began cascading from the sky, this time truly disabled as the teams powering them lay drained on their decks. Even the regular crew were affected, as most Urvalin possessed at least a modicum of Allpower.

Malalia had seen her take power before, but nothing on this scale. And across these distances? In space, no less? It was nothing short of incredible. While Malalia had to drink blood to take another's power, Rika was under no such restriction where the Urvalin were concerned.

"Marban, can you hear me? Are you okay?"

"Aye, we're still in one piece, if that's what you're asking. Just a little banged up."

Rika let out a sigh of relief.

Malalia turned to her. "How *ever* do you do that?"

Rika's rage settled, and her murderous link fizzled out. "I have no idea."

Whatever the method, it didn't matter. The tide had turned. The larger Urvalin fleet that had been supporting the bombardment from above abruptly pulled back and away from the moon base.

"Their ships are retreating," Sid transmitted to her. "Thank you. Thank you both."

"Happy to help," Rika said.

"My people are mopping up inside the array, now that the bombardment has stopped. There's space for you in hangar two if you like."

"I think we could use a little break," Rika said, feeling the aches of battle as well as the brimming of newly acquired Urvalin Allpower.

She guided the mech over the battlefield. Urvalin, human, and Chithiid bodies lay strewn about the moon's surface. Mostly Urvalin, she was glad to see. Sid's team was elite, and the enemy had underestimated them, to their own detriment.

Heading into the hangar, she saw a pair of dragons just outside, roasting and eating their Urvalin victims.

"They are eating the dead," Malalia noted.

"Well, dragons gonna dragon, right?" Rika replied with a laugh. "Speaking of food, I'm starving. Let's hit the mess hall." She set the mech down and popped the hatch. "Hey, Sid. We're gonna grab a bite. Would you mind sending Kara and Vee to meet up with us when they're free?"

"Of course," the AI replied. "Enjoy your meal."

He then reached out to the teens and their cyborg escort, offering them the use of some vacant quarters if they wished to clean up from the sweat of battle before meeting with Rika.

"Okay, we'll go meet her," Kara said. "But then we need to talk with Joshua. Without his help, I'll never get back to find my father like this."

CHAPTER TWENTY-ONE

Deep in the belly of an Urvalin command class warship, Visla Nikora Palmarian, his longtime enemy and member of the Council of Twenty, Visla Samanna, and a fiery young woman with shining, galactic eyes, sat in their cell, the three of them locked together not only physically, but magically as well.

All were power users of incredible strength, and all had fallen victim to the Urvalin threat. Visla Nikora Palmarian ruled an entire system, keeping his homeworld and its citizens safe under his immense power. When his second wife turned out to be a magic-sucking she-bitch, draining his daughter of her potency and leading her to believe she was lacking his familial power, he cast her out of his life.

That the woman was also Malalia Maktan, the several hundred years old daughter of the late Visla Maktan of the Council of Twenty, seeking galactic domination under the guise of Visla Dominus, made the decision all the easier.

His daughter, Karasalia, had suffered for so many years without his knowing. Now that they were both free and Kara was coming into her own, he redoubled his focus on doing good, solidifying his relationship with his only child.

Then he had been captured and it all went to shit.

As for Visla Samanna, his was a far simpler tale. One of power hunger and a thirst for conflict. He had butted heads with Visla Palmarian on more than one occasion but found his own significant power insufficient to overcome his adversary. Palmarian banned him from ever setting foot in his system again, and after their final encounter, Samanna had wisely done just that.

Nipsenni was the wild card of the bunch. A seemingly feral young woman with quite a temper and a foul mouth. She also proclaimed herself the great-great-great-great-granddaughter of a rather legendary pirate. A similarly hotheaded woman named Henni. One who was rumored to possess incredible powers not unlike those of a Zomoki.

Of course, no one believed those legends, but in a moment of distress, Nipsenni's grasp on her power slipped, and she jumped their entire ship a short distance before being knocked unconscious by the golden control collar around her neck. How she had managed the feat was a mystery. Fortunately, it was one the Urvalin had not realized was caused by her alone. At least, not yet. And that was her saving grace.

In any case, as they were all connected, Palmarian and Samanna succumbed to the shock as well.

It was a clever use of the collars by the Urvalin invaders, taking the device developed in this galaxy and using it against its originators. But that was precisely what they had done, and on many occasions as they rounded up any power user they might have use for in the coming conflict.

The powerful ones were bound together in casting trios. Triumvirates, as the Urvalin called them, and they were forced to help subjugate others of their realm. At least, that was the plan. Nipsenni, however, had other ideas about that, most of which resulted in her and her bound companions suffering a variety of unpleasant shocks.

Palmarian and Samanna both begged Nipsenni to please at least pretend to go along, if only to not be subjected to the pain their collars produced when they were disobedient, but so far their words had fallen on deaf ears.

It was ironic, Visla Palmarian had noted when Visla Samanna first tried to use his power to break the collar's bond, only to find himself impotent against it, that a Council of Twenty favorite had now been used against one of the members of the Council itself.

Samanna had wisely ceased his efforts when the mechanical aspect added to the collars was explained to him by the Urvalin guards. Aside from shocks and power-dampening properties, which he was very familiar with from his own use of the collars over the years, there was also an Urvalin addition. A final fail-safe that could be triggered remotely by their Urvalin overseers. A small explosive device that would end their lives in a fast, and rather disturbing, manner.

At least Nipsenni's stubbornness would not trigger *that* aspect of the device. She was troublesome, no doubt, but the Urvalin still saw value in this trio, and for that the two enemies were grateful.

"It is pointless for us to fight one another," Palmarian said. "For the time being, at least, we must put our differences aside and do what we must to stop her from continuing to antagonize our captors."

"Much as I dislike the thought, I am afraid you are correct in your assessment," Visla Samanna replied.

The two had suffered a great deal of pain and discomfort because of her constant testing of her restraints and lashing out at the confining magic holding them prisoner like a trapped animal might bash against its cage. If she was simply battering herself bloody they could have lived with her acting up, but she hurt others when she hurt herself, and that simply would not do.

Of course, any violence against her on their part would, as always, result in an even greater shock from their collars. So, it seemed, the two men were stuck in a rather unusual situation. One for which neither had a solution.

They had finally regained their strength after the last shock event when Nipsenni began testing her collar yet again.

"Nipsenni, *please*, stop," Samanna pleaded with her. "You must cease this futile struggling."

"You're a quitter, huh?" she said, shooting an angry stare his way. "You *like* being the Urvalin's plaything."

"You know that is not—"

"Well, I'm not putting up with it."

"As we have seen," Visla Palmarian said. "Far too many times at that."

"You saying you big, strong men can't handle a little shock collar?" she sniped. "Would the mighty Vislas Palmarian and Samanna rather be in a nice, comfy bed? Maybe if you lick their boots *real* good the Urvalin might even draw you a hot bath."

Palmarian couldn't help but admire her spirit, even if it had been causing him nothing but pain. In a strange way, it reminded him of his own daughter's relatively newfound confidence.

"Nipsenni," he said, "you know we are as opposed to our indentured state as you are, but think logically. There are a great many other casters imprisoned in the Urvalin armada for them to look after. If we do not give them reason to focus on us, our stay may at least be a tolerable one."

"You're talking as if you think they're just going to let us go when this is all done."

"He is not so foolish," Samanna said, flashing a wry grin at his former enemy. "And trust me, I would know."

Nipsenni started pacing the cell, tiny flashes of power lashing out, testing the chamber itself. A faint buzz began to be felt from all three of their collars.

"Please, think this through. Talk with us rather than blindly casting. Use your mind as well as your power," Palmarian pleaded. "You have so much potential, but you must learn to harness it."

She spun on him, eyes ablaze. "Oh, I already know how to harness it," she spat. "But these damn collars won't let me!"

She tried casting again, the shock level rising in response to her efforts. Palmarian and Samanna shared a pained look as they too felt the effects from their own collars. Then, with a frustrated grunt, Nipsenni let go.

The men slumped a little as the shock subsided, looking at one another with mutual amazement at how this diminutive woman could be so strong. To actually possess the power to jump an entire ship, regardless of how short a distance? It was unheard of, to say the least, and in better times it would have been a mystery both would have been very anxious to unravel.

"One thing is for sure," Samanna said, sliding over to sit closer to Palmarian. "We definitely know why the Urvalin took her."

"That we do. She's *strong*," Palmarian agreed.

"And thick-skulled, and stubborn, and a royal pain in my—"

His words cut off as another shock blasted his body.

"Nipsenni, please!" Palmarian managed to get out. "Stop before they blow our heads off!"

Nipsenni stopped, the shock vanishing in an instant. She spun on the men, an angry scowl they had become very familiar with plastered on her face.

"They won't kill us," she growled, tugging angrily at her collar. "We just need to get these damned things off!"

"They can trigger these devices remotely," Samanna pointed out. "They do not even need to be in the chamber to do so."

"I'm telling you, those bastards sitting over in their cozy command ship still want us alive. They'd have killed us already if that was the plan."

"Are you so sure? Do you really want to tempt fate?"

As if the gods had been listening, the chamber door opened. Three Urvalin guards stepped in and opened their cell.

"Your continued disobedience has been observed," their leader said, pointing to the small optical device in the corner of the room. "Your refusal to submit to Urvalin authority has angered the captain."

"Well, boo-freaking-hoo," Nipsenni shot back, hurling a glob of spittle at the guard's feet.

He stepped inside the cell and slapped her across the face, knocking her to the ground. Palmarian felt Samanna's hand clamp on his arm, preventing him from intervening.

"Do not," he said quietly.

Visla Palmarian, protector of millions, reluctantly stood down.

"Get up. All three of you," the guard said.

"Why? Where are you taking us?" Samanna asked.

"None of your business. But since you're so curious, you've screwed up big time. The captain is throwing you in general holding with all of the filth and lesser power users."

Samanna winced. They'd all started out in those cells when they were first taken, before they'd been pulled out and bound together. There were all manner of beings with some sort of power, and the Urvalin had taken them seemingly at random to experiment on to better learn how this galaxy's Allpower functioned. Drooks and casters, the dregs and the forsaken, all were represented in those cells. It was not a pleasant place.

"Please, don't put us back there. She will behave, won't you, Nipsenni?" Samanna said.

"It's too late for that," the guard said, pushing them out into the corridor. "Now, move."

The trio marched along, Samanna and Palmarian frowning dejectedly, but Nipsenni wore a mischievous grin on her face. The guards had no idea what to make of it, but knowing how stubborn this one had been so far, it came as no surprise.

"Do as you're told and get your triumvirate in order and perhaps you will be allowed back out to your own chambers. But until then, enjoy your stay," the guard said, then shoved them in with all of the filthy prisoners.

Palmarian looked at Samanna and sighed. "This really is turning out to be a bad day," he said.

Samanna couldn't help but let a little chuckle slip out. "Yes, Nikora, I'd say it is the worst."

CHAPTER TWENTY-TWO

A lone ship sat quietly in a clearing on a small, moderately forested planet orbiting binary stars, all alone but for the single human passenger sitting in the command module. This world, they had ascertained, was not populated. But the power of its suns was reasonably strong, and that was perfect for their needs.

While some people used magic as easily as they breathed, there were those for whom it was not a natural thing. Those who had grown up with magic only being a storybook tale, not something from reality.

But when faced with the unexplainable, some took a different path than most. And as Freya was herself considered an impossibility at one time, the AI stealth ship approached the problem with a rather different perspective.

She had instructed her swarm of nanites to focus on the use of galactic energy people called magic. Back home she would never have thought to even pursue such folly, but having seen it work firsthand, and having taken readings of every single spell-casting and power-using event she'd witnessed, Freya was getting an idea of what might make this magic stuff tick.

Being trapped in a magic-run galaxy also didn't hurt.

The constant ebb and flow of magical energy all around them in this galaxy gave the nanites plenty to work with, and it was Freya's sincere hope she could learn to cast without the need for a magic-storing konus attached to her framework.

Daisy was helping, when she could, though she no longer brought her sword along for Freya to test out ideas on. Stabby had been a bad, bad sword, and he was getting a time out because of it.

"How's it coming, Kiddo?" Daisy asked. "We're going to need to get back with Korbin and the others pretty soon."

"The nanites have been learning at an exponential rate," she replied with a burst of excitement. "It's so cool, Daisy. They've been applying what I extrapolated about this galaxy's power and what seemed to be the root nature of what they call magic here. They've really made a ton of progress."

"I know, but is it enough to help you do more than just boost your shields or cast some offensive spells?"

"I really think it could be. It's just going slower than I want it to."

"*Life's funny like that, Freya,*" Sarah noted, linking with the ship via Daisy's neuro band worn threaded in her hair.

"Yeah, I know, Sarah. But I just thought that being in *this* galaxy things might move a little quicker."

"Careful what you wish for. You never know what might happen with magic involved."

Daisy couldn't believe it had become such a regular part of their lives since Charlie had stumbled across time and into their world. Magic. Other galaxies. And now, new enemies from those other galaxies. It made her almost long for the days where they simply had the Ra'az Hok to deal with and anything else was trivial by comparison.

"You up for trying out some of your spells?" she asked.

"I think this is as good a time as any," Freya replied. "There's no one around, so if anything goes wrong, at least we won't risk damaging our friends' ships."

"Which would be rude, to say the least."

"I'll say!"

"*So, what do you think, Freya? Can you pull magic right out of the air without accessing a konus?*" Sarah asked. "*No pressure.*"

"I think so. The nanites are running throughout my entire body. This ship is essentially made of them now, so there's a massive surface area to collect and redirect it with."

"What about the spells?" Daisy asked.

"I've been experimenting with those," Freya replied. "From what I can tell, the words are important, in that in some phonic way they interact with a caster's intent. You remember what they told us about intent being an important key to casting."

"Yeah. It was also why AIs weren't supposed to be able to actually cast, only use konuses for defensive purposes."

"*But our girl is no ordinary AI, isn't that right? She was born differently than the other AIs. She can do what they can't.*"

"I like to think so, Sarah. I hope so. I'm pretty sure that with practice I might be able to cast without verbal cues at all. You know, using the resonance along with intent to direct the energy to release its potential as I want it to."

Daisy felt a surge of pride in her AI kid. Freya had really come so far from when she'd first woken her in that research lab all those years ago.

"Okay, then," Daisy said. "Let's try one out."

"Now?"

"You have other plans?"

"Well, no. But I don't know if I'm connected enough."

"Give it a try. Something simple. Worst-case scenario it doesn't work and you go back to the drawing board."

"I guess. Okay, I'm going to disconnect from my konus and try casting a basic illumination spell with just the nanites."

"Sounds like a safe one to start with. Good choice."

"Thanks. All right, here goes nothing."

Freya intoned the words, attempting to cast the spell. Nothing.

"Huh. I thought that would have worked. Maybe if I do it this way."

She cast again, but no dice.

"Okay, I feel the beginnings of something, but it's just not connecting. There's no *oomph* to it, you know?"

"Not really, but I'll take your word for it," Daisy replied. "Listen, I didn't mean to pressure you. If you're not ready—"

"No, I can do this. Hang on, I want to try something."

The ship shuddered slightly and the lights dimmed, slowly returning to their normal brightness.

"Freya? What was that? Freya?"

"*Something's wrong, Daze.*"

"Freya, can you hear me?" Daisy called out, increasingly worried.

"I-I. Hang on," the ship finally said, her voice breaking up.

"She didn't sound all right."

"*What did she do, Sis?*"

"I have no idea. Freya? What's going on?"

"Wow, that was weird," the ship finally said, returning to her normal self, her senses regained.

"What was weird?"

"Linking with the nanites like that. It was a weird sensation, but they're not just in my ship now. They're in my processors too."

Daisy felt a flash of adrenaline surge through her body. Even tucked away in his case, Stabby started to hum with sympathetic energy. "You did *what*? That's your brain, Freya! You can't do things like that. What if something went wrong?"

"It seemed like a good idea. And look, I'm okay!"

"But you could have lobotomized yourself."

"But I didn't. I ran the calculations. You said it yourself, I *am* a supercomputer among supercomputers, after all."

Sarah wasn't sold on the idea. "*That was too risky, Freya. It's not worth losing you.*"

"No one lost me," the ship replied. "And remember, there is risk in everything in life. That's what living is all about. And if we ever hope to get back home to our family, we're going to need to take more risks, like it or not."

Daisy hated to admit it, but the kid was right. "When did you get so smart?"

"Always have been."

"You little shit," Daisy said with a chuckle. "But listen, I don't want you worried about Joshua and Marty, okay? I'm sure they're doing just fine back home. Joshua's the smartest AI I know, next to you, and I know he won't let anything happen to him."

"Thanks, Daisy. And you shouldn't worry about Arlo and Vince and the others either. I'm sure they're okay as well." Freya paused and ran some calculations. "Look, this might be our best bet for getting home, or at least finding an edge against the Urvalin, but I can't say for sure. My simulations can't compensate for magic. I'm just going to have to practice. There's no road map for any of this."

"Since when did you care about maps anyway?"

"Since never."

Daisy knew firsthand that was the truth. "So, Kiddo. Whaddya say? Want to try another spell?"

"Why not?"

Freya's feel for the magical power the nanites were pulling from the fabric of the galaxy itself was growing stronger now that they were connected directly into her brain. Daisy and Sarah were right, of course, it *was* a risky thing to do. But with war against the Urvalin underway, it was a necessary chance to take.

Freya pulled on the connections, feeling where the power surged and ebbed and settled on a spell. A fire spell, this time. It was war, after all, and that might come in handy in a bind.

"Here goes nothing," she said, then cast the basic campfire spell.

"Jesus, Freya! What are you doing!" Daisy blurted as the trees around them burst into flames. So too had the brush surrounding them for nearly fifty meters.

"Oh, shit!" Freya said. "Uh, hang on, I've got this."

She cast what should have been a simple extinguishing spell, but instead of blowing out the flames, it spread wide, fanning them even more.

"Okay, enough casting for right now. Get airborne and deploy the CO_2 units, quick!"

Freya did as she was told, shooting up into a low hover and spraying CO_2 all around, sucking the air out of the fire, leaving an extinguished, charred circle.

"*So,* that *happened,*" Sarah said with a grim laugh.

"Yeah, that was no bueno," Daisy added. "Freya, what do you say we take this practice session out into space before we accidentally burn this planet to the ground?"

"I say that sounds like it's probably a good idea," the AI replied. "I think I know what went wrong, but it's going to take a while to sift through the data and run scenarios."

"Good thing you can multitask, then, isn't it?"

"That's for sure," she replied. "Okay, hang on. We're going back into orbit."

CHAPTER TWENTY-THREE

Grundsch would have much preferred to simply carry his pregnant charge to the medical facility, but with her Magus stone threatening to act up at the slightest hint of trouble, be it external or internal, he wisely relented and settled for a compromise.

Urvalin were all over the area, but once they had managed to connect with Cal, and not before having to play a rather harrowing game of hide-and-seek with a few recon patrols that very nearly saw them, they had ascertained the location of the nearest properly stocked medical facility that would suit their needs.

"You will require a significant amount of sterile medical supplies," Cal said. *"Most facilities are sealed up, their supplies being held in larger, centralized distribution centers. As you do not have the luxury of having what you need delivered to you, I am afraid you will have to travel a bit farther than I'm sure you would like."*

"Whatever it takes, Cal," Sarah replied. "Just get me the coordinates and I'll get us there."

He transferred the information to her forearm tablet along with the latest recon data his eyes and ears had for the area. While he was cut off from the remaining satellites in orbit, the guerrilla raiders had kept detailed logs and tactical video footage and uploaded it all to his remote servers whenever they were able.

None of them connected with Cal directly. All but a few still believed him dead, and that was just how they wanted it. Only the most trusted commanders possessed that knowledge, and even fewer of them knew where his uplink sites were.

As for accessing the remote stores of data they compiled, *that* was something he could do with ease, and without requiring direct contact with another soul.

"Cal, I see a pretty sizable Urvalin camp set up not far from the site you selected."

"Yes, I am aware."

"Then you are also aware we're moving with a *very* pregnant lady."

"Sarah, I have the utmost confidence in your abilities in this regard. That, and that building was already reported to have been thoroughly searched just two days ago by an enemy recon team. The Urvalin are persistent, but they do not like inefficiency."

"So, we'll have a window to be left alone before they'd repeat the same routine."

"Precisely. So long as you do not draw attention to yourselves, you should be safe there. Of course, I do not need to tell you that you will have to refrain from killing any Urvalin as you approach the area. Their eyes are looking in the other direction, but doing something like that would change their focus in an instant."

"Copy that. Have you had any word about the others? Anything about Ripley?"

"No news at the moment," he said. *"I'm confident they are fine,*

wherever they are. Drombus and Duzza are strong dragons and will do an admirable job protecting them should they need to."

"Let's hope they don't," Sarah quietly said. "Thanks for the help, Cal. And thank you for what you've been doing for all the rest of us."

"It's what I do."

"Yeah, but you shouldn't have to. Retirement was suiting you."

"You as well. But life has a funny way, does it not?"

"Indeed. Thanks again," she said, then cut the line.

Grundsch had pulled apart an old wheeled cargo dolly he found as they trekked and managed to fashion it into a sort of rolling litter. One with a long rope affixed to one end so the person pulling it would not have to be close to the very dangerous pregnant woman riding it.

"We can't use that," Sarah said. "Not yet, anyway. No wheeled tracks. The Urvalin would see them with all the dirt blown into the roads."

"But she is close to birthing," he replied.

"Yeah, I know, but we're just going to have to carry it with us and do this on foot for now. If we find a patch of clear pavement, then we can give her a lift but otherwise it's too risky."

The Ra'az was rather protective of Leila. She'd treated him well before many others had, and he appreciated her friendship and trust. She wasn't his hivemate—they were all dead now anyway—but she was the next best thing.

Baloo and Bahnjoh lurked ahead of the group, their konus collars pinging back to Grundsch any time they encountered Urvalin. It was in this manner that they played a life-size game of Battleship, hopscotching back, forth, and side to side as they probed and avoided the Urvalin forces.

Finally, after a great many hours, they arrived at the medical building. To their dismay, a small patrol of Urvalin was standing right outside the front doors. One seemed to be much higher ranked than the underlings around her. She had a communications device in her hand and was talking to someone. Someone named Torgus, from what Sarah's enhanced ears could hear.

"No, Commander," the Urvalin said. "The targets *were* there, but they had moved on before our forces arrived. They are close, but they have proven very hard to pin down."

"I do not want excuses," the man on the other end of the line said. "Failure is not an option."

"I understand, sir. I will double our patrols."

She almost saluted the device, so respected—or feared—was the man calling the shots.

"We can try the emergency access to the rear," Sarah whispered. "Leila, are you good to move?"

"As good as I'm going to be," she said, her pale-green skin even lighter than usual. She was focusing all of her willpower on maintaining her equilibrium and not allowing the Magus stone to react. They were so close, they just had to make it inside.

"Bahnjoh, Baloo," Grundsch whispered. "Scout."

The animals took off in silence, which, given their size, never ceased to impress Sarah. She was more than a little glad the beasts were on their side. A minute later Grundsch led the way to the emergency entrance with Sarah following at the rear.

"All clear," the Ra'az said quietly. "The doors were sealed, but I unsealed them."

Sarah looked at the bent frame. By unsealed he meant pried open, but in times of need there was little else to be done. So long as whoever patrolled the area next didn't come right up to the doors, no one would be the wiser.

"Come on, we need to get her inside," she said, covering them until everyone was in the facility, then closing the doors. "Okay, according to Cal's schematic, the delivery and maternity area is up one floor through those doors. I'm afraid we'll need to use the stairs. Are you able, Leila?"

"If there's a bed I can lie down on up there I'll do it on my hands," she said with an exhausted grin.

Sarah was glad to see her friend still had a sense of humor even in the most stressful of times. "Okay, this way."

They slowly scaled the stairs and made their way down the long corridor to the clearly marked suite of rooms. Fortunately, they were located on the inner portion of the building. No windows meant they could turn the lights on without risking being noticed.

Leila slid down onto the procedure chair with a relieved sigh and reclined to a comfortable position. The treatment space itself was extremely sparse, but that was because this particular location didn't need all of those supplies. Most of it was taken care of automatically by the single, large machine occupying the room. It was an extremely basic AI that powered the unit and functioned as a doula, midwife, or whatever else an expecting mother might require.

Sarah powered the device on.

"Hello! I detect a patient with a full-term pregnancy! Congratulations!"

"Shh!" Sarah hissed.

"I'm sorry, you'll need to clarify your request!"

"Be quiet!"

"I'm sorry, in order to best serve you, I must verbally engage with all patients."

"This machine is too loud," Grundsch grumbled.

"I know, I'm working on it," she shot back. "Okay, listen, Machine. You can talk, but we need you to be quieter."

"It is a known fact that forty-three percent of expecting mothers require more volume than other patients, as they are distracted by their pain."

Sarah was ready to pull her hair out. That or smash the machine to bits, but that would be too loud for their purposes, and they needed the damn thing. She looked around desperately at the maternity ward when inspiration hit her. She couldn't very well explain the Urvalin threat to the machine. She had to speak to it in terms it understood.

"We know you are just doing your job, but there are sleeping infants just outside this medical suite, and you are going to disturb them."

The machine almost winced, if that was actually possible.

"I am *so* sorry," it said in a much quieter voice. "My sincere apologies."

"That's okay. We just need you to stay quiet while we work. Can you do that?"

"I would gladly maintain reduced volume levels for the duration of your stay. Shall we begin the C-section?"

The Magus stone flared slightly. Even the suggestion of cutting by a machine seemed to trigger its defenses.

"No, no, we do *not* want to perform a C-section," Sarah quickly corrected, watching the stone's glow dim almost immediately.

"But this patient is ready for birth, yet she has not dilated and her water has not broken. Most unusual. I also detect non-human genetic material."

"Yeah, that's because she isn't one. And listen, we're not trying to facilitate the birth. Not yet, anyway."

"But she is clearly—"

"Can you give her some meds to ease the pain? Slow the labor down?"

The machine was designed to assist in childbirth and was more than a little confused. "Slow it down? You wish to slow the process down? I-I do not know if I can—"

"She's an alien, right? Your scans told you that much. Well, uh, her kind requires a slower birthing process to ensure the child is healthy, get it?"

"Oh, I see," the machine replied. "In that case, yes, I can assist. I will administer the proper medications."

A syringe slid into place from within the device and began moving toward Leila.

"Whoa! Hang on!" Sarah blurted just as the Magus stone began to glow. "You're going to have to let her do that herself."

"But it is my purpose."

"We understand that, but for, uh, *religious* reasons, only she can give herself injections. I'm sure your sensitivity protocols cover religious objections."

The AI whirred quietly a moment as it scanned its memory banks. It was amazing how this unit was not even a shadow of its brilliant cousins Sarah called family and friends.

"I will provide the syringe and instruct the patient," the AI finally said.

Sarah eyed the Magus stone, its glow dimming but not quite going out. "Okay, that's great. Leila, you got this?"

"Yes, I can do this."

"Great. We're just gonna wait out in the hallway until you're done."

Sarah and Grundsch cleared out fast, moving not only into the hallway but several rooms down, just in case. The sound of crumpling metal reached their ears, but it was over in an instant. They both hoped the walls insulated them enough and no one outside heard it.

Carefully, they stepped back into the room.

Leila was still reclined on the chair, the Magus stone calm now that her pain was reduced. The AI was still functional for the most part, but a few other items in the room had felt the stone's wrath.

"You feeling better?"

"Much," Leila murmured. "Charlie. I need to see him."

"Soon, hon. We'll get him to you soon. You rest now. We'll be right next door if you need us." With that, she and Grundsch quietly stepped out of the room and left her to get some much-needed sleep. "Dammit, Charlie. Where the hell are you?"

CHAPTER TWENTY-FOUR

Charlie stood in the red soil on the out-of-the-way planet they had selected as a safe rendezvous rest point for their team to eat, recharge, and go over incoming messages. What had just come through left him fuming mad.

"What do you mean, going dark?" he bellowed in frustration.

"Calm, Charlie," Ara said from her spot lounging nearby. "There is no need to yell."

"But this is bullshit!" He spun to face the alien leader of the nascent fighting force. "Well? What does it mean, Nakk? Huh?"

Nakk shook his head. "It means exactly that, Charlie. Several of the Urvalin craft we have commandeered are powering down unexpectedly."

Charlie threw his hands in the air, exasperated, but he didn't know what else to say. His friends watched him quietly a moment as he fought for control of his emotions. This was a blow he had not been expecting, and it could not have come at a worse time.

"Kill switches," Bawb muttered. "They have outfitted their craft with kill switches. Honestly, I would have almost lost respect for them if they had not."

"Screw the respect, Bob. We need every last one of those ships we took if we're going to have an effective fleet. What good are a bunch of spaceship-sized paperweights?"

"Paperweights? But paper does not weigh much at all."

"No, it's a pointless thing you put on top of paper to keep it from flying away."

"One would not want their important papers becoming lost," Bawb said.

"Indeed. That does not sound pointless," Nakk added. "In fact, it seems like a very logical thing to—"

"The point is, we need those ships *functional*," Charlie cut him off.

Bawb patted his friend on the shoulder. "Clearly. But I am sure there is a remedy for this problem. We have but to take a moment, calm ourselves, and discern what it might be. And that starts with understanding the problem better. Nakk? What is your assessment?"

He scratched his head a moment, glancing at Skohla for moral support. Finding it sadly lacking when she simply gave him a shrug, he ventured a wild guess. "Well, if the Urvalin were concerned about their ships falling into enemy hands, they'd have placed kill switches, which they did, obviously."

Charlie leaned closer. "I sense a but."

"*But* they have a massive amount of ships. The effort required to do so, as well as maintain a system that ensures they are not accidentally triggered by something as simple as a basic emergency crew change or system reboot, tells me they would probably only have installed them on the key craft. Things like simple shuttles, cargo ships, and fighters? No point. That's small stuff and not worth the added expenditure of effort. But the big prizes? Yes, those would be the most likely ones."

"And yet the ones we captured thus far have all been functioning just fine," Hunze pointed out. "Up until now, that is.

And even so, you said only a few have gone dark. Is there any pattern you can see?"

"Not really. It spans across several types of ship." Nakk scanned the report again for any other details that might be relevant. "The only other thing I can see is that the affected craft were the first ships we—of course! It's happening on a time delay!"

It made sense. If there was some sort of key or code that had to be entered to keep the ships running after a specific length of time, those that had been captured first would have reached their trigger points the soonest.

"But if this technology is already embedded in their craft, it seems unlikely the Urvalin would allow us to use their ships against them. I mean, wouldn't they likely also have an activation system that can be triggered by a simple signal or spell?" Skohla wondered.

Charlie turned to her as the realization hit. "Oh crap. You're right. These guys are all about sneaky little tricks, and the ships are just another part of it."

"Which means, what, exactly?" Nakk asked.

"Which means the Urvalin *know* we've taken their ships."

"Obviously. They were there when we took them."

"No, you're not getting the point, Nakk. What I'm saying is they're *letting* us use their ships."

"But we are taking more of them with their own craft with them."

"Yes, but they're letting us. They're lulling us into a sense of false security. Like when we first stole their weapons and they suddenly crapped out on us. They wanted us to think we had a windfall that could give us an edge against them, when they suddenly became useless when we needed them most. They'd planned it that way all along."

"But you modified those weapons so we *could* use them. At least for a while," Nakk noted.

"Yeah, but guns are one thing. Jury-rigging an entire ship, let alone a fleet of them? That's a whole other matter. They could take out nearly all of us in a single blow. We'll need far more than a little patch to block their devices from killing power to them when we least expect it."

Nakk began pacing, muttering to himself as he ran numbers and possible scenarios through his head. The man was a great tactician and had engaged the Urvalin long before the visitors to this galaxy had ever heard of them. Charlie knew that look on his face and left him to it, not saying another word until he had finished processing whatever was on his mind. Knowing Nakk, he'd be done soon enough.

"Okay," Nakk said a moment later, stopping in his tracks. "We know it will be the largest of our ships that are most likely to have these devices. That reduces the places our techs will have to look. I can send word to have them start picking them apart stem to stern immediately, pulling skilled members of the crews of other ships in the fleet to those to help speed the process. They're on standby now anyway, so this is the perfect time."

"Great!" Charlie said. "Finally, some good news. How long will it take? And how many ships do you think we are down?"

Nakk's excited grin faltered. "It will take a while, I'm afraid. And it is a *lot* of ships."

"What about trackers?" Hunze asked. "If they have kill devices—"

"No, that's something we learned to counter a long time ago. We already installed strong blocker units on each and every one of those craft as soon as we captured them. No way a beacon signal could get out. But the kill switches are another beast entirely, and until we clear the fleet, it will be extremely risky to fly those ships."

Charlie was getting tired of the up and down of this conversation. "So, we *are* screwed after all, is what you're saying."

Nakk's smile broadened as another thought dawned on him. "Not necessarily," he said. "There is one way to override this sort of Urvalin Allpower-fueled tech, although it is hard to come by. Extremely hard, as it is a *very* particular type of device that could get our fleet up and running in a fraction of the time."

"Great. Where do we get them?"

Nakk's eyes darted across the expectant faces of his comrades. "Ah, yes," he said. "Uh, that might be the tricky part."

CHAPTER TWENTY-FIVE

Kip and Dukaan separated from their friends and pulled ahead as they approached the coordinates Nakk had provided. It was an asteroid field of impressive size and density, the enormous rocks drifting to and fro, occasionally bashing into one another, fracturing, thus adding more dangerous rocks to the already dense field of floating debris.

And they were heading right into it.

"Okay, you guys, we're going to head in," Charlie transmitted. "Ara, keep an eye out. We'll be back as soon as we can."

"Of course," the Zomoki said. "Our position should allow us to detect anything coming our way long before we are seen."

"She's right," Skohla added from the command deck of Nakk's ship. "These asteroids have a high metal content. It will scatter scans long enough for us to spot new arrivals first. To anyone coming from a distance we will be lost in the readings."

"Especially if we operate on low power," Tamara suggested. "But don't worry. Shelly and me, we'll take the little Urvalin ship we stole out and run some patrols just to be safe. Watch your backs in there, fellas. And if you need us, just whistle."

"Will do," Charlie said, nodding the go-ahead to Nakk. "Let's do this."

"Follow this heading," Nakk directed Dukaan. "It is a rough course. From what I know of Vixx, his ship is deep in the asteroid field, but the route constantly changes by small amounts due to the natural shifts in the rocks themselves."

Dukaan glanced up from his controls. "I thought you said you knew him."

"I know *of* him from those who have done business with him. Multiple trusted sources have confirmed his location."

The pilot was still a little concerned. "And he lives in the middle of an asteroid field?"

"When you deal in costly, rare, and often illegal items such as he does, making it harder for pirates and other unsavory types to reach you, let alone find you, makes perfect sense."

"Nakk's got a point," Charlie agreed. "I mean, look at all these rocks. It's gonna be a hairy ride."

"But we have his most recent ident beacon frequency. With that, once we are close, he can guide us in through the densest part of the field. Few survive exploring so deep into the field, and none have ever found his ship without an invitation. And believe me, a good many have died trying."

It was going to be a rough ride with a lot of dodging of ship-killer-sized asteroids, which was why they were making the trip aboard the small AI ship. Anything larger would be pummeled to pieces long before it could find the elusive Vixx.

"This is going to be fun," Kip said. "I *love* asteroids."

Charlie shook his head. "You love asteroids? What do you have, some sort of death wish?"

"Nah, I've got a feel for them. Me and Dookie used to make runs through the belt out between Mars and Jupiter. We played around in the Kuiper belt too, but that was a while ago. Anyway, my point is, we've got this."

"I hope you are as good as you claim," Nakk said.

"Oh, we are, right, Dookie?"

The Chithiid pilot merely grunted, his eyes fixed on the displays in front of him as they began their entry into the danger zone. Charlie was as nervous as the rest, but he'd seen the AI and Chithiid work together plenty of times now, and in some pretty difficult situations. Say what you might about their odd friendship, the pair were a highly talented team, each filling in the little gaps in the other's skill sets.

"You all may want to tighten your harnesses a little more," Kip said as they dodged their first of many asteroids. "This could get a bit intense."

"Intense? But you possess gravity dampeners," Nakk said. "We should be—"

A sudden burst from the thrusters spun the ship into a sharp dive before pulling up abruptly into a corkscrew maneuver as they twisted and turned around a trio of rather large rocks. Nakk hastily pulled his harness straps tighter just as they banked hard left, then down.

It wasn't actually down, since there was no up or down in space, but with the gravity dampeners attempting to compensate for the maneuvers, down was at their feet at the moment, though only slightly. The machinery was working hard, doing its best to keep the crew firmly planted in their seats, allowing the cushioning to take most of the brunt of the maneuvers.

Even so, just as in fierce dogfighting, sometimes it was simply not possible to compensate fast enough.

The ship bucked violently with a loud crash.

"What was that, Kip?" Charlie asked as calmly as he could.

"Just a rock. Nothing to worry about, our shields handled it."

"I thought you were trying to avoid those."

"Yeah, the big ones. There's no way to dodge *everything* in here. But don't sweat it, I've pumped up the forward shields to compensate."

Charlie sank back into his seat and shook his head as another crash shook the vessel. "Worst. Road trip. Ever."

They carried on like that for some distance, flying deeper and deeper into the asteroid field, always staying roughly on the course Nakk had plotted for them, with key variations for survival's sake, of course. It was a stomach-churning ride, but Kip was living up to his promise.

The scanners were a mess, thanks to the strange magnetic resonance from the asteroids. Whatever they were made of, something was wreaking merry havoc on their instruments. It was no wonder no one could find Vixx without an invitation. Flying blind in this place was suicidal.

Without warning an alarm sounded in the cabin, and multiple angry red flashes appeared on the displays.

"That's not good," Dukaan grunted as they dodged another massive rock.

"What is it?" Charlie asked.

"Target lock."

"From where? Who?"

"You need ask?" Nakk replied, opening the comms system to the frequency he had been provided. He just hoped the information was up to date. "This is Commander Nakk of the Liberated People's Front. We have come to meet with Vixx."

Silence on the airwaves, then a gruff voice spoke. "Be gone now or die. We don't like the People's Liberated Front. Bunch of worthless tossers."

"No, you are mistaken," Nakk said. "We're the Liberated People's Front."

"Still doesn't matter. We have no desire to speak with you."

"But we have come with trade."

"Don't need any trade."

"But we come with Urvalin spoils of the highest quality. Stripped from top-tier command ships. Very difficult to come by."

"We've got that already," the voice replied.

"You have Urvalin command componentry? How in the stars did you come by that?"

"None of your business. Now, be gone."

Another pair of lights flashed on. "They're targeting us with more weapons," Dukaan said.

"Can we fight back?" Bawb asked.

Dukaan's hands flew across his controls. "All I see are these massive asteroids. I can't get a fix on where they're locking in on us from."

"Dammit," Charlie growled, keying open his comms. "Hey, don't shoot, okay? We bring trade the likes of which you have never seen."

"We have seen it all. This is your last warning. Turn back or be destroyed."

"Not like this, you haven't. That I can guarantee. We bring technology from another galaxy. Did you hear me? Another *galaxy*. Our cargo hold is loaded with that tech, as well as food and drink."

Another long pause hung in the air. "Food and drink?"

"Yes," Charlie replied.

"Alcohol?" the voice asked.

"Cases of it."

"From another galaxy, you say?"

"Yes."

"You did say *galaxy*?"

"Again, yes. And we are eager to trade."

Another pause, but this time the sinking feeling was no longer present in Charlie's gut. He could tell by the voice's curious tone. They were hooked. Now he just had to reel them in.

"I'll tell you what. Meet with us and we will give you a bottle to sample at no charge as a sign of good faith. If you don't like it, you keep it and we'll be on our way. What do you say?"

Static hissed over the line a moment, and a higher-pitched voice could faintly be heard in the background. A moment later the gruff one came back on the line. "In that case, you may come in."

"In?" Charlie asked. "Where exactly are you?"

"Follow my beacon, and do not deviate," was the only reply.

"I have the signal," Kip called out. "We're locked in on course."

He flew on for a few minutes, easily avoiding the obstacles now that he had the assistance of Vixx's people. Apparently, they had managed to map the asteroids in this area and calculate all of their trajectories, allowing them free movement in all directions in this little pocket amidst the chaotic rocks tumbling around them.

"We're approaching now," Kip announced.

"I don't see anything," Nakk said. "There is no ship. I only see asteroids."

"This is where the signal leads us," the AI repeated.

"Are you sure?"

"I'm an AI. Believe me, I can read a transmission."

"Then where is it? Where is Vixx's ship?"

A light suddenly appeared on one of the larger asteroids.

"There. It must be on the surface of that asteroid," Dukaan said.

They flew ahead in awe. The enormous rock was nearly the size of the largest ships in the Urvalin fleet, but as they drew closer, Charlie noticed something odd. Odd and amazing.

"Uh, guys?" he said. "That's not light from a little ship's beacon. Those are hangar doors."

Nakk and the others looked carefully at the rock growing steadily closer and realized he was right.

Bawb sat back in his seat with a grin on his face, quite amused, it seemed. "Oh, what a clever, clever man," he said. "Don't you see? The *asteroid* is his ship. How marvelous."

"Marvelous, yeah, that's a word for it," Charlie said as they flew into the opening, the doors closing behind them as they did. "But I tell ya, Bob, I can't help but feel a little like Pinocchio heading into the belly of the whale."

CHAPTER TWENTY-SIX

Malalia, Marban, and Rika watched the two teens inhaling mass quantities of food with a great deal of amusement. Poric had spoken with Sid and had seen to it they were provided whatever they could possibly desire in the way of food.

The AI didn't make it public knowledge, but ever since this galaxy had connected with theirs, the AIs overseeing things had made a point to begin cataloging and adding as many food items to their replicator databases as possible. After all, they had all fought together across both fronts, and the likelihood that their forces would blend at some point was high. And any good leader knows that your troops would fight far better with a good meal in their stomachs.

It was something the ancient Earth submariner fleets learned ages ago, providing the absolute best food to the men and women working in relative isolation deep beneath the sea for months at a time. It was enough to make some people snap, but top-notch gourmet meals helped keep that to a minimum.

Things were different at Dark Side base, of course. For one, there was ample space to move around, as well as an already impressive selection of food available as simply a normal part of everyone's lives. Food replicators made that possible, and now, thanks to the wonders of technology, Kara and Vee were enjoying all of their favorite treats.

And they had certainly earned them.

The fighting on the ground would have been exhausting in regular gravity, but in the greatly reduced gravitational environment of the moon it made maneuvering much more difficult. It was counterintuitive, how weighing less could equal more work. But for those not accustomed to the conditions, an inordinate amount of energy was expended doing little things, like simply turning around without spinning too far.

Fortunately, with Poric looking after them, Kara and Vee could focus more on the casting and less on fancy footwork on the dusty lunar surface. Both had demonstrated impressive skills with their magic, and while Rika and Kara's former stepmother had turned the tide of battle in space, the teen and her friend had very nearly done the same on the surface, and without aid from above.

Kara glanced up and saw the woman she hated looking at her from a table across the room. A flash of emotion rose within her, but she pushed it down. It was a good thing she'd just used so much of her power or else she'd have been at risk of some of it leaking out in her anger.

Malalia rose to her feet.

"You sure that's such a good idea?" Rika asked. "Maybe this isn't the best time."

"There will never be a best time," Malalia replied, heading over to join the girls.

"We should probably go with them," Marban suggested.

"Oh, you're damn right we're going," Rika agreed, grabbing her tray and following.

Malalia sat down directly across from the girl from whom she had stolen so much power over the years and said nothing.

She just looked at her, a quiet, sad look on her face. Rika and Marban joined a moment later.

"So, uh, nice job out there," Marban said when the silence grew unbearable.

Kara did not reply. Poric slowly turned his gaze on the pirate with a what-the-hell-are-you-doing stare. It flew right over Marban's head.

"Yep, you two sure did manage to put those Urvalin in their place," he continued. "Hell, I reckon that—"

"What is *she* doing here?" Kara hissed.

Rika leaned a little closer. "Malalia is helping us fight the Urvalin."

"She tried to kill you. Me. *Everyone.*"

There was no real comeback for that and Rika knew it, just as she knew the teenager would not let the anger of betrayal go so easily.

"Yeah, that she did. But the Urvalin are too much to handle on our own. We needed a caster."

"I'm a caster. Vee's a caster."

"Yes, but she is much more powerful."

Malalia took a sip of her electrolyte beverage, gently placed it on the table, then spoke. "Kara has every right to hate me. I did unspeakable things to her and do not deserve her forgiveness." She locked eyes with the girl. "Just know I am truly, deeply sorry for what I did. I should have been a mother to you. Helped you harness your powers as you blossomed into a young woman."

"*Step*mother," Kara growled.

"Yes, *step*mother," she said quietly. "Things would have been so much different had I but chosen a different path."

"My father wouldn't be imprisoned right now, for one," Kara shot back.

Malalia cast a confused look at Rika.

"Yeah, that. We didn't mention it before, but it seems the Urvalin have been rounding up vislas in your home galaxy."

"A conquest starting at the top. I have to admit, it is a wise strategy."

"That's my father you're talking about!"

"And others as well, I am certain. But the powerful have value. I am sure he is being held somewhere safe where he can be ransomed at a later date."

"Actually," Rika said. "There's the rub. The Urvalin are trying to use them to bolster their own Allpower. Making magic users do their bidding."

Malalia nodded as she took it all in. "Then it is a good thing you are in this galaxy, Karasalia. If not, I fear you would have been taken as well."

"I'm just a kid."

"You are far more than that and you know it. Seeing you in action today, even with all we have been through, I could not help but feel proud of you. You have truly grown into your power, and I feel it will only increase in time. And you, Visanya, a casting Ootaki? Using your own power, no less? While you could still use a great deal more training, what you've accomplished is exceptional. Really, you are both such remarkable young women."

Kara dropped her fork and pushed her chair back. "Okay, I've lost my appetite. Come on, Vee. We're going."

"Going where?" Poric asked, rising to accompany them.

"I don't know," she said, shooting a hateful look at Malalia. "Away from here. We talked with Joshua, and he says even if his ships were able to get out, we couldn't get to the portal. Not without a proper diversion, and that would take planning and intel they don't have yet."

"So why not stay here?" the cyborg asked. "I'm sure we could use your help."

Kara felt her stepmother staring but avoided Malalia's gaze like it was poison. "No. We need to get out of here. C'mon, Vee, let's get Nixxus and Gazz and go mess things up for the Urvalin somewhere else."

"Is that wise?" Malalia asked. "Just the two of you all alone? Let me help. I can borrow a ship and accompany—"

"Screw you!" Kara shouted, power crackling from her fingertips. "You're not my mom, you're not my stepmom, and I wish they'd killed you when they had the chance!"

She turned and stormed off, Vee close behind.

Rika placed a hand on the woman's arm. "Let them go. She needs time to process and cool off. Kicking some Urvalin ass might actually do her some good."

Malalia gave a sad nod of agreement. "I can only imagine how upset she is with me. And with good reason. But you are right, they need time."

"Yeah, and they'll be okay. They're getting pretty good at this casting thing."

"Oh, that much is most definitely true. I could feel the power wafting off of her, just as happens to her father, and that was *after* a battle no less. She is growing incredibly strong. And with Visanya's talents coming to fruition, they could prove to be a most powerful duo, if they would just learn to focus their potential."

Rika couldn't help but agree. Having seen the two in action, there was no doubt she was witnessing some next-level casters in the making. If they survived long enough to fully become them, that is.

Kara and Vee strode through the base quickly, Poric at their side, shooing away any who might want to pester them with questions about magic. They'd made quite an impression out there and were something of celebrities in Dark Side base. But they wanted nothing of that. They wanted to leave.

The dragons were still in the hangar, taking a well-deserved siesta after eating their fill of both Sid's replicated delicacies as well as slaughtered Urvalin.

"Hey, are you two good to fly?" Kara called out. "Or will it give you indigestion?"

"We have digested enough," Nixxus said with a satisfied belch. "Quite ready to fly, if that is the plan."

"Good. I need to get the hell out of here," she replied, seating her helmet in place and climbing up onto the dragon's back. Kara paused and looked back at Poric. "Hey, I want to thank you. For everything. You saved our lives back there."

"Just part of the job, and my pleasure. Now, you two be careful out there. And don't forget to come visit again, okay? This has been the most fun I've had in ages."

"You're what, a year old?"

"Yeah, but we don't have epic space battles every day, you know," he said with a laugh.

The dragons turned and headed out of the hangar, flying up and out of the dampening array. Once clear, the dragons turned on their harnesses, and the girls reactivated their suit power and took a look around. What they saw was a little unsettling.

A trio of Urvalin ships were nearby, and the sudden power readings from the reactivated tech gear had drawn their attention.

"We have company," Gazz called out.

"Good," Kara said with an angry determination. "Head for them."

"You want to *what*?" Nixxus asked.

The power began to crackle all around them both as Kara's bottled rage had finally found an outlet. "I said, head right for them!"

The dragons didn't need to be told again and quickly shifted course, heading directly for the Urvalin ships. Spells and weapons blasts flew past them, but their shielding deflected the few that got close.

"Vee, let 'em have it," Kara said as she unleashed her own power.

A wave of magic burst from the duo just as the dragons engaged the railguns mounted to their harnesses. It was a massive barrage of power and supersonic metal, and it tore the nearest ship to pieces, crippling another. By the look of it, no one aboard either had survived.

The third ship then did a very un-Urvalin thing. It turned tail and ran.

"Do we pursue?" Nixxus asked.

Kara looked at the trajectory on her readout. "No. Let it go," she said, much calmer now that she'd had a good old-fashioned serving of violence. "It's heading to their fleet. We can't go there. Not yet, anyway."

"So, now what?" the dragon asked.

"Now? There are plenty of other Urvalin in this system. We're going to go make their lives hell."

CHAPTER TWENTY-SEVEN

The sweet little old lady sitting on the porch of the rustic cabin well removed from the nearest city on this quiet planet sipped her tea, taking in the subtleties of the brew as it flowed over her taste buds. She drew in a deep breath, enjoying the fresh air of this place. But this woman was not what she seemed. Not by a long shot.

She put down her cup and turned to her visitors.

"What brings you to me, Daisy? We were not to cross paths for some time yet."

"I know, Master Farmatta, but I need your help with a couple of things. Korbin and Amazara have been doing their best, but they both think you will know more about this than either of them do."

"Ah, would this be about your sword, or your child?"

"Arlo? What have you heard?"

"Not that child," the assassin said, nodding toward Freya with an amused grin. "*That* one."

Daisy shook her head, amused. Of course Farmatta knew about Freya's latest blossoming abilities. The woman's spies were everywhere, and little escaped her network of eyes and ears.

"Yeah, I was going to ask about my sword, but Freya is dealing with some growing pains of sorts and could use some help."

"Help because your ship—a remarkable craft, I must once again commend you—is doing what should be impossible. She is learning to cast."

"Yeah, that pretty much sums it up. The thing is, she's having kind of a hard time with it."

"It's to be expected, though," Korbin said. "We all go through the same trials and tribulations when we first learn to cast. It's a rite of passage of sorts. No one is proficient at the beginning."

Amazara nodded her agreement. "She needs our support and guidance. But there remains the question of how one trains a pupil like her."

Daisy couldn't help but feel a swell of happiness in her chest. Yes, they were discussing a serious matter while in the middle of an intergalactic war, but these wonderful people—even the woman who had surely killed hundreds, if not thousands—were talking about Freya as a person. She was no longer a thing to them, she was part of their unusual little family.

"*Maybe she has some pointers,*" Sarah said in Daisy's head.

"Do you have any pointers for us? We've been hitting something of a roadblock progressing her casting," Daisy said. "She can access the power now, but it doesn't quite come out right when she says the words."

"I have tutored her in pronunciation and intent, and she speaks the words perfectly," Korbin added. "However, for whatever reason, it just does not seem to be taking. The magical potential is most certainly there, of that there is no doubt, but the ability to harness it? That is where we are experiencing problems."

Farmatta laughed. "Oh, you wonderful man. So powerful, so

experienced, yet so blind to the one thing you have not taken into consideration."

"What is that? Please, enlighten me."

The old woman rose from her seat and began walking toward the parked ship. She moved as though she were somewhat frail, but all present knew she was far, far from it. She was the Ghalian's most powerful caster, in fact, and that was precisely why they had come to see her.

She reached Freya and reached her hand out, pressing it against her hull. "It is good to see you again, child."

"Hi, Farmatta!" Freya chirped. "Thanks for taking the time to help us out. We all really appreciate it."

"For you, my dear, it is my pleasure." She closed her eyes a moment, her hand pressing even harder against the hull. Then, abruptly, she stopped. "As I thought," she said with a knowing grin. "Korbin, you have been teaching her like she is a person."

"Well, she is, is she not? Despite her origins, that is. She is one of us."

"Oh, most definitely. But you have not taken into consideration her rather unique physiology. She is a machine whose entire body has been attuned to magic and readied to cast. Think of what you have learned of this other world machinery. She does not have a mouth or vocal cords as we possess. She has an entirely different mechanism for speech. And it is that difference that is causing the issue."

Korbin realized what she was getting at immediately. "I feel like such a fool. Of course, she makes the sounds, but not the way we do. No wonder she is having casting issues. Thank you for your help. I believe I understand what I need to do now."

Farmatta smiled and patted him on the shoulder. "Good. Now, why don't you and your pupil practice for a while? I believe Daisy has something else she wishes to discuss with me."

"Are you ready, Freya?" he asked.

"Oh, yeah. But what are we going to do?"

"We're going to cast some basic spells, just as I taught you before."

"But they didn't work."

"No, they didn't. But that was my fault in the instruction. I told you to speak the words, but you rely on mechanical devices to produce the sound. It is not the same as when a flesh-and-blood person speaks."

"Well, I'm a ship. There's no other way for me to do it."

"Ah, but there is," he said with a grin. "Freya, I want you to cast silently. Speak with your entire being, projecting the spell and your intent with whatever impulses course through your body. Do not worry about forcing a machine to form the words for others to hear. Just project. Can you do that?"

"I think so."

"Then let's begin."

As she walked back with Farmatta and Amazara, Daisy turned and watched with swelling pride as Freya began casting in a completely new way. The first spell was the most basic illumination spell. One that she knew but that had been giving her trouble to no end.

This time, however, the area in front of her brightened despite it being broad daylight.

"Good," Korbin said. "Very good. Now, try the brighter version."

She did, and the light increased immensely.

"Excellent. That's enough of that one," he said, placing a small branch in front of her. "Now, I want you to try a fire spell. Just enough to ignite that branch."

Daisy could almost feel Freya's hesitance. "But the last time I tried that—"

"This will be different. Do you trust me?"

"Yes."

"Then trust that you can do this. Just like the illumination spell. Cast with your whole being. Let the spell flow from you effortlessly."

Freya didn't say anything, but a moment later the branch burst into flames. More importantly, nothing else around them caught fire.

"I did it!" she exclaimed.

"That you did."

"Daisy, did you see?"

"I did."

"I want to try a bigger spell!"

"Hey, now, Kiddo. Don't get carried away. You do what Korbin tells you, okay?"

"Right, right. I will," she said, the enthusiasm clear in her voice. "It's so cool—Magic works! I can't wait to tell Joshua..." She fell silent, a moment of glum reflection casting a shadow on her elevated mood.

"Don't worry, Freya. We'll get back. One way or another. I promise."

"But fighting Allpower is so different."

"It is. And that's kind of what I want to talk to Farmatta about. So you go practice some more, okay?"

"Okay," the AI said, then set her attention squarely back on her tutor.

"She is a handful, I will give you that," Farmatta said with a warm laugh. "And I feel one day soon she is going to become quite the force to be reckoned with. More so than she already is, I mean. You shall prove a worthy match for the Urvalin and their Allpower."

"Yeah, about that," Daisy said. "The Allpower, I mean. The thing is, I'm getting a little bit worried about my sword."

"A marvelous being, that blade. I've never seen its like before and likely never will again. The bond you share is impressive."

"Well, he was grown specifically from my own reinforced bone matrix, so that's kind of to be expected."

"Then tell me, is his bloodthirst troubling you?"

"So, you know about that."

"I have heard of his proclivities," the Ghalian replied.

"Yeah, and I was fine with that when he was draining vislas and whatnot. But the thing is, ever since he got a taste of Allpower, he's gotten, I don't know. Unstable. Like, he acts up, trying to do his own thing. Frankly, it's been getting harder to control him."

"And yet, he is yours to control."

Amazara cleared her throat. "Excuse me, Master Farmatta, but if I may, I am a reader, and I have sensed some disquiet within her blade. A battle raging within itself."

Farmatta nodded knowingly. "You say he battles your will, but is it not true that he still will not cut for anyone else?"

"That much is true, yes. His edge is dull for anyone but me," Daisy said.

"Then, perhaps this is a passing phase. Once you are back in your own galaxy, I suspect things will return to normal."

"I hope you're right, but how do we even get back? So far we've not been having a very good track record with our efforts."

"Give it time, dear. We have a plan. If Karasalia Palmarian and her friend managed to deliver the Bakana rods as promised, it should only be a matter of time."

"But how do we know if they even got there?" Amazara asked.

"Ah, yes, that. I am certain at least one has arrived. There was a massive power draw from another realm, though I could not determine which. None of our people were handling the rod still in this galaxy, fortunately—it is still in my possession in preparation for the final steps of our plan. But even so, the pull from it was tangible. I would say without a doubt that one of them, if not both, have reached their intended recipients."

"Then what happened? What was the power draw from?" Daisy asked.

"We will not know the answer to that until we defeat the Urvalin and are once more able to cross between realms."

Daisy sighed. "So, it's a Catch-22."

"A what?" Amazara asked.

"Long story. Basically, if you lose, you lose, but if you win, you lose."

"I do not think I like this Catch-22."

"Nobody does," Daisy said with a chuckle. She looked over at Freya and Korbin, the ship casting bigger and bigger spells under his guidance. She wanted to get home more than anything, not just for her own family, but for Freya's as well. "You said the power draw was unexpected."

"Yes," Farmatta said.

"Could the Urvalin have captured it?"

"There is a chance, yes, and I have wondered this myself."

Daisy could see the woman was thinking the same thing she was. "We need to find out, Farmatta. Is there any way at all to get more intel?"

The old woman nodded slowly. "There is an outpost not too many systems from here. A place the Urvalin have used as a base of operations for some of their intelligence ships. There are officers there. People with access and clearance. If anyone outside of their commander would have heard of such a thing, I suspect they would."

A smile slowly spread across Daisy's lips. "So, you want to go pay them a visit?"

Farmatta's grin matched her own, only hers sported pointy

fangs ready to drink the blood of her enemies. "Oh, most definitely," she said. "Allow me a moment to clean up my teapot and we will depart at once."

CHAPTER TWENTY-EIGHT

It was surprisingly easy to reach the planet Farmatta had pointed out as the location of the Urvalin intel coordination center. It seemed that having so thoroughly dominated this section of space, the invaders were a bit lax in their confidence. That was something their little group could take advantage of.

Korbin had left his ship behind at Farmatta's retreat. It was too well known by now to be able to avoid notice should anyone look their way. Farmatta, however, had her shimmer ship and could come and go invisibly. At least, she was reasonably sure of it. The Urvalin possessed novel tech and a different enough variant of magic that the threat always lingered that they might be able to pierce that particular spell with their scans.

Freya, however, had not only her new magical skills to test, but also a full suite of stealth options with which to hide herself, the most impressive of which being her active camouflage, courtesy of her clever little nanites, no magic required.

They would simply project an image along the entire ship of what was on the other side, making it appear invisible. The tech was bleeding edge, but so far it had worked against the Urvalin. And with it, they could safely make it down to the chosen world.

And it was the planet's surface rather than any of the vessels above that was their destination.

The Urvalin intel equipment and key systems were all positioned in a low orbit aboard a trio of massively armed ships. Surrounding them were a multitude of lesser craft, all ready to defend them at a moment's notice. Ships came and went regularly, delivering intelligence that could not be entrusted to regular communications methods.

The Urvalin were also concerned about the overlap of their technology and magic and whether the locals could actually crack it, it seemed.

But it wasn't the machinery Daisy's little group was after. They sought something far more susceptible to pressure. They were seeking officers.

"You think they'll have Nikora's location?" Amazara asked as Freya quietly landed just outside of town after tucking under a large tree for additional cover.

"I would think so," Korbin replied. "From what Farmatta said, these people pretty much know everything that's going on in the Urvalin fleet. Whatever information of importance there is within their armada, it passes through here."

"All clear," Freya announced as she silently landed and popped the hatch.

The team stepped outside, clothed in local attire so as to blend in as much as possible. They were still heavily armed, of course, but most of their weapons were hidden by their clothing. To any looking they were just another group of locals. At least, all but Daisy. She still stood out a bit, but a little bit of makeup, courtesy of Amazara, and she looked less human than usual. Hopefully that would be good enough.

The group began walking toward town. Thanks to Freya's stealthy approach, it was going to be a much shorter trek than they had initially feared.

"Korb, how is it Farmatta knows so much about this top-secret Urvalin operation?" Amazara asked.

"Because I have spies," a voice said out of the thin air ahead of them. Farmatta removed her shimmer cloak and fell in with the others.

"Nice trick," Daisy said.

"It comes in handy."

The group chuckled quietly and continued on their way. A few minutes later they reached the town's borders and stepped into the city limits. Farmatta motioned for them to follow.

"This way. There will be several establishments in which we have a good likelihood of locating one of the officers."

"And the plan is to drag them out and question them?" Daisy asked.

"A bit more subtle," she replied. "All it should take is one little indigestion spell applied to their food or drink to motivate them to head home. And once they are on their way, we will be able to take them."

"Okay, I guess that works for me," Daisy replied. "Freya, you see anything on scans?" she asked over her open comms.

"Nothing so far. You look clear."

"*I don't see anything either, Daze,*" Sarah added

"Thanks," she replied. "Hey, Korbin."

"Yes?"

"I was wondering. You guys always talk about just how powerful Kara's dad is. Do you think he might be able to help me and Freya cross back over?"

Korbin flashed an apologetic smile as he shook his head. "Unfortunately, despite his considerable power, Nikora does not possess the same magic as a Zomoki. Not even someone as strong as he can enter a sun's flaming plasma and survive. Only Zomoki, and your galaxy's dragons, appear to have that power."

"So, *only* dragons and Zomoki can do it."

"Yes."

"And they're currently *all* on the other side of that portal."

"That's the situation, yes."

"Aww hell. Then what good does anyone's power do me?" Daisy griped.

"Don't worry, Daisy," Freya interjected. "I'm working on it."

"Thanks, Kiddo. I appreciate the support, but what we need is a damn Zomoki."

The group walked deeper into the town, chatting casually amongst themselves, making a very good show of simply being a bunch of friends out and about. Farmatta had told them that her spy had informed her there would be only a small contingent of Urvalin troops on the ground but there was no barracks. They all stayed aboard their ships, rotating down as duty required.

As for the officers, they simply enjoyed visiting the surface to partake in the spoils of war. Food, drink, sex workers, all were on the table when their duty shifts ended. And with so massive a fleet in orbit, no one would dream of harming a hair on any one of their heads.

That is, almost no one.

The team spread out and made quick passes of the local taverns and bars until one of them came across an officer. Amazara was the lucky winner, and she signaled the others over their comms patches.

"In there. A group of three officers are dining together," she informed them when they converged on her location.

"*Three*?" Korbin said. "That's great news. Improves our odds several fold."

"Yeah. Now we just need to figure out how to get them out of there and where to snatch them," Daisy said.

"I will handle that," Farmatta replied with the friendliest of smiles. She stepped into the tavern, calling warm greetings to the nearest patron as she did.

"Should we go in after her?" Amazara asked.

"She's a master Ghalian," Daisy replied. "I wouldn't bother."

Sure enough, just a few minutes later she popped back out, waving a warm farewell to someone who had been a complete stranger only a few minutes prior.

"It is done."

Korbin did a double-take. "Already?"

"It is a trivial spell. Now, when they exit they will almost certainly head for their transport back to the ship. We must ambush them along the route."

"We passed that landing area on the way here," Daisy said. "We can get set up there in just a couple of minutes."

"Then let's not waste time," Korbin said.

True to Farmatta's word, they did not need to wait long at all for the three officers to come hurrying along their way. Two men, one woman, all of medium build. It would be a bit of work, but it would not be impossible to make them appear to be drunk and passed out, merely being helped back to their ships by helpful passersby.

"Hey, friend. Do you need help?" Korbin asked, stepping out into the pathway.

"Out of the way," the nearest man said.

"Rude!"

"What did you say to me?" the man said, turning in anger despite his rumbling belly.

"I said rude. But not as rude as what we're about to do to you."

"*We?*"

The three fell in a heap as Farmatta blasted them with a stun spell. "Now, quickly, help them up and make for the ship. The path should be clear."

They did just that, lifting the slumbering officers, but when they rounded the corner they noticed a problem. A *big* problem.

"Uh, guys?" Daisy said, staring at the dozens of Urvalin guards they had just run smack-dab into. "Weren't they not supposed to be here?"

"What are you doing?" the captain of the unit shouted. His name was Doxin, and he was a broad-shouldered, burly sort, the long scar running across his face only adding to his ferocious look.

"Shit," Daisy said, dropping the officer and drawing Stabby from beneath her cloak.

The others had already pulled their weapons and engaged as well. It was about to be a four-on-who-knew-how-many fight, but the Urvalin didn't know one key detail. There was a Ghalian in the mix. And a Stabby as well.

"Get some!" Daisy shouted as she tore into the Urvalin ranks with her sword. He cut with glee, severing limbs from bodies, drinking in their Allpower-laced blood like a drunk on a bender. There were so many of them to take the energy from, it was like a serial killer's Christmas come early.

Korbin and Amazara fought back-to-back, alternating between the pulse weapons they had become accustomed to using as well as their own magic. It was enough to throw the Urvalin off a bit, as they'd so far only faced magic users in this galaxy, and those had been handled easily.

Korbin, however, was a caster of significant power, and the Urvalin would have lost in no time had they not had a caster of their own among their ranks. The man's power flashed back against the intruder, locking horns with Korbin's impressive strength.

Farmatta flowed through the crowd, dodging weapons fire while dealing death to those in her path. "Korbin, the officer!" she shouted to him.

He glanced at the man at his feet and tried to shift his

casting to allow him to pick up their prize, but the caster was too strong. He had to maintain all of his focus possible.

"Daisy, a little help please!"

Daisy heard him and spun through the swarming troops, blocking spells and laying waste to those around her. Stabby was getting a bit too worked up for her comfort, but it was too late to pull back now. It was do-or-die time.

She stepped in front of Korbin and let Stabby engage with the caster in a battle of power. Magic and Allpower flowed as they clashed, and the sentient sword was loving every second of it.

"Get him out of here!" Daisy shouted at Korbin.

He gathered up the fallen officer and pushed ahead. But it would be near impossible to make it all the way back to Freya. There were too many Urvalin flooding the area.

Suddenly, without warning, a large group of them went *squish*, bodies exploding in a gory mess, crushed flat by the arrival of an invisible ship. Freya's nanites had shielded her from detection. They also now painted a picture of the bloody mess resting beneath her hull.

She de-cloaked her airlock and slid it open. "Come on!" she called out.

Farmatta saw her arrival and took that as a sign to make for her own shimmer ship. Korbin and Amazara piled into the opening, dropping the caster in a heap. They then began casting all the spells they had to give Daisy a clear path. But she was stuck.

The Urvalin caster was now focused entirely on her. Worse, Captain Doxin was shoving his way through his men, a menacing wave of dark Allpower wafting off of him. He wasn't just a soldier, he was a caster as well, it seemed.

"Oh, shit," Daisy said when she realized what was happening. She was locked in battle and had no way out.

"Guys, I'm stuck," she called to the others.

Freya reacted at once, powering up her railgun and letting loose a single blast. The caster exploded in a red mist, his resistance suddenly gone. Daisy turned to run for the ship, but Stabby was furious. He wanted that man's blood and had been denied.

"Not now, dammit!" Daisy growled.

"*He's not letting go, Daze!*"

"*I know, Sarah. What do I do?*"

"*You make him.*"

"*What the hell do you think I'm trying to do? How about you help me?*"

Sarah latched onto her sister's hands and did her best, but she was a ghost in the shell, and this sword was far, far too powerful.

With a sudden yank, Stabby dragged her forward, lunging into greatly outnumbered combat. Daisy hung on tight as the Allpower-charged sword swung and cut, powering his way into the troops, killing and drinking in a bloody Bacchanal of carnage.

She let go with one hand, pulling her pistol free to at least try to stop the Urvalin coming at her from the other direction. Freya had taken out the caster at a distance, but she couldn't risk a shot this close to Daisy. She was on her own.

Another caster, though not as powerful as the other, began bombarding them with spells. Stabby felt the power, and a surge of excitement rushed through him, into Daisy's arm. He was too far gone now, she could tell. Stabby yanked hard in the direction of the caster.

"*Daisy, he's pulling you into their ranks! Get out of there!*" Sarah shouted.

She hated it, but she knew Sarah was right. Daisy popped off a series of shots, clearing the narrowest of paths to her ship.

Then, with great reluctance, she let go and took off running for the airlock. It was the sword or her life, and there could only be one answer.

Stabby flew out of her hand, embedding himself in the caster's chest, drinking greedily, pulling the man's life force out like a teenager finishing a milkshake, slurping for every last drop. He was so engrossed in his carnage, he didn't even notice she was gone. In retrospect, as they made their escape, Daisy wondered if he would even care.

She dove into the airlock and looked back one final time. Doxin was standing over the fallen caster, drawing a sword, *her* sword from the man's body.

"I'm in. Go, Freya! Go!"

The door slammed shut and the ship bolted for the sky. "They're deploying dampening fields," Freya announced as they gained altitude. "Hold on, I'm gonna try something new."

"New? Freya, what are you—"

The ship tumbled violently to the side, and the instruments and displays went dark. They were powered down but still flying somehow. Daisy had no idea what had just happened. They should have crashed. They should have been dead.

Korbin, however, recognized the feel of the power around them. "Drook," he said, amazed. "She is mimicking Drook power to fly the ship."

They were thrown about as the ship popped out of the atmosphere. A moment later they jumped.

Far away in a distant system, Freya reappeared. She powered her systems back up, releasing the Drook magic.

"Damn," Korbin said, looking at the caster on the floor. He'd woken long enough to kill himself rather than be captured, it seemed. "All of that was for nothing."

"Freya, how did you do that?" Daisy asked, climbing into a seat.

"It was like Korbin taught me. Don't cast, but instead *be* the spell. Cast with my whole self."

"But you're a machine. How did your brain not shut down when we passed the dampening field?"

"Well, that's a little trickier, but so far as I can tell, when I incorporated Drook magic into every bit of myself, I ceased being a machine. At least so far as the dampening devices were concerned."

"Remarkable," Korbin said. "Freya, you have done exceedingly well."

"Thanks. But, Daisy, what happened out there? Why didn't you come when I cleared the way?"

Daisy looked at her hands, empty, lacking something she hadn't realized she'd become so accustomed to having.

"It was Stabby," she said quietly. "He went rogue."

CHAPTER TWENTY-NINE

After more than a few run-ins with the locals on a disparate assortment of worlds, Arlo and Ripley had come to realize that, while they might stand out as off-worlders, it was the dragons that were really freaking people out.

More than once they had fallen under attack the moment they landed, the inhabitants opening up on them with both weapons and magic before they could even say they meant no one any harm. It was a bit of a rude wake-up call, but the writing was on the wall. Dragons were not normal here.

Of course, dragons weren't normal back home either, but at least plenty of worlds they'd visited had stories about them. And as for Ara's galaxy, Zomoki were still a part of everyday life, though nearly all of those were unintelligent, brutal animals lacking the intellect and wisdom of their friend.

As a result, when they approached the next inhabited world, the teens decided to try a new approach.

"Are you sure this is a good idea?" Drombus asked when Arlo suggested he and Ripley be dropped well outside of town. "We can take you much closer than this."

"Yes, I agree with Drombus," Duzza said. "There is no need

for such a long walk when we have wings."

"Just take us down," Arlo replied. "We keep getting our asses handed to us everywhere we show up. We're tired, we're hungry, and we need to try something new."

"Ripley, do you concur?" Duzza asked the girl riding on her back.

"It's nothing personal," she said. "But yeah, I think we should change it up just this once and see what happens."

"Very well."

The two dragons descended into the atmosphere, protecting themselves and their passengers with their magic as they pushed through the planet's protective bubble. Once clear, they took a wide route down, making sure to approach from an angle where people on the ground were not likely to observe them.

With a few flaps of their wings, they settled down in a small clearing a few kilometers outside of the nearby town. It was quiet there, and the spaceport where ships were coming and going was clear across the other side of town. No one would notice them here.

They stripped off their armor and stowed it in the compartments on the dragons' harnesses.

"How do we look?" Ripley asked.

"Like humans on an alien world," Drombus replied.

"Well, at least we're not marching into town dressed for battle. That's probably another reason people freaked out on us. C'mon, Arlo, let's get walking."

"Just a minute," he said, reaching into Drombus's harness and pulling free the tightly wrapped Bakana rod.

"Why are you bringing that? We can't use it, you know."

"Yeah, but this wrap isn't going to hold up much longer. We need to find some kind of tube or something it'll fit in. We know what could happen if it winds up touching one of the dragons again."

"It should stay here. Just take measurements."

"Rip, don't worry. No one knows what this is. Hell, they'll probably just think it's a walking stick. And this is something we really should take care of."

Though Ripley was not thrilled about the idea of carrying the rod with them, she couldn't fault his logic. The wrap *was* wearing in places, and the possibility of another accidental contact with whoever was holding it on the other end was a substantial risk. Even more dangerous, the power could flow both ways, and that could be catastrophic.

"All right. Fine. But don't let that out of your sight."

"You have my word."

It was a long walk to town and a longer walk before they passed from the sparse residential area into the more bustling city center. It was good, though. They needed to stretch their legs and get some fresh air.

They also hadn't really figured out what their next steps were going to be now that things had gone so sideways on them.

"I don't know why they can't seem to get a lock on Ara," Ripley said now that the dragons were far from earshot. "I mean, they should be able to smell her, right?"

"Right. Ara does that kind of thing all the time. But I wonder, are Zomoki noses more sensitive than dragons?"

"How am I supposed to know?"

"It's a rhetorical question, Rip. I'm just wondering out loud."

"I knew that," she lied. They walked silently for a few minutes before Ripley glanced over at the rod in Arlo's hand. "Do you really think that thing will be able to get us back home?"

"If it works as promised, I hope so. I mean, Charlie and Ara are hella powerful, and if they link with the others across all three galaxies, the theory is, it should be enough power to not only defeat the Urvalin, but also get us back where we belong."

"God, I hope so," Ripley griped. "I'm sick of this."

"Me too," he said. "Hey, you want to stop in at a tavern and get some food?"

"You think that's a good idea?"

Arlo shrugged. "We can't live on roasted alien monster alone."

"On that we agree. Okay, let's find a place."

Ripley led the way, selecting a run-down but clean tavern on a busy street. All manner of alien creatures were in the roadway, and only a few were remotely humanoid in shape. Like the infamous Donnie, the two earthlings were very much out of their element.

"Kinda smells in here," Arlo said.

"I don't care. I just need to sit a minute. Oh, yeah. That feels *good*," Ripley sighed as she sank into a cushioned seat.

The proprietor took a moment to adjust their translator to the newcomers' language but finally managed to take their orders after making a few suggestions.

She drank deep from the juice cooler placed in front of her. "I can't remember the last time we sat down to a proper meal."

"It hasn't been that long, Rip."

"But it *feels* like it."

Arlo wasn't about to argue. And to be honest, he also felt the stress of their voyage slowly ebbing from his body as they took a load off.

Despite the pungent smell of the tavern itself, the meal was delicious, full of flavor and ingredients that simply couldn't be translated. It made no difference; the teens were thoroughly stuffed.

When the bill came, Arlo placed his chit tab on the tray.

"What's this?" the alien asked. "We only take money here."

"That *is*—aww, shit," he said as he realized his mistake. "Hey, Rip. You have any coin?"

"Coin? Really, dude? We don't use that where we're from."

"Look," the proprietor said, "I don't care where you're from, you have to pay for your meal."

Arlo rose to his feet, hands in front of him in a non-threatening way. "Hey, listen, friend. We made a mistake and left our other wallets at home. Uh, how about I leave this scanner with you for collateral while we run back and get it?"

"I'm not falling for that scam. Morkan! Get out here!"

A rustle from the back of the tavern was followed by several loud footsteps, each shaking the floor as the grew closer. An enormous being that looked like a cross between a yeti and an elephant stood over them, thick hands on massive hips, staring down at the teens.

"What's the trouble, Boss?"

"These two can't pay."

"Oh yeah?"

Arlo didn't like the sound of that and pulled up a defensive spell. At least, he thought it was. Unfortunately, the magic flew awry and knocked several tables over, sending the patrons tumbling.

"I'm sorry! I didn't mean to!"

Morkan was already reaching for him when Ripley let loose with her own spell. This wasn't a defensive one but an offensive type. And it almost worked.

Almost.

The force impacted the creature square in the chest, driving it backward into the wall, where it smashed the furniture with a crunch.

"Arlo, we need to get out of here!" she said.

"One step ahead of you," he replied, snatching up the Bakana rod and turning for the door.

A pair of Urvalin guards stood there watching the events.

"Oh, shi—" he managed to say before their stun spells

dropped them to the ground.

"Again, Argus?" one of the guards said to the proprietor, tossing him some money. "That'll cover your bill."

"Much obliged, Darvax. I hope these two work off their debt quickly. They seemed nice enough."

"Nice enough for freeloaders, you mean," the Urvalin said with a laugh. "We'll put them to work, don't you worry."

The Urvalin hoisted the teens over their shoulders. Darvax noticed the wrapped walking stick on the ground and, after a moment's consideration, picked it up and brought it with.

Far away, the two dragons were sitting quietly in their clearing, waiting for the teenagers to return. This was a populous world, so they couldn't just go hunting for something to eat anywhere they pleased like they could on uninhabited planets. Fortunately, they were well enough fed of late. But this was getting boring.

"Hey, do you smell that?" Drombus asked, sniffing the air.

"That smells like their magic," Duzza replied. "And something else."

"Urvalin!" they exclaimed in unison.

Drombus activated the comms link on his harness immediately. "There are Urvalin here! Arlo? Ripley? Do you hear me? I said, there are Urvalin. You need to get back here at once."

Silence hung heavy in the air.

"We need to go get them, scaring the locals be damned."

"I agree. Let's—"

Duzza was cut off when an Urvalin ship lifted off and shot by overhead, the lingering traces of Arlo and Ripley's magic trickling behind it. They looked at one another and took flight. The ship was too big for them to take on themselves, so that meant there was only one thing they could do.

They would follow.

CHAPTER THIRTY

While Charlie, Bawb, and Nakk were off doing whatever it was they were doing deep in the asteroid field, the rest of the team stood by in Nakk's command ship. They hadn't detected any signs of explosions or impacts within the belt of floating rocks, so at least it looked as though the away team was all right.

That, or at the very minimum Kip and Dukaan had managed not to crash and burn in a massive blast.

As for their meeting with the elusive Vixx, however, their guess was as good as anyone's.

"Ara, any word from Charlie?" Hunze asked the Zomoki casually floating beside them.

"He informed me they had made contact," she replied. "Apparently, he and Bawb decided it best not to communicate via magic once inside Vixx's craft for fear he may have Allpower detection units of some kind they might trigger. They are all right last I heard, but trying not to cause a stir."

Hunze felt the slight tension in her shoulders release. Bawb was still in danger, but people he could handle. Million-ton floating rocks, however, were something even the most skilled fighter could not battle their way past.

She and Skohla had been monitoring the clear space leading up to their entry point into the asteroid field for any possible threats, but thus far they appeared to be quite alone. Ara was also keeping an eye out, taking in the scents of the region. The crushed rocks bashing into one another, however, made for a bit of interference.

It seemed that whatever ore was within them, fracturing an asteroid released a tiny charge of Allpower. Individually it wasn't a lot, but when millions of rocks were floating and colliding with no particular pattern, it wreaked a bit of havoc on her ability to detect Allpower of the Urvalin variety.

Tamara and Shelly had taken a small stolen Urvalin fighter out to do some longer-range recon of the system, scouting out the nearby planets and moons for the enemy. There was a lot of open space between them and the asteroid field, but the planets were still close enough to pose a potential problem. And as they drew near the fourth planet from the sun, it was a problem they indeed found.

"Hey, guys," Shelly transmitted via her portable comms unit rather than the Urvalin tech. "We picked up traces of some Urvalin scout ships snooping around. Looks like they're at the fourth planet here, but maybe also one or two of its moons. How are the boys doing?"

"Still not back," Hunze replied.

"All right, then. We'll handle these guys."

"But you said there are many."

"Yeah, but we've got a plan."

Hunze and Skohla shared a look. They knew Shelly and Tamara's shared penchant for violence. "What are you going to do?"

"Don't worry about us," Shelly replied. "We're just gonna go be decoys and lure them away in the other direction. Maybe mess their shit up a little in the process. We're a bit outnumbered here, but it looks like they're spread thin, so we shouldn't have too much of a problem drawing them into pursuit."

"In the wrong direction," Tamara added.

"I already said that," Shelly could be heard over the open comms.

"I know, I'm just reiterating."

"Anyway, that'll force them to be shorthanded as they seem to have some away teams on the surface here. I don't know what they're doing, but it looks like they're setting up some kind of camp. Piles of crates, possibly weapons. We're not exactly sure."

Hunze and Skohla were already thinking the same thing, strapping into their seats. "We will fly out to assist you," Skohla transmitted. "Once the ships are away, we will deal with the forces on the ground."

"Sounds like a party. Have fun. We'll check in if there's an update."

"Thank you," Hunze replied. "You be careful out there."

"Never," Shelly said with a laugh.

Skohla plotted a course to fly in behind the departing ships as they pursued their friends. If she timed it right, they would slip in and land without anyone being any the wiser. And when they returned, they would have their hands full with the carnage on the surface. That would hopefully buy them more time for Charlie and the others to finish doing whatever they were doing.

"Ara, can you stay here and monitor for our friends and protect their exit route?" Hunze asked. "I would ask you to join the fight, but if they see you, they will realize this is not just a resistance attack."

"Of course," the Zomoki replied. "I was listening to the conversation. The plan is sound. Good hunting."

"Thank you. I hope it will be productive."

With that Skohla redirected the ship away from the

asteroids, skimming the rocks to disguise their signature until they were ready to shift course for the planet. From their vantage point they were able to observe the faint signals of the Urvalin ships pursuing their friends, as planned.

Skohla ducked behind a moon, using its mass to hide their approach. Only as they grew extremely close to it did she shift course, driving into the atmosphere.

"I see they possess a few small transport ships still on the ground," Hunze noted.

Skohla had noticed the same thing. "We will land far from them and take the smaller jump ships closer. Number one is pre-programmed and ready."

Despite the size of Nakk's command ship, they landed unnoticed. The planet was uninhabited save for the Urvalin camp, and they had set down a fair distance away. The small jump ships launched almost immediately, each woman at the helm of a craft. Only a few minutes later they landed on the rocky terrain close to the Urvalin camp.

As they approached, they were better able to see the details of the ground work. There were several teams deployed to a few areas, each setting up camps. What the Urvalin were up to they did not know, but this was an opportunity to put a serious crimp in their plans, whatever they were.

As Bawb had often said, in war one must seize the opportunity to disrupt one's enemy's supply and logistics hubs. Even the slightest inconvenience could mean a shifting of the tides and lead to eventual victory.

The jump ships landed a few hundred meters apart from each other. Hunze and Skohla quietly made their way to each other. The two women had suited up in light armor, armed themselves to the teeth, and were ready for a fight. The Urvalin wouldn't know what hit them.

Hunze nodded to Skohla when they reached the camp's

perimeter. There was no need for words. She had been training the woman in the ways of the Ghalian for some time now, and Skohla had proven a worthy pupil. She was nowhere near as proficient a killing machine as Hunze or Bawb, but she had more than a few new tricks up her already full sleeves.

"What do you think you—" was all the sentry managed to say before he fell to the ground, his head nearly severed from his neck by a wicked-sharp blade.

For this fight, Hunze had brought her Vespus blade, the sword's glowing length ready for a battle. With only Skohla with her it would be easy to ensure its power was directed away from her friend's direction. In a fight with her allies all around, she was still unsure if the weapon's power could be fully trusted in this galaxy.

"Intru—" another guard began to call out before a dagger pierced his throat.

It was enough, though. The Urvalin laboring to prepare the camp realized something was wrong.

Fortunately for Hunze and Skohla, they had all been hard at work, and thus were not carrying their usual load of weapons. Rifles were nowhere to be seen, and only small arms and blades rode on their belts. The guards were there for the off chance some wild animal might appear, but on this empty world no one had expected an actual fight.

Unfortunately for them, that was exactly what they now faced.

Hunze's blade flashed bright as she tore into the Urvalin troops, felling the men and women in her path as Skohla did the same at her flank, but meting out death with the dual pistols she was currently wielding.

At first, the Urvalin were slow to respond to the threat with the urgency it warranted. A woman with a sword? They could take her. Then shots rang out, and they realized there was more to this attack than it seemed. A few managed to return fire, but Hunze was casting defensive spells against tech while her Vespus blade unleashed brutal offensive magic.

The Urvalin numbers were dwindling rapidly as the pair tore through their ranks.

"Skohla, on your left!" Hunze called out.

Skohla pivoted and dropped to one knee, unloading her weapons in that direction without fear of hitting a friendly. Three Urvalin fell, but her pistols were now empty. She holstered them quickly, not about to leave behind evidence of exactly who had done this, and drew her blades. Now it was time to put what Hunze had taught her to use.

She rushed ahead closer to her friend, engaging the enemy in a sweeping arc as the two of them settled into the back-to-back fighting position Hunze had shown her. And the foolish Urvalin were rushing right to them like livestock to the slaughter.

The two slashed and hacked, sending a great deal of Urvalin to their graves, but the other work teams had gotten word of the attack and were racing back to bolster the rapidly dwindling group at their main camp.

"Now," Hunze said.

The two women threw the stun-blast grenades they had stuffed in their pockets and turned and ran. The Urvalin fell as the charges went off. Only the light armor the two women were wearing prevented them from doing the same. But that was the plan. To give themselves enough of a head start to get clear.

They raced into the trees and across the rocky outcroppings as the Urvalin regrouped.

"Up there!" one shouted as jump ship one slowly lifted off and came into view as it cleared the treetops. Weapons fire rang out, pinging its hull. The ship wobbled, apparently damaged, but continued to climb.

"After it!"

The jump ship quickly shifted course and made for the atmosphere. Uninjured members of the Urvalin crews rushed to their ships and took off, carrying as many armed troops as they could. If they could down this ship, they would capture or kill its crew with overwhelming force, as was the Urvalin way. They would not be blindsided again.

The jump ship breached the atmosphere and engaged its jump system. It failed. The Urvalin were growing closer by the second when the craft shifted to its warp drive.

"It's attempting to warp!" one captain called out, but too late. The ship vanished in a crackle a moment later.

"We damaged it," another ship noted. "I am reading leaking warp residue."

"We can track that. Follow that ship!"

The Urvalin powered up their drive systems and warped after it, leaving the few survivors on the surface to deal with the wounded.

Hunze and Skohla silently emerged from the tree line and made their way through the camp, killing every last remaining Urvalin without a sound.

"They took the bait," Skohla said, popping open a crate. It was full of weapons. "I'll get the other jump unit and return to our command ship. We should take as much of this as is useful, then destroy the rest."

"I will do a search for other supplies and any intelligence they may have left behind," Hunze said. "It was a good plan, Skohla."

"Thank you. The ship should be executing its seventh warp by now."

It was a pre-programmed route. One that was heading far, far away from this system, leading the Urvalin on a wild goose chase. And if they called in the support of their comrades, it would free up Tamara and Shelly in the process. A win-win for Team Kickass.

An hour later they arrived back at the rendezvous spot outside the asteroid field.

"I smell traces of battle," Ara said. "A success, I assume?"

"It looks that way."

Shelly and Tamara's little fighter approached, flying low over the edge of the asteroid field, then docked aboard the command ship.

"Hey, what did you guys do?" Tamara asked as they reached the command center. "The ships on our tail abruptly peeled off in a hurry."

Skohla grinned broadly. "We sent them off to chase their own tails for a while."

"A decoy ship?" Shelly asked.

"Yep."

Tamara and Shelly shared a look and burst out laughing. "Oh, that's priceless. All of those big bad warships expending all that effort for nothing."

"And hopefully keeping them out of our hair for a while," Hunze added.

Shelly nodded. "You think it'll work?"

"I hope so," Hunze replied. "I suppose we will find out soon enough. Let us hope the others have been successful in their quest."

CHAPTER THIRTY-ONE

Yellow stripes adorned the stone and metal walls identifying the section of the massive asteroid ship they were currently located in. There wasn't a convenient key anywhere like in malls of the old days, Charlie noted, meaning from the time they landed Kip in the spacious yellow sector hangar until the time they met with Vixx himself, they were denied any idea of exactly how expansive this ship actually was.

The asteroid was huge, that much was clear, its craggy mass easily housing just about anything Vixx had seen fit to build within it. Frankly, Charlie thought, even not knowing all of the ins and outs, it was marvelous. A magnificent feat of engineering that appealed to his technical side.

Vixx himself, a deep-green, scaled being with a short vestigial tail protruding from his clothing, turned out to be quite the opposite of the gruff persona they had encountered on their way in.

"Oh, that was Ming," their host said with an almost manic laugh. "He's quite sweet, actually, but his demeanor helps deter the few who might be foolish enough to get this far without an invitation."

"He did have an intimidating presence," Nakk agree.

"I know, isn't it marvelous?" Vixx gushed. "And that voice! Oh, he could shatter rocks with it. Figuratively, of course. I wouldn't want to go breaking holes in my ship, now would I?"

He burst into laughter again. One thing was certain about their host; he was as flamboyant as he was powerful, and this led to a rather off-kilter footing for their trading session.

It was one thing to be social and jolly when greeting new trading partners, but when it came down to striking a deal, a cold, hard edge shone through his bubbly demeanor. It almost reminded Charlie of Bawb and his Binsala character. The drunken trader made friends wherever he went, and his jolly persona never made any enemies. But Binsala was a finely crafted act, while Vixx did not seem to be putting on airs.

In any case, when it came to trade, he was clearly out to make the best deal he could.

As guests in his realm, if you could call it that, Charlie and his friends had made good on their offer and presented him with the free bottle of alcohol up front, as promised. It seemed that Vixx was something of a lush in addition to being a purveyor of rare and often very illicit items, and the temptation of an entirely new variety of drink was too much temptation to pass up on.

The liquor was one of Charlie's favorites, a twelve-year-old whiskey of the Irish variety. Once upon a time such a bottle would have cost a small fortune back on Earth, but with the invention of food replicators everyone could afford the finest. He was just glad Kip's systems had the data he needed to make them.

Vixx sampled it while his men helped Charlie and company unload the trade they had brought him. Charlie and Bawb shared a knowing look as the muscular helpers moved crates onto a small, floating conveyance to take to the meeting room for a proper haggle session. These were laborers, yes, but not ordinary ones.

Their muscles were clearly built from years of combat training rather than static lifting. And the scars some of them bore spoke further to their use of their skills as a security force. They were not here for show. They were here to protect Vixx's interests. And with wealth like he possessed, he had clearly hired the best.

"This is incredible!" Vixx gushed as he sipped his sample glass. "And you say you brought more?"

"A few cases," Charlie replied. "We also have several other varieties for you to try, as well as a wide assortment of foods from my galaxy."

"Marvelous! You will have to tell me how you came by such rarities."

"If trading goes well," Bawb said with a cool smile.

Vixx found his directness endearing. "And what of this technology you spoke of? Also from another galaxy?"

"In those cases," Charlie said, pointing to the tall stack of things they had gathered that they could spare without concern. "And I guarantee you, they are nothing you have ever seen before. No one in this galaxy has. You will be the first."

The trader was absolutely beaming with delight. He poured himself another glass of whiskey, this time a far healthier portion, and downed it in a single gulp.

"You have impressed me," he said. "And let me tell you, that is not easy to do. People who come to trade with Vixx only bring the best, and yet, you have somehow outdone them."

Charlie took that as a very good sign. "Well, with what we are asking for, we thought it would be best to avoid all of the pussyfooting around and just break out the good stuff straightaway to show you we're serious and worth doing business with."

"Clearly, you are!" he exclaimed, pouring himself another drink. "This has a most wonderful, smooth burn to it. If the other items are even half as good, I think this will be a mutually beneficial trade indeed." He downed it in a single gulp. "Aaah! Delightful!"

Charlie was both impressed and mildly horrified by the man's appetites. "You might want to be more care—"

"Enjoy!" Bawb cut him off. "We have plenty more where that came from!"

"I shall! Now, come, let's head to the trading room so we can properly inspect your wares. Follow my men. I will be along shortly," he said. "Oh, and do make sure to stay within the yellow zone. We wouldn't want you getting lost."

With that, Vixx sauntered off, bottle in hand.

"Well, then. Let us head to the trading room," Bawb said, putting his arm around Charlie's shoulder. "Let him drink," he whispered through his smile. "Inebriated traders are the best sort." His attention shifted to the large men guiding their merchandise to the trading room. "Please, Gentlemen, lead the way!"

Dukaan stayed with Kip, ready to fight or flee should the need arise, while the others followed Vixx's goons. It was a short walk to the spacious and well-lit chamber. Long tables with what appeared to be embedded scanning tech of some sort stretched nearly from wall to wall. It was almost unnoticeable, but when the muscle began placing items on the tables they seemed to glitch, causing a temporary flash of color change.

Clearly, they were designed to weed out forgeries and fakes, which, in this line of work, made perfect sense. But in the case of items not yet cataloged, and from another galaxy no less, they had no frame of reference whatsoever.

Vixx left them alone to prepare their wares for nearly an hour before strolling back to his new guests. They'd been ready almost immediately, and it was a sure thing this room was being monitored, so Charlie's best bet was that Vixx was carrying out multiple trades at once. In an asteroid this big, who knew what other deals might be mid-negotiation?

"So," their host said, leaning on the nearest table, a little wobbly, "what do you come seeking?"

Charlie looked at his companions. It seemed very much like Vixx had actually imbibed the entire bottle. In an hour. If so, it was a miracle he was still standing. But then, he didn't know much about his race's disposition toward alcohol or if they perhaps metabolized it faster than other species.

Nakk stepped forward for this part, being the one familiar with the rare item they needed.

"We need something of a specialty item," he said. "Actually, we need as many of them as you can provide."

"Ooh, a quantity deal. Color me intrigued," Vixx said with a grin. "But what kind of special thing are you talking about? I have a lot of rare and—"

"We need Urvalin kill switch disablers."

Vixx's smile faltered, but only for a moment. His body language, however, remained more stiff than before. "Urvalin kill switches are tricky work. Only a handful of people know how to disarm them. And even fewer possess the skills needed to construct these devices."

Nakk nodded, never breaking eye contact. "We are aware. And that's why we came to you."

Vixx sized up his guests with new curiosity. "You do realize how difficult those are to come by, yes? To find the parts to fabricate them is hard in and of itself. It requires components from Urvalin ships, and not the easy-to-find stuff."

"Yes, and we have brought several cargo pods of stripped Urvalin command center tech we think may help."

Vixx stroked his hairless chin, looking over the tables of rare treats from another realm. Finally, he made a decision.

"I'm not saying I know someone who can make them for you, but if I did, you must be aware just how labor intensive it would be. To overcome both Urvalin Allpower and tech in one small device? It's a big ask."

"And that is why we came to you," Bawb interjected. "When we arrived in your galaxy, we were amazed by the technology and Allpower your worlds possess. But even as impressive as that was, Nakk has told us many times of the man who can accomplish the impossible. Who is arguably the most well-connected trader in the galaxy. *That*, Vixx, is why we sought you out. We required the absolute best at what they do, and you are clearly it."

Charlie refrained from rolling his eyes no matter how thick Bawb laid it on. He was a Ghalian master and had decades of experience reading and manipulating those around him. He just hoped this man was as susceptible as the rest.

"Well, when you put it like that," Vixx said, a broad smile spreading across his face. "I will do it."

"Excellent."

"*But*, my price is *all* of the delights you have brought with you today." He watched the visitors carefully, perhaps a bit more sober than he had initially appeared.

Charlie, Bawb, and Nakk looked at one another. They already knew they were going to give him all the otherworldly treats he wanted. Food fabricators didn't exist in this realm, and Vixx had no idea how trivial a thing it was to generate the wealth of novelties spread on the table before him.

"That's a lot," Bawb said to Charlie, on cue.

Charlie nodded slowly. "Yeah, but we know he'll do it right. He is the best, after all. Nakk, what do you think?"

Nakk hesitated as if in deep thought, even going so far as to pretend to count the items they had laid out, calculating their value on his fingers. "The price is steep," he agreed, "but none have the skill or reputation of Vixx. I say we agree to his terms." He turned back to their host and gave a nod. "Very well. All of it."

Vixx had expected a bit more pushback, apparently, and he was delighted to have scored so much so easily. "Very good," he said, not entirely successful at hiding his glee. "Now, how many did you say you needed?"

Nakk handed him a small tablet. "The numbers and details on each ship are on this."

Vixx took the device and scanned over it. "That's a lot," he said. "And it will take some time. But my team are up for the task."

"Wonderful," Bawb said.

"In the meantime, please, allow me to offer my hospitality. You are my honored guests. Make yourselves comfortable. There are dining chambers just down this corridor. My staff will prepare whatever you wish. And the other direction just past the intersection is a relaxation suite should you wish to utilize it."

Bawb gave a little bow. "Thank you, Vixx. We are most grateful."

"It is entirely my pleasure. But please, do not wander. My ship is a big place and easy to get lost in. And do not cross into the blue section where the corridors converge. That is not for you."

"Understood."

Vixx waved to his men, who promptly packed up all of the marvelous trade items and hauled them away, leaving the men to themselves.

"Dukaan, you read?" Charlie asked over their comms.

"I'm here. How is it going?"

"Good so far, but it could be a while. They've offered to feed us. You want me to send you a take-out bag?"

Dukaan laughed. "I'm fine here, thanks. I'll be standing by."

He didn't add the words *just in case* but Charlie knew that's what he meant. He hoped nothing would go wrong, for once. But with their luck, anything was possible.

CHAPTER THIRTY-TWO

Vixx's hospitality was as extreme as his personality. When he said his people would provide his guests with whatever they might want in the way of food or entertainment, he hadn't been kidding.

Nakk was familiar with the delicacies of this galaxy, but for Charlie and Bawb everything was still a novelty, and as a result, Nakk took great pleasure in ordering them an assortment of the most amazing foods, the availability of which even he found impressive.

They ate slowly, careful not to overfill their bellies to the point of discomfort as well as give themselves ample room to sample as many of the items spread before them as possible. Bawb showed more restraint, but that was just who he was. Charlie, however, couldn't help but dig in.

"I am so bringing a to-go container back for the others," he said as he polished off a plate of Kitzin fritters. "This stuff is delicious."

"Admittedly, the cuisine *is* far better than I had expected," Bawb agreed.

Nakk had taken a break from the culinary part of their

hiatus and had headed into the adjoining gaming chamber. "Hey, you should see this," he called out to his friends.

Charlie and Bawb wiped their hands and pushed back from the table.

"Ooh, I may have overdone it a little," Charlie said as he stood.

Bawb grinned, amused. "I warned you about overindulging."

"Yeah, but it was so good."

He raised a brow but let it go. He'd known Charlie long enough by now to know his weaknesses, and good food was certainly one of them.

They stepped into the gaming room to find Nakk on a platform, waving his arms and running in place.

"What's he doing?" Charlie asked.

"I have no idea," Bawb replied.

"Guys, you have to try this," Nakk called out.

Charlie was more than a little confused. "Try what?"

"Come up here and you'll see."

Charlie looked at Bawb and shrugged, then stepped up onto the platform. Immediately, he was surrounded by an immersive, life-like simulation. One set on a tropical jungle planet by the looks of it. Animals scurried by, looking at them then hurrying along. Large, tempting fruits hung from vines within arm's reach. Charlie raised up his hand to pick one.

"Don't," Nakk said. "I learned the hard way. They're poisonous."

"But they're not real."

"I know, but unless you want to lose a life, you should avoid them."

Charlie stepped down from the platform. Nothing. Not the slightest trace of the game. He stepped back up and was again right in the middle of the adventure.

"This is wild," he said. "No headsets required, no visible projectors."

"It's run by Allpower," Nakk said. "I'd heard of these, but I've never seen one in person. Only the most wealthy can afford this kind of casting."

"Well, Vixx most certainly seems to fit that bill," Charlie noted. "I tell ya, this would be really cool if they could broaden the scale, ya know? Like, make it hangar sized so you could really move in it."

"I suppose, but it's wonderful as it is," Nakk said. "A seamless artificial reality. Incredible."

Charlie popped out of the game and off the platform. "I suppose it is, but I think I ate a little too much to be running around right now."

Bawb cocked his head and strode out of the gaming chamber. Charlie knew better than to question him and followed at once.

"There you are!" Vixx said as his men placed a small crate on the table. He seemed even more inebriated than before. Clearly, he had been sampling the wares in the other crates. "Have you been well taken care of?"

Charlie smiled wide. "Oh, yes. And thank you for the food. It was delicious."

"I could say the same for the delights you have brought to me. But I didn't come to talk about food. I wanted to show you the progress we've made."

Vixx opened the crate, revealing a few dozen surprisingly small devices made of metal and what looked like grown crystal of some sort, the two melded into a single unit.

"The crystal is imbued with the Allpower necessary to drive the mechanism, you see. And the main unit itself acts as a linkage to the ship itself."

"*These* are the kill switch disablers? They're so tiny."

"Sometimes, despite what you may have heard, size does not matter," Vixx said with a wink. "Marvelous craftsmanship, if I do say so myself. Which, of course, I do. Anyway, what was I saying?"

"Uh, the crystals and the mechanism?" Charlie suggested.

"Oh, yes, right. So, the two work in conjunction to overpower the kill switches, blocking them on both a technological as well as an Allpower level. But that's not all."

"It isn't?" Charlie asked.

"No. It's even better. You see, my technician has made an improvement to the design. *These* units overlap their power moderation when in use. It makes them even more potent and also negates the possibility of a secondary kill system overwhelming the devices."

"Truly a marvelous design," Bawb said appreciatively. "And is this all of them?"

"What? Oh, no. That's about half of them. He's still working on the rest, but these came out so well I wanted to show them to you."

"You are even more impressive than your reputation," Bawb said, laying it on a bit thick, which the drunk man seemed more than happy to accept.

"You're too kind."

"But what I say is true. You have also been a magnificent host."

"Well, they say Vixx knows how to show *anyone* a good time," he said with a drunken laugh. "Now, if you'll excuse me, I must see to my other guests."

He motioned for his goons to come along and headed out, leaving the visitors and their crate of devices behind. Charlie picked up the container.

"Surprisingly light," he said. "These guys really know how to pack a lot of punch into a small device."

"Sometimes that is all it takes," Bawb noted.

Charlie looked at the stone and metal of the ship itself and couldn't help but marvel at the feat. It was something his engineer brain could study for weeks and never get tired of. He pulled out a small pocket scanner and took a few readings of the walls.

"What are you doing? Do not upset our host," Bawb urged.

"Don't worry, it's set to passive. No active signals being sent out. I just wanted to get a reading of—oh, cool."

Bawb shook his head as Charlie wandered off into the corridor, eyes glued to the device.

"Did I hear the devices were ready?" Nakk asked.

"Half of them," Bawb replied.

"Oh. Where did Charlie go?"

"He's being Charlie," Bawb replied, knowing that could be either a good or bad thing, depending on the day.

As far as Charlie was concerned, it was a very good day. There was so much amazing design work to study, he really didn't mind if it took Vixx's people a bit longer to finish their work. That just meant more time to explore and take notes.

Unfortunately, he became so engrossed in his readouts that he hadn't noticed he had passed into the blue corridor Vixx had cautioned against. But no alarms had sounded, no warnings shouted out. It seemed it was just a suggestion from the ship's captain.

"Ah, what's the harm? It's just a little peek," Charlie said as he continued farther into the blue section.

This part of the ship appeared to connect to another set of corridors. Blue met red not far ahead. Charlie figured that yeah, maybe this was a good time to turn back when he heard voices. Curiosity got the better of him, and he turned for the open door just ahead.

"I wonder what other visitors Vixx has—" he wondered as

he poked his head around the opening. He felt his stomach drop as he realized whom the voices belonged to.

Sitting at a table, eating a substantial meal, much as he and his friends had done, were a dozen Urvalin. Officers and their aides by the look of them. And there were guards as well.

"What are you doing here?" a guard shouted, taking aim at the intruder.

Charlie cast a stun spell on instinct, slamming the man into the wall and rendering him unconscious. Apparently, his magic worked just fine here. The only problem was he'd just kicked the hornet's nest.

"Guys, get to the ship! We've been double-crossed!" he shouted over comms as he raced down the corridor.

"What do you mean, double-crossed?" Nakk transmitted back. "Where are you?"

"Just grab the crate and run! Vixx is working with Urvalin!"

Nakk felt his stomach clench. Bawb had already snatched up the crate and moved to the door, ready to drop any who might stand in his way. Lucky for them, no one had come. Not yet, anyway.

"We must go," the assassin said. "*Now.*"

"But Charlie—"

"Will meet us at the ship. Now, move!"

Charlie was trying to do exactly that, casting spell after spell behind him as he ran down the corridors. He was getting turned around in this place, just as Vixx had warned, and the blue section appeared to have many more corridors than yellow. He raced ahead, looking for a familiar landmark.

"Dammit, where is it? Where's the damn yellow section?"

Allpower blasts hit the wall beside him, and small arms fire bounced off his defensive spell. Going straight made him an easy target. Charlie had no choice but to pick a corridor and run. He turned right and headed off at full speed. As luck would have it, up ahead the color changed. And it changed to yellow.

Meanwhile, Bawb and Nakk were rushing down the corridor toward the hangar where their friends were waiting.

"Kip, Dukaan, prepare for immediate dust off," Bawb transmitted.

"Is there a problem?" Dukaan replied.

"Most definitely. Urvalin."

"Oh, shit."

"Exactly. Have Kip ready to fly."

"On it."

He and Nakk rounded a corner and nearly ran right into Vixx and five of his burly protectors. This time, they were not here to carry cargo.

The two nearest Bawb lunged at him simultaneously, some sort of barbed brass knuckle thing wrapped around their meaty hands. The Ghalian bent aside in a way that should not have been possible, planting a solid kick on one's knee, dropping him with a sickening crack, while driving a hidden dagger up into the other's elbow, rendering his arm useless. A chop to the throat left him grasping his neck with the functional hand.

The three others moved in unison, encircling him and attacking at once. They were not using spells or guns. Not in these walls. Not where an errant shot might accidentally hit their patron. But they were all muscle, and no one had ever dreamed of overcoming them.

Until today.

Bawb ran to the side and jumped up on the wall, his legs pushing off hard as he flew over the two closest to him. He delivered an incapacitating blow to one as he passed, the man falling to the ground unconscious. The other spun, ready to take on the troublesome visitor, but Bawb was already moving, his fists rabbit punching into what he hoped were key nerve points.

With different species one never could be certain, but the morphology of the goons was similar enough to a few he was familiar with to make it worth a try. And succeed he did. The man fell in a heap, his limbs rendered immobilized, at least for the time being.

That left but one guard. Bawb turned toward him when a loud thud sounded. Nakk had smashed the butt of his knife into the man's head. It only staggered him, though, so he repeated the process a few times.

Thud. Thud. Thud.

Finally, the goon fell.

Bawb was on Vixx in a flash, his fangs sliding into place as he drew the man close.

"What is the meaning of this double-cross?"

"What double-cross?"

"The Urvalin. They are here, aboard your ship. Charlie encountered them and is now running for his life."

"I don't take sides," Vixx protested. "Business is business. We were just doing a transaction. And I told your friend not to venture into the blue sector."

Bawb had heard enough. He silenced the man with a non-lethal blow and lowered him to the ground.

"This has turned into a mess," he said. "Come, Nakk. We must hurry."

CHAPTER THIRTY-THREE

Charlie had managed to tangle up the pursuing Urvalin with a spell he hadn't wanted to cast. It was a violent blast, and that sort of thing was a huge no-no aboard any ship. Normally, one wrong spell and you could inadvertently blow a hole through the hull, and that meant a very quick trip from the inside to the outside for anyone nearby, including the caster.

But this ship was an asteroid, and a huge one at that. Adding in all of the metal woven throughout the rock, and Charlie felt confident enough the spell wouldn't pose a problem. At least, he hoped that was the case.

The rocks crumbled where the magic flew true, dumping a fair amount of debris into the corridor. It wouldn't take the Urvalin long to shift the rubble and continue their pursuit, but this gave Charlie some desperately needed breathing room.

He turned and sprinted as hard as he could, rounding the corner to the last stretch leading to the hangar in a hurry.

His feet caught on the nearest of Vixx's fallen guards and he went hurling headfirst, tumbling to the ground. Fortunately, years of training had honed his reflexes, and he managed to extend his arm and perform a very hastily improvised diving roll. It was ugly, but the impact spread across his arm and torso rather than his head, and he wound up back on his feet in a flash.

He turned and looked at the pile of men. They were still breathing, he noted. Vixx was there too, a bloody bump on his head. It was looking like his friends had a little encounter as well.

"Charlie! Come on!" Nakk shouted from Kip's open door.

Charlie heard the call and looked across the hangar. The others had made it to the ship. That meant he was the last man standing, and he had no intention of sticking around a moment longer than he had to.

Charlie took off at a run, crossing the hangar and diving into the ship just as Dukaan powered up the shields. It wasn't a moment too late as the pursuing Urvalin opened fire, not concerned one bit about errant shots in the heavily reinforced hangar space.

The hangar door was opening. Kip had hacked their system enough to at least manage that. There was still a force field keeping the air in, but with all of their power focused ahead, he should have no problem making it through.

"Punch it, Dukaan!" Charlie bellowed, barely making it into a seat and slapping on a restraint belt before the ship spun and burst out into the asteroid field.

Kip immediately shifted all of his shielding to the rear for the inevitable weapons fire from Vixx's people, but nothing came.

"What the hell?" Charlie wondered. "Are they just letting us go?"

Bawb smiled. "No. But we were granted free passage by Vixx, and until he rescinds it, his underlings do not dare counteract it. Even in this instance. And since their employer is currently quite unconscious—"

"Nicely done, Bob," Charlie said, slapping him on the shoulder. "Have I told you I love you? Because I love you, man."

"The sentiment is appreciated, and returned, my friend, but we need to focus on what lies ahead."

"More rocks, I assume."

"That, and Urvalin fighters. There are multiple hangars on that ship, and if there was an Urvalin delegation there, we are bound to be—"

The ship shook as a blast impacted the shields.

"Kip?" Charlie called out.

"Shields are holding. Sons of bitches got in a lucky shot. Hang on, me and Dookie've got this."

With that, the AI attack ship abruptly dove to the side, spiraling between asteroids in a stomach-wrenching maneuver. When he was able to see straight again, Charlie counted four Urvalin ships behind them.

"We've got company, all right."

"Little ones," Dukaan said. "They are just as hamstrung as we are in this space. Small ships only."

"Can we shake them?"

"Hopefully. But we won't be able to warp. There is too much debris, and we wouldn't get a clear shot out."

Charlie's jaw flexed, and he felt for his magic. "Then it looks like we're going to have to do this the hard way."

Kip zigged and zagged, opening up with his railgun periodically, firing where he calculated the nearest Urvalin ship would have to be in order to dodge the asteroid tumbling toward it. The first volley missed, as did the second. But the third flew true.

"Got one!" Kip exclaimed.

"Great. Only three more to go," Dukaan said.

"Yeah, *only*," Charlie replied. "Bawb, can you use your wand?"

"No. The metal content of these asteroids appears to react strongly to Allpower. There is no telling what they might do if an errant blast from my wand hit them."

"So, it's back to basics," Charlie said, adding his defensive spells on top of Kip's shielding. "Dukaan, can you lock onto one of those rocks with the pulse cannons?"

"Easily enough, but why?"

"The metal content," he replied. "What Bob pointed out. But if these things are full of metal, a significant enough blast just might turn one into shrapnel. Or, more accurately, a floating field of chaff."

"Nice idea." Dukaan lifted one of his arms and gave a thumbs-up. A benefit of having four, he could still operate the ship while having one or two to spare.

It was beginning to be a nauseating ride, this moving slalom through the ever-shifting asteroids. But Kip was an ace about mapping their trajectories, and that gave them an edge over their flesh-and-blood Urvalin pursuers.

Dukaan powered up the pulse cannons to maximum and stood by. "Kip, let me know which one in their path has the highest content of metal."

"Will do, Dookie," the ship replied.

Dukaan had long given up attempting to get the ship to stop calling him that. He just sighed and kept his fingers on the triggers. The ship rocked as another shot glanced off their shields.

"Anytime now, Kip," he said.

"Hang on, there's a good one coming up. I'm adjusting course to bring it between us and them. Stand by."

"I've been standing by."

"Okay, target is on your screen."

"I see it. Firing."

Dukaan let loose a double blast from the pulse cannons at

full power. The shots flew true, striking the asteroid and shattering it. More than that, the temporary heat from the energy melted bits of metal into deadly projectiles, just as they'd hoped.

The Urvalin ships flew right into the debris, the first two ships faltering and spinning out of control as their cabins were penetrated by the unlikely attack. Their shields had been calibrated for pulse weapons and Allpower as well as supersonic projectiles. Solid shards of metal floating inert in their path were not on the agenda.

"One left," Dukaan announced.

"We're almost out of the field," Kip added. "We'll lose our advantage in clear space, so if you've got an idea, now's the time."

Dukaan did, and it was a good one.

"They are adapting to our strategies."

"Clearly," the ship replied.

"On my signal, dump the water and waste tanks directly behind us."

"But why—"

"Then drop behind an asteroid and allow them to pass."

"Oh, I see," Kip said. "You got it."

He slowed his pace a little, letting the enemy get right behind him. The ship shook from the impacts, but the shields held. It was a lucky thing this was a small fighter. Anything larger and their goose would have been cooked.

"Get ready to brace," Kip said. "Here we go!"

He dumped the tanks and shifted course. The water, as well as a few floaters that hadn't been processed yet by the waste system, hit the Urvalin shields harmlessly, as expected. But when they did, they froze into a sheet of mucky ice.

The pilot's view was obstructed, and there was just one thing to do. He dropped his shields a moment to power through the ice and continue his pursuit. Only when he did, there was no ship to be seen. The Urvalin only had a split second to realize he'd been tricked before the pulse cannons tore his ship apart from behind.

"Yes! That's what I'm talking about! Good work," Charlie shouted with glee.

Nakk gave two thumbs-up, as he had learned was a good thing where his friends came from. "Yes, that was—"

The ship rocked hard as weapons fire hit them broadside just as they exited the asteroid field.

"Urvalin warship!" Kip announced.

"*Ara, where are you?*" Charlie called out over their magical link.

"*Waiting for you to provide a distraction,*" she said, flying right toward the much larger ship. "*Thank you.*"

She sprayed their shields with magical fire, the intensity forcing the Urvalin to split their attention between both adversaries. The ship was a big one, and tough. And after all they'd just been through, it was a fight neither Kip nor Dukaan were looking forward too. Fortunately, they were in clear space now, and that meant one thing.

Charlie smiled at Bawb and nodded. "Break out that bad boy, Bob. It's time to see what it can do."

Bawb drew his wand from its protective case and carefully touched its power. It was ready, but what it would do, exactly, was anyone's guess.

"Ara, Bob's gonna cast," Charlie announced over comms so everyone could hear. "You'll want to get clear. There's no telling what this spell will do. It might disable the ship, or it might make everyone's bones explode."

"That is horrifying," Nakk said.

"Just saying, we don't want any friendlies near that thing."

"I'll be clear in a moment," she replied, quickly pulling away from the ship.

Charlie looked at Bawb. "Okay, dude, it's your call."

Bawb chose a strong stun spell. One that should, in theory, penetrate the Urvalin shielding and knock their casters and crew unconscious. If so, they would have claimed yet another powerful craft as their own.

"*Oomanus dilepsi gomanna!*" he muttered, drawing a massive charge into the wand and directing it out of their ship and into the Urvalin vessel.

He felt the power rip out of the wand and across space, but beyond that he didn't know what it had done.

"Did it work?" Nakk asked.

"I do not know. Kip?"

"The ship is still powered up, but they've stopped firing. They're drifting. They look like they're dead in the water. I think your spell worked, Bawb."

Kip changed course, making a loop around the much larger craft. No weapons tracked his progress, and no smaller ships were launched. It appeared they'd actually done it.

A flash of light caught Charlie's attention as a large ship jumped near their position. He could sense its weapons powering up, ready to open fire.

"Oh, shit. It's Skohla. Tell her to stand down!" he shouted.

"Skohla, this is Nakk. Hold your fire! Hold your fire!"

He was a moment too late, and a pulse blast rocketed toward the Urvalin ship. Kip made a decision and accelerated, putting himself between the ship and the blast.

"What are you doing?" Dukaan shouted.

"We've got full shields. We can take it. That thing's got none right now," he replied as the impact hit. He shook and rattled, but with Charlie's quickly cast help, their shields held.

"Let's not do that again, okay?" Charlie said.

"What the hell is going on?" Tamara yelled over comms. "Why did you block our shot?"

"The ship is ours, Tamara. Bawb knocked their crew out."

A long pause hung in the air. "Oh," she finally said. "Well, then. Shit. Sorry. Uh, I guess Shelly and me should head over there and secure the crew."

"Sounds like a good idea," he replied. Charlie turned to Bawb and let out a sigh. "Man, it's been one of those days."

Five minutes later Tamara called them back from inside the Urvalin ship. "Uh, guys?"

"Yeah, what is it?" Charlie asked.

"What the hell did you do?"

"What do you mean? Bawb stunned them."

"Uh, no, he didn't. There's nothing here but piles of meat. The entire crew by the looks of it."

"I'm sorry, what?" Charlie said.

"Yeah. Looks like their bones just exploded or something."

Charlie glanced over at his friend. Bawb just shrugged. "I told you it was unpredictable."

Charlie keyed his comms open. "Yeah, sorry about that. Our bad. Hey, listen, we're going to have Nakk bring over one of the kill switch blockers so one of his crew can fly that thing to the rally point."

"So it was a success?"

"Of sorts. We'll tell you about it at dinner."

"After seeing this," Tamara said, "I don't know that I want any."

Ara had been drifting close by, keeping a wary eye out for any further threats. None had appeared, but something else caught her attention. She sniffed again.

"I have a trace of Arlo's scent," she said. "Hurry with what you are doing, the trail is hot once again."

CHAPTER THIRTY-FOUR

Rika, Marban, and Malalia departed from Dark Side base not too long after the girls had, but with a different objective in mind. The unlikely trio was going to utilize this window while the Urvalin were regrouping to take a better look at the dampening microsats up close, without the annoyance of pesky weapons fire interrupting them.

The technology was new to them, but the concept of demolition was not. If they could find a way to take out the dampening array over the base, even if just a limited quantity of them, the results might then be reproduced on a much larger scale with the array surrounding Earth.

But first things first. First, they needed to find a way to break Joshua and his small fleet of upgraded ships free from the constraints trapping them in the small area surrounding the base.

"How long until they come back to bother us again?" Marban asked as the *Coratta* and Rika's mech flew up toward the hard ceiling above the base.

"I have a feeling not long at all," Rika said, noting the swarm of smaller ships they hadn't noticed when the larger ones pulled back. "Looks like they left behind some expendables."

"Enough to hinder Joshua and his ships all the same, though," Marban noted. "Clever tactics. Annoying, and a total disregard for the lives of their pilots, but effective."

"Yes," Malalia said from her seat beside him in the *Coratta*. "The Urvalin have an impressively efficient fighting methodology. Provided, of course, they have the fodder to throw at their enemy in great enough quantities to support the losses. From what we have seen so far, they do."

"Seems so," Marban said, still a bit unsettled at having Malalia aboard his ship without Rika nearby to keep her in check. But when they departed Dark Side, the caster had opted to support Marban and his ship instead of Rika and her mech. *She* needed no magical help, that much was abundantly clear.

"Well, it looks like we're going to be a bit restricted in our tests," Rika said. She switched her comms to wide band. "Hey, Joshua. Can you guys give us some support from below? We've got a bunch of Urvalin fighters up here and need them distracted so we can get close enough to the array to get a better look."

"With pleasure," he replied. "Teams one through four, take up positions delta and omega. Aim up and put some pressure on the enemy."

Two small groups of ships shifted position and took aim at the sky, then began firing periodic blasts upward, keeping the Urvalin occupied avoiding the shots. It wasn't hard for them, but that wasn't the point. They just had to have their focus shifted long enough for Rika and her friends to accomplish their goal.

Several fighters dove in to engage anyway, quickly repositioning themselves in line with Rika and Marban so their ships could not fire at them without risking hitting the pirate ship and mech. The maneuver quickly devolved into a dogfight as soon as the Urvalin grew close.

Rika opened up with her magic as she was too close to the hard ceiling to safely keep the mech operating on regular power. Fortunately, in space it was so much easier as she didn't have gravity to fight against.

Marban let loose with his own magical weapons as well, while Malalia did her best to get a feel for the Urvalin devices that somehow negated technology if they came too close. It was not her area of expertise, but she was willing to do her best. In times of war, she had often said, you do what is required, not what is desired. This situation, it seemed, fit the bill.

Joshua and his fleet continued to lay down a suppressing barrage around the area their comrades were operating in, but it wasn't doing enough. The Urvalin had shifted position quicker than anticipated, greatly reducing the operation's effectiveness.

"Oh, screw this," Rika grumbled. "Marban, I'm gonna pop out of the dampening field and give these guys something to think about on their own turf."

"I'll accompany," he said. "Malalia's informed me she's got enough of a lock on one of the units to keep working on it even if we move a bit."

"Great. Then let's go give them a little surprise."

The two craft shifted course and powered straight up, exiting the dampening array with ease. *That* was not something the fighters were expecting. They had been expecting to fight a hamstrung opponent. This, however, was something far different.

"That's right," Rika laughed as she powered up her mech to full capacity. "Eat hot death!"

Her pulse cannons blasted out a spread of shots, damaging a few ships and forcing several more to rapidly pull back and regroup. Marban had also activated the tech weapons on his ship, the additions Cal had given him getting a full workout against the Urvalin foe.

Malalia struggled to maintain her grasp on the one microsat she had sequestered from the others. She even used her magic to pull it with them a bit as they flew. Interestingly, the others appeared to shift as she did, closing the tiny gap in the dampening field that she had nearly made.

"You see that?" Marban asked.

"Yes," she replied. "It seems to be a self-healing system. Disrupt one and others adjust to take up the slack."

"This is not good."

"No," she said, straining to maintain her hold on the device. "But I think I have an idea."

"Rika," Marban transmitted, "Malalia wants to try something."

"Great," she said. "Anything will help."

"I'm not so sure," the caster replied. "It will require a fair amount of magic, and I worry it is a bit risky. If something goes wrong, we are rather close to the base. Even the far edges are close enough there could be some unintended consequences."

Rika thought on it a moment as she lit up another Urvalin ship. "Okay, this isn't going anywhere anyway. Let's pull away and head out to the nearest dead zone minefield area. The only friendly ships there are long dead."

"Very well," she said. "I will prepare. Notify me when we are in position."

"You got it," Marban replied. "Rika, you ready to peel off?"

"Ready. Joshua, we're heading away from the moon to test something out."

"Best of luck," the AI replied. "And if I can be of any assistance, do not hesitate to ask. Of course, stuck in this cursed bubble, I really don't know how much I can do for you."

"Just keep doing what you're doing. The Urvalin just got

spanked big time, so you should have some breathing room for at least a little while longer."

"Thanks, Rika. And good luck out there."

With that the *Coratta* and the mech changed course and disengaged from the Urvalin fighters, pulling away at a high rate of speed before settling into a less rushed pace. The Urvalin were not pursuing them, so Rika landed her mech aboard Marban's ship and joined them in the command center.

"Well, that was interesting," she said as she took a seat. "They're persistent bastards, I'll give 'em that. Now, Malalia, what exactly is it you were thinking of doing?"

"These devices are a mixture of both technology and magic. While I am not terribly familiar with the former, I am intimately acquainted with the latter."

"And you think you can disrupt it?" Marban asked. "I mean, this is their own flavor of magic. Allpower is different than our own."

"Yes, but it is worth a try. However, I feel the mechanical portion of the device is designed to compensate for damage to the magical part."

"Only one way to find out," Rika said. "Marban, you wanna power off the tech stuff and go minefield hunting?"

"Great minds think alike," he said, already powering down his electronic additions. "Okay, we're good. Running on magic and ready to go."

"Then take us in."

He directed the *Coratta* to the dampening minefield they had mapped out, courtesy of Cal and the others. It was impossible to see on scans The camouflaged microsats simply blended in with other space debris and did not give off any signal traces that could help them pinpoint their exact locations. It was a visual search of the needle in the haystack variety, but at least they knew where this haystack was, and there were a lot of needles in it.

What Malalia had already learned about the microsats was an eye-opener in and of itself. They could be moved, it seemed, though with some effort. But if they were pulled out of position, the others would recognize the gap and shift their own locations, sending more to take up the slack and close the opening in a much larger shift of resources. It was frustrating, but that aspect of the devices seemed to be based in technology, not Allpower, and at least that was something they could potentially hack and work with.

They carefully circled the area marked as a dampening field, searching for the devices.

"Got one," Marban said a short while later. "Toward the edge, I think. Should let us position ourselves in the clear enough to be relatively safe while Malalia tries whatever it is she has planned."

"Yes," the caster agreed. "This will do just fine."

"Is there anything else you need us to do?" he asked.

"No. Just be ready to move quickly if something does go wrong."

Malalia then closed her eyes and began pulling her power to cast. Rika felt the hairs on the back of her neck stiffen in the presence of such power. She had almost forgotten just how strong Malalia was. It was frightening how she had regained her powers so fully. It seemed that feeding on Urvalin blood had given her an unexpected boost.

She loosed her power in a single burst, all of it directed at the microsat. The device faltered a moment, but it seemed to draw additional energy from the units around it, compensating for her spell. She stopped casting a moment later and slumped in her seat, dejected.

The microsat was unharmed.

"Hey, it's okay," Rika said, patting her shoulder, surprising herself that she was actually comforting Malalia Maktan. "You tried your best."

"And failed," Malalia replied. "I am not accustomed to failure."

Marban, ever jovial even in the most trying of times, chuckled and leaned over, wrapping both women up in a bear hug. "Failure is more common than you think. Welcome to the rest of the galaxy's lives."

CHAPTER THIRTY-FIVE

"I still do not understand why it didn't work," Malalia said, still dwelling on her failure with the dampening array.

"Hey, it happens," Rika said. "You can't win 'em all."

"Yes, it is a lesson I am painfully familiar with."

Rika shrugged. She was the one who had delivered the coup de grace at the end of the war against Visla Dominus, and she was the reason Malalia had wound up banished to a distant planet. But that seemed like a lifetime ago, and there were newer, bigger fish to fry than bad memories.

"Hitting the atmosphere," Marban announced. "We'll be down in ten minutes."

"Thanks, big guy. We'll be ready."

Malalia looked a bit uneasy.

"What is it?"

"You say you wish to connect with some of your elite fighters on Earth. I have a history with them."

"Yeah, tell me about it. But don't sweat it, things are different now."

"I hope you are right. I am sure a great many still wish me dead."

"I'm telling you, don't sweat it. They're friends. You'll be fine."

Ten minutes later the *Coratta* was on the ground outside of the city of Pasadena by the foothills of Southern California. It was here that the team of cyborg super soldiers had asked to meet, away from the main targets in Los Angeles but close enough to still reach them in a hurry if they needed to.

"Hey, Rika," a tall soldier with a ginger crewcut greeted when she and the others stepped off the ship. "Been a while."

"Yeah, it has. Glad to see you're holding up okay."

"As good as can be expected. Cal's been running us ragged, though. But don't tell him I said that."

"Mum's the word," she said with an amused grin. "Jerry, this is Marban."

"I've heard a lot about you. A pleasure."

"And, of course, you know Malalia Maktan."

"Naturally. Thank you for helping us out. This magic stuff has been a bitch to deal with. I mean, guns? Knives? No problem, we'll do that dance all day. But magic? Pain in our collective asses, that is."

"Where's everyone else? Where's George?"

"Sarge and the others were scouting out some reports of Urvalin activity not far from here. Probably nothing, but we have to check out every incident, just in case. They're sneaky bastards."

"That they are," Marban said. "We have plenty of firsthand experience in that regard, let me tell you."

Jerry grinned. "Yeah, I hear ya, brother. Well, come on, it's about a fifteen-minute trek from here. I didn't want you setting down too close to our area of operations, just in case."

Rika nodded her approval. "Good call. Lead the way."

The hike went quickly, the streets, while deserted, were not full of debris or obstacles like one might expect during an alien invasion. In fact, for the most part, it just looked like a quiet day on a quiet street. That is, until weapons fire rang out not far from their position.

"Shit, Sarge says they were ambushed. Urvalin, a lot of them from the sound of it. And he says there are casters."

"Casters, plural?" Rika asked.

"That's what he said."

"Then we need to hurry."

They rushed along, weapons at the ready, eyes scanning every building and every alleyway for potential threats. So far, none reared their heads, but that didn't mean the coast was clear. Marban and Jerry worked as a team, one sweeping left, the other sweeping right. Their schools of tactics may have been slightly different, one being a pirate and the other a cybernetic commando, but the basic principles were the same.

Rika and Malalia were also ready for action, though they were prepared to provide support of the magical variety if it was needed. Shielding from spells was a constant concern where the Allpower wielding aliens were concerned.

"There!" Marban said as they rounded a corner, staying low to avoid drawing attention.

It was George all right, along with Vince and Finn, and two more soldiers. All five were pinned down by the constant barrage of Allpower directed at them. It was fierce, and it wasn't letting up.

"The casters are overlapping their spells," Rika said. "It looks like they deployed all three of their triumvirate to one location."

"A show of overwhelming force, no doubt," Malalia said with a smirk.

Rika looked at her with confusion. "What's so funny?"

"I feel their magic in the air. It is all around us."

"Me too, but that doesn't—"

She looked at Rika, her expression like that of a parent

241

explaining to a child. "They are not terribly strong," she said, standing up tall and walking into the street. "Allow me."

"Malalia!" Rika hissed, but it was too late. The casters saw the lone woman in the street and turned their attention to her.

They launched spell after spell, a non-stop flurry of Allpower heading right for her. Malalia let her magic flow and simply batted their attempts away as though they were no more than a nuisance. She then turned the tables and struck all three down with a single spell, the magic knocking them to the ground.

She then turned her attention to the Urvalin troops. Grunts lacking much power at all. A single word was all it took to fling them into the buildings with great force. They made no effort to get back up.

Malalia walked past the sheltering cyborg and his friends, right to the downed casters, then bent low and sank her extending fangs into their necks. In short order, all three had been drained of their Allpower, and with it, her own magic swelled with renewed potency well beyond what she had expended.

Sergeant Franklin and the others stepped out into the street and surveyed the damage. It was impressive, what she had managed.

"Thanks," George said. "We were in a tough spot. Your help is appreciated."

Malalia turned to face him, self-consciously wiping the blood from her lips. "I'm sorry for my appearance. Please forgive me, I know how horrible it must look."

"Hey, Lady, I've seen a lot of messed-up things over the years, believe me. If that's what you've gotta do to do what you just did, so be it."

The others walked over to join them, impressed at her efficiency.

"Rika, any news?" Vince asked.

"Not much that Cal hasn't already told you," she said. "Dark Side is still blockaded, and we haven't figured out a way to take down their dampening array yet. Aside from that, it's kinda status quo. Meaning things suck. How about you guys? Anything new? I mean, aside from your little hunting expeditions."

"Oh, there's a good one in the works," Finn chimed in. "Tell her, George."

"George? Is there mischief afoot?" she asked.

"Heh. I suppose you could say that. Cal and the others came up with a plan. It's way out of left field, but I think it actually has a good chance of disrupting the Urvalin command structure. Maybe enough for us to shift the tides and take control of their ships."

"How in the world do you plan to do that?"

"Simple," he said. "Remember that Nasturian stuff you and Jo brought back from your adventures?"

Rika flinched at her inert cyborg friend's name but sucked it up. This wasn't the time for mourning. Victors had that luxury, not combatants. "Yeah, I remember it," she said. "Go on."

"Well, Cal thinks we can get it aboard the key Urvalin command ships."

"But how?"

"That's the clever part. The Urvalin have been taking supplies, raiding food depots and the like. Word is, the leadership is growing fond of our food. The spoils of war, and all that jazz. But what if we were to spike a load of food? I'm talking really high-end stuff we let them capture from us. The top-tier stuff that would only be fit for a commander's private larder."

Rika nodded as the plan became clear. "Of course. Then you'd have a potentially immobilizing agent aboard their ship just waiting to take down key personnel."

"Precisely. All we'd need to do is sneak into the fleet and

place the cargo in strategic areas where the leaders would be sure to notice them."

"But how do you propose this?" Malalia asked. "You do not look a thing like Urvalin."

"Easy," the sergeant said. "We'll just skin up Jerry here to look like one."

"*Skin up?*"

"Jerry's a cyborg, like me. Metal endoskeleton covered by a flesh exterior. But the thing is, we don't *need* the flesh to function. It's just to blend in with our comrades."

"And enemies," Jerry added.

"Yeah, and enemies. Well, Cal's been working on a new flesh covering for some time. A type that looks a hell of a lot like Urvalin."

"The joy of being a cyborg," Jerry said with a chuckle. "And of being the tallest on our team."

"Quit bragging," George joked. "We all know it was our designer's doing."

Finn was processing all of the information, but the one thing that stuck out the most was the Nasturian. He'd tried it once, not believing the magically charged spice was as hot as people said it was.

He had spent the next several hours curled up in a ball.

"If the Urvalin are even remotely as sensitive to Nasturian as the rest of us, well, we all know what happens when you eat it."

"Exactly!" Rika exclaimed. "Pain and incapacitation. They'll be suffering so much no one will be able to concentrate enough to cast. And when that happens we'll knock 'em right out of the sky." She turned to George, a big grin on her face. "I gotta admit, though, as much as I like the idea, it's a pretty iffy plan."

"But if it *does* work, we could end this whole mess right quick."

"Can't argue with that," she said. "Is there anything we can do to help?"

George looked at his comrades and the destruction in the street. It had been a lot of work just getting here, and looking at this mess, one did come to mind. "How about a ride," he said. "And if you know any depots, a good selection of fresh food we can use."

Finn perked at that last part. "Oh, food? I can help with that."

CHAPTER THIRTY-SIX

Commander Prin sat in her seat atop her casting podium, examining the strange artifact she had left systems bathed in blood to acquire. Frankly, she was unimpressed.

While the Korna tablet possessed the unusual power they had believed it would, Fraxxis, Torgus, and Prin had been experiencing a very difficult time making it do more than simply connect with their Vikann stones.

It was frustrating, to say the least, and the constant work to improve the connectivity with the tablet had been eating into Prin's fun time. Namely, the further conquest of the galaxy.

Torgus and Fraxxis, on the other hand, were always eager for their scheduled test sessions. When all three were working together, the tablet actually did seem to obey them, at least a bit better. But when she tried on her own, Prin met nothing but failure.

"I do not see why you are so down on the process," Torgus said during their next session together. "We have only had the tablet a short while, and while it is not functioning exactly as we had hoped, it *is* gradually strengthening the link with every use."

"Barely," Prin grumbled. "We are warriors. Conquerors of

worlds. We spend too much time tinkering with this thing we do not yet fully understand."

"And that is how we learn to understand it," Fraxxis pointed out. "Did you truly believe wielding such a powerful relic would be easy? These things take time and effort."

"Yes," she shot back. "Time and effort we could be applying to the ruin of our enemy and those who would support them."

Torgus took a deep breath and refrained from raising his voice at his friend. Prin was the most emotional of the three, and she had always been impatient as well. But she was a strong caster, and she had succeeded in finding the Korna tablet. More than that, though she was not willing to admit it to the others, Prin undoubtedly felt the increased power the Vikann stones were emitting even when the relic was not in use.

It seemed that once the connection had been made, something had triggered within the stones, and that something was now building steadily, growing in power. It was a heady feeling, using the stones, and their abilities had increased. But they were not invulnerable. Not yet. And their enemies were proving most clever. Clever and troublesome.

"What of the Ghalian pests, Prin?" Fraxxis asked. "Have you managed to eliminate them from the equation?"

"No, that will take far more time than we have. Once we have conquered these realms, then we can set about properly disposing of the pockets of holdouts, but for now it would divert too much energy to try."

"But we must prevent them from interfering with our plans."

"And we shall. I have plans underway that should accomplish that goal, stranding them away from support. A trap, if you will."

Torgus liked the sound of that. "A kill box of sorts?"

"Not exactly. But I will leverage my forces to crush the Ghalian leadership, driving them into a corner. They will be difficult to kill, but this will prevent them from interfering in the actual battle once we begin the final phase."

Fraxxis liked the idea, but he still had some doubts. "And their allies? They have connections across the galaxy."

"We will lure them out into the open and eradicate them with malice. Without the Ghalian to support them, their underlings should fall with relative ease."

He saw the possibilities her plan held, and ideas of his own sprang forth. "You can also utilize the casters you have collared so far. Deploy them far and wide to create multiple fronts to deceive the enemy. Confuse them as to our actual target."

"I have already put that plan in motion," she said. "There are a few holdouts who still vex me, but they will be dealt with."

Torgus chuckled. He knew just how much she enjoyed placing the yoke on her prisoners. "I understand some of those captured are particularly powerful," he said. "They will be a great asset to our cause."

"They will be. But because of a lifetime of power, they may also prove difficult to tame. At first, anyway. One way or another, they will do as I command. If they do not, I will do away with them. My patience has worn thin."

Torgus was pleased. "Good. And your favorite new visla pet?"

Prin glanced over at Visla Skirbal. The man had put up a good fight when her casters faced him, but he had been subjugated in the end. He was a man of many connections across the systems, and those were now hers. Now he was as loyal a servant as the Urvalin could ask for.

"Doing as I command, and performing admirably," she said. "And as he was very well known among his kind, he has proven a useful interface with reluctant newcomers." She waved casually at the man. "Skirbal, fetch me the latest conscripts. I would speak with them."

"At once," he replied, resigned to his subservient role. "Come," he said to his servants, both of whom fell in behind him silently, as was expected of them.

Margitt carried a tall cooler of refreshing juice for his master, as one never knew when the visla might become parched. Rovalla bore a small tray with his favorite snacks should he feel hungry while doing the Urvalin's dirty work.

When he was not at work for his masters, his servants would simply keep his quarters tidy, launder his clothing, and run whatever errands he required. It seemed he was having less and less free time of late, but, amazingly, he did not mind nearly as much as he'd thought he would.

It was quite a thing, having as much power within the Urvalin ranks as he did. Even as a defeated visla, he still wielded a significant amount of influence, and that was almost as intoxicating to him as any liquor could be.

Skirbal had of late been privy to a good many of Commander Prin's elaborate plans, and the Urvalin caster had even asked his input and opinion on a few occasions. He had aspired to ascend within the Council of Twenty. But now he was even better off, though under the control of their conquerors. It was better than the alternative, however. Most of the Council, if not all at this point, had been captured, collared, and forced to labor in groups of three, flying far and wide doing the Urvalin's dirty work.

By comparison, he was living a life of absolute luxury.

"Rovalla, I desire a bath. Prepare one for me. I shall return to my chambers when I have done as our gracious host has asked," he said.

"At once, Visla," she replied, her head bowed. Rovalla then hurried back to his chambers to prepare his tub.

Rovalla, or Soria, as she was known among her Ghalian family, had heard more than enough to warrant the risks of making contact with her order. She was the most deeply embedded spy in the entire Ghalian network and her intelligence did not come easy. Getting it out would take effort, and exceptional timing in no small amount. Bribes would quite possibly also come into play, which was always a risky proposition. But her people were in jeopardy.

She began drawing the visla's bath and let her thoughts wander for a moment to the poor vislas aboard the other ships, bound by their collars, forced to perform horrible acts for the Urvalin. And, by the sound of it, the more troublesome ones might very soon find themselves without a head, thanks to the explosives bound to their control collars. It was a fast death. At least they had that working in their favor. But very soon, dissenters in the ranks would be no more.

CHAPTER THIRTY-SEVEN

Nipsenni, Visla Palmarian, and Visla Samanna had been confined to the stench of the commoner cells for some time now, and even the normally good-natured Palmarian was becoming increasingly irritated.

The faint crackles of power that would leak out and spark across his body were beyond his control, but they were normally not an issue. He had learned to contain them for the most part, and when he was truly upset he would simply deploy some magic to drain off the excess.

Here, however, he was collared and restrained, and every surge of transient power activated all three of their collars, delivering a shocking jolt. It served its purpose, keeping them in check, but this wasn't even an escape attempt, and Samanna was starting to get really annoyed because of it.

"Nikora, will you *please* stop doing that," the visla grumbled.

"I am sorry. I just need to let off a little power and this would stop happening."

"Well, so long as our tiny friend there resists the Urvalin," he said, nodding toward the young woman crouched across the cell, huddled close with a filthy woman with mud-caked hair and clothes, "I do not think you will be getting that opportunity anytime soon."

Visla Palmarian let out a pained chuckle. It was such a ridiculous situation for two of the most powerful vislas in the galaxy to be in. Just as amusing was the fact that now that they were both essentially powerless, and with no reason to quarrel and facing a common enemy, the two men found they actually enjoyed one another's company. They weren't friends, but with the plotting and grudges stripped away, they were just two men passing the time talking about life, love, and everything in between.

And just as a friend would do, Samanna had a good laugh when Palmarian griped about his former wife.

"Oh, we all heard about *that*," he said. "To think, Visla Dominus was married to the great Visla Palmarian all that time. Stealing power, building her forces. I have to admit, much as I disliked her as a leader, you could not help but respect her drive."

Palmarian nodded. "Driven she was, but for evil reasons. She drained my daughter. For *years* she took so much of her magic that my poor Karasalia seemed to be a weak and powerless girl."

"Little did you know how much strength she actually had, eh?"

"That is an understatement. When I saw her in battle? Well, no father wants their children to fight, but I could not help but feel such a swell of pride."

"She's going to be impressive when she's fully grown into her power," Samanna agreed. "Perhaps we could introduce her to my youngest son. His own magic is only moderate, but he has much potential."

Palmarian shook his head with a little laugh. "I appreciate the sentiment, but I am fairly certain her interests lie elsewhere. Another galaxy, in fact."

"Ah, I see," Samanna said. "To be young again, eh?"

"Indeed."

Visla Palmarian leaned back and took in their surroundings for the umpteenth time. So many prisoners, but all with only moderate power. The Drooks had all huddled together, as their kind were wont to do. The rest sat wherever there was space. All were unwashed, and the smell was enough to make your eyes water.

His gaze traveled along the despondent prisoners until it fell upon his bonded companion. Nipsenni was still whispering with the mud-caked woman and had been for some time. Why she chose to befriend that one was anyone's guess.

His stomach twinged when he saw that the filthy woman was playing with the control collar around Nipsenni's neck. Visla Samanna saw him tense up and followed his gaze. He did not like what he saw one bit.

"Hey! Be careful with that! You'll get us all shocked," he called out.

"Shut it," Nipsenni barked, not even turning to face him, never losing focus on her new friend.

"I'm telling you to stop."

"Don't tell me what to do."

"Fine. I am *asking* you to please leave your collar alone. I know I speak for both of us when I beg you to please just stop. We are tired of being shocked for your irrational behavior."

"Irrational? Did you call me irrational?"

"Oh, no. Here it comes," Palmarian groaned, waiting for the inevitable shock when she lashed out. But, amazingly, nothing happened, and Nipsenni remained crouched where she was.

The doors to the holding area opened, and a trio of guards walked in. One for each of them, he warranted. It was almost insulting for vislas who had toppled armies, but helpless as they were, that was all that was required.

The guards opened the cell door and stepped inside, each taking position to escort one of the prisoners to the command chamber.

"You'd better think very carefully about what you do next," the one in charge growled. "The captain's had enough of your mischief."

"We wish we could help," Samanna said, "but you see how we're hamstrung."

"I don't care. It's time to perform or die. Now, get on your feet."

The two vislas rose and dusted themselves off. Nothing would remove the stink short of a long, hot bath, but at least they could attempt to look presentable.

"You too," the guard called out to Nipsenni.

She nodded to the muddy woman, squeezed her hands, and rose to her feet. Her eyes were positively sparkling with rage. Rage, and pent-up power begging to be unleashed. Palmarian saw her look and tensed for the inevitable shock.

"Nipsenni, please, don't do anything stupid."

"Yeah," the guard said, grabbing her by the arm and pushing her out of the cell. "Behave."

She looked down at the deck. She was outside of the cell. A little grin spread across her face, and even the two vislas were unsettled by it. "Behave?" she said with a frightening tone. "Oh, I'll behave all right."

Nipsenni clenched her fists tight, her knuckles turning white from the strain. Her eyes sparked even brighter as power crept onto her skin, the air buzzing with magical potential. The guards were mere underlings and had no idea what to make of this. No one had told them what to do if the prisoners acted up. This wasn't even supposed to be possible.

"Why isn't her collar working?" the guard asked just as they all felt a gut-wrenching lurch.

The others were not as sensitive to the expenditure of magic as the two vislas were and had no idea what had just happened. Palmarian and Samanna, however, did.

They had just jumped. And a very, very long distance by the feel of it. They looked at one another, sharing the same thought at once. This far from the fleet, the Urvalin could not trigger the remote explosive device on their collars, they were almost sure of it.

"Well?" Nipsenni said in an exasperated, exhausted voice. "What are you waiting for?"

Palmarian hesitated, but Samanna leapt at the opportunity, casting hard and fast, dropping not only the three guards that had come to take them, but the others who had been standing watch in the holding area.

"We're unbound!" he exclaimed, reveling in the flow of unrestrained power once more at his fingertips.

Palmarian let his magic flash out, testing his collar. Not only was the explosive not activated, his collar had ceased to work as well.

"But, how did—"

"No time for talking," Samanna said with renewed vigor. "Come on!"

The two men raced out of the chamber and into the corridors, pulling up their vast reservoirs of power, layering defensive spells on top of one another as they ran ahead.

The Urvalin they encountered first had no time to react and were blasted to either unconsciousness or death in a flash as the men passed. Palmarian and Samanna were free, and no Urvalin was safe.

The Urvalin realized something was wrong faster than they would have liked, but after such mistreatment, a good fight was just what they needed.

"You ready?" Samanna asked with an excited grin.

"Never been more," Palmarian replied, his smile growing as he felt his comrade's power blending with his.

The two had fought against one another on so many occasions that they knew each other's magic almost as well as their own. This was familiar. And that familiarity meant almost seamless intertwining of their spells as the two cast repeatedly while advancing on the command center.

The Urvalin were throwing everything they had at them from both ends of the corridor, though the majority lay ahead of them, and for good reason. Both men had learned long ago, never leave an enemy capable of attacking from the rear.

Of course, the ship was vast, and there were bound to be accessways to the area behind them, but defensive spells were firmly in place, and at the first sign of aggression one of the two would spin and eradicate the threat with extreme prejudice.

Nothing was going to stop them from reaching the bridge.

They were moving fast, not pausing for a second. They were, in a way, working as a triumvirate, their powers far greater together than individually. The third of their party, while not present for the advancing attack, had somehow freed them all. But how long they had before the collars might drop them to the ground, or worse, they did not know. Time was of the essence.

The rank and file Urvalin possessed some Allpower, but they were no match for the raging vislas. And worse, their lone caster on this ship was cut off from the other two in his triumvirate. How they had suddenly wound up so far from reinforcements he did not know, but as he rushed to face the escaping prisoners, he realized this would require much more than just Allpower if they hoped to stop them.

Conventional weapons were handed out rapidly, and the guards took up positions, ready to fire the moment the men rounded the corner on the final stretch to the command center. But no one came. Death and destruction had visited much of the ship, but this final corridor, the last stand, was quiet. The troops held firm, weapons aimed, ready to engage. Eventually, the enemy would make their move. And when they did, hopefully their powers would be unable to stop the non-magical attack.

"Where are they?" the caster whispered. "Does anyone see anything?"

"No sign," the captain said, ready to defend the bridge along with the rest of the troops.

The farthest dozen men screamed out as their bodies collapsed in on themselves, their weapons crumpling into worthless scrap. The others looked around in a panic. There was no one there. The corridor was empty.

Ten more cried out as the same happened to them. Their guns were as destroyed as their bodies. The caster looked in horror as he realized what was happening.

"Your armor! Shed your armor!" he called out, but it was too late.

The enemy had somehow figured out the precise materials of their weapons and armored suits, and they were directing their attack at only those things. It was a brilliant tactical move, he hated to admit. The two vislas were able to eradicate their opponents with simple spells rather than brute force in a head-to-head firefight between magic and tech. And they didn't have to be line-of-sight to do so.

The caster stood alone, surrounded by the dead, the only one who never wore any armor. He was part of an Urvalin triumvirate, why would he? It was the only thing that saved him. For a moment, anyway.

Two dirty, angry men were now running down the corridor right at him as he desperately drew upon his Allpower, hoping to stop them. His defensive magic was strong, but he didn't know how long he could hold them back. Hopefully long enough to reach the comms unit just inside the command center. The crew had suited up for battle and died for it before they could signal the fleet. But if he could just get to the control panel and send their coordinates, help would be on its way.

A length of metal pierced his chest, impaling him right against the wall.

He looked down at the improvised spear, formed from a piece of piping, and laughed. All of that preparation, all of his Allpower directed and focused to stop their magic, and they had attacked with one of the oldest weapons in the galaxy. And an entirely unpowered one.

The caster slumped forward, and cast no more.

Visla Palmarian and Visla Samanna strode into the command center and surveyed the carnage. Not a soul was left alive.

"A good plan," Samanna said. "I would never have thought to use their own protective apparatus against them like that."

"You do enjoy a frontal assault," Palmarian said with a chuckle. "And I should know."

The two men clasped hands in celebration and newly forged friendship, their powers complementing one another.

"The ship is ours," Samanna said. "And we are free."

"Yes, but how?"

CHAPTER THIRTY-EIGHT

Palmarian and Samanna set to work doing cleanup throughout the ship. There were still crew who had not been part of the fight, and they would need to be dealt with. They left the bodies strewn on every level where they lay as they quickly made a complete sweep of the ship.

By the time they were done, only six Urvalin techs and mechanics were found to still be drawing breath. This was an entirely new type of vessel to the vislas, and it was lucky they found that many, Samanna noted. The Urvalin had a nasty habit of killing themselves rather than be captured.

Lower-ranking techs, on the other hand, tended to be far less zealous than their violence-prone comrades. For many of them this was simply a job, and that meant that as their leaders had failed to scuttle the ship, taking their lives along with everyone else's, they were quite happy to have survived the ordeal.

Of course, they would need to be watched closely if and when they were allowed out of their cells to do work on this vessel. For now, at least, they could rest quietly, safely locked up in their own prison, treated far better by these former prisoners than they would have been at their own people's hands.

"Do you see her?" Samanna asked after they released the last captives and made sure their new prisoners were secure.

"No. She is not down here," Palmarian replied.

The men looked at one another with a knowing glance. In the short time they'd known her, they already both had a very good idea where she would likely be. They headed up a few levels and entered the ship's galley.

Sure enough, Nipsenni sat at a long table, eating everything in sight. Sweet, savory, it didn't matter. She was an eating machine. Food disappeared into the diminutive woman as though she was fueled by a black hole in her belly. And after what they'd seen her do, Palmarian and Samanna wouldn't have been surprised if that was actually possible.

Across the table from her, the woman covered in dried mud, whom she apparently called her friend was slowly sipping a bowl of broth, her own hunger far less ravenous than her companion. Other former captives had found their way there as well, or had followed Nipsenni. In any case, people were free, eating, and in the best spirits they'd been in since their capture.

"Shall we?" Palmarian asked.

"Don't mind if I do," Samanna replied.

The two vislas loaded up a pair of trays with a healthy selection of food from the kitchen and headed over to the table their cellmate was at. The food was good, by the smell of it, but they were sure the top-tier stuff was likely locked away in a special larder, reserved for the captain and the ship's caster. But there would be plenty of time to find that later.

"Mind if we join you?" Palmarian asked.

"Suit yourself," Nipsenni replied between bites.

The men sat down and quietly tucked into their food. Both ate faster and greater quantities than they'd anticipated. Apparently, they had burned through quite a bit more power than either had realized in the fray. The intertwining of power had given them a sizable advantage, but it also led them to cast a bit too much a bit too fast, at least, without practicing first.

In any case, both powered into their meals. Only once the fires of hunger had been somewhat quenched did they turn their full attention to the third link in their chain.

Palmarian took a sip of his juice cooler and turned to his young counterpart. "Nipsenni, what you did was astonishing."

"Yeah, yeah," she muttered.

"No, truly. I mean, we have seen what you can do on a far smaller scale, but to jump a ship this size such an incredible distance? The sheer power required to do such a thing is incredible. Why, I doubt even a fully grown Zomoki could accomplish such a feat."

Nipsenni swallowed her mouthful and looked at him, her eyes back to their normal state of low-key galactic sparkling. "I told you, my great, great, great, great grandmother Henni could do it."

"Yes, the pirate of legend," Samanna said.

"Yep. Now, you don't think she'd teach her kid, right? And then her kid's kid?"

"Are you saying it's a generational thing?" he asked.

"Now he gets it," she said. "Each generation has more practice. More trial and error. And each generation passes that knowledge on to the next. I would have gotten us out of there sooner, but things got kinda messy with these stupid collars."

Samanna's fingers reached up to feel the golden ring around his neck. It was still intact, the fine runes traceable under his fingertips. "And there is another mystery," he said. "That you were able to jump the ship while collared. How you were able to cast at all without being shocked, in fact. The collar should have stopped you."

Nipsenni smiled at the woman seated across from her,

reached out, and squeezed her hand. "Have you met my new friend, Zoralla?"

"Uh, no. Nice to meet you," he said with a courteous little bow, despite the woman's incredible filth.

Palmarian smiled to himself. Seeing Samanna being kind to someone he would have scorned and likely demanded be removed from his presence just a few weeks prior was heartening. The man was changing for the better, even if he wasn't entirely aware of it. Samanna turned his attention back to the young woman.

"As I was saying, the collars are quite powerful devices. How in the world did you manage to—"

"You know, I saw Zoralla here when I was first taken aboard," she interrupted.

"Oh?" the visla said. "I hadn't noticed."

"It's funny, that."

"What?"

"How people overlook us. Ignore the small and the plain. The dirty."

"Well, with good reason on the last count," Samanna joked.

Nipsenni shot him a disapproving look. "Oh, is that so? You think that just because someone isn't as regal as you, they aren't worthy of respect?"

"I mean, yes, to an extent. But I fail to see what—"

"Hush," Nipsenni said.

"But—"

"What did I just say?" she asked, her eyes sparkling a little brighter as they fixed on his.

"Samanna, I suggest you hold your tongue," Palmarian quietly said.

Nipsenni tore a strip from her tunic and dipped it in her glass of water. She leaned in toward her new friend but paused.

"May I?" she asked with such care and respect it floored both men hearing it come from her lips.

Zoralla nodded.

Nipsenni took the woman's hand in her own, brushed off the majority of the dried mud, and began wiping the back of it tenderly.

Samanna looked at Palmarian, confused, then back at the two women. Zoralla was not just dirty, she was filthy if ever there was an example of the word. Head to toe, it seemed, she was covered in mud and grime. Her long, long hair was matted with dark filth that had stained her clothing where it touched it, and her skin looked almost as though she were a golem, raised from the soil and brought into the world of the living.

"A bit late for that, don't you think?" Samanna said with an amused grin. Then the smile fell from his face, replaced by a look of absolute shock.

"What is it?" Palmarian asked. "Are you all right?"

"Her hand," he gasped. "Look at her hand."

Visla Palmarian shifted his gaze, focusing on what had stunned his comrade, and almost fell out of his seat in surprise. Where Nipsenni had wiped a spot clean, her true skin color became apparent. Pale yellow.

Nipsenni saw their expressions and reached up and wiped clean a small lock of Zoralla's hair. It was bright and golden as any they'd ever seen.

"An Ootaki!" Palmarian exclaimed.

"Taken in with the others," Nipsenni replied. "The Urvalin felt some sort of power to her, but when she didn't cast defensively they just took her in and tossed her with the others."

"But Ootaki cannot cast," Samanna said.

"Something the guards were apparently unaware of," she replied.

"But how did you know? She looks like, well, *this*. No offense."

Zoralla merely gave a little nod and continued sipping her broth.

"Thank you," Nipsenni said, letting go of the woman's hair.

She turned her gaze upon the two vislas. Powerful men who ruled over millions but failed to see them as individuals. She took a sip of water and carefully set the cup down.

"Life isn't easy for the rest of us. Not everyone lives in a majestic estate with servants waiting on us hand and foot."

"We cannot be blamed for possessing power," Samanna said.

"And yet, I can do things neither of you can. But I am seen as less than you. Unimportant. Well, let me tell you, when you're used to being treated like you're worth nothing, you tend to pay more attention to the details. The things your supposed betters overlook. And poor Zoralla here has been held, quietly, in those cells since before any of us arrived. Unnoted and ignored."

Zoralla gently put down her bowl and quietly spoke. "It's better that way," she said. "We are not seen as people, but possessions. Being Ootaki is more of a curse than a gift."

Samanna sat quietly, a curious look on his face. He was a member of the Council of Twenty and had used Ootaki like disposable magic repositories for as long as he could remember. And now, here with this strange young woman and this filthy Ootaki, for the first time in his life, he questioned his decisions.

Visla Palmarian, on the other hand, was a just man and never took power from Ootaki. His daughter's best friend was one, though her adoptive parents had done an admirable job of hiding it from others.

"That still doesn't explain how you managed to negate the collar's hold on us," he said. "How did you do it, Nipsenni?"

She smiled and flashed a little wink as she pulled her collar out of her neckline for him to see. There, wrapped around the bright metal was a single, long hair. It was filthy, yes, but much of the mud and grime had worn off, revealing the hair's golden sheen.

He had heard of Ootaki hair being used to dampen a collar's effects, but that was normally a great many of them woven into a ribbon or length of fabric. This didn't make sense.

"Just one strand?" he asked.

Zoralla looked at Nipsenni with the warmth and affection of one who had found a friend after so many years of abuse. "Freely given," she said quietly.

The two vislas blanched at her words, realizing the incredible amount of power she had willingly given to this wild young woman. Zoralla was clearly possessing a lot of stored magic in her hair. Whoever had possessed her had groomed her to be a vessel for their power until a rainy day. Likely a member of the Council of Twenty, judging by the length of her hair.

And now, this formerly captive Ootaki had provided Nipsenni a single strand of hair possessing enough power to block out the collar's hold on them. Nipsenni watched the two men's faces shift as they processed the information.

"Good, you get it," she said. "And as all three of us are bound by the same spell linking these collars—"

"Negating one negates all three!" Samanna realized. "This is amazing!"

He reached up and felt his collar again, daring to test it with a tiny spark of power. No reaction. The collar was inert. His fingers reached the Urvalin explosive mounted to it a moment later, and his mood shifted a little.

"But the explosive—"

"Is conventional Urvalin tech," she said. "And I jumped us well out of range of their command ship, so whatever signal they would have used to trigger them is not going to reach us for a very long time."

"But we will need to move eventually, and when we do, we will come across the Urvalin again," Palmarian said.

Nipsenni shrugged. "Then I suggest you two figure out a way to deactivate them." She pushed back from the table and held her hand out for Zoralla. "As for the time being, I think we all could use a nice, hot shower."

CHAPTER THIRTY-NINE

"What is that smell?" Charlie asked, wrinkling his nose as they stepped into the tavern. "It smells like something died in here."

Bawb, Hunze, and Nakk followed him in and caught a noseful of the watering hole's pungent aroma.

"For all we know," Bawb said, "something might have."

"Lovely. That's nasty, Bob. People eat here."

"And who knows what they may be eating. This is an unfamiliar galaxy for both of us, after all. Who can say what passes for normal cuisine?"

"I'm missing Vixx's place already," Charlie groaned.

"Even the people trying to kill us part?"

"At least they smelled better." Charlie reached out to Ara, safely tucked away outside of town. *"Are you sure this is the place?"*

"Certain. And I have found very strong traces of dragons out here. I think their plan was similar to ours. They landed far from the city center, and Arlo and Ripley walked in."

"At least they're finally realizing the dragons might be causing a bit of a stir when they come swooping in. I'm glad they adjusted their actions accordingly. Now to find out where they went."

He looked around the tavern, taking stock of the patrons, all of whom seemed rather rough and tumble, but one stood out head and shoulders above the others. Literally. A massive beast of a creature that Charlie thought looked like someone tossed a yeti and an elephant in a blender and this was the result.

It, because he couldn't tell its gender at a glance, was an impressive specimen. And a little bit disquieting, the way it just stared back at him.

"You looking for something, friend?" the proprietor asked, approaching from the bar area. "I'm afraid Morkan's not much for conversation, if you know what I mean."

"Actually, it's funny you should ask," Charlie said.

"The two young ones, I assume?"

"How did you—"

"You look like the same race as them. That, and I had to adjust my translator to understand them, so I'm familiar with your unusual language already. Quite a coincidence, eh?" There was more than a hint of aggression in the question.

Bawb noticed the remnants of broken furniture and felt the air around them. They were faint, but there were traces of magic still lingering in the air.

"Was there a problem?" the Ghalian asked, all smiles and cheer, slipping into the Binsala role in a flash. Fortunately, Charlie and the others were very familiar with it by now and knew to play along.

"I'll say," the proprietor grumbled. "Damn kids come in here and eat my food without paying. Offered me some useless garbage they said was currency. Can you believe it?"

"The nerve! How dare they?" Bawb said with a startlingly convincing shocked face.

"It gets worse. When Morkan confronted them to pay up their bill, they tried to cast some God-awful spells."

"What do you mean?" Charlie asked.

"Just look at the place. Broken chairs, busted up tables. Dishes shattered. They cost me a lot, those two."

"That's terrible," Bawb said.

"Yeah. Luckily the Urvalin took care of 'em before they could cause any more damage."

Charlie kept his face neutral, but he felt his pulse quicken at the words. "Oh?" he said. "Did they kill them?"

"What? Kill someone for not paying their tab? Don't be ridiculous. Nah, they covered their bill and then took them away to work off the debt. Scrawny things they were. I bet it'll take them years."

Charlie's mind raced. If Arlo and Ripley had been taken prisoner without mention of the dragons, that meant they had been separated. Worse, tracking them down would be a logistical nightmare. They needed a plan, but for that, they needed more information, and quick.

Fortunately, the Ghalian in their group was thinking exactly the same thing.

Bawb lurched forward and put his arm around the proprietor. "Well, let me tell you something. Those kids?" He pointed to Charlie. "They're his wife's niece and nephew. Nothing but trouble, I tell ya. She's the one who begged, I mean actually *begged* him to go find them before they got into more trouble. You know what they say about keeping your wife happy, though, am I right?"

The alien laughed. "On that we're definitely in agreement. And don't get me started on my own nephew."

"So you know what he's dealing with, poor guy. Now me? I'm just here for moral support. Well, that, and he promised to feed me if I helped him."

"Feed you, eh?" the proprietor said.

"Yes. What can I say? I like to eat. And unlike those two little miscreants," he said, pulling a jingling pouch from his pocket, "we can pay."

The alien's expression softened, and he waved over a server. "Well then, I welcome you to my establishment. Ingus will be right over and will be glad to get you taken care of, friend. Please, have a seat."

"Don't mind if we do," Bawb replied. "I tell ya, I'm famished."

"We all are," Hunze added. "You build up an appetite chasing after teenagers, and I'm starving."

The proprietor liked the sound of that. "I'm sure we have something to all of your liking. And as for drinks, the first round is on the house."

Bawb, aka Binsala, gave him a big bear hug, grinning ear to ear. "I knew I liked you for a reason. Thank you for your hospitality. I'm sure the meal will be divine."

The group sat down and reviewed the offerings then ordered a far larger spread than they'd planned on. But with Bawb winning over the owner's good graces, it was important to further the relationship in an organic way. And spending coin, which they had stolen from the Urvalin anyway, was a surefire way to ingratiate oneself to any business owner.

It was also their best bet to find the kids. If the locals had a good relationship with the Urvalin, then paying for information would not only not work here, it would also raise suspicions. They needed to be tactful. Fortunately, tact was Binsala's middle name.

Along with drunk, handsy, and gregarious.

The travelers ate well and played up their love of the cuisine, as well as warming up the establishment's staff and owner, building goodwill and loose tongues in the process. It seemed Binsala could not help but make friends with everyone, no matter where he went.

As the evening progressed, Bawb flattered the hell out of

their host, playing his ego like a fiddle as he coaxed information out of him. It seemed the Urvalin had set up a few bases of operation on this planet some time ago, and the locals had come to not only accept them but actually had a fairly good interaction with them.

It had been a rough world at one point, but with the Urvalin there, crime dropped dramatically. It was trading one evil for another, but at least this one would punch you in the face rather than stab you in the back. And if you kowtowed to them just right you could even have what bordered on a pleasant relationship with them.

"Well, it looks like this is going to be more difficult than we thought," Nakk said as they sat digesting their meal.

At least they had eaten well on the Urvalin's coin. It wasn't what they'd come here for, but sometimes you had to take one for the team. Or, in this case, *eat* one.

"The nearest Urvalin garrison in this city is pretty well fortified," Hunze noted. "It sounds like at least thirty troops, if not more."

Charlie didn't like the sound of that. And there was something else bothering him. "*Ara, are there any Urvalin ships lingering nearby?*"

"*Only a few on the ground. None in orbit,*" she replied over their silent link.

He mulled over that tidbit a long moment then turned to the others. "Guys, I think it's time we head out," he said loudly in a reluctant voice. "My wife's gonna kill me if we don't find those two and bail them out soon."

The others took the hint and rose to their feet. Bawb walked to the patron and handed him a handful of coin, and a decent amount more than their bill.

"Thank you for your hospitality, friend. It was a fantastic meal."

"It has been my pleasure," he replied, his eyes widening as he counted the currency.

Bawb patted him on the shoulder. "For the damages the children caused, which we are truly sorry for."

"Kids will be kids, I suppose."

"That they will," he replied.

"Well, I hope to see you again under better circumstances. And please, if ever you need anything, do reach out."

Bawb stroked his chin. "Now that you mention it, you could do us one favor. Could you point us in the direction of the nearest Urvalin garrison?"

CHAPTER FORTY

Binsala and his friends staggered out of the tavern and into the night, leaning heavily on one another as they called out their cheerful farewells to the proprietor. Even Morkan stepped out to wave goodbye, which was highly unusual for the enormous creature.

"What a lovely bunch," the owner said, watching them wander off into the city.

As soon as they were clear of the establishment and well out of sight the four of them sobered up immediately.

"I was really hoping that spell would work," Charlie said of their favorite drinking trick.

"Fortune was with us on this occasion," Hunze said.

The spell in question was a simple transit spell. One that teleported inanimate objects short distances. In this case, any liquids swallowed would reappear approximately one hundred meters away. But with their magic behaving so unusually, using this bit of magic was something of a crap shoot. Fortunately, it worked, though they had no idea where the liquid mess eventually wound up.

"I wish I had a spell like that," Nakk said, leaning over and making himself throw up. He wiped his lips and stood tall. "Ah, that's better. Nothing like the old classics."

"Vomiting is a classic?" Hunze asked.

"Not that part. The first bit. You see, when the food came out, I ate the fattiest, oiliest thing first. I do not know about your physiology, but for my kind that forces the gastric sphincter to contract to force the fatty food to stay in the stomach longer, giving the acid more time to break it down. And with it, anything else that follows, alcohol included, is kept out of the intestines where it would be absorbed. If I get to vomit soon enough, I can keep nearly all of it out of my system."

"That sounds horrible," Hunze said. "But practical, I suppose. Remind me to try to find a version of our spell that would work for you for future occasions."

"You know," Charlie said, "I actually read about this same practice on my planet. Back in the old, olden days bar girls would drink a few shots of olive oil before going out on the floor to trigger the same response."

"But if they were bar patrons—"

"Not patrons. Employees. Scantily clad employees who hustled men into buying them overpriced drinks. Every once in a while they'd go to the toilet and force it all out, staying sober enough to keep working."

"That sounds horrible."

"I'm sure it wasn't fun. But my point is, our physiology must be at least a little similar, right?"

"Apparently so," Nakk said. "Unfortunately, that does not help us with our next predicament."

Charlie groaned. "Ah, yes. The part where we need to find the Urvalin garrison and get those two out. This should be interesting."

They followed the directions given to Bawb, and within just ten minutes arrived at what resembled a small fort. Only this fort was made of metal, and it looked considerably more formidable than any of its wood or stone cousins.

"This must be the place," Bawb said. "Note the few ships out in the landing area beside it. Nothing large enough for a long haul."

"That's a good sign," Nakk said. "Or a bad one, if a bigger ship is coming back soon."

Charlie didn't like the sound of that. "Let's just hurry and not wait around to find out, okay?"

Bawb nodded. "Agreed. Charlie, you're the human, so you're up."

"Just my genetic luck," he grumbled. "Okay, here goes nothing. Follow me."

The group walked into the lone entrance to the facility, passing a pair of sentries on their way. Fortunately, this was a quiet world where trouble was simply not a regular occurrence, and they were waved through without issue. Once inside, there did not appear to be any further guards present. At least, not at the moment.

Charlie walked right up to the lone man at the tall counter barring access to the garrison's depths.

"What do you want?" he asked, a bored look on his face.

"Hey, I was hoping you could help me out here. I'm looking for my wife's niece and nephew. They would have been brought in a little while ago. Teenagers, about this tall, kind of look like me, complexion-wise."

"Yeah, the two freeloaders. I know the ones. What do you want with those two?"

Charlie felt a rush of relief flood his system. "Oh, thank God you have them. We've come to pay their bail. Oh, those kids are going to be in so much trouble when they get home."

The Urvalin laughed. "Bail? There's no bail. They committed a crime. Several, in fact. And now they're going to pay their debts with sweat and blood. The transport ship should already be at Moslof internment camp by now."

"Wait, you sent them offworld?"

"Of course. This isn't a penal colony. They needed to go somewhere to work for their crimes."

"Damn," Charlie grumbled. "So, where exactly is this Moslof?"

The desk guard leaned forward and gave Charlie a once-over. "Say, your kind are kind of strange-looking. What planet are you from?"

"Oh, us? Uh, just a little place. Far away from here. We immigrated only recently."

Bawb's ears picked up the sound of running feet in the distance. He threw a dagger, piercing the Urvalin guard's forehead.

"Bob, what the hell, man? You've gotta let me work my mojo. I was talking my way out of that."

The assassin pulled his knife free, wiped it on the dead man's clothes, and slid it back into its sheath. "He triggered a silent alarm, Charlie. Prepare for battle. Others are coming. A *lot* of them, by the sound of it."

"Aww, shit," he replied. "I guess we do this the hard way, then." He reached out for his Zomoki friend. "*Ara, it's about to get ugly here. Be ready to move if we need you.*"

"*I am ready. What happened?*"

"*They've taken the kids offworld. We were trying to find out where and, well, I'll have to explain later. If we survive this,*" he said as at least twenty Urvalin guards came storming into the room, surrounding them.

The four put their backs toward one another and prepared for a fight. At nearly eight-to-one, in a relatively confined space, no less, this was not going to be pretty.

"Well, don't just stand there," Charlie called out. "Let's dance!"

He didn't wait for the confused Urvalin to move. They were just processing the fact that their comrade at the desk was not merely taking a nap when Charlie and his friends pushed off of one another and into the fray. The Urvalin didn't seem to know what to do for a long moment. They were so used to being the respected and feared enforcement arm on this world that actual resistance was a total shock.

That surprise wore off quickly enough when bodies started hitting the floor. These were Urvalin, not some poor conscripted soldiers. They were true believers, and that meant one thing. They were all fair game.

Charlie whipped into the nearest two, his concealed knives making themselves known in a bloody flurry. The pair fell, but several more took their place, and these were ready for the fight.

Bawb and Hunze were only holding back to ensure they did not accidentally harm Nakk as they fought. Their comrade was doing his best, but fighting outnumbered like this was not his forte. Bawb grabbed him by his collar and hauled him out of the way of a swinging blade. Hunze struck fast, finishing what that attacker had started with brutal finality.

The Urvalin knew better than to use their Allpower in such close quarters, especially when the vast majority of bodies in the room were their own people. And while Charlie, Bawb, and Hunze's magic was working better, they still didn't dare cast at anything approaching full power.

"*Ara, we're going to need to make a hasty exit here,*" Charlie messaged the Zomoki just as a large fist nearly dislocated his jaw.

He rolled aside and back to his feet, lunging right toward the nearest Urvalin despite his equilibrium still being a little off. He had learned the lesson in gladiator training all those years ago.

Even dazed, *especially* dazed, staying still meant getting dead, real fast. And he had no intention of joining that particular club.

Charlie hoped no friendlies were in the mass of Urvalin in front of him as he cast a hard force spell. His magic backfired somewhat, ramping up and going wild. The spell pushed hard, all right, but it did so in all directions.

Everyone in the room tumbled to the ground from the shockwave. No one was injured, but all were surprised. It was an odd pause in the fighting as they all assessed the situation and scrambled back to their feet. They were about to re-engage when a loud shrieking sound rang out from above as the roof was violently torn free.

Ara had come to pay a visit. And she was not amused.

The Urvalin, stoic to the last, were staring down precisely that. Their demise.

Ara took advantage of the spacing Charlie's spell had created and used the weapon she had the most control over. Her magical flames. She spat out a steady stream with relative accuracy, engulfing a good half of the Urvalin. Bawb and Hunze took the opportunity the distraction handed them and flew through the panicked troops in a whirlwind of blood and gore.

Limbs dropped and heads flew. Blood pooled on the ground as the last Urvalin fell. Ara leaned in and scooped up several of the still-smoldering bodies and downed them whole.

"Ara? Seriously?" Charlie said.

"*You* already ate," she replied. "And *I* was hungry. Now, hurry and climb on before reinforcements arrive. I will get you all back to the ship as quickly as I can. Kip and Dukaan are creating a diversion at the other side of town and will meet us in orbit."

"We didn't get the location," Charlie said. "We can't go yet. We need to find—"

"I have a trace," Ara said. "The dragons departed this planet in a hurry, by the strength of the jump residue they left in their wake. I believe they were pursuing the Urvalin ship that took Arlo and Ripley."

"And you can follow it?"

"I can."

"Well, hot damn, Ara! Why didn't you say so?"

"I just did, Charlie. Now, please, hurry."

Charlie and the others scrambled onto Ara's back as quickly as they could, holding tight to the harness as she took to the air. The flight to Nakk's ship would be a short one, and once there, the pursuit would begin in earnest.

"Tell me, Charlie," Bawb said. "What in the world was that spell you cast?"

"Just a simple force spell."

Bawb chuckled. "A *simple* force spell? Perhaps test it first next time. As we have learned, magic does not work quite right in this galaxy, and even worse under duress. And we will be having a lot of that if we are to rescue the others."

"I know," Charlie grumbled as they approached the ship. "Stupid galaxy."

CHAPTER FORTY-ONE

Captain Doxin had led his men on a destructive rampage in pursuit of the enemies who had dared kidnap one of their own. He was doing so with not only his own Allpower and vast assortment of weapons claimed over a lifetime of battle, but also with his newest addition. A weapon that seemed to have the most remarkable powers.

That is, if only he could tap into them.

"You will bend to my will and do as I bid you," he had growled at the bone-white sword on several occasions now.

It was sentient, that much he could feel, and it possessed a vast reservoir of Allpower far greater than any banda he had ever worn. But there was something else there. A different sort of Allpower than any he had ever wielded. And the stubborn sword would not let him access it no matter how hard he tried.

As if the sword's refusal to give up its secrets weren't enough, the blade had somehow become dull as a club since he had claimed it. This was impossible, of course. He had seen that cursed woman slice through scores of his men with it as though they were no more than paper dolls. But when he felt the sword's edge, there was no denying it. This blade was so dull it couldn't cut a piece of soft fruit, let alone an enemy combatant.

Minnitz, his squad leader, entered the training chamber.

"Still no luck?" he asked as he watched his captain bash Stabby into a training dummy to no avail. Though he tried over and over to cut it, the weapon merely thudded off it like a club, not a sword.

Doxin nearly threw the blade in frustration. "It has Allpower, Minnitz. I can feel it. An immense reserve that is just waiting to be tapped. Yet for some reason this blade will not do as I command."

"Curious, to say the least. I was part of that skirmish, and I also saw what it was capable of. This weapon sliced our men's limbs clean from their bodies with little effort and deflected spells with similar ease."

"And yet it is now dull as a rock. And it will not cast or even allow me to touch its power."

"That makes this a truly unusual conundrum. If the enemy possesses the Allpower skills to craft a weapon such as this, what else are they capable of? And moreover, what sort of trickery did they use to create it? We need to understand its nature if we hope to ever craft weapons of our own in its image."

"But sharp," Doxin added.

"Yes, but sharp." Minnitz pondered what else he had seen in battle that day. "We know it was wielded by that strange woman, and we know it both cast and defended against Allpower with ease. What else was there about it?"

"It seemed to absorb the essence of those slain," Doxin replied.

"I did not see that."

"I did. It drained our caster dry."

"Well, that would explain how it has attained such power. But how does it work?"

"I honestly do not know."

"May I?" Minnitz asked.

Doxin handed him the blade. He carefully touched the edge, then again with more force. It was so dull there was no danger of harming himself. But he had an idea.

"What if it only functions when in actual battle?"

"You mean a limited use weapon?"

"Of sorts. Perhaps a fail-safe spell restricting its use."

Doxin mulled over that thought a moment. "It would explain why it has been inert all this time." An idea dawned on him. "Minnitz, bring in a prisoner."

"At once," he replied, hurrying out of the training room.

Doxin focused his not insignificant Allpower on the sword and pushed hard, trying his damnedest to make it react. To make it do something. All the sword did was sit quietly in his hands.

Little did he know that Stabby, bloodthirsty as he was, also felt discombobulated. He felt off. Something was not right, and it was more than the stranger trying to wield him.

Minnitz returned a short while later with a bound woman with thick, leathery red skin and piercing yellow eyes in tow. He shoved her into the chamber and closed the door behind him.

"Whatever it is you want, I've told you, I don't know anything," she said. "Your men have questioned me for days. I'm just a simple shopkeeper."

"You were present when the strangers fought my men."

"Yes, but only because I heard a commotion and stepped outside."

"So, you have seen what they are capable of. That they dared assault Urvalin officers."

The woman stammered. "I-I don't know what I saw, sir? Surely, no one could possibly stand up to the Urvalin. It must have been—"

She cried out in pain as he swung the sword hard, impacting her arm just below the shoulder. The bone snapped, he could feel it give, but the sword still failed to so much as break her skin, let alone cleave her in two. Apparently, a live target wasn't what it needed to work.

"What did I do?" she howled. "I'm just an innocent bystander."

He had already determined that part of her story was true some days ago. She didn't know anything. But the woman possessed a small amount of Allpower, what the locals here called magic. A trivial, middling bit of power, really, but he wondered.

"Please, don't hit me again," she begged.

"Then cast," he replied. "Cast against me, as hard as you are able."

The woman cradled her arm and looked at him like he was mad. For all she knew, he actually was. "I wouldn't dare cast against you, sir. I'm just a shopkeeper. Please, let me—"

"I said *cast!*"

She did as she was told, casting the only offensive spell she knew. It was a little thing, no more than a shove spell her mother had taught her as a young girl. Something to create distance enough for her to run away from trouble. But here, aboard this Urvalin ship, there was nowhere to run.

Doxin swung as she cast, commanding the sword to defend itself as he connected with her leg. It was a powerful blow, enough to send her to the ground, but it did not break her bone. Among her kind, bone density was a genetic trait, and her long bones were unusually strong.

Doxin looked spitefully at the sword. "Cast again!"

"But I don't—"

"Do it!"

She cast as best she could, bracing herself for the ensuing

blow, but this time Doxin tried something different. This time he drove the point right into her chest.

The sword plunged into her with ease, the pointy bit not requiring all that much effort to penetrate soft, un-armored flesh. The woman gasped with shock then felt a strange tug on her magic just as she died. Doxin watched with almost bored indifference as the light went out in her eyes, only then did he pull the sword free. He and Minnitz watched in amazement as the blade actually absorbed the blood, drinking it in until nothing remained.

Stabby had done what he was made to do, but this wasn't Allpower. This was magic. And this wasn't Daisy wielding him, it was someone else. Absorbing the power felt good, but for some reason it also felt wrong. Still, he drank, as he always did, but he felt another unusual sensation coursing through him. One he'd never felt before.

Stabby was feeling pangs of doubt.

This wasn't what he was crafted for. At least, as far as his primitive instincts could tell him. He had started life as a mere extension of Daisy, crafted from her own reinforced bone matrix until he grew into his final form. A sword. A sword made of her own bone, connected to her and her alone, his edge shifting to molecule-fine sharpness only when in her hands.

He needed blood to repair himself and survive, but once he'd tasted magic blood, he had begun to evolve into something more. He wasn't sentient like a person, but there was enough there for him to have instincts, and drinking this innocent woman's blood felt wrong.

Had he possessed the power of truly rational thought he might have comforted himself that he was only doing what was natural, drinking her blood, and that she would have been dead in a moment anyway. It would have been a shame to let that power go to waste.

"Interesting," Doxin said, testing the dull edge once more. "It reacted to the blood. Perhaps it merely needs a more powerful adversary to trigger it."

Minnitz pondered the new information. "We do have word of a pocket of resistance fighters not far from here. A group that reportedly has a powerful caster with them. And possibly that tech ship as well."

Doxin slammed the sword into the makeshift sheath he had crafted and smiled. "Well, then, ready the men. It is time to fly out to battle."

CHAPTER FORTY-TWO

Down on Earth, a lone Urvalin landing ship made its way across the blue skies, heading upward toward the dampening array, and beyond that, the armada amassed near the sun's protective fleet.

This in and of itself would have been an unremarkable event if not for the most unusual cargo the craft contained. Jerry, the formerly human-looking cyborg, had been stripped to his bare metal and carefully re-skinned with an experimental new flesh composite.

Cal had obtained plenty of samples from fallen Urvalin from which to base his work, but unlike with human tissue, he did not have centuries of experience dealing with this alien cellular makeup. As a result, it took time to get the flesh to hold together. The vascular system required had to be invented on the spot as the standard human pumps and tubes simply were not compatible.

As for the skin itself, that was something of a hybrid, with elements of artificial dyes added to the cellular matrix to achieve the precise coloring of the Urvalin invaders. It was a rush job, and it was far from perfect, but unless Jerry received an extreme amount of scrutiny, he should be able to pass as Urvalin long enough to carry out his mission.

That mission was both complex and relatively simple. All he had to do was deliver the cargo of nasturian-laced food to the command ship and ensure it was placed in the leadership's special cache of prime plunder. Then he would gather all of the intelligence he could before departing back to Earth to report his findings.

In theory, it had the potential to go off without a hitch. The cyborg had downloaded all of Cal's latest translation files and could speak as fluently as any Urvalin. What's more, Cal had devised an ingenious way for him to appear to possess the slight background level of Allpower that so many Urvalin had. Especially those in the fleet's guard forces.

He had taken one of the captured bandas, stripped from a fallen soldier, and wrapped it around Jerry's endoskeleton before the skinning process began. From the outside, even stripped naked, there was no sign of the accessory device providing him Allpower. Should anyone be sensitive to such things, they would feel his Allpower and think nothing of it. And as one of their own, they would have no reason to stop and question him about his destination and where he got the food items.

Once the nasturian was ingested by the Urvalin commander and his minions, the incapacitating pain they experienced would leave their fleet ripe for the taking. All they needed was access to their own ships with which to surround and board the enemy vessel and take their leader captive.

If all went to plan, they might just manage to turn the tide of battle with hardly any more bloodshed. But first, their ships had to be freed.

That was where Rika, Marban, and Malalia came into play.

"How's it looking?" Rika asked Sid and Joshua as she and her team hovered just above the lunar surface near a bottom-most dampening microsat.

"We're getting there," Joshua replied. "I'll be first to come your way, and I'll have the devices with me."

"You sure that's a good idea?" Marban asked. "You are kind of one of the key leaders of this place."

"That's Sid's job. Me, I just experiment, build things, and fight. You'll have what you need shortly."

"All we can ask for," Rika replied.

He had been hard at work constructing a half dozen of the devices in a burst of inspiration. If they worked, these tech-based units should be able to trick the Urvalin microsats into believing another unit was active where it actually was not. It was with this Trojan horse that they would be able to carefully remove a few of the *actual* microsats while preventing the gap created from being sealed by the others in the array.

Sid had told Zed the basics of the plan via their Morse Code communications method but had not even tried to send him the details of Joshua's design. If they had a normal connection then sure, it was no problem. But to relay detailed schematics of an alien tech-mimicking device across millions of miles using nothing more than a big mirror? It simply couldn't be done.

"Any word on Jerry?" Rika asked as she continued to map the most likely microsats that would need to be dealt with as they opened the gap.

"He has departed the planet," Sid replied, their proximity allowing his comms to reach her despite the Urvalin blocking technology. "He should be shutting himself down to cross the array and be pulling out of the atmosphere shortly. He'll power back on when the reboot spell embedded in the ship triggers once he's clear."

"That's great news," she said. "Hopefully, by the time he

reaches his destination we'll have our team freed up and ready to strike. Any news on the dead zones out there?"

"Nothing appears to have changed. If that holds true, then the maps we drew up of the dampening fields should be accurate. Jerry will confirm as many details as he can while he is flying to their fleet. Once he is on the return flight he'll relay further information about the specifics of the Urvalin commander's ship."

Rika let out a little whistle. "Damn, now, you've gotta admit, that's ballsy."

"Ballsy?" Malalia asked. "I am not familiar with this term."

"Uh, it's about possessing a set of brass—well, it means someone's doing something extremely brave."

"What is?" Marban asked.

"Flying straight into the heart of the enemy fleet in a stolen ship. That takes some major cajones."

"Yeah, it's risky, but he *is* a cyborg," the pirate noted. "Their kind doesn't really do the whole fear thing."

"Hey, an AI wants to keep on living just as much as the rest of us, buddy."

"I am aware of that. I just mean—"

"I know what you mean. Just fuckin' with ya."

Malalia rolled her eyes. "The two of you are ridiculous."

Rika grinned. "A badge I'll wear with pride. Hang on, I've got a ping from Joshua. Looks like he's on the way."

Sure enough, the AI's ship was flying toward them, skimming the surface of the moon just high enough to not kick up a trail of moondust. While he was the stealthiest ship in the galaxy after Freya, and this portion of the moon was still in shadow for another few hours, there would be no way the Urvalin would miss a giant dust plume, even from their altitude.

"I can't get any closer than this," he transmitted as he grew near. "I'm dropping the microsat decoys and pulling back. Let me know if there's anything I can do to assist from here."

"Will do," Rika said, her mech launching out of the *Coratta*'s hangar to retrieve the devices. "It's just plug and play, right?"

"In theory, yes. Once in position, they have been calibrated to detect the distance of all nearby Urvalin satellites and then broadcast a similar signal back to them, confirming location while spoofing their activity codes. If they work, they should trick the Urvalin tech to stay in position, keeping them from being affected by the dampening array."

"So, these devices will truly allow you to escape the Urvalin trap?" Malalia asked as she attuned her magic to the microsat nearest them, readying to take it out.

"They should. And once that happens we all sneak out and make our way to back up Jerry's play on the commander. If all goes according to plan, they won't know what hit them. Now, are you certain you can block that thing from squelching an alert signal when it comes free?"

"Rika and I have already attempted it on units in the minefield. I am confident of our likelihood of success."

"Well, okay then. I guess it's time to do this. Sid, how's Jerry doing?"

"He has exited Earth's atmosphere and is moving toward the enemy fleet. I have my telescopes tracking his movement. So far, so good."

Rika gathered up the devices Joshua had built with the mech and hurried back to the dampening array. "Nice construction," she commented. "Small enough that I can carry them all at once."

"Bigger isn't always better," Joshua said. Rika suppressed a giggle. "Especially when it comes to technology. You'd be surprised just how much we can cram into a small package."

A laugh-snort leaked out. "Sorry," Rika said as she began to reach for her magic, her tattoos starting to glow. "Had something in my throat. Anyway, I'm powering up on my end and moving into position. Malalia, you ready to go?"

"Ready when you are."

"Okay, now remember to suppress any bursts of Allpower from that thing while I put these in place. Once the decoys are in, you can destroy it. Clear?"

"Crystal."

Rika set to work, using her power to untether the Urvalin tech from its interlaced position and pull it free just as she slid a decoy device in its place. It was like a magician's sleight of hand trick, only the stakes were much higher.

The first one pulled free, and Joshua's unit fell into a comfortable, stable hover.

"Okay, it's in. Kill that one, Malalia."

The caster shifted her magic, crushing the Urvalin device until it was no more than a ball of metal. "Done."

"On to the next one," Rika announced.

Five more times she and Malalia did their little gambit, and each time, to their great pleasure, it worked.

"Okay, Joshua, you have that drone to test it?" she asked.

"Coming your way," he replied, launching a small drone to measure the size of the opening and confirm the dampening array was indeed pierced.

The unit flew straight for the gap between the surface and the array, passing through with ease before looping back.

"We did it! It worked!" Rika exclaimed. "Great job, Joshua."

"You as well," he said, watching the data stream as his drone flew back and forth until it finally hit the new edge of the dampening field and fell silent. "It might be a little tight, but if we're careful I think we've got a clear way out." He signaled the others, not wasting another second. "They will be here shortly."

Joshua then carefully slid forward through the gap, his large ship detaching into smaller segments to better make the transit. Once out, he quickly reconfigured back to his normal warship setting.

"Sid, I am out."

"I see. The others are on their way."

"Good news, my friend. How close is Jerry to their fleet?"

"I see him drawing closer. I think he will be able to dock in less than—" Sid fell silent. "Oh no."

"What is it?" Rika asked.

"This is terrible."

"What is?"

"Jerry's ship was just blasted out of the sky."

Everyone sat in stunned silence.

"What happened?" Rika finally asked. "How could they possibly have known?"

Joshua had just lost a dear friend, but he put his emotions aside. They had a job to do. Mourning could wait for later. "We have no way of knowing," he said. "Regardless, my fleet is almost out, and with the newly mapped routes to the portal he sent before his destruction, I think this fight is about to get very interesting."

CHAPTER FORTY-THREE

Ara had set the course for Nakk to follow as soon as she'd dropped her friends off at his ship. Skohla had been monitoring Urvalin communications chatter from there the entire time they'd been away and had heard of a commotion in the city before they had even reached out to her. Naturally, she had already prepped the ship for immediate liftoff as soon as they were aboard.

Kip and Dukaan were safely in the vessel's hangar almost as soon as it cleared the atmosphere. They'd run several sneak attacks on Urvalin troop positions then streaked across the city to misdirect the enemy before quietly shifting course and heading up to space. They'd only been waiting for the others a few minutes when Ara and the ship arrived.

Ara led the way with Charlie safely riding on her back, the two of them ready to unleash an ungodly amount of their dangerously unpredictable magic if anyone dared interfere with their escape. Fortunately, while the Urvalin had several smaller ships on the ground—several of which Kip had damaged in his attack—nothing had made it to space. At least, not before they jumped out of the system, leaving the enemy licking their wounds.

It was a series of smaller jumps they wound up making rather than a single longer one, as it turned out. Not a normal way to travel, but Ara was following a scent of magic, and it ebbed and flowed in spikes.

"They were somewhat erratic in their flight," she said after their third jump. "Why they were behaving like this, I am unsure. But their scent is very strong now. I believe we will catch up with them on the next jump."

"And then?" Charlie wondered. "Where are we jumping to, Ara?"

"I am not certain, but it feels like a small solar system with binary stars. We will find out in a moment. Nakk, are you ready?" she transmitted.

"Ready when you are."

"Then jump."

The Zomoki and ship performed a tandem jump across the remaining distance, flashing into existence in a solar system with two suns, just as Ara had predicted. There were seventeen planets here, most of them uninhabitable gas giants, several with thick rings surrounding them.

At this density of worlds, they had settled into an intricate orbital dance with each of them affecting the other as they circled the suns at the center of the system. It was something of a marvel to behold, and Charlie would have a field day going over the recorded readings at a later date. For now, they were on a mission.

"Ara?" he asked.

"Hold on." She sniffed the void. "I have them. Two dragons, and close."

She sped along toward the blue-green planet nearest them. It had four small moons orbiting it but no asteroid belt like the gas giants. This was a habitable world, located firmly in the Goldilocks Zone. And even without seeing the surface one could tell it was a fecund place, green and vibrant.

Ara veered away from the planet and toward the largest of the moons. Charlie felt her magic bubbling with agitation and ready for a fight as she descended in a flash, not knowing exactly what they might find. Nakk followed close behind, his weapons primed and ready.

Drombus and Duzza merely looked up and watched her land as she zeroed in on their scent. No Urvalin were present, and the two dragons appeared to be intact and unharmed. Both, she noted, were wearing harnesses similar to hers.

"Ara," Drombus said. "We have been searching for you."

"Yes, and it's been quite a bit more difficult than we'd have imagined," Duzza added. "Magic does not seem to work properly in this galaxy."

"Yet you both appear to have refined your use of it," she said.

"Necessity is quite the motivation," Drombus noted. "But where are my manners? We know who you are, of course. The famous Ara, last of her line of Zomoki. The Wise One."

"Just Ara, please."

"I am Drombus, and this is my cousin Duzza."

Both dragons gave her a respectful little bow.

"I have heard of you. Friends of Nixxus, if I recall correctly."

"You do."

"Sorry to interrupt, but what are you doing in this galaxy?" Charlie asked. "Oh, and I'm Charlie, by the way. But you probably already knew that too."

Duzza laughed. "Of course, Charlie. And it is a pleasure meeting you. Ripley and Arlo have spoken much of your adventures."

"I bet they have," he said, wondering just what tall tales the teens had told. "But this galaxy. It was an Urvalin trap that led us here. How did you wind up sucked into it? And how did you manage to escape the black holes?"

"Ah, that," she said. "You see, we were supporting Marban in his attempt to cross over to bring you one of the Bakana rods. An item of great power, apparently."

"That's putting it lightly."

"His ship was under fire and could not reach the portal, so we made the choice to bring it to you ourselves."

Arlo, Ripley, and these two dragons had actually *chosen* to come to this galaxy. It made Charlie's stomach uneasy. And if their parents found out? Oh, there was going to be hell to pay.

"I'm assuming the Urvalin are creating a problem back home," he said. "You wouldn't have come here, let alone brought a Bakana rod, if not."

Drombus nodded. "They have taken control of the portal to the other galaxy, dropping it into the sun and guarding it with a large contingent of their strange ships. They use both magic and technology to operate them."

"It's called Allpower here, but yeah, we know."

"Did you also know they have encircled both Dark Side base as well as Earth with energy-dampening devices that make technology power off?"

"Oh, shit," Charlie said. "That I did *not* know."

"It is why we are here," Duzza said. "Why Marban was attempting to bring you the rod. His ship is not from our galaxy. It does not rely on technology."

"Yeah, I know. The *Coratta* is powered by several strong Drookonuses. A tech-dampening field wouldn't affect them."

"Correct. Magic is the only thing we can effectively fight the Urvalin with. That is also why Marban, Rika, and Malalia have been so instrumental in the protection of—"

Charlie felt his face flush red in a burst of adrenaline.

"Whoa, whoa, whoa! Hang on a second. Did you say *Malalia*? As in *Malalia Maktan*?"

"That is her name, yes. An old enemy of yours, from what we have been told."

"Buddy, that's the understatement of the millennium. Who in their right mind would let that crazy bitch free?"

"She has been fighting with our forces quite effectively," Drombus noted. "And, from what Rika told us, despite her working for our side willingly, she has also had a fail-safe of some sort placed on her."

Charlie felt his blood pressure slowly coming down to only severely hypertensive. Malalia freaking Maktan? The woman had hectored him across two galaxies and multiple timelines. He'd thought she was gone forever, but now the most powerful caster he'd ever faced had been let out of her cage, and that worried him almost as much as the Urvalin.

But if Rika and Marban were working with her the fail-safe must be pretty damn impressive. Rika had more reason than anyone to hate that woman, and for her to side with her, let alone not drive a knife into her heart, meant his home was in more trouble than he imagined.

"Oh, God. Leila," he gasped. "If the planet is under attack—"

"She is the one with the powerful stone around her neck?" Duzza asked.

"That's her."

"Ripley mentioned something about her once. I am afraid I do not recall the details."

"Is she all right?"

"From what I recall of the conversation, she was well enough that her magical device was a concern for those around her."

Charlie felt a wave of relief wash over him. Leila was safe. The Magus stone was apparently acting up even more than before. Much as he hated not being there with her, at least he knew almost nothing could touch her now.

But he wanted more information. *Needed* it. And for that they needed the kids.

"Where are Ripley and Arlo now?" he asked.

"The Urvalin took them off the planet they were snatched from to rendezvous with a larger ship. We followed and watched it dock. When the small craft left and returned to the surface, their scent remained behind. We kept our distance and followed that ship, and that led us here."

"I do not see a transport ship," Ara noted. "Only warcraft orbiting that planet. Nakk, is there anything else on your devices?"

"Nothing on scans," he replied.

"Oh, the transport ship left, but not before depositing them on the surface. We did a little bit of reconnaissance, but the Urvalin are everywhere. Apparently, this is some sort of farming system they use to feed their forces. And out in the fields? Thousands upon thousands of workers, all under some sort of pulse grid above them."

"A laser cage or something," Charlie wondered. "It makes sense. Remember what the shopkeeper said? They'll pay for it with sweat and blood. This is a freaking prison labor camp."

"Several, by the look of it, all across the planet," Bawb noted. "And as the dragons have pointed out, a great deal of Urvalin both in the sky and on the surface. Far too many to take in combat, even if we had several more craft with us."

"It's why we are up here," Duzza said. "Trying to figure out a plan from somewhere they wouldn't stumble upon us."

"So, we need to figure out how to bust them out of there," Charlie said.

"Yes," Bawb replied, "but one thing first. You said they brought a Bakana rod with?"

"Oh, yes," Drombus said. "I think I connected with it by accident when we crossed over. I'd never felt that strong before."

"Hmm. Likely true. And likely the only reason you survived the transit. But with that rod, we might be able to—"

"Arlo was carrying it with him," Drombus interrupted. "When he was taken, I mean. We don't have it."

Bawb and his comrades felt their spirits sink. Another powerful tool that could help them, and one they were confident their own power would not accidentally destroy, and it was out of their reach.

"This is bad," Hunze said. "If the rod is lost—"

"Hang on," Charlie blurted. "This is a prison camp, right? And the Urvalin love playing police to the galaxy."

"What are you thinking, Charlie?"

"I'm thinking that unless they're powerful people, whoever took them in likely had no idea what it was. It doesn't show any signs of power when not in use, right? So odds are it would have simply been tossed in prisoner possessions storage upon their intake, like any good little rule followers would do. All we need to do is somehow get in there and take it back."

"While rescuing Arlo and Ripley," Duzza added.

"Well, obviously. But while we're at it, we get the rod back."

"But it is a heavily fortified Urvalin facility," Nakk pointed out. "And so many guards."

"Yeah, sure," Charlie agreed. "But it's also just a prison camp. There's no strategic value. No simple wealth for anyone to try to steal. All of that imposing stuff down there isn't to keep people out, it's to keep prisoners in. And if this place is anything like on Earth, the people staffing it are likely bored and tired. And we know what that means."

"No. What does that mean?" Duzza asked.

"It means they're sloppy. And that means we can break in."

"*In*," Skohla said. "You wish to break *in*."

"Like I said, it's how we get them back."

"But you forget, it is an entirely Urvalin facility. And you do not look like an Urvalin. None of us do."

Charlie grinned. "Yeah, but we have a solution for that, don't we, Bob?"

The assassin chuckled. "Yes, we do." He turned to Hunze and flashed a bright smile. "How is the child?"

She rested her hand on her belly. "Calm. The pain was temporary. This phase should continue to go much more smoothly."

"I see."

"Are you thinking what I'm thinking?" she asked, her smile growing to match his.

"Of course," he replied. "So, dearest, what do you say we go on a little outing?"

CHAPTER FORTY-FOUR

Kip had deposited the away team as close to the target as possible, using every trick in his limited arsenal to avoid detection. His active camouflage hid him from view, and fortunately no one was casting scanning spells up into the sky. At least, not where they were heading.

The Urvalin were in complete control of this planet—this system, for that matter—and the thought of an attack was so slim none would have considered it possible. And that allowed him more access than any of them expected.

Kip found a quiet spot on a low rooftop, and he and Dukaan guided the little ship into position, settling into a low hover, cloaked, camouflaged, and silent. "We'll be here," Kip said. "Just holler if you need us."

Charlie headed for the airlock door. "Thanks, guys. If this doesn't devolve into a shit show, we'll be back soon."

The small group descended to the street and began walking. It was only Charlie, Bawb, Hunze, and Skohla for this mission. Any more would have drawn attention.

As they moved closer to the labor camp that Drombus and Duzza had zeroed in as the holding site where Arlo and Ripley had been taken, Charlie felt something odd. There were Urvalin everywhere, but the amount of Allpower in the area was minimal.

"Ara, do you feel this? Drombus? Duzza?" he quietly commed his hiding comrades. "There don't appear to be any serious casters here."

"We noticed that too when we first arrived," Duzza said.

Nakk joined them on the line. "This is a farming labor facility. They produce huge amounts of food with which they feed the troops who are stationed here awaiting their next deployment."

"I suppose that's a pretty big win/win for the leadership," Charlie mused.

"It is. And with this many Urvalin constantly coming and going, there is no need for a particularly strong casting triumvirate here. They have the advantage of huge numbers present, ready to help put down any insurrection among the prisoners."

"That, and any prisoner possessing significant Allpower would be brought to a different type of facility," Skohla added quietly.

"What sort of facility are we talking about?" Charlie wondered.

"The kind where they break your spirit to force you into the service of the Urvalin," she replied. "That, or make you so traumatized that you wouldn't think of lifting a finger against them."

"And those who don't fall into those categories?"

"You've met a few in our rebel fleet," Nakk said. "We didn't all wind up on that prison planet when our ships were lured in, you know."

"It is time for silence," Bawb whispered, his lips not even

moving as they approached the front entrance of the labor camp intake area.

Bawb and Hunze had spent hours refining their disguise spells, casting slowly at first, using limited magic as they began dialing in their new appearances. This sort of magic seemed to work better than their combatives here, but it was still a bit tenuous. Nevertheless, by the time they were ready to go, they looked just like Urvalin and were relatively sure the spells would hold. At least, as long as they were not forced to cast any other spells along the way.

They had clothed themselves in actual Urvalin uniforms, taken from the fallen. It was a small detail, but one that would make their passage easier, especially with Nakk showing them which of the uniforms bore the correct markings for troops who would likely work in these facilities.

It was dually beneficial, as it allowed them to focus their magic on maintaining their bodily appearance without having to camouflage the look of their clothing as well. The less they had to cast here the better. They were doing this mostly old-school. It was a Ghalian adage. When in doubt, revert to practical versus magical, when at all possible.

Each of them was escorting a single prisoner to the camp. Charlie was with Bawb, and Skohla with Hunze. Two teams with two objectives.

Charlie would be processed into the facility and brought to the fields to find the teens. He was an unusual race in this galaxy, and since he looked like them, more or less, he made the ideal prisoner to be introduced to the fields.

Hunze and Skohla, on the other hand, would divert while in processing and seek out the personal possessions of the prisoners. Their lone task was to find and retrieve the Bakana rod.

"Heads down and mouths shut," Bawb said as they stepped

into the large structure serving as the entry, exit, and housing facility for the prisoners.

They walked in slowly, but with a practiced gait that made it appear they were moving faster, and with utter confidence as to where they were going. Pulling along reluctant prisoners only helped the effect.

It was a Ghalian trick when entering unfamiliar territory that allowed the highly trained assassins to take in as much information about their new environment as possible without obviously standing around gawking at everything.

The prisoners, however, were expected to do just that, and Charlie and Skohla played the part perfectly, craning their necks this way and that with a worried expression on their faces.

It was surprisingly easy for Bawb to bluff their way past the simple guard post standing between them and the inner workings of the facility. After that one checkpoint they were free to move about.

The lone guard seemed bored with her duty station, and who could blame her? Anyone coming in was brought by an escort, and once inside, the labor overseers and the facility's overall design would prevent prisoners from escaping.

She waved them through without even checking credentials. It was two Urvalin guards, after all. And they wouldn't be coming in without a reason. The whole place was designed to keep people in, not out.

Charlie and Skohla were both led to the intake area and stripped of their clothes. For this occasion, both had worn throwaways they would be fine with losing.

"This one has a lot of personal items," Hunze said, shoving Skohla forward toward the storage area. "This is my first time to this particular facility. I need to sort her things."

"Been working at Camp Ixnis?" the man asked.

"For a little while, though I'm hoping to deploy out shortly."

"Aren't we all."

"So, where is the personal item processing area? I need to get her possessions logged in before I take her to the fields."

"I can take care of those if you like," the property intake guard said, looking up from behind his desk.

"Thank you so much. But you are clearly busy, and I wouldn't want to take you from your work. If you can point me in the right direction, I will handle it," Hunze replied.

This was the dangerous part. If she had to she would kill the man and hide his body, leaving his station unattended. Odds were it would be noted but his absence would not raise an alarm, but there was simply no way to know for sure.

Bawb watched out of the corner of his eye, ready to jump in and help if need be, as Charlie finished dressing in his work attire before being taken to the fields. Charlie had taken a particularly long time donning his clothing for precisely that reason, though he simply played it off as being a rather clumsy man who was just slow with his hands.

"Yeah, fine," the guard said after a moment. "You see that door over there?"

"Yes."

"That's where you need to go. You know the filing system for intake?"

"Of course," Hunze bluffed. "Thank you again. I'll bring this one to the fields as soon as I'm done."

"Yeah, yeah," the guard replied with a lazy wave, his mind already returned to other more interesting things.

Bawb and Charlie saw her progress and hurried off on their own task, quickly making their way toward the work field access doors. Bawb waved to the guard operating the locking system. The man saw him escorting a prisoner and waved back, unlocking the doors as he approached.

A moment later they were back outside, only this time inside the tall fencing surrounding the field areas, and under the intertwined defensive grid above. It was the only thing that actually seemed to have been put in place to thwart attackers, though Charlie couldn't help but wonder if it wasn't more to prevent a jail break. In a big open field like this, without it a ship could theoretically drop in, grab a prisoner, and fly out before anyone could stop them. It was what had kept the dragons from even considering the idea.

Unfortunately, Arlo and Ripley had no idea help was on the way, and even if Kip could fly in, he wouldn't know where among the tens of thousands of workers to land. By the time he did, he'd surely be targeted and possibly blasted from the sky.

So, on foot it would be.

Bawb led Charlie out into the field to begin their search.

Meanwhile, Hunze was guiding her prisoner into the storage area. Surprisingly, there were a few Urvalin milling about, sorting boxes and shifting them to different racks. She noted that a few items seemed to be unattended on the tables with no box around.

These workers would never dream of stealing from the Urvalin. But from lowly prisoners? Well, there was bound to be some good pillage in their personal items.

Hunze reached out with her magic, testing the air, trying to sense the Bakana rod. It was something no one else could do, as the device was undetectable in its dormant state. But Hunze was different. She had been broken free of captivity by a Bakana rod, and her connection with it under such an extreme situation of duress and power had made her sensitive to it even when not in use.

To anyone else it would just look like a regular old rod. A metal walking stick, perhaps, or some such useless item. She turned slowly, feeling for it.

"There," she said. "It is in that row."

Voices drew closer. More Urvalin, carrying boxes, it seemed. And they turned right into the area they needed to go.

"What do we do?" Skohla whispered. "They're blocking the way."

"Leave that to me," the Ootaki replied with a little grin.

Hunze pulled a tiny thread of her magic and cast it into the racks of personal effects, tugging hard. The racks buckled as though from an improperly placed load, and boxes began to tumble.

"Look out!" she called to the workers.

The Urvalin looked up and realized what was happening just in time to duck aside, dropping their boxes as they fled. A mess of stored items rained down from above for a good twenty seconds before things stabilized and the debris ceased falling.

"Are you okay?" Hunze asked, rushing forward.

"Yes, thanks to you," the nearest woman replied.

"I saw it beginning to go from where I was standing," Hunze said, slowly scanning the fallen items, but not in the way the Urvalin thought she was. There it was. She could feel it. The Bakana rod was here. "What a mess," she said, wading into the pile and pulling boxes free, making it seem as though she was looking for anyone trapped underneath.

Her fingers felt a hard length of metal, and her body nearly reacted from muscle memory. She fought it down, keeping her disguise in place, but only just. The other Urvalin were already at work doing the same, pulling the boxes up and starting to straighten out the area.

"I still have a prisoner to finish processing," Hunze said. "Once I have finished, I'll return to help you."

The thankful Urvalin flashed her an appreciative smile and thanked her, then turned to work with the others. Hunze shoved the Bakana rod, as well as a random box she had grabbed, into

Skohla's arms and ushered her out of the area. Once clear, they turned for the exit.

As they'd suspected when they came in, no one gave them a second glance on the way out. And with a prisoner carrying items like manual labor, why would they?

"Do not drop those," Hunze barked, as they exited the compound. "Come one, now. Keep moving!"

She was playing the part to the hilt, and it was working. None of the other Urvalin suspected a thing. She had managed to retrieve the Bakana rod without detection and would be back at the ship in a few minutes.

Now it was up to Bawb and Charlie.

CHAPTER FORTY-FIVE

Bawb gave Charlie a rough shove on the back as they walked deeper into the fields. "Keep moving," he growled as they passed one of the Urvalin overseers keeping an eye on the workforce.

They trudged along, passing through several different varieties of crops on the way. They started off weaving through tall stalks of something that looked like a bulbous version of corn, though that was only a guess as they would have to snap one of the pods off and look inside to confirm that theory. Something the Urvalin would undoubtedly take exception to.

They stepped from the shadows of those plants into open sunlight and long mounds of what appeared to be a tuber of some sort, judging by the way the crop seemed to be underground, not above.

Next were groves of trees, their branches laden with unripe fruits. Then came waist-high shrubs, bursting with bright-red berries. Judging by the thorns on the plants, Charlie wondered if perhaps they hadn't taken on that color from all the blood they'd absorbed from the workers picking them.

Bawb shoved Charlie hard again, making him nearly trip. The Urvalin overseer in this section chuckled to himself and gave the disguised assassin a knowing nod. He hated the prisoners too, it seemed. But Bawb had different reasons.

"What the hell, Bob?" Charlie grumbled. "No need to be so rough, it's just an act."

"And you are meant to act meek."

"I *am* acting meek."

"As meek as a Zomoki-riding visla, you mean." Bawb let out a little sigh. "You are emotionally involved in this, Charlie. And, despite our mission, you are itching for a fight."

"I am not."

"You forget how well I know you."

"Okay, fine. I guess maybe I do want to kick someone's ass right about now. But can you blame me?"

"Not at all. They have captured our friends. More than that, they have invaded our home, cutting you off from your loved one. But you have trained for this, Charlie. You know what you must do. Take all of that out of the equation. Let it wash from you like the blood will rinse off your hands when we have finally ended the Urvalin threat."

"Stop talking dirty. With all that blood talk, you're getting me worked up," Charlie joked.

"We will have our day," Bawb continued. "But this is not it. Now, do as you have practiced."

Charlie knew Bawb was right. He had to settle into his role. He took a deep breath, letting his ego slip away as he fell into character. His shoulders hunched, as though he were a broken, beaten-down prisoner. His footfall became less sure, belying a wary state of mind. And hardest of all, he let his worries for Leila slide to the back of his mind, never gone entirely, but not distracting him from his work.

He had done an admirable job of it so far, but with every day the likelihood of her giving birth increased. And now knowing the Urvalin had actually invaded his homeworld, he was nearly beside himself with worry. But Charlie couldn't let that show. He had to bring his A game. Many more lives than just theirs depended on it.

"I think I see them," Bawb said. "There, ahead on the right."

Charlie squinted, but even from a distance it was pretty clear who they were looking at. "Yeah, that's them. The only humanoid-looking people in this area."

It was a stroke of luck that the teens had not been moved to another field as of yet. When Charlie was walked out to begin his first shift, the guard had told Bawb to bring him to this section to start harvesting Walla berries with the other newcomers. The thorns were a bitch, he said, but at least they were easy to pick.

The harder crops, it seemed, were saved for after the new arrivals had become acclimated to a life of labor. It was the first mildly compassionate thing they'd heard the Urvalin do so far. Though that was likely only because if they wore out the prisoners on their first day they would have to divert resources getting them back on their feet rather than benefiting from their labor in the fields.

The two men made their way toward the teens, casually scouting out the location of any other Urvalin in the area. As these were new arrivals and more likely to be a problem, there were several overseers in the general vicinity, but even then they did not seem overly concerned with their charges.

"Keep working, and do not look up," the disguised assassin said as he shoved Charlie toward the others.

"Bawb?" Ripley asked.

Charlie settled in beside her. "Speak quietly, Ripley. And keep working."

"Charlie? What are you two doing here? Did they capture you too?"

"We've come to get you out of here."

"But how?" Arlo asked. "It's great to see you and all, but in case you hadn't noticed, we're in a prison camp."

"You let us worry about that," Bawb replied.

Arlo tensed up. "Oh, crap. Charlie, we had something for you, but the Urvalin, they—"

Charlie nodded slightly. "Yeah, a Bakana rod. We know. Drombus and Duzza told us."

"Then you know the Urvalin took it from us."

"Do not worry," Bawb said quietly. "It is being retrieved as we speak."

"But, how?"

"Leave that to us. We've got it all under control," Charlie said. "I'm just glad you're okay."

Ripley heard the slight hitch in his voice and, against Bawb's directions, looked up at him. She could see the look in his eyes, the worry, the sadness. It was apparent to anyone who knew what to look for.

"Oh, you don't know," she said. "Leila is okay."

"I heard she was unharmed. For now, at least."

"No, it's more than that. My mom and Grundsch are with her. They've been looking out for her, keeping her away from the Urvalin. And Baloo is with her, of course. And Bahnjoh. And from what I heard, they've been seriously messing up anyone who comes after them."

Charlie felt a rock-hard knot of tension release in his chest for the first time since their arrival. Others would still linger with his myriad concerns, but this one, the most important one, was gone. Leila was really okay. She was safe.

"She's okay," he said with a relieved sigh.

"Yeah. Ready to pop from what I heard, but safe and in good health."

Hearing that she was so close to giving birth steeled Charlie's resolve and fired his desire to get back home. And with the Bakana rod, that would be sooner than later.

"We're getting you out of here," he said. "Just follow our lead."

"How?" Arlo asked as he picked the sticky berries. "There are guards everywhere."

"Not so many as you think," Bawb noted.

"Is Ara with you? Are you going to have her fly in and blast them all with fire?"

"No, Arlo, nothing so brash," the assassin said. "We are going to walk right out of here. Casual and unnoticed, not raising any alarms."

"But if Ara's here—"

"Not fighting is the best option if at all possible. We have been having our own interactions with the Urvalin since we have been in this galaxy, and a lot rides on our remaining unobserved. The Urvalin do not know we are here, and we must keep it that way."

"So what do we do?" the teen asked.

"You fight."

"What?" he asked just as Charlie tackled him to the ground.

"He said *fight*," he quietly growled. "And make it look good."

Arlo was no match for Charlie, that he knew all too well, but he was determined to make a good show of it, if that's what was required. Charlie, for his part, could not display any of his customary skill and allowed the boy to strike him more than once.

"Good. Just like that," he said as he delivered a quick jab to Arlo's jaw. It was a pulled punch, but the impact still made the boy's head recoil.

"Enough!" Bawb bellowed, stepping between them, grabbing them both by their collars and hauling them up onto their toes. "You will be disciplined for this disobedience." He pulled them forcefully back the way they'd come. "Girl, you are to come as well. Do not fall behind!"

Ripley gathered her basket along with Arlo's and hurried after them.

"Where are we going?" Arlo whispered. "That's their base of operations."

"I am aware," Bawb replied.

"We can't go through there. That's where they all are."

"As I said, I am aware. And that is our way out. Now, silence. Not a word."

"What could we say? We don't speak their language. And hang on, how are *you* speaking it?"

"Bone-conduction comms patches," Charlie said. "We've got Kip tied in making real-time translations for us. That, and we've had a bit of practice by now."

Bawb yanked on their collars a bit harder. "Hush, both of you. We are nearly there. Ripley, you may drop the baskets."

She did as she was told, wiping her hands on her work clothes as Bawb led the three prisoners toward the building.

He nodded to the guard at the door, who, just as before, opened it for him without question. He did not hesitate, quickly ushering the workers through the building toward the facility exit.

"Hey, where are you taking those?" a guard asked, stepping in front of them.

Charlie tensed up, ready for a fight, but Bawb just carried on as though this was no problem at all.

"I was told to bring them for transport. This lot are being relocated," he improvised.

The guard looked him over with what could only be described as disdain. "What are you, some kind of idiot?"

"I—"

"You know the rules. All prisoners have to be taken out of the worker exit."

"Of course. How foolish of me. With these two giving me a hard time, it slipped my mind."

"Well, don't let it happen again. And if they act up any further, let me know and I'll give them a good reason to behave."

"Thank you," Bawb said, already moving in the direction the guard had noted. "I've got this."

The guard watched them walk for a moment, then he turned and went back to his duties.

"Almost there," Charlie whispered as the doors came into view.

Bawb led them outside into the fresh air with the confidence of someone on a mission. No one thought to stop him. Why would they? Prisoner transfers were a common occurrence, after all. He pushed on, leading them toward the transit area. Eyes were on them now, and there was simply no way to change course to reach Kip. They would have to play this out.

"There," Charlie hissed. "A small transport vehicle."

Bawb saw it and hauled them toward it, ordering them to climb into the back before he jumped into the front seat.

"You know how to drive one of these?" Charlie asked through the divider.

"I will learn quickly," Bawb replied.

He powered the floating transport on. There were no keys required. After all, who would steal from the Urvalin? He pulled away from the facility and headed out of town as quickly as possible.

"Kip, we are going to have to meet you outside of the immediate area. We are in an Urvalin transport vehicle. Follow my signal and rendezvous when we are in the clear."

"On my way," Kip replied, silently taking flight.

He saw the course they were on and hurried ahead, landing

beside the roadway where no one would see him. A few minutes later, Bawb pulled up where he was directed and let the prisoners out of the vehicle.

"Thanks, Bob," Charlie said. "Well done."

"But where's our ride?" Ripley asked.

"Hey, Rip," Kip said as his airlock hatch uncloaked and opened for them. "So glad to see you guys."

"Kip!" she squealed as she hopped into the craft. "Oh, man, it's great to see you too!"

The others quickly piled inside and sealed the hatch. And with that, they took flight, the Urvalin none the wiser that they had ever been there.

CHAPTER FORTY-SIX

Charlie had opted to stay aboard Kip when they rejoined the others. While he preferred riding with Ara on most occasions, this, most certainly, was not most occasions.

"Tell me everything," he said as soon as they had cleared the atmosphere undetected and rendezvoused with their friends hiding out on the nearby moon.

Arlo and Ripley were exhausted from their relatively short stint at working hard labor in the fields, but both perked up once they had a few electrolyte pouches and some snacks in them.

"Thanks," Arlo said, tossing the crumpled beverage packet into the waste receptacle. "They really didn't give us much to drink out there."

"Of course, happy to help out. But what news do you have from back home? Why did you come here? We only got a partial story from the dragons."

"Ah, yeah, that," Ripley said as she finished her nutrition bar and washed it down. "We were with Rika and Marban trying to get the Bakana rod to you, when things went kinda sideways."

"I thought Malalia was with you."

"Her? Nah. She was back on Earth with Fatima. I tell you, she's been messing with the Urvalin something fierce. Hard to believe, right?"

"Beyond that," Charlie said. "But why didn't she fly with you to the portal if she's got her power back? She'd be quite an asset, if what you've said is true."

"Because no matter how she may have reformed, a Bakana rod is a lot of power," Ripley said. "Rika didn't want to tempt her with it. You know how easy it is to fall off the wagon."

"I see. So, she's working with Fatima and dealing with the Urvalin on Earth. Now, tell me again, how exactly is this Urvalin tech blocking thing working?"

"It's a bunch of microsats," Arlo said. "Cal told me how it works. Well, he told Marty, who then told me. Same difference, though. Anyway, they deployed them to look like a bunch of inert space rocks. You know the kind, just random debris. But when they got into position they powered up and interlinked. Something about the Allpower and tech they use working in tandem that let them create what amounts to a force field or something. If anything running on conventional power flies through it, blammo, it all goes dead."

"And a lot of our ships were lost that way," Ripley added. "We just got lucky that Cal and Sid figured it out and warned as many as they could before they wiped out our fleet. Now Cal's blocked off, just like Dark Side, and Zed's out by Mars last we heard, trying to coordinate his ships and figure out a way to deal with the Urvalin. Unfortunately, they also blocked comms when their dampening array went active, so those three have been pretty well cut off from one another."

"And Cal? He's okay?"

"They destroyed his command center in LA, but he wasn't really there anyway."

"Yes, we were aware it was a decoy location," Bawb noted.

"Hey, how did you know when we didn't?"

"Because, that sort of information could do a lot of harm if it leaked out. Only a handful knew."

Charlie patted her on the shoulder. "Don't take it personally. We're talking, like, *literally* three or four people."

Ripley shrugged. Growing up with her mom and aunt being who they were, it wasn't the first time she'd been out of the loop on some pretty significant details. At least she knew now.

"Well, we wound up in NORAD, where Uncle George had set up a secure base of operations. Food, water, equipment. We've been pretty well stocked."

"Hang on, NORAD's open again?" Charlie asked.

"I guess Cal's list for that was even smaller," she joked. "Anyway, we've been running guerrilla ops with George and his guys for a while."

"And our dads," Arlo chimed in.

"Yeah, obviously. They were with us too. We actually took out a lot of Urvalin ships by sneaking up and planting charges on them. It was clever. They wouldn't trigger until they'd hit a specific altitude—"

"To disguise the origin of the attack as well as possibly disable others in their fleet at the same time," Bawb mused. "I like it."

"And Leila is good?" Charlie asked yet again. "You're sure of it."

Ripley saw just how concerned he was. It had to be a horribly helpless feeling being trapped in another galaxy while your partner was in danger. "Believe me, my mom and Grundsch are taking good care of her. But from what my mom said, the Magus stone thingy is really doing a number on anyone who even thinks about harming her. Like, it turned some Urvalin into puddles of meat."

"Nasty," Arlo said.

"Seriously," she agreed. "But what about you guys? How did you wind up with a whole freaking fleet at your disposal?"

Charlie sighed. "That's a long story. Let's just say that we weren't lucky enough to have a Bakana rod on us when we were sucked through the portal, and when we arrived on this side we wound up crashing on that lone planet just outside the reach of the black holes' pull. There was one of those dampening arrays there too, and it knocked out Gustavo. And the power drain from the black holes drained Griggalt as well."

"But they're okay, right?" Ripley asked.

"I'm afraid they're dead, Rip. Sorry, I know you and Gus were friends."

She was clearly hurt, but it was wartime, and she'd seen others she cared about fall in recent days. Ripley pulled herself together and dealt with it. It was something Charlie felt no kid should have to do.

"Anyway," he continued, "we met up with Nakk, and our friend Skohla, here, kicked the Urvalin's collective asses, and got the hell out of there. We've been building up our fleet and fighting back ever since, trying to find a way home."

"That's where the Bakana rod could come in handy," Hunze said. "It is an item of extreme power."

"That's why we brought it to you," Ripley said. "Kara and Vee brought two of them through the sun portal, one for the Ghalian master hiding on Earth—"

"Master Leif," Bawb noted.

"Yeah, him. And the other to get to you. She said Master Farmatta believed that to counteract the Urvalin's weird Allpower stuff we would need to do what they did. Namely, connect power across all three galaxies."

"So, just like the Urvalin," Skohla mused.

"Not exactly," Bawb said. "The Bakana rods connect individuals with power, but not actual power systems. It is

320

entirely based on the particular casters in possession of them at the time of their use."

"That's why they sent it to me," Charlie said. "Me and Ara, we're linked, and we share a huge reservoir of magic. Unfortunately, sometimes magic from our realms doesn't quite work right here."

"Yeah, we noticed," Arlo grumbled.

"We've seen the aftermath," Charlie chuckled. "No need to tell us about your misadventures. But you learned quick, and that's the first step. This place makes it hard to cast, and there are even entire worlds that react negatively to our flavor of magic."

"That can't be good," Arlo said. "But we can't cast anymore anyway. They took our konuses when they captured us."

"We were unable to retrieve your belongings when we found the Bakana rod," Hunze said. "But we have spare konuses in Kip's storage containers, as well as additional items aboard Nakk's ship that I am sure will be of use to you."

"Yeah, I think maybe it's time to head over and land," Charlie said. "We clear, Kip?"

"No Urvalin anywhere to be seen."

"Then take us in."

Kip and Dukaan guided the ship into Nakk's landing bay, joining the two dragons and Ara, all three of whom had come aboard as they quietly flew away from the Urvalin-controlled system.

"A Bakana rod, Bob," Charlie said, carefully unwrapping the end of the device. "This could actually help us defeat the Urvalin."

"That it could," he agreed.

"But more than just that, this is the sort of power we've been looking for. If we hit the trap portal just right, we might even be able to force it to reverse and let us back to the other side."

"If the casters linked together are strong enough, then yes, it would be a possibility. Especially if the amplification of power across all three galaxies is as strong as Ripley said it is."

"Yeah. And then I could get back to Leila. I could be with her when our kid is born."

"As you should be, my friend."

Charlie's spirits dimmed a little. "But if we use the rod to cross over, it won't be in this system any longer. And that's the whole point."

Bawb glanced at Hunze then back to Charlie, nodding slowly as he considered their options. "This is true. But we will deal with that problem once we have rejoined our fleet and can better assess the situation."

Kip set down in the hangar and settled to a halt. His doors opened, and the passengers stepped out into the alien ship.

"Ara!" Ripley exclaimed.

"Good to see you both," Ara replied. "Drombus and Duzza here have been telling me of your adventures. You have had quite the time of it, from what I hear."

"I'll say," Arlo agreed with a laugh. He turned to their dragon friends. "You two made it out okay, I see."

"When you were taken, Duzza and I managed to follow without being detected," Drombus said.

"Man, it's humiliating. They took all our stuff."

"We still have these," Drombus said, activating the release on the small cargo container on his harness.

Arlo's armored space suit fell to the deck.

"Oh, thank God we still have these!"

"That's some really fine-looking armor," Charlie admired.

"Thanks. Uncle Cal had it whipped up for us special. But other than that, we were cleaned out."

"I am Nakk," the ship's commander said as he entered the hangar. "A pleasure to welcome you aboard my ship."

"Nice to meet you," Ripley and Arlo replied in unison.

"You know?" Nakk said with a grin. "I think perhaps I can help with your problem. Please, if you will follow me."

They all dropped in behind him and walked to the storage compartment at the far end of the hangar. Nakk opened the door and gestured for the teens to step inside. Their eyes widened at the sight of the treasure trove of captured gear piled high.

"Please, take what you like. Hopefully this will help replace at least some of what was taken."

The two teenagers dove in, amazed at all of the fantastic items present. There were weapons and scanners, knives and bandas. There were even a pair of particularly strong konuses Charlie and Bawb had contributed to the stash.

"Look at 'em," Charlie said with a laugh. "They're like kids in a candy store with that pile of goodies."

Ripley flashed him a gleeful smile. "Pile of candy? It's not a pile, it's a candy mountain, Charlie!" she chirped, digging into the stash, marveling at every new discovery.

Charlie decided he would leave them to it and stepped out with the others.

"So, we have the rod. Now what?" he asked.

Bawb thought a moment. "Now we should rejoin with Tamara, Shelly, and the rest of our forces and see what progress they've made deactivating the Urvalin kill switches. We have the Bakana rod, yes, and that is a win. But the Urvalin are up to no good, and in multiple galaxies. Now is the time to plan exactly how we will fight back."

CHAPTER FORTY-SEVEN

By the time Nakk arrived at the rally point, his fleet was already in an entirely new configuration than when they had departed. The largest, most powerful of the vessels were deployed in a staggered formation, the other craft likewise clustered beside it in smaller battle groups, each containing larger, mis-sized, and smaller ships.

Tamara and Shelly had been hard at work while they were gone, helping the technicians install the override devices in the most valuable of their assets as swarms of engineers, techs, and simple laborers did a rapid but thorough search of every accessible portion of the vessels.

The Urvalin had left behind well-hidden kill switches, and now the vast majority of those had been rendered inert, but it was not at all impossible that they might have left a backup for their backups. But after two dozen searched ships, it seemed apparent that, in this one thing, they had not added an additional layer of sneaky to their tricks.

Of course, they were also so overconfident and cocky that they likely never thought it possible they would actually ever need to rely on the kill switches in the first place. And that cockiness had cost them a lot of ships. Ships that would now be used against them.

Kip flew down to the surface of the small planet they were calling home at the moment and set down.

"Hey, gang," Tamara greeted her returning friends. "Like what we've done with the place?"

Bawb looked at the armada with pride. "I like it," he said. "I like it a lot."

Charlie nodded his agreement. "Yeah, nice work. I assume the biggest, baddest ships are clear for action."

"Yep. And we've arranged a support system for the smaller ones as well as any that were taken a relatively long time ago but we didn't have an override device for. Big ships protect while mid-sized ones rescue the crews of any ship that should go dark. We've also come up with a plan to scuttle anything we have to leave behind. No sense giving the enemy their warships back, right?"

"Amen to that," he agreed. "How long until we'll have a solid handful of ships to take on a mission?"

"Now, if you need 'em. Shelly's just doing a final rounder of that group over there, but most of these are ready to go. Just say the word."

"Word. Pack your things and get ready to go. We've got something interesting in our possession."

"Hey, guys!" Arlo called out as he and Ripley exited the attack ship. "Good to see you're okay."

"You found them! That's excellent! Not exactly what I'd call interesting, but good news all the same."

"They're not the interesting part," Charlie said, unwrapping the top of the Bakana rod for her to see. "*This* is."

"Holy crap. Where did you get that?"

"They brought it over with them. Apparently, things are much worse at home than we realized. The Urvalin have invaded Earth. Dark Side too. And they blocked off the portal at the sun."

"That's not good, Charlie."

"No, it isn't. What's worse is they've also invaded the other galaxy. That's three galaxies under simultaneous attack. And, apparently, once they're properly joined, it will let the Urvalin ramp up their Allpower exponentially."

"That would be *very* bad."

"Which is why we're going to stop them. We have the Bakana rod, and if I can connect with the others, we should hopefully be able to put a stop to their efforts."

"Well, hell, Charlie. You know you can count me in. I'll get Shelly on the horn, and we'll be ready to be wheels up in ten."

"Great. We leave as soon as we can."

"Where are we going? If you don't mind my asking."

A worried look flashed across Charlie's face. "We're going back to the portal."

Charlie and his friends loaded up onto one of the larger of the captured Urvalin warships and settled in for their flight. Tamara and Shelly had joined them, parking their commandeered Urvalin attack ship in the large landing bay.

Ara and the dragons were also safely aboard, as was Kip. They would be flying in as a single unit aboard that ship, but all of them were ready to deploy at a moment's notice. Two dozen other heavy-hitting ships were flying with them, ready to buy them the time they needed to do what had to be done.

The plan was to open the portal with the Bakana rod and send them back through to their own galaxy. Once they had gone through, Nakk's ships would adjust positions and engage the Urvalin protecting the portal with everything they had. It was a risky move, but they only had one chance at this. The portal was already far more protected than it had been previously, and after this it would undoubtedly be impossible to reach.

"Hang on," Arlo said as they began their series of jumps to the narrow entry path between the black holes that would lead them to the portal. "Isn't that a trap?"

"Yes, the portal was a trap," Charlie replied.

"Okay, so I'm not crazy. And correct me if I'm wrong, but, like, those black holes? They're what pretty much screws up everyone's magic in there, right?"

"Again, yes. But when we lose our power, so do the Urvalin. It evens the playing field."

"If we get lucky, sure. But this is crazy risky."

"Shut up, Arlo," his cousin snapped. "We don't have another choice."

"This is death we're talking about, Rip. Falling into a black hole and dying is not something I want to do."

"But if you've gotta go, you have to admit, that's pretty badass," she quipped.

"Sure, but only if there's someone alive to tell people about it."

Charlie rested his hand on the nervous teen's shoulder. "Our ships have technology, and that will not be affected by the magic drain. And we have the Bakana rod. It also shouldn't be affected at all by the black holes. It only activates when grasped, so it will have its full potential when I use it. And, if we're lucky, it'll have enough power to reverse the portal to let you through. Don't worry, Arlo. I'll get you home. I promise."

Bawb and Hunze looked at one another, holding hands, but said nothing.

It was a ballsy plan. Audacious. And there was no way the Urvalin would fall for the same trick twice. Once they flew down the narrow accessway to the hidden portal, they would effectively be stuck there. And then the Urvalin would come, ready to pick them off.

The plan was for part of Nakk's fleet to peel away immediately and destroy the dampening array from orbit with an overwhelming amount of firepower. They had already proven that this particular system was not nearly as robust as what had been deployed around Earth. If enough of the microsats were eliminated, the whole system would fail with no additional units to reconnect with.

This time they had another advantage. This was a battlefield Nakk and his people knew intimately from years of imprisonment on that world. The Urvalin might have numeric superiority, but Nakk had the edge nonetheless.

"Don't you worry about us," Nakk transmitted from his ship. "We've already spent ages there and know it well. The Urvalin are going to have one hell of a fight on their hands."

"We know you'll give 'em hell," Charlie sent back. "Now, keep clear of the portal. Once this is done, you know what to do."

"Good luck, Charlie," he replied. "Nakk out."

The ships exited their jump just at the entrance to the pathway to the portal, taking the Urvalin fleet by surprise. They wasted no time and immediately barreled ahead at full speed, knowing the enemy would be reacting by now and launching into pursuit. And there were a lot of them from what they'd seen. Far more than they'd expected.

Onward they raced. The clock was ticking.

Charlie walked through the hangar toward the small shuttle standing by to launch. He reached inside and pulled out the Bakana rod and began to unwrap it. As the covering fell away, he touched it with just his fingertip. The connection was instantaneous.

"So much power," he gasped, pulling his finger free. The rod was doing as he'd hoped. It was functioning perfectly despite the black holes.

Ripley came running up to him. "Charlie, what are you doing?"

"I told you, I'm getting you home."

"But if you use the Bakana rod, it won't be in this galaxy any longer, and that was the whole point!"

He gently rested his hand on her shoulder. "I know," he said quietly. "And this is the sacrifice I have to make."

"No! That's not fair!"

"It has to be done, Ripley. It's the only way."

"Ahem," Bawb said from behind him.

Charlie turned to see his dear friend and his mate standing side by side, fingers entwined. They were looking at him with such deep affection he almost had to look away.

"What, Bob? You know I hate goodbyes."

"But goodbye it is," the Ghalian said. "For now, at least. Now, hand us the rod."

"Wait, what? No. You're going to be a father."

"And you have your own little one to welcome into the universe."

"I can't let you do that, man. It's me the Urvalin were after. This is on my shoulders, not yours. You'd be stranded here."

Hunze smiled with disarming warmth. "But we will be together, Charlie. As you should be with Leila. Now, please, hand us the rod. We share my power, and who knows? Perhaps we might prove even stronger than you when we cast together."

Charlie felt his heart in his throat. This wasn't the way it was supposed to happen. Bawb walked up to him and wrapped him up in a warm hug. "You are my brother, and always will be," he said, stepping back, the Bakana rod in his hand, only a scrap of the wrapping keeping it from his skin. "Go," he said. "Save your world. And give Leila our love."

With that, he and Hunze stepped into the shuttle.

"Wait!" Charlie called out before they could close the hatch. "I'll come back for you!"

Bawb flashed a bright smile. "Not if we come for you first." Hunze stepped close, wrapping her arms around her love. Despite the circumstances, the Ghalian looked happy. At peace. "Now, go," he said. "We've got this."

The doors to the shuttle closed and it lifted off, pulling away from the massive warship, giving it space to maneuver.

"They can't do this," Ripley cried. "They just can't. It's not fair!"

Charlie wrapped her in his arms and held on tight. "I know," he said. "I know."

Comms crackled open loudly. "Whatever you are planning on doing, it has to be soon!" Nakk shouted. "They're coming, and I mean fast!"

Charlie knew there was no more time.

"Come on. We need to get to the bridge."

As they ran they felt a wave of incredible magic wash over the ship, making their knees weak from the power.

"The portal has reversed!" Tamara called out from the helm. "I'm taking us in!"

The Bakana rod's power had done it, forcing the portal to reverse, even if but for a moment. The ship powered ahead, vanishing from this galaxy in an instant, spit out billions of light-years away in a distant realm.

Charlie reached the bridge just as they arrived, falling to the deck as the ship lurched back into normal space.

"Enemy?" he asked, pulling himself to his feet.

"None," Shelly replied. "We're alone out here. Looks like they had better things to do than baby sit their trap."

"They've moved past this phase of their plan," he replied. "Set a course for Earth."

Charlie watched as the portal became a smaller and smaller dot on their mapping array until it faded from sight.

"I'm coming home, Leila," he said. "Thank you, my friends. Thank you."

Far across space, the Ghalian and his mate released the Bakana rod and slid it back into its wrapping.

"It worked," Hunze said.

"It did," Bawb replied, resting his head on hers a moment before opening his comms link. "Nakk," he said, "make for the planet at once and take up your positions. We are in for a fight."

CHAPTER FORTY-EIGHT

Drombus and Duzza felt the effects of the transit back to their own galaxy the least of the winged members of the team. They had originated from that realm, for starters, and they had only been in the Urvalin's galaxy a relatively short time.

It had taken a minute, but Ara felt the return full force, her equilibrium taking a mighty blow as they crossed back into familiar space. As they were bonded by blood and their powers shared, Charlie felt the effects equally as strongly.

As for Arlo and Ripley, the konuses Kip had provided them seemed to function perfectly, but then, they were not natural magic users.

"What the hell was that?" Charlie asked, his head still spinning. "I feel like my whole body just went through a rock tumbler."

"We crossed through the portal, Charlie," Tamara said. "Nothing special about that."

"Speak for yourself. I feel like hell. Ara, what's going on?"

"We have adjusted our magic for the Urvalin realm," she replied. "Our bodies are attempting to adjust to our return to where it works normally. Unfortunately, our power is fighting with itself."

"Oh, that's just great. We're flying into the hornet's nest and I can barely stand."

Ara was about to speak when her stomach flip-flopped one time too many. A stream of bile coated the hangar deck. "My apologies," she said, attempting to cast a clean-up spell. Despite being a painfully minor spell, it failed miserably, only spreading the liquid across more of the area.

"Don't worry," Shelly said. "We'll get it the old-fashioned way. I think there's gotta be a mop around here somewhere."

"Allow me," Kip chimed in, lifting off and hovering over the pool of sick. "This'll just take a second." He dropped low and activated his pulse cannons, but on a low setting.

"What the hell are you doing?" Shelly hollered.

"Don't worry, I'm just spinning them up to vent the excess power. You'll see." A moment later he purged the weapons' energy, dumping it from the lower release valves directly onto the vomit. The liquid bubbled and vaporized in an instant.

"There, see? All better."

"No, not better. Now the whole hangar smells like boiled puke," Shelly grumbled.

"Well, at least you won't dirty your boots," he called after her as she stalked out of the compartment. "No respect, Dookie. Some people."

Dukaan just shook his head. "Whatever you say, Kip. Whatever you say."

Up in the command center, Charlie managed to keep his last meal down, but only barely, as he rose to his feet.

"Set a course for home, but be careful of Urvalin dampening fields. We've got Kip aboard, and we don't want to fry him."

"We're on it," Arlo said. "We flew out with the dragons and know where the hot spots are."

"Yeah, they're pretty easy to dodge once you know what to look for," Ripley added.

"Good. Then you've got the bridge."

"Hang on, what?"

"You heard me. You're not little kids. You two just went up against a massive alien threat, traversing galaxies at great risk to yourselves on a crazy rescue mission. Trust me, you can handle it."

Arlo felt a little flush of pride in his chest. Ripley did as well. The two were just doing what needed to be done. To have someone of Charlie's stature give them such accolades, well, it was pretty heady stuff.

"Okay, you two do your thing. I've gotta go lie down for a minute."

"We'll call you when we get close," Ripley called after him.

"Uh-huh," he replied weakly, heading for anywhere he could get horizontal and close his eyes for a bit.

By the time the stolen Urvalin warship was coming within striking distance of their home solar system, Charlie and Ara were both feeling worlds better. They had taken a brief detour along the way to an uninhabited planet so the two of them could try casting in a safe environment to get their magic firmly under control again.

The first several attempts were outright disasters, but they improved rapidly. Far quicker than when they had been trapped in the Urvalin's realm. Once casting was more or less solid, Ara took them up for a few quick test jumps. Just around the solar system, nothing long. That was more of an instinctive thing for her, and it fell into place after only a few jumps.

"Looking good, Cousin," Drombus said after her fourth jump.

"Thank you for the words of support, but this was as natural as breathing not so long ago."

"You survived that galaxy," Duzza said. "Nearly died, but somehow made their weird Allpower work for you. It's only natural you'd feel a little off after that."

"I appreciate the sentiment. Charlie, are you feeling all right?"

"I'm not at one hundred percent, if that's what you're asking, but yeah, I think I'm good. And we need to get back sooner than later now that we're okay."

They decided to fly aboard the Urvalin ship for a bit longer, allowing the craft to do the heavy lifting for them while they rode in relative comfort. Only a few jumps later and they arrived at the very outskirts of their home solar system.

"You're sure any signaling tech has been turned off?" Arlo asked.

"Trust me, kid, we went over this thing with a fine-toothed comb," Tamara assured him. "Until they see us, they won't know we're here."

Charlie climbed up onto Ara's back and settled into his harness. "Then it's time for us to take our leave. Ripley, Arlo, you two ready to fly?"

"We are," Ripley said.

"Then let's go. You know the plan. We're going to take the roundabout path and fly to Earth, logging all the Urvalin we see on the way in. You two head in fast and hit Dark Side and Zed's flotilla. We need to let them know the situation. That the Bakana rod is in place and we need to begin our counterattack, whatever that may entail."

"Yeah, it kinda sucks not knowing what the next steps to the plan were," Arlo muttered. "We left before we found out."

"We'll know soon enough."

With that, Ara and the two dragons lifted off and departed the ship, jumping toward their destinations.

"Uncle Zed," Ripley called over comms as she approached his command ship. "We've got news."

"Ripley! You're all right! We heard you'd crossed the portal."

"We did. But we're back now. The Bakana rod worked. Bawb and Hunze have it in the Urvalin galaxy and are ready to connect as soon as the others are."

"I see," the AI said. "I'll relay the information to Sid now."

"Arlo's on his way there."

"Then we'll have a nice redundancy," he replied, his mirrors already flashing out a message for his comrade.

Sid picked up the message just as soon as Arlo and Drombus swooped down through the dampening field and into his hangar.

"I had to kill my suit comms for the descent," he called out to Poric as the cyborg rushed to greet him.

"Yeah, that dampening field is a bitch, right? But what's the news? We all heard you were gone to the other side. Galaxies, I mean, not the metaphorical death thing."

"You're weird, Poric. Anyone ever tell you that?"

"All the time. So what's the news?"

Arlo relayed the information to him as quickly as he could. The Cyborg was also receiving the update from Sid wirelessly as it came in via Zed's message, but Arlo was so excited telling him about their adventure he didn't want to interrupt.

"Anyway, the point is, Bawb and Hunze are ready to go. We need to launch our counterattack now. Are we ready?"

"In this galaxy? Yes. Rika's got the rod now."

"What happened to Master Leif?"

"Dead, I'm afraid. Something sucked him dry."

Drombus's head drooped. "I fear that was me. I received a surge of power when we reached the other galaxy."

"No sense worrying about that now," Poric chided. "This is war. You can mourn the dead after we've won."

"And if we do not?"

"Then I guess you can hope someone will mourn you instead."

"The Bakana rod was powerful enough to reverse the portal long enough for us to cross back over. Does that mean the other galaxy is ready as well?" Arlo asked.

"I'm not sure. Hang on, let me see if the relay line we ran under the edge of the dampening field can reach them. Hello? Kara? Vee? Can you hear me? It's Poric."

A blast of static hit the line, followed by a familiar voice.

"Yes, what's up, Poric?" Kara asked.

Arlo felt a rush of joy at hearing her voice but kept it in check while Poric was communicating. The cyborg, however, read his heightened temperature, elevated pulse, and a release of teenage pheromones.

"Arlo is here with me and wants to let you know he is okay. There's a lot more to say, I'm sure, but there will be time for that later. We need to get a message back to your galaxy, Kara. Do you think you and Nixxus are up for it?"

"If we can get past the Urvalin, yes. What's the message?"

"The Bakana rod is in place. They need to begin the counterattack immediately."

"Got it."

"Great. Be ready to move. We will deploy an attack fleet to distract the Urvalin on this side. You're the only ones who can cross back over, so when you get there, pass along the message as soon as you can. Tell Korbin it is time to enact the final push. I've sent a ping to your chronographs to help with a countdown. The Urvalin are strong, but if all three rods connect at once, it will be difficult for them to use their power-sharing trick to handle the threat against all three fronts at the same time. It should even the odds. But remember, their leaders are incredibly strong. Under no circumstances should you underestimate them."

"We understand, Poric, and will be standing by."

"Also, remember there will be a lot of Urvalin on the other side when you emerge."

"Oh, we know."

"All right, then. It will take a little bit for our ships to get in position, but when they strike, you'll have to move fast."

"Got it."

"Okay, then. Good luck," Poric said.

"And come back safe," Arlo added. "Just please, come back safe."

"You know I will," Kara said, her heart pounding a little harder. "Okay, Vee, let's get ready. We're going home."

CHAPTER FORTY-NINE

Back in Kara and Vee's home galaxy the Urvalin were already hard at work, the pieces of their plan sliding into place as they executed the last stages of their takeover efforts.

The Wampeh Ghalian had been fully engaged in this battle, no longer silent participants who only dipped their toes in the waters of war when it suited them politically and financially. This was bigger than that. This was the freedom of their entire galaxy, and they could not stand idly by while an invading force staked claim to their home.

But clever and secretive as the Ghalian were, the Urvalin seemed to have outplayed them, luring the bulk of the assassins into a corner then springing their trap, casting furiously, layering spells and preventing their escape. The convergence of so many fighting forces into one system seemed fortuitous, an opportunity to lay waste to the Urvalin. But that was precisely what Commander Prin had wanted.

She was there herself to personally oversee her greatest victory in this galaxy to date. And it was going to be a decisive one.

Scores of Urvalin ships jumped into the system once the

battle was fully underway in space as well as on the surface of the one inhabitable planet fourth from the sun. With their Allpower linked in such numbers, the casting triumvirates and vislas laboring in their service were able to block any jumps out of the area. Not the whole system—that would have required a fleet larger than any military might possess—but they were able to hinder the Ghalian and their allies where it counted.

Daisy, Korbin, Amazara, and Master Farmatta were in the thick of the ground fighting on the planet, engaging with the Urvalin as well as their visla conscripts in the middle of the largest city on the main continent.

Many of the locals had fled for cover, but a few had decided death was preferable to servitude. Those had taken up whatever arms they could and had joined the resistance forces in the fight. On their own they wouldn't have stood a chance, but with the aid of the galaxy's deadliest assassins and a motley band of resistance fighters, they became part of something bigger than themselves as individuals. A fighting force which, while not extraordinary in magnitude, was nevertheless giving the Urvalin a run for their money.

Even so, the ground forces were slowly being beaten back and forced to retreat, while the Urvalin ships swarming the system, which outnumbered the defending craft, were slowly wearing them down.

More of the Ghalian were moving to join the main battle group, the normally lone killers banding together to bolster the defensive forces. Each one of them was worth ten or more of the other combatants in battle, but it seemed that with the veil of mystery and intrigue lifted, the Ghalian, while deadly and widespread, were not in nearly such great numbers as rumors had led the galaxy to believe.

They achieved their goals through grit and skill, not brute strength, and their successes over the centuries had become a psychological force multiplier more than mere physical bodies. But it was clear to the Urvalin as they closed in, even the Ghalian couldn't stop this tech and Allpower assault.

"I thought this was supposed to be a milk run," a particularly skilled Ghalian fighting nearby said over a wide-open skree link, not caring if the Urvalin heard.

His name was Kort, and he was in line to become one of the Five someday. But for that to happen, first he and his kin would have to survive.

Master Farmatta opened her skree and replied. "Our intelligence told us this was a minimally defended location. Not much resistance and a great deal of valuable intelligence were supposed to be here."

"It would seem that was not the case," he replied.

In her command ship, Commander Prin listened to the exchange with glee. Her network of traitors and turncoats had provided her with a link to the Ghalian's communications system, and she had been listening in for some time now, plotting and planning, waiting for just the right moment to seize control of this realm once and for all. And this battle was shaping up to be the linchpin in that plan.

"We cannot withstand this much longer," Kort said. "I am coming to your position, Farmatta. I will be there momentarily."

With that he made a push through the ranks of Urvalin, cutting down many and leaving both troops and casters in his wake. He was expending a great deal of magic doing so, however, and despite drinking deep from the Urvalin casters as well as the collared vislas in their service, his power was running out.

This was a sign, Prin thought to herself. "Send in the rest of our troops to finish them," she commanded.

Her second-in-command hesitated. "But we have not yet secured—"

"Are you questioning me?" she barked, her Vikann stone flaring along with her anger.

"No, of course not. Sending in the reserves now."

Prin watched with great joy as the rest of her landing parties headed for the ground while the peripheral ships moved in closer for the kill.

Daisy was fighting with her usual ferocity, her pulse rifle growing hot from the use. Unlike her typical fighting style, she was holding back and picking off the attacking Urvalin. Without her sword, she was forced to rely on a konus for defensive spells, and that was simply not her strong suit.

Korbin and Amazara fought alongside her, overlapping their spells to help protect her in the process. They were the magical component of this group, while she specialized in the technological aspect. Together, they were giving the Urvalin a taste of their own medicine, mixing the two styles as they fought, but just as they thought they were getting a foothold, another wave of Urvalin landing craft touched down, releasing more troops into the fray.

"We can't keep this up forever, Daze," Sarah said.

"No shit. There are just too many of them," Daisy replied, letting off another volley of rifle fire. "Damn, this one's overheated," she said, tossing it aside and picking up the spare she had thought to bring along.

She had quite an arsenal aboard Freya, and she had brought a lot of gear with, just in case, but things had gotten out of hand. This was a much bigger fight than they had expected, and Freya was now fully engaged in the battle above. She had her own problems to deal with for the moment. Daisy was on her own.

Kort charged through the swelling Urvalin ranks, riding the surge of battle the local fighters were bringing to the invaders. It provided him an opening to get closer to Farmatta and the others, and he was within sight, but he was cut off as even more ships landed nearby.

He fought hard, letting loose with his magic until it was almost gone. These weren't casters he was fighting. Not strong ones, anyway, and they didn't possess enough Allpower to be worth it for him to pause to drink from them.

The Urvalin encircled him, pushing closer. In exhaustion, he bent and picked up an Urvalin rifle and swung it like a melee weapon.

"Oh, look," an Urvalin trooper said. "The Ghalian attempts to use technology like a club. Foolish, backwater killers are no match for—"

His words ceased as the top of his head left his body, the weapon's blast taking it clean off. Kort managed to get another shot off before the weapon's kill switch rendered it inert, but he was fine with that. The fallen lay all around him, and each of their weapons would provide at least one shot, if not two, and the Urvalin were suddenly realizing that perhaps they had underestimated the man.

Kort unloaded on them again, dropping the snatched weapon and grabbing another as he moved, seamlessly firing and running, dropping and picking up, casting the last of his magic as he simultaneously blasted the troopers to bits.

Confusion set in, and a small path opened for him as the Urvalin regrouped. Daisy and Master Farmatta were fighting near one another as he moved, both of them watching as he made quick work of the enemy. Then he did the truly unexpected. Kort raced into the nearest Urvalin ship, slaughtered the two-man crew who had just dropped off their load, and shut the hatch.

A moment later the ship was in the air. Kort spun it sharply, activating its weapons systems and targeting the thickest pockets of Urvalin. He accelerated rapidly, strafing the ground, killing dozens upon dozens of Urvalin before spiraling up into the sky, blasting Urvalin ships as he flew.

Daisy's mouth hung open. "Where in the world did he learn to do that?" she marveled.

Master Farmatta chuckled even as death rained all around them. "You introduced us to your fascinating neuro-stim technology," she said with a grunt as she sliced a man in half with her blade, though magic was her strong suit.

"You've been using neuro-stims to learn Urvalin tech?"

"Since the moment they arrived," the older woman said with a pointy-toothed grin. "And we have become quite proficient."

"But you're all about magic and casting and swords and stuff."

"Yes, that is our way. But we are the Wampeh Ghalian, and you should know by now, we will utilize *every* tool at our disposal to gain an advantage."

A moment later, Daisy, as well as the rest of their allies, found out just what she meant by that.

Hundreds of Ghalian ships uncloaked, dropping their shimmer spells and seeming to pop into existence as they engaged the enemy. More than that, a great many Urvalin ships abruptly turned on their own people, opening fire on the Urvalin fleet with their own weapons. Anyone close enough to try to target them would very quickly realize they were now sporting a new defensive signature. Ghalian magic, to be precise.

Daisy stared at Farmatta in shock. "You knew it was a trap," she said.

"Let's just say we heard of the possibility," Farmatta replied as she finally let loose a *real* blast of power, knocking down dozens of advancing troops with a single spell. She winked at Daisy as she pulled upon more of her magic and cast again. "Now the *true* battle begins."

CHAPTER FIFTY

Commander Prin was beside herself with rage as she watched her carefully laid trap implode on itself, her forces falling into disarray as the enemy swung the tide of battle in their favor. It was clear she had been tricked. Worse yet, if she didn't retreat she would lose.

But Prin did not give up so easily.

"Bring me the big guns!" she screamed at her command staff.

"But they guard the portal, Commander. Torgus instructed us that under no circumstances—"

"I do not care what Torgus said. He is not here. *I* am. And this is *my* fleet."

"But—"

"No buts! The dragons have already gone, and no one else can even enter the portal anyway. We need those ships. Now summon them at once. Leave a handful behind if you must, but bring all of the rest!"

"As you command."

The message was relayed, and a lone ship jumped away from the battle to get within closer relay range. Without doing so, it would take far too long for the order to reach them, and judging by the commander's rage, that simply was not an option.

The ship flew hard, nearly burning out its warp drive as it did, forcing them to switch to jump Allpower mid-flight. But they made it soon enough, and relayed the order. The portal fleet heeded the command and warped away at once, heading straight for battle, leaving only a few craft behind as a token symbol to defend the portal.

Prin felt a rush of excitement as the large ships began arriving. This was what she needed. This would put an end to this battle in short order. She directed them into the fray, ordering them to fire on their own ships if they displayed so much as a trace of local magic instead of Allpower.

Her trap had been turned on her, but now it had been turned back yet again. The tide was shifting in her favor.

In space and the skies above, the fight grew even more heated as the newcomers engaged the jumble of craft already in the midst of battle. On the surface, the Urvalin forces were abruptly freed from having to defend against airborne attacks from their own ships, freeing them up to charge the local resistance once more.

Daisy and her comrades in arms had enjoyed the respite, but now the battle was surging again, and the fighting was even more intense. And for all her years of training and skill, Daisy was beginning to wonder if this might be her last battle.

Taking on magic armed with nothing but a rifle and a konus she didn't really have much skill in using? Things were not looking good. But Daisy pressed on anyway, fighting with a frenzied urgency. If she was going out, it would be on her terms.

"There may not be any way out of this one, Sis," she said through clenched teeth as she slammed the butt of her rifle into an Urvalin's jaw, shattering it.

"*I know,*" Sarah replied. "*But it's been a good run, hasn't it?*"

"That it has."

Saying it out loud, the reality of the situation actually set in. They'd put up a good fight, but this would be her final—Daisy froze, something tugging on her senses. Something familiar. A sensation of connection, and it was growing stronger.

"Stabby?"

She spun in a circle, eyes scanning the battle.

There, not more than thirty meters away, a large, scarred Urvalin was stabbing people in his path. Stabbing them with *her* sword. And he was being wielded by the enemy. But something was wrong. Something didn't feel right. Stabby, she realized, was not a willing combatant.

Daisy dropped to one knee to make herself a smaller target on the battlefield and closed her eyes, hoping no one would get in a lucky shot as she reached out with her mind. She concentrated hard, feeling for her sword's connection.

Stabby hadn't noticed her at first. The amount of blood he was taking in had distracted him as much as the loathsome man wielding him. But then he felt it too. Daisy was here! It was the closest thing to a feeling of joy, love, and home he had ever felt, and he'd never even known he missed it. Until now, at least. His home was here, and he wanted to go back.

"Damned blade," Doxin growled as Stabby swung to and fro, pulling his arm hard, forcing him to miss as he tried to impale another resistance fighter.

He drew his pistol and ended them the old-fashioned way, then resumed his fight with the sword. But Stabby wasn't having any of that. He had drunk a lot of blood while in the Urvalin's possession, and his power had grown even more as a result of it. And now, finally, he felt free to use it.

"Curse you, stupid swor—"

Stabby abruptly ripped free from Doxin's grip, flying through the air of his own accord. The Urvalin watched in shock

347

as the blade spun in mid-air, the grip landing firmly in the hand of the woman kneeling on the battlefield.

"Kill her!" he bellowed, directing his forces to focus their attack on the lone woman. Allpower tore through the air, as did weapons fire, but the sword flared bright, a burst of magic powering out and deflecting it all harmlessly aside.

Daisy slowly opened her eyes and rose to her feet. The feeling in her hand was one of warmth and love. Connection. Stabby had gone rogue, yes, but he now realized where he truly belonged. Daisy smiled wide. "I'm glad to see you too," she said. Her gaze shifted to the approaching troopers. "Go get 'em, boy."

She loosened her grip and Stabby flew out of her hand like Thor's hammer, impaling and slicing those in his path, leaving dead and dismembered Urvalin in his wake before flying back to her hand, happily at home, and happy in battle, the last traces of blood already absorbing into him. Powering him further.

Daisy locked eyes with the shocked Urvalin. Doxin had no idea what he'd just witnessed. It was unlike anything he'd ever seen before, and in his many years fighting for the Urvalin cause, he had seen a lot.

His human adversary smiled a scary grin, and the normally unflappable Urvalin actually felt a pang of fear as he realized he should have approached this fight differently. Namely, by running away. But it was too late for that, and he had numbers on his side. Or so he hoped. It seemed he would find out soon enough.

"Advance!" he shouted, urging his men forward.

Daisy ran at them, her exhaustion gone, revitalized and actually looking forward to the far more visceral nature of hand-to-hand combat. And Stabby was sharp again, cutting through the enemy with ease.

Doxin felt his rage bubble to the surface. This woman could make the sword do what he could not, and it infuriated him. He wanted her dead in the worst way. Judging by the speed at which she was clear-cutting her way through his troops, he would have his chance sooner than later.

They reached the captain, but Stabby actually missed for a change when they lunged at him. Doxin may not have been his master, but he'd felt his magic and knew it a little. Enough to counter with his Allpower, at least for the moment.

Daisy and Doxin circled each other like feral animals, each waiting for the other to flinch before launching into a flurry of claws and teeth.

The Urvalin drew his long dagger and swung at her while casting a powerful killing spell. His Allpower was no laughing matter and was a good part of the reason he'd survived so long, climbing the blood-soaked ranks.

Stabby swatted aside the spell like a giant might brush off a fly, so uneven was the contest. Doxin's eyes went wide with shock as he felt the sword's true power. Felt it just before the blade plunged into his chest, pulling his substantial life force out with glee. A moment later, Doxin's corpse fell to the ground, no more than a dried-out husk. Stabby, it seemed, had taken this one personally.

Daisy felt a rush of energy flow into her and shuddered. Despite all of the fighting thus far, she felt revitalized and ready to go.

"*He's feeding energy into you, Daze. Into us. He's never done that before.*"

"*I know, Sis,*" Daisy replied as she raced back into the fight.

Her beloved sword sliced through their enemies like a hot knife through butter, sucking their power in a flash and then moving on as the two of them worked together in perfect harmony, the blade and his master finally fighting as one.

"*Our boy is home.*"

CHAPTER FIFTY-ONE

The tide of the battle raged and shifted repeatedly, both sides seeming to pull ahead toward victory only to have their forces pushed back and be forced to regroup yet again. It was a contest not only of the will and strength of the combatants engaged in a life-and-death battle, but also of the minds behind the day's bloodshed.

The greatest tacticians were putting their skills on display, pulling tricks out of their hats they had been reserving for a rainy day. It was pouring, it seemed, and everyone was wet today, though with blood, not water, and it was time to leave no maneuver unused.

Korbin, Amazara, and Daisy had remained close to one another, fighting as an improvised triumvirate of their own in a manner of speaking. With Stabby back in her hand and running high on Urvalin Allpower, Daisy was nearly as strong as they were.

It was a fortunate thing. After so many hours the two natural casters were relying more and more on their konuses to bolster their own magic. It would recharge in time, as it always had, but they were pushing themselves hard. Too hard. For the sake of not only victory, but their survival there was no other option.

"This is getting ugly," Daisy said as she deflected a group of attack spells, the Urvalin casting them having learned to stay a healthy distance away from the crazy woman with the white sword. "They're not engaging us normally."

"They've learned your tricks," Amazara said.

"Yeah? Well, Stabby needs to get closer if he's going to keep feeding to keep his power up."

Korbin spun and unleashed a stun spell, knocking the three Urvalin who had been trying to sneak up on them from behind to the ground.

"Thanks, Korb," Daisy said with a grin as she loosened her grip, letting Stabby fly into the downed warriors. "He needed that."

"Glad to help," he said, winded and just for a moment wishing he had decided to stay with his ship and perhaps fight from a seated position.

But the battle up above was raging just as intensely as down below. There was no escaping the fighting anywhere in this system. Not today.

"Zara, how are you holding up?" he called out.

"Tired, but making do. And you?"

"The same."

They watched as yet another Urvalin transport ship landed out of their reach, depositing still more ground forces. Their own allies had been slowly thinning under the attack. The Ghalian were using shimmer cloaks, disguising themselves as they slipped through the peripheral ranks, fanning out to cover more ground.

But the fighting was too thick in most places for that tactic to work. They would be just as likely to be hit by friendly fire as be discovered by the enemy. Still, the assassins were doing more than their share of the work.

Farmatta had remained close to the trio, keeping her power levels maxed out as she picked off the strongest casters one by one. It not only helped their cause, it allowed her to stay ready for what was to come. If that was ever going to happen.

"Aww, hell. Here they come," Daisy groaned as she braced herself for another onslaught.

Suddenly, a massive plume of flame blasted the ground from above, sending the Urvalin scattering. As they ran, a second burst joined in, the two scorching the enemy, laying waste to a wide swath of combatants.

Korbin knew that smell. Magical flames. He watched with amazement as the two dragons swooped in, landing hard, snatching up several still-writhing Urvalin and downing them whole. Off behind them, a dozen flaming ships began impacting the surface, falling from the sky along their arrival path. But where they had cleared away enemy ships, more were shifting course and filling in the gaps.

Two armored shapes leapt from the beasts and raced toward him as he cast a protective spell around them.

"Uncle Korbin!" Kara cried out with joy as she embraced him with a somewhat uncomfortable armor-clad hug.

Vee joined in, wrapping her arms around them both.

"Girls, you've returned. How did you find us?"

"Nixxus and Gazz," Kara replied. "They know the smell of your magic. Though, there's so much going on here, it would be hard to miss. It's an epic battle."

"Believe me, kid, we know," Daisy chimed in. "We've been fighting it for hours."

"Yes, it looks like the Urvalin have committed almost all of their forces here. We were wondering why the portal was so poorly guarded when we emerged. Now we know."

A blast of powerful magic shook the ground, narrowly missing the dragons. It seemed the casters on the ships above had taken note of their arrival and had begun an aerial bombardment, their own forces be damned.

"You've got to get out of here," Korbin urged. "It is about to get very, very ugly down here."

"No, we have a message. The final push against the Urvalin has begun in all three galaxies."

Master Farmatta suddenly appeared out of thin air, shedding her shimmer cloak and startling everyone, even Korbin. With the way she could get so close without him noticing her, even with all the power he possessed, it was clear why she was considered the most powerful of the Ghalian casters. With skill like that, she must have had the blood of thousands on her hands by the time she joined the Five.

"You were successful in your efforts? You got the rods to both Charlie and Master Leif?" she asked.

"Well, yes and no," Kara said. "There was an incident with the rod. Master Leif is dead."

"Dead? Then who—"

"Rika is in possession of that rod."

Farmatta nodded her approval. "An extremely powerful caster, and with magic from two realms. She can handle the strain. And the other?"

"Delivered to the Urvalin galaxy, but it is not with Charlie. He returned to his own galaxy."

"Again, an unfortunate surprise," Farmatta said.

"Yes and no. He left the rod behind when he crossed back. It is with Bawb and Hunze."

"Together?"

"Yes."

Farmatta had been anticipating the human and Zomoki contributing their magic to the equation, but Hunze and Bawb shared an incredible wealth of Ootaki magic. It wasn't what she had planned on, but it would work.

"Charlie also brought an Urvalin warship with him when he crossed back. Arlo and Ripley flew with him as well."

"Arlo is okay?" Daisy blurted, her heart leaping with relief.

"Yeah. He and Rip were out at Dark Side last I heard. There was an attack there as well, but we managed to fend off the Urvalin, though they seem to be readying for a final push as well."

"Freya, did you hear that?" Daisy asked the ever-monitoring stealth ship.

"I did. Arlo and Rip are going to need help."

"I was thinking the same thing."

"*You thinking what I'm thinking?*" Sarah asked.

"*You know it,*" Daisy replied. "Freya, you think you can do that thing we were talking about?"

"I'm damn well willing to try, but it's getting really hairy up here. A lot more Urvalin ships showed up for the fight."

"How many more?"

"I don't know. Looks like *all* of them, maybe?"

"Do you think you can get through this mess and get down here?"

"I'll do my best."

"Thanks, Kiddo."

The fighting above grew thicker, the magic and Allpower flowing steadily as collared casters, Ghalian and resistance fighters, and Urvalin triumvirates all vied for control. It was a stalemate, all sides locked in desperate combat.

Then, out of nowhere an Urvalin command ship jumped into the middle of the battle. Prin let out a little sigh of relief, and her troops felt their spirits rise, but something was wrong. This ship's Allpower was strange. It was clearly one of the command ships carrying captured vislas, but it had not arrived via an Allpower jump, nor had it used warp tech. It felt like something *different*.

The Ghalian also noted the strange arrival. It was a ship, but it felt of Zomoki magic, which everyone knew was simply impossible. But whose side was this odd vessel on?

The answer became quickly apparent as the magic from the ship began flowing hot and fast along with the other weapons at the vessel's disposal. And all of it was aimed at the Urvalin.

"Defend yourselves, idiots!" Prin shrieked as her ships began falling to the barrage.

Down on the surface, Kara spun, the hairs on the back of her neck standing up inside her armored suit. "My father!" she gasped, feeling his distinctive magic. "He's here!"

Aboard the commandeered Urvalin command ship, Visla Palmarian and Visla Samanna worked in tandem, blasting their shared enemy with everything they had. Nipsenni sat at the helm, flying the ship with surprising skill. All three of their control collars gave a sudden pop as the Urvalin explosives detonated, but they merely left a small char mark on the deck in the compartment the broken bands had been left in.

These three were flying free.

"Target the larger ships," Nipsenni ordered the raggedy crew manning the guns.

They weren't former captives, they were something else. Friends of the family, in fact, come to help their dear Nipsenni. Pirates. *Coalition* pirates, no less. And they had not come alone.

Hundreds of pirate vessels large and small flashed into the battle, jumping in with the take-no-prisoners enthusiasm that had made them the most feared and respected of the pirate conglomerates in the galaxy.

Nipsenni watched the Urvalin flying in disarray, unsure exactly how to engage the new combatants.

"That's right," she said, turning to her two visla comrades

with a wild grin. "You see? I told you not to question my family line."

"An error in judgment I apologize for wholeheartedly and with great pleasure," Samanna said. "Now, if you don't mind, we have a battle to win."

Nipsenni opened a skree line to the pirate fleet. "This is it, my friends. A haul the likes of which none of you have ever dreamed possible. No prisoners! Go out there and claim all the booty you can carry!"

It was space, and there was no sound, but the raucous cheers aboard the pirate ships felt almost loud enough to violate the laws of physics just this once.

The newcomer ships flung themselves headlong into the battle, engaging the enemy not with standard tactics, but their own unconventional pirate ways. It was guerrilla war in space, and the Urvalin didn't know quite how to react to it.

"Daisy, I'm almost to you," Freya called out over comms. "These guys opened up a nice big hole for me to make an approach. See you in a sec."

True to her word, the stealth ship rocketed to the surface, pulling up at the last second, a little game she was so amused by, then gliding to a soft landing by her friends, crushing a few Urvalin beneath her in the process.

Daisy shouldered her weapon and turned for the open hatch.

"Where are you going?" Korbin called after her.

"Back home," she called back. "My kid needs me."

"Mine too," Freya added.

"But the portal is still in the sun," he reminded her. "Only Zomoki possess the magic to survive it. You'll die, Daisy."

"Maybe yes, but maybe no. But if Freya's nanites have learned from what they've seen Ara do, we should be fine. That's something else they've been practicing, you see."

"It's not the same. Zomoki magic is unique in all the galaxy."

"Perhaps," Freya chimed in. "But it's really not *that* different. Not to me, anyway. Now, come on. We need to get back. Marty and Joshua need me."

Daisy hurried aboard, waved farewell to her friends, and then was gone as the ship shot up toward open space.

"*She's sounding a lot like someone I know,*" Sarah said. "*Pushy, confident, and fiercely protective of her family.*"

"*Yeah, yeah, she takes after her Mama, I know. Now let's just hope that, like her Mama, she can back up all that big talk.*"

CHAPTER FIFTY-TWO

Freya hurtled through space at breakneck speed, alternating between warps and jumps as she pushed hard for the portal's hiding place.

She had used the confusion caused by the swarming pirates to blast her way clear of the fight with the Urvalin and had hit clear space in no time. Under almost any other circumstances she would never dream of leaving her friends in need, but in a battle such as that, one small ship, no matter how skilled, would not win or lose the day.

"Almost there," she announced as they dropped out of warp. "One more and we'll be on them."

"I'm ready, Kiddo," Daisy replied, her weapons station fully charged and ready to go.

They were going to warp in just clear of the burning plasma and engage the enemy with everything they had. If what Kara had said was correct, is would hopefully be enough to create a gap for them to make their attempt. If not, they would have to engage in a drawn-out fight, and without support, that only hurt their chances of making it through.

"Here we go," Freya said. "Hang onto your bootstraps."

"My boots don't have any—" Daisy began to say when the ship lurched into warp.

Freya exited in a flash, the burning plasma stream dead ahead. The Urvalin really had left a skeleton fleet behind, they were pleased to see. Less than that, even. Just a handful of ships that didn't even really constitute a flotilla, let alone a fleet or armada.

"Light 'em up!" Daisy shouted, firing all weapons in a blistering burst of pulse and railgun fire.

Strangely enough, the Urvalin ships didn't seem to want anything to do with her. In fact, she noted, several appeared to have suffered significant burn damage from the dragons as they had come through, and there was floating debris where a few others had been torn apart.

Apparently, Kara and Vee and their friends had made quite a showing of themselves when they arrived, and the surviving ships were just doing all they could to keep from decompressing and losing what was left of their atmospheres.

Freya went silent as she focused on her connection with every nanite within her, drawing their magic from not only the galaxy but the sun's plasma itself, powering up for her most ballsy attempt yet.

"You sure you got this?" Daisy asked.

Freya's attention narrowed to the plasma ahead of them and the portal it was spewing from. "One way to find out," she replied. Then she formed the spell, sending it out hard and with everything she had, casting as she had recorded the Zomoki doing, directing her nanite-powered magic to do her bidding.

Freya ramped up her shields to maximum, just in case, and punched it, barreling forward into the flames.

"Love you, Sis," Sarah whispered in her head.

"Love you too. But this is going to work. It has to," she replied, then held on for the ride of her life.

Freya plunged into the sun's plasma, driving ahead and into the portal itself. The transit was unlike anything Daisy had ever seen before. They were surrounded by swirling plasma hot enough to fuel a solar system. The heart of a star. And yet they were unharmed. It was amazing, this incredible power, and for a brief instant she felt at one with the universe.

"Freya, evasives!" she shouted as they burst out the other side, plasma spraying as they entered her home galaxy.

The ship was already on it, firing off not only railgun and pulse cannon fire, but also a massive spread of potent spells, several of them flying true and impacting the Urvalin fleet.

"Powering down," Freya announced, wrapping her mind in a protective bubble of magic, switching entirely to magical systems. There were dampening arrays out there, and this was the only way. Freya's nanites had apparently learned to not only channel the sun's power, but also store it for later use as well. Now she just had to be sure to cast the jump spell right.

"Hang on," she said. "This part is still a work in progress."

Before the Urvalin could even properly react, she jumped to Dark Side base, arriving just outside the dampening array. She plunged right through it without hesitation. She'd just flown through the goddamn sun. If she could do that, she could do anything.

The microsats left her unscathed as she hurtled to the surface. A few Urvalin ships were present, but not a terribly imposing fighting force. She blasted them from the sky regardless and made her way to Dark Side base.

"Sid, we're back!" she announced. "Joshua, I've come to get you out of here."

"Arlo? Do you read me?" Daisy added.

"Welcome back," Sid replied. "I'm so glad to hear your voices."

"Where's Joshua?" Freya asked, a jolt of worry flashing through her. "I don't sense him. He isn't responding."

"He's fine, Freya. They all are. Do not worry."

"What happened to them?"

"Happened? Nothing. He and a group of others escaped out of a gap Rika, Marban, and Malalia managed to make in the dampening array before heading back to Earth. Joshua and his ships flew out some time ago to meet up with some of Zed's ships and engage the Urvalin fleet to draw them away from the sun. The idea was to provide Kara and Vee with a window to cross over to the other side. Shall I assume they were successful?"

"They were," Daisy chimed in. "Holy crap, Freya, they're still back at the portal. And we were just there."

"I just jumped for Dark Side as soon as we came through," she said. "I didn't think there would be any of our people there. Oh, no. Do you think I harmed any of them? I was firing indiscriminately."

"I don't know, Kiddo, but I do know one thing. We need to get our asses back there, and pronto. If there's a fight going on, we need to be a part of it.

"Sid, are you okay on your own?" Daisy asked.

"I still have plenty of resources at my disposal, but thank you for asking. Now, go get your families."

"Don't have to tell us twice. Freya, let's go."

The ship changed course heading back out of the dampening array in a flash. It seemed that just as they had done in the other galaxy, most of the Urvalin had left to join the main fight. Even so, there were still a few for Freya to blast as she flew by. Then she jumped.

"There they are!" Daisy blurted as they emerged from the jump at the edge of the battle. "Arlo, are you okay?"

"Mom? What are you doing here?" a confused voice replied. "I thought you were stuck on the other side of the portal."

"Long story. Are you okay?"

"We're fine, Aunt Daisy," Ripley chimed in. "The majority of the fleet turned tail and ran. We're mopping up here at the sun."

A large ship unlike any other in the fleet broke free from the battle and sped toward Freya. It broke into pieces and reformed itself as it drew near, taking on a protective, defensive configuration.

"Freya, you're back," Joshua said, overjoyed. "But how? I saw what I thought was you streaking from the sun, but the energy signature was all wrong. It was Zomoki."

"Yeah, I know."

"But how did you do that? It should be impossible."

"Simple. You needed me," Freya replied. "So I made it work. Now, come here. I have something for you."

Joshua slid up close until their wings lay on top of one another. Nanites leapt from Freya's ship onto his, blending with his own personal swarm in a flash, relaying all they had learned to their cousins.

It would take time for the process to spread to his entire ship, and the learning curve for casting with them would be steep, but Freya knew the greatest tactical AI ever to live would be more than up for the challenge.

"Is Marty okay?" she asked.

"He is, last I heard," Joshua replied. "He has been leading raids across the planet, engaging Urvalin, operating with commandos. Oh, Freya, I am so proud of him."

"As am I," she said. "Now, tell me. Where exactly did the rest of the Urvalin fleet go?"

CHAPTER FIFTY-THREE

After a long-way-around approach to Earth that had taken far too long for Charlie's liking, he and Ara had finally arrived. They were expecting to use their lack of a tech signature to freely map Urvalin forces as they made their way to Earth. But, to their surprise, there were none to be found.

A few were still at Dark Side base, they were sure, and a small battle group of others at the moon, but the rest of the fleet? They hadn't seen them anywhere. That is, until they reached home.

"Oh, crap," Charlie gasped. "Look at all of them."

It seemed the Urvalin were amassing forces just outside of Earth's orbit, staging for what looked to be a final assault. While he didn't see a kitchen sink floating around out there with all of the Urvalin ships, large and small, he wouldn't have been surprised to find it out there with them.

"This is a full-fledged invasion force," Ara noted. "It appears we have arrived just in time."

"Looks that way," Charlie said. But the threat of his planet falling under attack took a back seat to the number one concern on his mind right now.

Ara sensed his agitation and inhaled the mixed magic and Allpower swirling around the planet.

"I have located Leila's scent," she said a moment later. "Hold tight, we are heading to her now."

With that, she dove straight into the atmosphere, not caring one bit if the enemy might notice a lone streak of orange burning through the sky. Once in the atmosphere she cooled back to normal temperatures but did not slow at all, powering down toward what appeared to be an outskirt of Los Angeles.

"There is a pitched battle taking place," she said as they drew near. "It appears to be only ground forces at the moment. I do not detect any enemy ships in the air. Her scent is coming from that medical facility, but it appears the fighting is all around it."

"Then get me as close as you can and I'll fight my way in."

"Oh," she replied with a toothy grin, "I will do much better than that."

Ara took a deep breath then let out a scorching blast of magical fire, roasting a good number of the Urvalin forces, sending them temporarily scrambling for cover. She hit the ground and Charlie jumped off, racing for the building's doors.

Ara covered him, her flames acting as quite the distraction as he forced his way into the locked facility. Charlie ran through the corridors. He could feel her. She was here, but where? He paused, sensing his love.

Upstairs.

Charlie took the steps two at a time, bounding up to a happy reunion. He burst out of the stairwell and was promptly tackled hard into the floor.

Charlie pulled up a killing spell and nearly cast it when he saw who it was crouched above him, her nanite arm likewise ready to deliver a killing blow.

"What the hell, Sarah?" he said, releasing the magic and dusting himself off.

"Holy crap. Charlie, I wasn't expecting you."

"Clearly."

"Hi, Charlie," Grundsch said, peeking out from a room down the hall.

"Hey, Grundsch," he replied, a bit taken aback by the odd situation. "Where's Leila, Sarah?"

"She's in there."

He moved for the door, but she grabbed his arm. Hard. "You don't want to go running in there."

"She needs me."

"That may be true, but a lot's happened while you were away."

"A lot, like what?" he asked, a sinking feeling forming in his gut.

"The Magus stone."

"What of it?"

"It's gotten, well, *protective*."

"I know, Sarah. I've already taken a couple of zaps from it."

"It's liquefying anyone trying to get close to her."

Charlie paused. "*Liquefying*?"

"Yep."

"Oh."

"Yep."

Charlie stood there, torn, when the building shook from the battle raging outside. Whatever they were going to be doing in here, the fight outside didn't care one whit. He keyed open his comms.

"Rika. Rika, this is Charlie, do you copy? If you're in atmosphere and can read this, I need backup at my signal coordinates."

"Charlie! You made it! Welcome back!" she replied a moment later.

"It's good to hear your voice, Little Brother," Marban chimed in.

"You too, Marban. And guess what? I'm about to be a dad!"

"We are happy for you, my friend. Now, what can we do for you?"

"There's a big fight going on right outside our position. I'm gonna need some support. I need to get Leila out of here."

"I'll be there in a flash," Rika said, turning to her companions.

"Charlie, a father?" Malalia mused. "Who would have guessed?"

"Yep, he's just full of surprises. Marban, I'm going to take my mech to go help. Malalia, I want you to take one of the ships in the *Coratta*'s hangar and cover me while I descend into the fight. Our people need a strong caster backing them."

"Of course."

"I should get to George," Marban said. "I want to divert, but—"

"I've got this, Big Guy. You go and help our friends. I've got Charlie and Leila covered."

Malalia and Rika both raced to their respective craft and launched. Marban high-tailed it out of there on a bee line to the cyborg and his forces while Malalia began casting, creating a diversion so Rika could slip down relatively unnoticed.

The mech flew fast, touching down outside the medical facility just a few minutes later. Rika's tattoos glowed as she jumped out and raced toward the building, the tightly wrapped Bakana rod in her hand, her own powerful magic laying out anyone in her path. She barged right in, slamming the doors behind her.

"Up here," Charlie called down the stairwell.

She ran up the stairs and leapt onto her friend, wrapping him up in a fierce hug. "It's good to see you, Charlie."

He looked at the rod. "Wasn't Master Leif supposed to have that?"

"Things went bad. I've got it now," she replied. "And weren't you supposed to be wielding the other one back in the Urvalin galaxy?"

"Things went sideways. Bawb and Hunze have it now."

"Ah. That explains the massive power draw I felt not too long ago. It was strangely familiar, but not yours."

"Yeah, they pulled from the rods to get us through the portal. But listen, we need to get Leila out of here."

"It's too dangerous to move her," Sarah said. "Oh, and hi, Rika."

"Hey, Sarah."

Charlie was shaking his head. "Look, I know it's dangerous, but it's Leila. We need to—"

"Charlie?" he heard her call from her room.

Charlie looked at the others and made a decision. He took a deep breath, nodded what might be his farewell to them both, and stepped inside.

Leila was in the final stage of labor. It seemed she had been holding on as long as she could, but the time had come. Her hair was plastered to her head with sweat, and the assistant AI that had been trying to help in the process lay in a crumpled heap on the floor, the massive machine reduced to nothing as if it were no more than a ball of paper.

"Hey, babe," he said, watching the pulsing green stone around her neck cautiously.

She let out a relieved sigh. "You made it." Another contraction hit her hard, and the stone flared up. Charlie stood absolutely still. Any movement at all and he might be seen as an intruder, and that would end *very* badly.

Leila let out a cry and pushed hard, the infant sliding out of her in a rush onto the birthing table. She leaned down and gathered up the child and brought it close.

"It's a boy, Charlie," she said, marveling at the palest of green hue to their son's skin. A mix of his dad and his mom, and, from what they could tell, perfectly healthy.

The baby cried out, using his lungs for the first time, and Leila pressed him to her breast. The infant latched on immediately, instinct taking over as he completed the birthing bond with his mother.

The Magus stone flashed even brighter, the glow spreading through the entire room.

"Uh, babe?" Charlie said with a worried tone, but the light did not harm him. Rather, now that the child was outside of the mother's body, it had shifted its protective nature. The family unit was under its watch, and Charlie was most definitely a part of it.

He moved to her side and kissed her head gently. "He's beautiful."

She squeezed his hand hard, emotions flaring every which way. This was a mess of feelings the likes of which she'd never encountered before.

"We're going to be okay," he reassured her. "Everything is going to be just fine."

The building shook again, snapping him out of the moment.

"I'll be right back," he said, stepping out into the hallway to the expectant eyes of his friends. "It's a boy," he said. "A healthy boy."

"May he live many happy days," Grundsch said.

"Congratulations, Charlie," Rika added, tears welling in her eyes.

"You'll be a great dad," Sarah told him.

"I hope so," he replied, his face betraying the fierce

protectiveness of a Papa Bear. "The stone will protect them, of that I'm sure. But we're getting them the hell out of here."

Rika grinned. "I know just the place." She keyed on her comms link. "Malalia, I'm getting Leila and the baby out of here. I need you to stay here and cover our departure."

"Where will you go?" the caster asked.

"Cal's secret location. It'll be safe there, but I can't risk us being followed. It's imperative you distract the Urvalin."

"Consider it done."

Rika turned to her friend. "Okay, we're good. Just gotta push through some assholes outside to get to the mech and we'll be set. Ara's nearby?"

"She is."

"Great. You can fly with her, since the mech's gonna be a little bit crowded. Now, are you absolutely sure the Magus stone won't melt me?"

"As sure as I can get. It's still in protection mode, but not nearly like you said it was before."

"I guess we'll see soon enough. Come on, this is going to take both of us."

Charlie helped Leila to her feet, the baby swaddled in her arms. He saw that the afterbirth had already delivered and had come out intact. She was out of the woods. Now she needed to get somewhere safe to rest and regain her strength.

They made their way to the ground floor where the others were waiting for her.

"Sit here," Charlie said. "I'll be right back."

The Magus stone had gone dark again, and both Baloo and Bahnjoh were allowed close to sniff the new addition to their little family. Seeing that, Rika felt a whole lot more comfortable loading them into her mech. Now they just had to clear a path to it.

Rika and Charlie stepped out, defensive spells cast and

ready. The Urvalin apparently had added air support to their forces after Ara had made her impressive appearance. Weapons fire rained down from above while Allpower battered them from all sides.

It was all they could do to just stop the attack, but moving forward would be a problem.

"Come on, Chuckles, show us some of that magic of yours," Rika said.

"It's still not firing quite right, but I'll try." He cast a mid-range stun spell and sent it toward the enemy. The spell flew true, but it broke apart on their defenses. A blistering response was launched their way. Apparently, they had some powerful casters with them and were pulling out all the stops.

"Gah!" Rika grunted as she barely deflected the attack. "Enough of this bullshit!" she bellowed, pissed off and emotional. It had been a long day, and she was over it.

Charlie watched with shock and awe as she violently ripped the Allpower from the nearest Urvalin, taking it for herself and leaving them barely moving on the ground.

"What the hell, Rika?"

"Yeah, so that's a thing now," she said with a shrug. "Doesn't help with those ships, though."

A moment later two of the Urvalin craft blew to pieces, and the third took a healthy dose of railgun sabots before spiraling away as fast as it could. Pulse cannon blasts peppered the forces on the ground, forcing them into a hasty retreat.

"Who the—" Rika wondered when she saw a familiar shape. A ship. *Her* ship. The *Fujin*.

"But it was dead. The array took it out. How the hell—"

The ship dropped down right in front of them and the hatch popped open. Jo rushed out of the opening, a pulse rifle in each hand, blasting at any Urvalin who showed their faces.

"Come on, you slackers! You don't want to miss your ride!"

Rika raced to her friend, hugging her hard even as she continued to fire. For a cyborg, multitasking was just part of daily life.

"You're okay! But you were fried."

"It took a while, but Cal and his team did a bang-up job on me. Managed to do a full restore and reboot. I got me a few nifty upgrades in the process too. But there's no time for that. We've gotta go."

"You don't have to tell me twice."

Rika rushed back inside with Charlie and gathered up the new mother and hurried her to the ship. "You guys can come too," she told Sarah and Grundsch.

"Nah, we're good here," Sarah said. "Someone needs to keep messing with the Urvalin's plans. Now get out of here, and keep our girl safe."

Rika gave her a quick hug then ran to her mech, powering it up and taking to the sky. Charlie rode with his family aboard the *Fujin*, the knot that had lived in his stomach for so long gone entirely.

"*Ara, meet us in the air. We are leaving,*" he told her. "*It's time to get out of here.*"

"*I shall. And congratulations, Charlie. You're a father now.*"

He let that thought sink in as he held Leila and his son in his arms. "I'm a dad," he marveled, now more ready than ever to do whatever it took to keep his family safe.

A little flash of sadness hit him as he thought of Bawb and Hunze, their own child on the way. He had hoped their children would grow up together, but now all of that was up in the air, to be decided in the heat of battle, and far sooner than later.

CHAPTER FIFTY-FOUR

Far across space, millions of light years away, a master assassin and his mate were laying waste to Urvalin troops by the dozens. They had saved their vespus blades' immense power for their final battle with the enemy, but now, here on this God-forsaken planet, the weapons were no more magical than anything else in this place.

But they didn't care. And the gleaming blue metal was still more than sharp enough on its own to make quick work of any who were foolish enough to draw within their swords' reach.

The Bakana rod remained wrapped but for one small section, the length of it strapped to Bawb's back as he and Hunze fought, ran, ambushed, and fought some more. He would just barely touch it from time to time, waiting to see if the final connection had been made.

Rika had one of the rods, he had learned as much when he pulled power from her to help force their friends back through the portal. It was amazing just how much magic was within her, and as she bore power of multiple types, it had managed to be just enough to achieve their goal, at least that one time.

But to take on the Urvalin they needed the third caster. That would be Master Farmatta, and she was *powerful*. For some reason, however, she had not yet connected. But Bawb knew her well, and if she had delayed, it was undoubtedly for a good reason.

As for Nakk and his rebel fleet, they had managed to disable the dampening array surrounding the planet. Suddenly, the entire world was fair game. An open battlefield above and below upon which they were fighting to the bitter end. And it was a good thing, because Commander Fraxxis had led a massive portion of his fleet down the narrow path to safety between the wormholes and taken up a position blocking anyone's escape.

From there he had dispatched his forces in waves, launching attack ship after attack ship to weaken his enemy before he himself would move in for the coup de grace.

But it wasn't working out quite as easily as Fraxxis had hoped. With the dampening array down, the planet now acted as something of a buffer zone, its mass separating the two fleets. Grudgingly, Fraxxis ordered even more ships into the fray while maintaining his safe distance aboard his command ship. It would only be a matter of time.

"Anything?" Hunze asked as she and Bawb stepped from the battlefield to catch their breath.

Bodies were falling all around as the Urvalin and rebel ground forces fought. It wasn't just Nakk's people, the enemy had discovered when their landing craft arrived, spewing forth their troops. It was all of the countless others who had been stranded here by the Urvalin over the years as well. Those who hadn't made the escape with Nakk and his new comrades.

He and his people had lasting issues with some of them, the rival factions warring for longer than any cared to remember. But now the Urvalin had come to their home turf, and all other conflicts seemed of little importance. The ones who had stranded them here had foolishly landed, and they were more than eager for revenge.

Bawb took a sip from his water flask and wiped the sweat from his brow. He reached back and touched the bare spot of the Bakana rod. Rika was still connected, but no Farmatta.

"Anything?" Hunze asked.

"Not yet," he said, stroking her cheek tenderly.

"What is she waiting for?"

"She has her ways," he replied. "But what of you? This fighting has been strenuous. How are you faring? Your form appears sound as ever."

"For a pregnant woman, you mean."

"For a majestic Ghalian warrior," he replied.

She leaned close and kissed him gently. "I am fine, my love. But I fear we cannot continue like this much longer. The Urvalin greatly outnumber us, and eventually they will deploy the rest of their forces."

"I know," he said. "But there is little more we can do than—" He fell silent. Something felt different. Different in a good way.

"Bawb? What is it?"

"I believe it is time," he said, pulling the rod from his back and unwrapping its length. As he did, he could feel Farmatta's considerable power flowing into the rod along with Rika's formidable magic. And linking like this across the three galaxies, it was only compounded.

He and Hunze each grasped a portion of the rod, feeling their shared magic flare to life despite the black holes. This was something so much more powerful than just this system's Allpower.

Immediately, they cast hard at the ships above, straining the tenuous wisps of magic Fraxxis and the others in his triumvirate had managed to somehow maintain even in this place. It was the Vikann stones and their bezels, connecting them across the galaxies that gave them power as well. But they had not managed to make the Korna tablet do its work for them.

The commanders were stronger than before, no doubt, but not nearly where they needed to be. Especially not if the enemy had this sort of power up their sleeve. Incredibly, Fraxxis felt his power slipping.

"This is impossible," he growled, pulling harder from the stone and his comrades. "How can they do this? Here in this place? It is not possible!"

"I do not know," Torgus said, straining against incredibly strong magic targeting him and his fleet as well. Down below, Rika held the other Bakana rod, channeling its power and casting hard from the remote safety of the desert while the Urvalin commander high above felt the sting of her power, his forces now fighting without their commander's support.

The battle still raged in the magic galaxy, but the Ghalian and pirates were making quite a fight of it, and Commander Prin was on the ropes. Her power was weakening as well as the old Ghalian woman on the surface poured her magic into the third Bakana rod.

Prin was on the verge of collapse when the onslaught abruptly ceased. Whatever had been attacking her power had relented. In fact, across all three galaxies something had happened, ceasing the assault, and the Urvalin were not about to ask why.

"Attack!" the commanders ordered almost in unison.

Commander Fraxxis poured more of his fleet toward the prison planet, readying to overwhelm the resistance with sheer numbers.

"How many more?" Nakk asked as his ship took another strong hit.

"I cannot count them all," Skohla replied. "Too many."

"We are going to have to fall back. There is no way we can—"

A barrage of pulse and projectile weapons fire lit up Fraxxis's ships from behind as hundreds of attack craft streaked down the narrow gap toward the Allpower-free world. The Urvalin had their defenses projecting forward, not back, and there was limited room to maneuver in this tight space. They were under attack, but they risked hitting their own ships if they fired recklessly. As a result, the craft barreling through their ranks had almost free rein as they powered through the armada, leaving behind a wide swath of damage.

The ships then bombarded the craft lurking behind the planet, staying out of the line of fire of Nakk's fleet.

"What is this?" Nakk wondered, utterly confused by the strange craft.

A familiar voice crackled onto the comms system, overriding their own encryption settings with ease. "Hold back for a moment," the familiar voice of the high priest said. "We will be to you shortly. We just have a few things to do with these Urvalin scum beforehand."

It was the void dwellers. The technology-based people from the Allpower-free realm. They had come to help, and they had come *very* highly armed. Nakk and his people watched with rising spirits as the newcomers wreaked havoc on the Urvalin ships, scrambling their tracking systems as they flew strafing runs.

Some of the smaller Urvalin ships succumbed to the intensity of the attack, while the larger ones adjusted their shielding to better protect themselves. Once that happened, the newly arrived fleet abruptly broke free and sped around the globe to join the other rebel forces.

"I thought you did not want anything to do with this fight," Nakk transmitted. "You have our gratitude, whatever your motives."

The head priest came on the line once more. "What was said

had validity. No one would be safe if the Urvalin succeed in their plot. They must be eradicated, for all of our sakes."

Nakk felt his heart swell with joy. These new allies and their highly advanced tech ships had turned the tide of battle, at least for the time being. It was a delicate balance that had been struck, and the day could fall to either side. What they really needed was Bawb's Bakana rod to help them once more.

On the surface, the Ghalian was trying to do just that, but one of the rods was no longer connected, and he had no idea why.

"What is going on in the other realm?" Hunze wondered.

"I wish I knew," he replied. "All we can do now is hope, because if they broke the connection, Heaven only knows when it might be restored."

CHAPTER FIFTY-FIVE

"What in the name of the Ancients do you think you are doing?" Torgus bellowed from his casting podium, his Vikann stone flaring bright in its bezel. "You are taking much more than your share. Korna tablet or no, this is not the plan."

"I am doing what needs to be done," Prin yelled back, casting furiously at the resistance forces swarming her fleet as she did so, drawing even more power than she already had from the three commanders' shared link.

"Disengage, fool!" Fraxxis hissed. "You have overcommitted. You are putting us all at risk."

"No! I have them cornered. *We* have them cornered."

Torgus and Fraxxis were livid, beside themselves with fury. Prin had gotten too caught up in the moment, giving in to the heat of battle, and it was endangering all of their plans. Unfortunately, separated by galaxies, as they were, their only recourse was via discussion. Had they been in the same system, it very well may have come to blows.

"You felt their Allpower," Torgus continued. "They have also somehow learned to connect across the galaxies. You must withdraw while we adjust our tactics."

"No!" she repeated. "I can defeat them!"

He wasn't having it. "Don't be a fool. You have very nearly cost us our victory."

"And now I will ensure it. I will end these pests once and for all. Soon the Ghalian and all of their pesky resistance fighter friends will be dead or subjugated to my will."

"Prin, stop this madness!" Fraxxis yelled as he felt her pulling even more power from the Vikann stone.

It was unbalancing the power between them, tipping the flow unevenly to the galaxy she was occupying. They already learned she had committed nearly all of her forces into this battle, foolishly believing herself to be walking the enemy into their final trap. But, it seemed, the fight was far from over.

Whatever had happened, however the enemy had managed to cast so ferociously against them, they likely only had a brief window in which to regroup and redeploy their forces.

Prin, however, saw her opportunity to crush the enemy and seized it with both hands.

She cast hard, battering the resistance craft with her magic, giving her other casters the surge they needed to push the resistance fighters, Ghalian, and pirates back on their heels. Victory was close, she could taste it. She just needed to draw from the Vikann stone a little longer.

The fighters on the surface were reinvigorated by their leader's display of force and were pressing their attacks, and try as they might, the resistance was faltering.

Korbin and Amazara were leading the fight, Kara and Vee flying through the battlefield atop their dragons offering aerial support, then landing to pick off individual pockets of resistance before launching back into the air. This one pocket of combatants was making a good showing of it. Unfortunately, the rest of the resistance forces did not possess the same degree of power.

Worse, Korbin was tiring. It was inevitable, and the teens could feel it.

"We need to help him, Vee," Kara transmitted over their helmet comms.

"I'll cover you," Vee replied, sweeping wide with Gazz blasting a path with his magical flames.

Nixxus landed beside Korbin, and Kara quickly dismounted, rushing to his and Amazara's side.

"Quite a day," she said, casting a protective spell just as a new barrage from above rained down. Her magic held, and they remained unscathed. But for how long was anyone's guess.

"Quite a day indeed," Korbin replied. "You should leave, Kara."

"Never."

"There are too many of them. This is getting—"

A sonic boom shook the air as a massive stolen Urvalin warship blasted into the atmosphere, dropping straight out of the sky. At the last moment it powered up hard and reversed its fall, decelerating and landing on the battlefield, crushing a fair number of Urvalin in the process, a few of their legs sticking out from beneath it like the Wicked Witch of the East.

The hatch flew open, and a barrage of Allpower and weapons rained down upon it. But nothing happened to the tall men calmly exiting the ship. In fact, their combined magic was so strong it not only deflected the assault, but actually threw much of the enemy's attacks back at them, sending them fleeing in disarray to regroup and find some new means of attack.

"Father!" Kara called out.

Visla Palmarian spun, locking eyes on his daughter, and ran to her, sweeping her up in his arms as Visla Samanna covered him, casting vicious spell after spell into the Urvalin ranks. He and Palmarian were working well together. Quite well, in fact, their former disagreements a thing of the past now that the Council of Twenty was no more.

"Nipsenni, this way," Samanna called out. A small woman with wild hair and wilder eyes scurried out of the ship and made her way to his side as they hurried toward the reunited family.

"I can't believe you're okay," Kara said, tears in her eyes. "We tried so hard to find you, but every time we hit one of their ships, you weren't there. But we never stopped looking."

Palmarian nodded his thanks to Korbin and Amazara, his dear friends since longer than he'd care to admit, but did not let go of his daughter. The two of them were crackling with magic as their emotions ran high. Like father, like daughter, it seemed. They felt the rush of magic and decided now was a fantastic time to put it to good use.

"Shall we?" he asked with a proud smile.

Kara nodded once, then cast her hardest. Her spells flew out, smashing through the Urvalin ranks almost as powerfully as a visla might. Palmarian beamed with pride as he joined his magic with hers, increasing the power and clearing some breathing room for their ground forces.

A small group of Urvalin casters made a brazen attempt to flank them, all of them drawing deep for their spells as they cast against them. Flames engulfed them as they were distracted by the people fighting on the ground. Vee and Gazz swooped by overhead, laying waste before dropping behind the protective spells of their friends.

"We felt a massive surge of power from down here," Visla Samanna said. "It was pushing back the Urvalin with incredible force. But then it ceased."

"That would be the Bakana rod," Kara informed them. "They are connected across all three galaxies."

"They are our best chance at defeating the Urvalin," Korbin

added. "The Ghalian provided them in hopes of turning the tide. Master Farmatta has been using it to—oh no!"

All eyes turned to see the old woman lying on the ground, badly hurt, but not dead. She was a tough one to kill, it seemed, but she was clearly out of this fight.

A ruined ship, or what was left of one, had nearly crashed on top of her as it fell from the sky. Only redirecting her power at the last moment had kept her from being crushed. But while she had amazingly managed to deflect the massive hunk of debris, the rain of sharp bits of shrapnel that fell with it had struck her down.

She now lay on the dirt, bleeding out slowly, a length of metal on the ground just out of her reach.

Nipsenni saw the hurt old lady and rushed to her side.

"It'll be okay," she said. "We'll get you help."

"Don't mind me, child," Farmatta said, somehow managing a bloody smile. "I will be all right. But you must take the Bakana rod. Get it to Korbin's hands."

"The *what*?"

"The Bakana rod. It is a relic of great power connecting our fiercest warriors. Get it to Korbin, quickly. It requires a powerful caster to complete the link. It is our only hope to defeat the Urvalin."

Nipsenni hesitated a moment, then turned toward Korbin and picked up the rod. As soon as her fingers wrapped around it, though, she felt what the old woman was talking about. The sheer power flowing through it. Through her.

More violent spells smashed into their defenses, shaking the ground despite Palmarian and Samanna's casting. Nipsenni's anger flared, and her eyes sparkled brighter than before. She looked at the fallen woman, the magic flashing behind her incredible eyes shocking the woman, which, considering who Farmatta was, was really saying something.

"Don't worry," Nipsenni said, her anger rising and her power surging like never before. "I've got this. Just tell me, how does this thing—"

Vast power surged across three galaxies as she joined with Rika, Bawb, and Hunze. This time the magic was much stronger than before. A new type of power had joined the trio, and its potential was incredible.

Commander Prin fell to her knees aboard her command ship in pain as the wave hit her. She nearly vomited from the force as her senses spun around her. "What sort of Allpower is this?" she cried out from the deck.

Her ship was shaking, her own spells no longer defending any of her fleet as she struggled to simply maintain consciousness. Slowly, she rose to her feet, her Vikann stone flaring bright as it struggled to protect her from this new magic.

Men and women were screaming, she heard, as her senses cleared. There was a fight, and it was here in her ship. In her command center. She blinked hard, pulling all of her remaining power to herself rather than her fleet.

Pirates surrounded her casting podium, she realized. She didn't know how long she had been incapacitated, but it had been long enough for them to board her ship. She was weakened, but by no means out of the fight. And like a cornered animal, she was even more dangerous in her home turf.

"Listen, Lassie. Your ship is ours," a gregarious pirate with a great, bushy red beard growled. "Now, you can fight if you like. Nothing would suit me better. Killing you? That would be less paperwork, after all."

"Paperwork?" Prin asked, legitimately confused. She had been ready to smite them all with her remaining power, but that comment, for some reason, had taken her aback. "How dare you?" she spat, regaining her composure. "Do you realize who you are dealing with?"

Sharp fangs sank into her neck, her power falling away from her as the Ghalian behind her drank deep. "Yes, they do," Master Zilara said with a bloody grin. "We all know who you are."

Prin realized her mistake, but there was nothing she could do about it. The pirates, the loud bearded man, they had been a distraction. All to allow the assassin to sneak close enough to strike.

"Don't worry," Zilara said. "I will not drain you dry. Not yet, anyway. Now, be a dear and just lie here for a while. I need you alive to maintain your connection. It is not quite time to break it. Not just yet."

Prin was too weak to reply, but her fading mind took in those words. "Not just yet." It seemed the enemy had a plan in motion after all. And she was likely never going to learn what it was.

CHAPTER FIFTY-SIX

Commander Fraxxis had regrouped his forces and pulled back into the gap as soon as the massive power he and the other commanders had been fighting had broken. It might only be a brief respite, but he was going to make the most of it.

Somehow, the rebel forces had come to possess Allpower, even in this place where it should not be possible. It had sent his ships into disarray, but then, as quickly as it had appeared, it had vanished.

Of course, having another fleet of attack craft come barreling into his own ships from behind had been another nasty surprise, but their shields were strong, and the damage sustained, while significant, was not by any means enough to stop their assault.

They were going to crush the rebels once and for all, both in space as well as on their prison world's surface, and that would be the end of the rebellion.

The fighting intensified as Urvalin streamed to the planet. They had expected something of a rout when they got there. Tales of their enemies being forced to live like animals on this prison world were common in their fleet. A bit of self-congratulatory ego boosting to make themselves feel important and powerful, not to mention striking fear into the hearts of would-be rebels who heard them.

But they found out the hard way that the people they had stranded all of those years ago were far from broken. In fact, as their troops were slaughtered in those first waves, they realized that perhaps a land war against the rebels was not such a wise idea now that they were embedded with the local forces.

But Fraxxis demanded they press onward, so onward they fought, killing as many as they could as they pushed on across the planet.

Nakk and his fleet had stayed in space, fighting the Urvalin off as best they could, but Bawb and Hunze were partaking in the more visceral form of combat, fighting in tandem in true guerrilla fashion.

They had possessed the advantage for a brief moment, the Bakana rod forcing the Urvalin into a retreat, but that connection had abruptly ceased, leaving them exposed and without many options. Even the arrival of the high priest and his ships was only going to be a bandage. A temporary means to staunch the bleeding before the Urvalin moved in for their final stroke.

"I fear we are running out of time," Bawb said as he and Hunze scurried for cover as a squad of Urvalin raced by. "If only —" The power in the rod suddenly flared once more. "Hunze, take hold!" Bawb said, swinging the rod from his back once more.

The two of them connected at once, the power flowing through them with an intensity like they had never felt before. They directed it at the main Urvalin caster, Commander Fraxxis. He felt the wave hit, but his own Vikann stone somehow managed to draw power in this place as well, fighting back and keeping this new force at bay, but only just. It was so strong, though. So intense. He wondered what he might do to stop it.

For now, it was a stalemate.

The battle raged on across the planet as well as in space. With Fraxxis now focusing all of his efforts on defending against the magical attack on himself, the other ships were left on their own. Normally, this would not have been a problem, but with the combined forces of their original targets as well as the newcomers dividing their attentions, it was difficult to fight effectively, especially with their commander otherwise occupied.

"We are not making progress," Hunze grunted. "He is able to resist."

"This place reduces our potency," Bawb replied.

"What can we do?" she asked. "Neither side is making progress. The black holes are draining too much power."

An idea dawned on the assassin. "Nakk," he transmitted. "Can you hear me?"

"Loud and clear. What's going on, Bawb?"

"We need you and the other ships to retreat. Disengage from the Urvalin and pull back behind the planet."

"But we're driving them back. They're being pushed into the space around their command ship. It's an ideal firing scenario."

"I know, and you have bought us a lot of time. But you must trust me. Pull everyone back and get clear."

Something in the Ghalian's voice made Nakk put aside any hesitation. "Recall all ships. Everyone, get clear of the Urvalin immediately!"

The ships did as commanded, though a great many were confused. But Nakk had not steered them wrong so far, and they obeyed his commands.

Bawb and Hunze's knuckles whitened as they clenched the

Bakana rod, casting as hard as they could. But they had released Fraxxis from their attack.

The Urvalin felt the assault cease and grinned. "All craft, regroup at my location," he commanded, drawing his ships to form an impenetrable blockade of the exit route. They had numeric superiority, and with their enemy's slip-up, now they could slowly separate them from their comrades one by one, taking them out until there were none left.

Fraxxis wondered a moment where the massive power he had felt had gone. It was still in play, that much he could feel, but it was no longer a threat to him or his ship. That was twice he'd nearly been overcome by it, and twice he had come out on top. His ego swelled. He was even better than he had thought. "Not bad," he said to himself. "Not bad at all."

Bawb and Hunze, however, had continued to cast with all their might, but not at the Urvalin command ship, and not even at the fleet. They had targeted the Urvalin portal, forcing it to open wider, pulling energy through it ever faster. The surge of galactic tide rushing between realms heeded their spell and began flowing faster and faster as it did.

The reaction was subtle at first. Just a push here, a nudge there. But when the floodgates finally opened, a wave of space time energy slammed into the Urvalin fleet. Normally, they would have had no issues with such a thing, their shielding protecting them from damage. But packed in tight as they were, this pushed them off course, crashing into one another until they started to teeter at the edge of the safe zone, ship after ship falling out of the path of safety and into the pull of the black holes.

Fraxxis realized what was happening only a few seconds too late when he ordered all engines full. The ship possessed massive amounts of thrust, but that would be no match for the pull of a single black hole, let alone several.

Fraxxis frantically pulled from his Vikann stone, trying desperately to escape the gravitational well he was on the edge of falling into. But with his other craft smashing into the command ship as they slipped into the gravitational pull, it would only be a matter of time before the engines gave out and they all fell to their doom.

But he was a stubborn man, and with his stone he would hold on as long as he could, not caring that his connection stayed open the entire time he did.

Just as Bawb had hoped he might.

"You may send your people to mop up," he transmitted to Nakk. "The day is ours."

"Thank you, my friend. We will come and retrieve you at once."

"Not just yet," the Ghalian replied, still locked in and casting with the Bakana rod. "We are not quite done here. The others still need us."

CHAPTER FIFTY-SEVEN

While Bawb, Hunze, and Nipsenni were bringing the hammer down on their respective Urvalin enemies, Rika had been on guard duty in the desert, watching over her friends while channeling her power to both of the other Bakana rods.

They simply couldn't all share in the magic at once as the Urvalin were attempting to do with their Vikann stones. One would have to selflessly pull back and let the others focus on their battles. It was the only way to win.

The Urvalin, however, were not ones to possess such a team player attitude, and each commander was pulling as much of the Allpower as they could for their individual battles. It had cost them much, and had not gone as planned for two of them, but they were all still linked, and that gave Torgus the power he required to push aside the resistance fighters like toy ships.

His moment had arrived. This was the time to lay claim to this realm. Prin and Fraxxis were faltering, he could feel it, but they were so locked into their own battles they were ignoring the other casters. Fine. He would do it himself, becoming the first of the three to conquer an entire galaxy.

"Take the ship down," he commanded. "Bring me to the hub of the resistance fighters' operations."

"Immediately, Commander," his first officer replied, setting the course for Los Angeles, the former home of the leading AI mind in the resistance.

The ship was massive, and the spectacle it created when it pushed into the atmosphere was one to behold. An enormous craft descending for the surface, its smaller support ships swarming around it like angry remora looking for scraps.

As he flew, the dampening array prevented the escape of his enemy. Now was the end game, and they would all pay the price. But something was afoot not so far away, and it would shake up his plans something fierce.

"Testing now," Joshua said, firing a small probe impregnated with the magic-casting nanites Freya had given him.

It was a single bit of magic they had been instructed to cast. Power the probe, nothing more. And as it flew into Earth's atmosphere, remaining functional as it cleared the array, he knew he was on the right track.

"It worked, Freya."

"Of course it did. But that was just a small probe. Are you sure you want to risk this? You haven't had much time to prepare."

"Marty is down there, as are all of our friends. You saw the command ship descend. This is it. What choice do I have?"

"I can enter now," Freya said. "You can help Zed break his fleet free. We still need to deal with the dampening array blockading him, and you are the one who can disrupt it."

"I suppose," he said. "But Marty? And the others?"

"I've got this." Freya flew close and touched wings with him once more, as much a gesture of affection as a test of his nanite swarm.

They were charged and adapting incredibly rapidly. More than the other AIs in their extended family, Joshua was a special mind, much like she was. Unique and one of a kind. He had been thinking outside of the box since the day he was created, it was what he'd been made to do. And as a result he was able to adjust to impossible things like magic-casting nanites linked to his brain far better than anyone else might.

His ship was made up of dozens of smaller pieces, each heavily armed and armored, and each ready for a fight. He just had to separate them and dismantle as many of the microsats at once as possible to break the array's lock on his friends. Do that and he could finally make up for so many days of seeming impotence, locked in a bubble on Dark Side.

While Joshua prepared for his difficult task, Torgus's ship landed with a massive plume of dust and debris, right in the heart of the city. He wasn't going to defeat these peons from a distance. He wanted to feel their loss up close and personal, watching their faces as he forced them to bow to his command.

He swept through the city on his personal skiff, arriving at the burned-out remains of Cal's command center. He smiled. What better place to lay his ultimate claim to this world? To this galaxy, for that matter.

He brought the skiff to a halt and stepped off, walking to the raised courtyard in front of the ruined structure as he began casting with great destructive power. His fleet felt the Allpower flow and increased their attacks, swarming to his location then spreading out, seeking any pockets of resistance.

Of that, there were many.

"Yes," he said to himself with great pleasure, his Vikann stone glowing bright. He cast a projecting spell, throwing his voice out across the city. "This is Commander Torgus of the conquering Urvalin fleet. You are defeated. Feel my power and kneel before me!"

A sonic boom shook the air nearby, followed by a loud reply blasted over Freya's external speakers.

"Yeah, that's totally not happening, dickweed," Daisy shouted back. She killed the comms and opened fire, blasting the Urvalin's skiff to pieces, along with a few dozen of the tightly packed troops who had come to witness their leader's glorious victory.

"Drop me off, Kiddo, then have at it."

"Copy that," Freya said with glee, activating her camouflage and dropping to the surface unseen as the enraged commander scanned the sky to no avail.

Daisy hopped out and took off running toward Cal's old home, weapons clattering on her back and hips as she ran. For this fight, more was better than less, she'd surmised.

Freya leapt back into the air, powering her railguns with magically enhanced sabots, and let off a volley, the powerful rounds punching right through most of the Urvalin defenses, the mix of metal and magic proving too much for the lesser casters.

Torgus shifted his power to counter her, zeroing in on her location once the railguns fired, batting aside her next attack, keeping his forces safe.

"Oh, hell no," Daisy growled, drawing Stabby from his sheath, the sword pouring out his magic into the fight, adding to Freya's attack.

Still, Torgus managed to block them, holding them off with relative ease. He actually smiled at the battle surrounding him. He'd forgotten just how much he enjoyed smiting his enemies personally like this.

Daisy felt a surge of Allpower push back against Stabby's power, and incredibly, the sword almost seemed worried. This was not good. Torgus still had too much power at his beck and call.

"No, you don't," a voice said just as multiple high-velocity rounds flew at the caster's head, forcing him to slightly shift his defenses to block the shots.

"Hey, Sis," Daisy said as Sarah ran to her side, weapons blasting away.

"Hey, yourself. What the hell are you doing? You and Freya can't possibly take him on your own."

Daisy smiled. "Nope. And we're not trying to. We're the distraction."

A pair of winged shapes flashed down from above, magical flames blasting from their mouths, laying waste to any Urvalin they contacted and sending many of their ships tumbling from the sky. Torgus shifted his casting yet again, now dealing with yet another angle of attack, this one from above. Ara and Orgalius moved quickly, casting defenses as they continued to bombard his ships.

While he was occupied, Marty flew in hot and fast and dropped off his cargo then hauled ass back into the fight up above. Sergeant Franklin and his guerrilla team rushed to Daisy and Sarah's aid.

"Hey, babe," Vince called out to Daisy.

"We're here to cover your flanks," Finn added. "George and his boys are gonna go hunting."

A massive Ra'az Hok, flanked by a pair of enormous beasts, strode out from behind cover. "Did someone say hunting? Can we come?"

George almost burst out laughing, which, even in battle, was actually pretty much in character for him. "This is marvelous," he said. "Hell yeah, Grundsch. Come with us; we're gonna go smite us some Urvalin."

The ground troops hurried on their way while the Zomoki, the dragon, the magical AI ship, and the deadly sisters all pressed the attack on the Urvalin commander. He was holding his own, but the stress of defending and countering against so many fronts was showing. Still, his Vikann stone glowed brightly, keeping him solidly in the fight.

"I don't know if we have enough firepower," Sarah said. "He's too strong."

"Oh, ye of little faith," Daisy replied. "Look."

Two new plumes of dragon fire shot out of the sky, accompanied by a brutal barrage of pulse and railgun fire. Drombus and Duzza had joined the fray, and their riders were eager for battle.

"What in the world?" Sarah gasped.

"Our kids are doing good, Sis," Daisy replied with a proud grin.

"They really are," Vince said from her side as he blasted a pair of approaching Urvalin goons. He was absolutely beaming with joy. "Just look at our kids go!"

It was getting to be too much for Torgus. He realized he had perhaps claimed a premature victory. He was cut off from his ship, but if he could somehow make it back to his casting podium, he could increase his connection with the others, and then overpowering these troublesome resistance fighters would be simple. But first he would need to open a path. And the best way to accomplish that was to smite a few of these casters harassing him dead. It would only take a few to weaken their combined attack, and then he could—

Torgus felt a cold pain in his chest and fell to his knees. He looked down, his hands searching for blood, but there was no wound he could find. But something had happened. Something had—he realized what it was and fear washed over him.

Prin was gone. Her connection had been severed, and not by her choosing. She was dead, there could be no doubt.

Torgus reached for Fraxxis, trying to bolster his own power at the expense of another, but he, too, was slipping from reach. Not abruptly, like Prin, but fading quickly, petering out until there was no more.

The Vikann stone fell to a minuscule little shine, sitting quietly on his heaving chest as he knelt there, exhausted. All around him his loyal troops, ready to give everything for him, watched in shock as Daisy walked toward their fallen leader.

"You've lost," she called out. "Give it up."

The Urvalin realized she was speaking the truth. One look at their leader and it was clear. Torgus had failed. The caster slowly rose to his feet, much to the joy of his men. He had lost, yes, but he would go out like a true Urvalin.

"I surrender," he said, raising his hands in the air.

A shocked stir rippled through the bloodied Urvalin ranks. Suicide rather than capture was their way. Their creed. Many had chosen that sacrifice without hesitation for their cause, and now their leader was taking the coward's way out? It seemed what was good enough for the commoner was not suitable for the ruling elite.

"You give up?" Daisy asked, her sword ready to act if need be. "No funny stuff?"

"You have my—"

A single weapon blast slammed into his chest, deflecting off his Vikann stone, which was impervious to such trivial things, striking him dead. Daisy and the others spun, but the assailant was already dead as well. He, and his comrades, had triggered their suicide spells once their traitorous leader had been executed. They would not be prisoners. They would die on their own terms with their honor intact.

Daisy and Sarah shared a look as they gazed across the scores of Urvalin now dead on the ground. Apparently, their leader's failure was a rather triggering event. It was one hell of a sight.

"Well," Daisy said with a morbid laugh, "I guess we don't need to build bigger prisons now after all."

CHAPTER FIFTY-EIGHT

Rika felt the shift in the galaxy's power as Torgus's pull abruptly ceased. The leader of the invading forces had fallen, and none too soon. The subtle influence she had been exerting all across the system, gently pushing Urvalin ships out of position and hampering their communications, had been an enormous expenditure of the Bakana rod's shared power.

Had she come at Torgus head-on, he would have undoubtedly reinforced his position and dug in for a long fight. She had to be tactful with this one, and do the one thing he wouldn't expect. She opted *not* to engage directly. To lure him out with a false sense of victory. And from what she could tell, it had worked.

Of course, the majority of the Urvalin fighting forces had not yet learned their leader had fallen, and that was going to pose a problem. The power vacuum could be a dangerous thing, and word of his demise would take time to spread.

Rika released her grasp on the Bakana rod's power and wrapped it tightly. "Heya, Jo, would you do me a solid and tuck this away in the *Fujin*?"

"No problem," her cybernetic friend replied, taking the rod from her hands. "Nice work, by the way."

"Thanks," she said, looking out across the sand to the shady spot Charlie where and Leila had settled down for some bonding with their new addition. "It's been an interesting day, that's for sure."

Jo headed back to the old, beat-up hangar where they had tucked their ship and mech away, keeping them both out of sight from anyone who might fly by overhead. This was the perfect place for it. There were a dozen large hangars, as well as a length of old runway from who knew when, long out of use and fallen to disrepair.

Aside from that, all around them was essentially nothing. Just a vast expanse of desert way out in the middle of nowhere.

Or so it should have been.

Two Urvalin troop carriers dropped down fast, their soldiers spilling out and forming a firing line as they moved in on the new parents. Rika's tattoos flared, but she didn't need to worry. The Magus stone sensed the hostile nature of the newcomers and lashed out hard, smiting all who had dared venture near, leaving nothing of them but bubbling puddles of melted flesh.

The remaining troops hurried back, looking for guidance, not boarding their ships and fleeing, but not engaging either. Now things were getting interesting, it seemed.

Rika looked up as another shape streaked through the sky. The small ship Malalia had been flying. It circled hard and swung low, landing in a cloud of dust. The Urvalin turned as the hatch opened and the powerful woman stepped out onto the cracked tarmac. They watched her walk, but, Rika noted, did not make any attempt to subdue her. In fact, they were almost deferential in their posturing.

Malalia glanced over at Charlie and Leila and the newborn

in their arms, taking in the glow from the Magus stone and the puddles of what had just recently been Urvalin. She shrugged.

"Just leave those ones alone. We don't need them anyway," she said, striding toward Rika, her full power restored and then some.

"Malalia? What are you doing?"

"Doing? Why, I'm taking what's mine, obviously."

"But you were reformed. You were good. That wasn't an act."

Malalia's eyes softened, but only for an instant. "Perhaps, in a fit of weakness," she said. "But we both know I was meant to rule. You better than most, if I recall correctly."

Rika's tattoo's flared, but she held back. Casting this close to Leila and the baby could be risky, regardless of the Magus stone's power. Instead, she reached into her pocket and pulled out a small cylinder with a button on top. She popped the cap off and held her finger over it.

"Don't make me do this," she said.

Malalia just laughed and kept walking toward her. Rika pushed the button, triggering the explosive in her neck. Only nothing happened. She pushed it again to the same result.

Malalia grinned. "Oh, the explosive device? My friend Torgus removed it for me at our first encounter. I must say, it was not an easy feat, and it required a great deal of power on both our parts."

"That's why you were so weak," Rika realized. "You two weren't battling. You were working together. You used your power up helping him disarm it."

"I'm afraid so. You see, I couldn't risk using my own power to take it out or it would have detonated, just as you planned. But, you see, you missed a crucial loophole in your plan."

"Oh? And what was that?"

"Nowhere was it said that I was unable to have another caster do it for me."

"So you partnered with Torgus? Became his lackey?"

"He made me quite the offer. One too good to reject. You see, it is far better to join and rule than to live out my life in exile. Worse than that, without all of this delicious power at my disposal."

"You told him about the Nasturian. That's how they knew our ship was coming."

"Afraid so."

"But there were no transmissions. You were with us the whole time."

"Ah, that is where *this* comes in quite handy." She pulled out a glowing stone from her pocket. "A Vikann, they call it. One of only four known to still exist. Quite a marvelous device for linking power across galaxies, akin to the Bakana rods you are so fond of. Shame you sent yours away just now or you might have stood a chance."

Rika's tattoos flared with agitation.

"Oh, don't bother. My power is now linked with the remaining stones. And with you being so kind as to remove Torgus from the equation, his power, and his forces, are now mine."

"You don't have to do this, Malalia. You can still be good."

"I don't think she knows what that word means," Charlie said, walking slowly to his friend's side. Leila was safely protected by her Magus stone. At least he hoped so. But now it looked like Rika needed him.

Malalia flashed an amused smile. "Oh, I tried the whole good thing, and you know something? For a minute it actually felt nice. But then I came to my senses and remembered. Power is so much better. And now? This world is mine, just a little later than I had originally planned."

Rika's tattoos flared bright, and Charlie pulled upon his own magic as well.

Rika raised her hand, energy crackling across her fingertips. "You know I can't let you do this. This is your last warning. I will stop you if I must."

Malalia scoffed. "No, you will not."

Her Vikann stone lacked a bezel, but that was inconsequential. She wasn't using it to drive the Urvalin fleet. She was using it to feed her own power. She pulled hard, drawing as much of the stone's energy into herself as she could, and cast a brutal smiting spell, intending to strike her enemies from this very plane of existence with a single blow.

Charlie cringed, his defenses flaring strong, but Rika just stood there, her tattoos actually fading as Malalia cast.

The woman let out a startled shriek as her spell misfired horribly, the power discharging harmlessly, draining her as it did. Her youthful skin dulled and grew ashy, her hair flashed silver-gray then white as she crumpled to her knees.

Charlie seized the opportunity, releasing his spells on the remaining Urvalin troops, knocking them unconscious in a single blast of magic, negating Malalia's backup entirely. The defeated woman looked up, spent and withered.

"I don't understand," she gasped. "How..."

Rika walked over to her and looked down on the powerless shell of what had been one of the most powerful vislas to live with a look of both pity and disgust.

"I told you, we had mechanisms in place should you go rogue. You forget, we know you, Malalia. We hoped you might actually have reformed, but it was a fleeting thought. You see, we didn't worry that you would betray us. We counted on it."

"But I cast before. I've used so much power."

"Yes, you did. But not here. That explosive in your neck? That was just a decoy. A distraction. You were so weak when we put the device around your neck, there was no way you could have felt the true purpose of it."

"What have you done to me?"

"Nothing that you haven't done to yourself. But while that machine was whirring away, making all sorts of sounds and sensations on your neck, I was implanting a powerful trigger spell as well, hiding it deep within your own power, concealing itself as you gained strength. A spell that would only trigger in a specific place, and only if you attempted to cast against us. A spell that would negate your power and drain you every time you tried to harm us. Little did we know you would side with the Urvalin and add their power to your own, though I must say, the result has been quite impressive."

Malalia took in the information and slumped lower, defeated. "Of course," she said. "Cal's lair. You knew I would eventually come here. What I had thought was a careless breach in security—"

"Was a test. Yes. And you failed it. We *let* you hear about this location. There was no other reason you would ever come here but to do harm and gloat. It's why I selected this location in the first place."

"I thought—"

"Oh, sweetie, did you actually think Cal was based here?" Rika chuckled. "We chose this spot because of how remote it is. Aside from a few old empty hangars, there's nothing you could damage for miles."

From the nearby shade, Leila and the baby watched with quiet amusement. "Hi, Malalia," she called out with a wickedly mirthful grin. "Nice to see you again."

CHAPTER FIFTY-NINE

Commander Torgus's body was burned without ceremony along with the scores of Urvalin who had fallen in battle, their ashes scattered into the sun.

As for the remainder of his troops, while a great many had succeeded in killing themselves, Rika and Charlie had combined forces, taking the Vikann stones from Malalia and the deceased commander, using them to seize control of the Urvalin suicide spells, blocking them entirely. If the troops wanted to take their own lives, they would have to do it the hard way.

Some did just that upon finding themselves denied the easy way out. Many found easy methods, like blasting themselves out of airlocks, while others flew their entire ships directly into the sun. But some Urvalin found themselves simply alive. Alive and without a cause to fight for the first time in their lives.

Cal had a fair bit of practice at setting up rehabilitation centers, and large camps for the remaining prisoners were established all across the planet. Torgus, Prin, and Fraxxis were diabolical beings, no doubt, and their elite fighting forces were true believers. But the rest of their ranks were just people caught up in the fight. Puppets manipulated by their masters.

With patience, and a good amount of luck, a decent amount might even come out of rehabilitation as new people, free from the bonds of their warlike ways.

As for the rest? Well, that remained to be seen.

But that was an Earth problem, it seemed. On other worlds, as soon as Torgus's support vanished, the locals rose up, slaughtering every last Urvalin they could find.

A small victory gathering was being held in Malibu at Charlie and Leila's home, with Vince providing ample food for all. It wasn't an all-out party, though. A lot of good people had died fighting this battle. But while the mood wasn't exactly off the rails festive, neither was it somber by any means.

They had defeated the enemy, banishing Malalia back to live out her remaining days on her distant planet, alone and powerless, while overcoming an entirely new alien threat the likes of which they had, up until recently not considered possible. The sheer size of the Urvalin forces was incredible, though admittedly, there were far fewer left behind.

"How many we talking here, Cal?" Charlie asked over regular comms now that the AI had come back out of hiding.

"I would estimate upward of one hundred thousand Urvalin remain."

Daisy whistled. "That's a helluva lot of prisoners."

Charlie nodded. "Yeah, but considering the size of their armada, that's just a drop in the bucket. We got lucky here. I mean, if you consider them all offing themselves and saving us the trouble luck."

Rika nearly laughed her beer out her nose in a gush of foam. "Morbid, Charlie. That's just straight up, cold-blooded morbid," she said with a laugh.

"Hey, when it fits, it fits. And besides, I am *tired*. Cut a guy some slack."

Rika smacked him on the arm. "Yeah, new papa's gonna be a lot more tired pretty soon. But he's a beautiful kid, right, Jo?"

"Took the words out of my mouth," the cyborg replied. "Hey, George, I think Rika needs a fresh one."

"On it," the commando replied, shirtless and gleaming in the beachside sun. He didn't need to get a tan, but it was a beach party, and he was always one to fit in. "Poric, my brother. Beer me," he called to his new friend, the moon-stationed cyborg getting his first taste of beach life.

"Here ya go," Poric replied, passing a cold one to George, who relayed it to Rika. "Hey, Ara, Orgalius. You guys need anything?" he called down to the Zomoki and Dragon lazily floating in the kelp bed just offshore.

"Thank you, Poric, but we are quite fine as we are," Ara replied, enjoying the relaxing feel of the surf on her scales.

Charlie walked to Leila and kissed her tenderly, then raised his glass to the assembled group. "Everyone, if I may. A toast. To the victors, to the fallen, and to absent friends."

"Absent friends," the group responded, their thoughts drifting to the many who were not with them, spread across the galaxies.

Across the portal, which had been pulled from the sun as soon as Torgus had fallen, another sort of celebration was taking place. Smaller, but no less festive than their counterparts on Earth. Visla Palmarian had offered the use of his estate, but Korbin, in a rare show of social behavior, offered his private retreat instead.

The group sat at a long table, enjoying the hospitality of their host to the fullest, with an impressive spread, courtesy of Korbin and Amazara.

"This is really good," Nipsenni said as she ate enough food to feed a small army.

"Where does it all go?" Amazara asked, amazed by the display.

Samanna shook his head with a laugh. "I honestly do not know."

Korbin handed the wrapped Bakana rod to Master Zilara with a thankful bow. "We could not have done it without the Ghalian," he said.

"We do not often take sides," she replied. "But when our entire galaxy is at risk, we side with our own."

"And how is Master Farmatta?"

"Wounded, but healing. It will take some time, but we expect a full recovery."

"I'm glad to hear it. And the Urvalin? Any survivors?"

"None that we have found. There are so many dead, it will be spoken of for generations."

"So, the spellblock to their suicide spells?" he asked.

"No luck. We discovered it too late. They killed themselves rather than be captured. At least, nearly all of them did. A few stragglers may have had cold feet, but they are of no concern to us now. Their forces are no more than a memory, and they are little more than castaways in an alien realm."

"What a waste," Palmarian said, shaking his head.

Visla Samanna nodded somberly. "I agree, my brother," he said, placing his hand on Palmarian's shoulder. The most unlikely of friendships forged in the most unusual of circumstances.

Nipsenni was also a part of their new circle, and both Palmarian and Samanna had invited her to visit their estates whenever she saw fit. Given her proclivity for fine dining, they were relatively sure she would take them both up on the offer.

When the fighting finally ceased and the bodies began to grow cold, she had made sure her pirate brethren were well paid for their efforts beyond the mere spoils of war they were claiming in abundance. Given that the galaxy had just been saved with their help, the grateful citizens of countless worlds were glad to chip in with their thanks. At this rate, the pirates would be out of a job. There was simply no joy in pirating from one's friends.

A shadow flashed overhead, then another, as two dragons circled, flapping hard as they landed nearby.

"I understand there is an offer of food," Drombus said with a grin.

"Arlo! Ripley!" Vee chirped as the two dismounted and removed their helmets.

"Hey, Vee," Ripley called out. "We crossed back as soon as we could. Heard you guys kicked some serious ass!"

Korbin waved them over "You know," he said, "I'm impressed with both of you. Your skills are maturing rapidly."

"Thank you, Korbin," Vee said.

"Yeah, what she said," Ripley said, beaming.

"*But*, your skills still need work. Vee, you are learning to control your blossoming power well, but Arlo and Ripley have lacked proper instruction for far too long."

"What are you saying?" Ripley asked.

"I am saying that, if you are interested and willing, I would be proud to teach you to *really* use your powers, joining your magic with your dragons to become something truly magnificent."

Ripley swallowed hard. "Wow. I-I don't know what to say."

"Think it over. There is no rush."

Arlo nodded his thanks then stepped over to Kara and her father. "Sir, I am glad you made it out all right. I know Kara was terribly worried about you."

"Thank you, Arlo. It has been quite an ordeal. But I have

something I need to discuss with my friend here. Come, Samanna, we should talk."

"What do you mean, Nikora?"

Palmarian flashed a look and made a little gesture with his head.

"Oh, yes. *That*. Yes, we should leave these two to catch up and go discuss that thing. The one we need to talk about."

Kara rolled her eyes as the two men walked away.

"So, you're good?" Arlo asked. "What am I saying? Look at you. Clearly you're good. What I meant was—"

Kara leaned in and silenced him with a kiss. "Come on," she said, taking his hand. "There is so much I want to tell you."

Vee and Ripley watched them go, leaning on each other with a happy embrace.

"It's so romantic," Vee said.

"I know, right?"

"Wait. You're not 'busting his balls,' as you say?"

Ripley flashed a little grin. "Nah. Not today. He earned this. But don't worry, no balls will be safe come tomorrow."

The two laughed and laughed, and all was right in the galaxy.

"You girls up for some dessert?" Amazara asked.

Ripley perked up immediately. "Oh, hell yeah. Come on, Vee. I'm starving!"

CHAPTER SIXTY

A ripple of power flowed across three galaxies, a tenuous link connecting them via a trio of magically created portals. The contact had been established. It was slim, but it was there.

Bawb and Hunze carried the Bakana rod uncovered at all times, one of them always close to it in case the others might resume their connection. With it, they hoped they might manage to somehow find a way back to their home.

Days stretched on as they lingered, at the prison world, waiting for the chance to reverse the portal if the stars aligned. But finally they departed, accepting a ride with the head priest aboard the majestic command ship of their fleet.

There was not a single thing powered by Allpower on it, these people did not use that sort of thing. Technology was their way of life, and this was the pinnacle of their efforts.

The combined forces had cleaned up the prison world, going so far as to rescue all of those who had been trapped there and wished it. Some had gone native, however, and had no desire to leave their way of life. Nakk and the priest understood and left them to it.

As for the Urvalin fleet, there wasn't much cleanup required at all, as nearly all of their ships had been bumped out of the safe passageway and into the grip of the black holes.

Nakk and the priest flew out together, as all but a handful of their newly allied ships remained behind to evacuate the last of the survivors and rescuees.

They had stopped to transfer craft before parting ways a few systems away in a calm, beautiful part of the galaxy, linking the two ships to make their final farewells. Nakk would take the Ghalian and his mate wherever they wished to go. This was their home now, and no matter where they went, they would be welcome with open arms.

"Thank you for your assistance," Bawb said to the priest. "And for your friendship."

"It is quite a thing," the priest replied. "And here when we first met I had such serious doubts about you and your associates."

"And now look at us."

"Indeed. You are a good man, Bawb. I wish you and Hunze nothing but the best."

"Thank you. I look forward to visiting you in—" Bawb fell silent.

Hunze had frozen still, her hand clenching the Bakana rod hard. "It is active," she gasped.

At long last, it was time. But they were nowhere near the Urvalin portal. This was not how it was supposed to go. But now there was little to do for it. They would have to make the best attempt they could.

"Bawb? What do we do? We're far from the Urvalin portal. Can you reverse it from here?"

"No, it is too far. We must form a *new* portal," he said. "We have to try. It is the only chance."

"Can we do that?" Hunze asked. "The power required—"

"We must at least make the attempt," he said, grasping the

rod with her, both of them channeling their magic together, directing it into the empty space around them.

The couple released their power, pulling from the Bakana rod and straining to shape a new portal back to where they had come from. Back to their home.

Space around them buckled and warped as they struggled to mold the beginning of a portal into a solid shape.

"It is slipping!" Hunze gasped as the tiny speck of a portal threatened to close once more.

Bawb's forehead beaded with sweat from the effort. "We cannot allow that to happen. More power, Hunze."

"I do not know if I can."

Suddenly, the portal expanded enormously, the energies of not two but three galaxies merging, weaving together and solidifying into a secure link. The tickle of shocking energy they had felt between the galaxies surged as the circuit completed, the magical flow intact and smooth.

Bawb and Hunze dropped the rod, exhausted, but also confused.

"Did you do that?" he asked.

"No. Did you?"

"No. What was that? How is it possible that—"

"Oh," the head priest said with a little chuckle. "That was me."

"*You*?"

"What? You seem so surprised."

"But, you. Your people," Hunze blurted.

"My dear Hunze, we may not have Allpower in our system, but that does not mean that some of us were not born with it—a significant amount, in some cases. Nor does that mean we do not know how to use it."

The priest pulled a bright stone out of a hidden pocket and

tossed it to Nakk. "You should bind this to the portal. It will keep it from collapsing."

"A Vikann stone?" he gasped. "But I thought the Urvalin possessed the only ones in existence."

"One should never assume anything, my friend."

Hunze and Bawb stood in awe of the new portal, safe and secure, basking in the incredible feeling of a new flavor of magic flowing through it.

"What *is* that?" Hunze asked.

"The Allpower, or magic, if you prefer, now moving freely from realm to realm. The dawn of a new age of power for all three linked galaxies."

Bawb pulled his mate in close and held her tight, staring deep into her eyes. "What do you say, love? Shall we go home?"

EPILOGUE

Word spread quickly to those who held the Urvalin's remaining Vikann stones as to the best way to safely lock them away from dangerous hands. In short order, all three galaxies had the stones magically bonded to the portals, an immense linkage of power that connected the three galaxies now and forever. Removing them would be nearly impossible, and with the benefits of the portals, no one would even dream of trying.

Magic and Allpower flowed easily between the realms, and travel became a thing of ease as the portals now possessed a new, and rather unusual, feature. Unlike the normal two-way transit created by the spells, these portals were interlinked in such a way the party crossing could exit at whichever realm they desired.

The first few to attempt a crossing were a bit shocked by this, getting turned around all kinds of ways before realizing what had happened. But now safe passage had been established.

With it, some of the more unsavory sort were bound to make their way to a new realm in which to try their luck, but so too were settlers and adventurers freed from the confines of their own galaxies. And best of all, even those without any magic or Allpower whatsoever could use the portals with ease.

It had been nearly a month since the portals had opened when a Ghalian shimmer ship quietly touched down on the bluffs of Malibu. Bawb and Hunze stepped out and breathed deep the salty ocean air. It was good to be home. Back to *this* home, that is.

Fingers intertwined, they walked the path toward the beach where they had seen their friends gathered on this beautiful day. All of their little extended family were there. Daisy and Sarah, along with their husbands, kids, and the two girls from Bawb's own realm, all playing in the surf, enjoying the ocean's gentle, salty kiss.

Tamara and Shelly were sunbathing, their metal limbs gleaming bright, while Fatima lay in the shade close by, sipping an icy drink.

Grundsch and the animals were playing fetch with a stick the size of a small tree branch, the two beasts frolicking and having the time of their lives, while Ara and Orgalius watched from the shore where the two were curled up, basking in the sun's warm power.

Charlie sensed them before he saw them, as did Ara. She raised her head, fixing her golden eyes on the couple, and gave a welcoming nod. Bawb and Hunze returned the gesture, their hearts brimming with love as they approached their friends.

"Been a long time," Charlie said, giving his Wampeh brother a warm hug. "I was beginning to wonder when you might finally come by. You look well, man."

"We had to take a trip to my realm," Bawb replied as Leila rose to her feet, the baby slumbering in her arms. "Things move a bit faster for our kind, and we needed to check in with a physician from our own world."

Leila handed Hunze her sleeping child, then gently rested her hand on her friend's growing belly.

"You really do move quickly," she said. "How long?"

"Not very, though the doctor was not quite certain. A Wampeh-Ootaki union is a very uncommon thing."

Charlie leaned over and gave Hunze a little welcoming kiss on the cheek. "But everything is good, right?"

"Fantastic."

"I'm so glad to hear it." He looked at the Ootaki's bulge and flashed a knowing grin to his friend. "So, Bawb, what's it going to be?"

He glanced at his mate.

"We decided to take a page from your book and let it be a surprise," Hunze said.

"She thinks it is a girl," Bawb noted.

Hunze beamed with happiness and squeezed his hand. "Time will tell, love."

Charlie laughed. "And relatively soon by the look of it."

Bawb grinned back at him. "It would seem that way. And yours? A boy, I see."

"Yes. We named him Bob, by the way. Earth spelling, of course."

Charlie watched in shock as the rarest of things happened. Had he not seen it first-hand, he would never have believed it. Tears welled up in the Ghalian's eyes, though only for a moment. But Charlie had seen, and that was all that mattered.

"A good name," Hunze said. "Strong."

The baby hiccupped in her arms, a strange burst of magic spewing out of him, igniting a nearby palm tree.

"Leila, it's your turn," Charlie said with a tired sigh, taking the baby from Hunze and rubbing his back.

Leila quickly cast an extinguishing spell, dousing the flames.

It was then that the newcomers noticed several other mildly scorched trees in the vicinity.

Charlie smiled a sheepish grin and shrugged.

Hunze was amazed. "Did your child just—"

"Yeah. He does that sometimes."

Bawb burst out in a belly laugh, his hands on his stomach from the force of it. "Oh, my friend," he said. "You are going to have your hands quite full."

"Well, they say it takes a village, right?" Charlie replied, looking warmly at their extended family. This was perfect. This was safety. This was home.

He glanced at Ara, who was watching with great amusement, then looked up at the sky. "You know, in our case, however, it may take a few galaxies. And that's fine with me."

AFTERWORD

Several years and a dozen books later, it amazes me how Charlie and his friends have come so far. It's been a fantastic journey and your support means more than you can imagine.

Every rating and review helps stoke the creative fires as well as helping make these books more visible. So, from me to you, dear reader, thank you from the bottom of my heart.

~ Scott Baron ~

ALSO BY SCOTT BARON

Standalone Novels

Living the Good Death

The Clockwork Chimera Series

Daisy's Run

Pushing Daisy

Daisy's Gambit

Chasing Daisy

Daisy's War

The Dragon Mage Series

Bad Luck Charlie

Space Pirate Charlie

Dragon King Charlie

Magic Man Charlie

Star Fighter Charlie

Portal Thief Charlie

Rebel Mage Charlie

Warp Speed Charlie

Checkmate Charlie

Castaway Charlie

Wild Card Charlie

End Game Charlie

The Space Assassins Series

The Interstellar Slayer

The Vespus Blade

The Ghalian Code

Death From the Shadows

Hozark's Revenge

The Warp Riders Series

Deep Space Boogie

Belly of the Beast

Rise of the Forgotten

Pandora's Menagerie

Engines of Chaos

Seeds of Damocles

Odd and Unusual Short Stories:

The Best Laid Plans of Mice: An Anthology

Snow White's Walk of Shame

The Tin Foil Hat Club

Lawyers vs. Demons

The Queen of the Nutters

Lost & Found

ABOUT THE AUTHOR

A native Californian, Scott Baron was born in Hollywood, which he claims may be the reason for his rather off-kilter sense of humor.

Before taking up residence in Venice Beach, Scott first spent a few years abroad in Florence, Italy before returning home to Los Angeles and settling into the film and television industry, where he has worked as an on-set medic for many years.

Aside from mending boo-boos and owies, and penning books and screenplays, Scott is also involved in indie film and theater scene both in the U.S. and abroad.

Made in United States
North Haven, CT
28 December 2024

63626804R00257